W9-BGU-327

Date: 8/25/20

J GRA 741.5 MIC
Mickey and Donald :
Christmas parade.

Disney

Mickey and Donald Christmas Parade

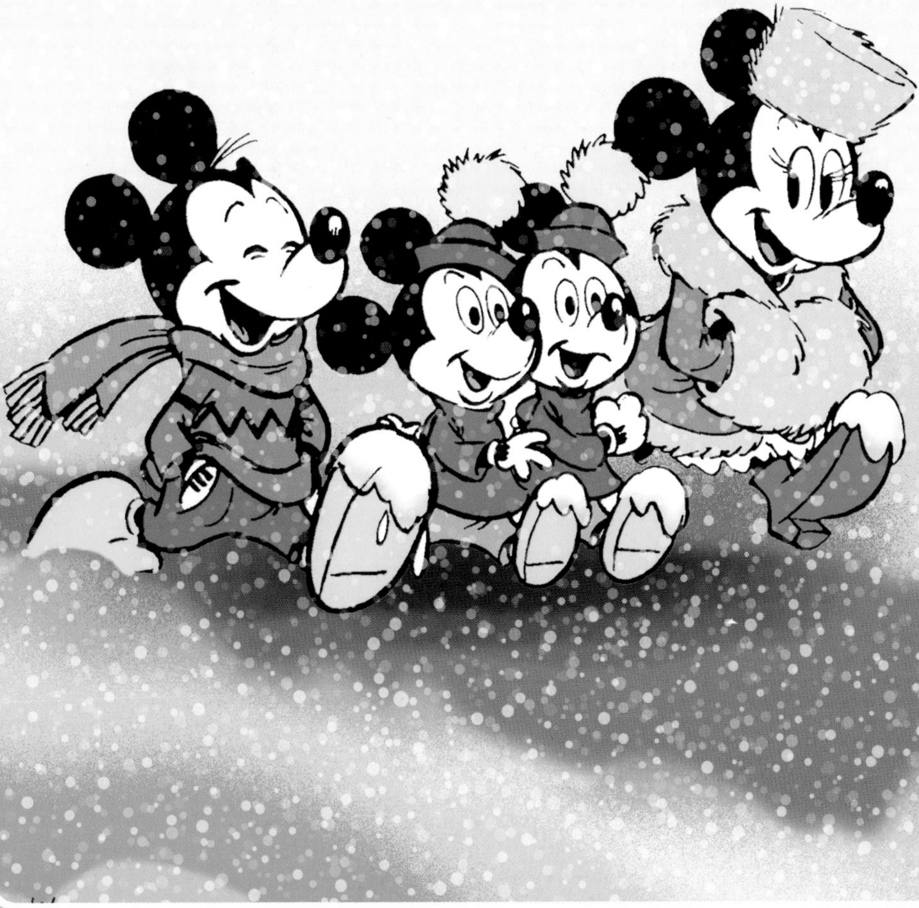

Contents

SERIES EDITORS: **SARAH GAYDOS** AND **CHRIS CERASI**

COVER ARTISTS: **CLAUDIO SCIARRONE & ULRICH SCHROEDER**

ARCHIVAL EDITOR: **DAVID GERSTEIN**   COVER COLORIST: **HACHETTE**

COLLECTION EDITORS: **JUSTIN EISINGER** AND **ALONZO SIMON**

COLLECTION DESIGNER: **RICHARD SHEINAUS** FOR **GOTHAM DESIGN**

PUBLISHER: **GREG GOLDSTEIN**   For international rights, contact licensing@idwpublishing.com

SPECIAL THANKS TO: STEFANO AMBROSIO, STEFANO ATTARDI, JULIE DORRIS, JULIA GABRICK, MARCO GHIGLIONE, JODI HAMMERWOLD, MANNY MEDEROS, EUGENE PARASZCZUK, CARLOTTA QUATTROCOLO, ROBERTO SANTILLO, CHRISTOPHER TROISE, AND CAMILLA VEDOVE.

ISBN : 978-1-68405-324-7   21 20 19 18   1 2 3 4

Greg Goldstein, President and Publisher
John Barber, Editor-In-Chief
Robbie Robbins, EVP/Sr. Art Director
Cara Morrison, Chief Financial Officer
Matt Ruzicka, Chief Accounting Officer
Anita Frazier, SVP of Sales and Marketing
David Hedgecock, Associate Publisher
Jerry Bennington, VP of New Product Development
Lorelei Bunjes, VP of Digital Services
Justin Eisinger, Editorial Director, Graphic Novels & Collections
Eric Moss, Senior Director, Licensing and Business Development
Ted Adams, Founder and CEO of IDW Media Holdings

www.IDWPUBLISHING.com

Facebook: **facebook.com/idwpublishing**
Twitter: **@idwpublishing**
YouTube: **youtube.com/idwpublishing**
Tumblr: **tumblr.idwpublishing.com**
Instagram: **instagram.com/idwpublishing**

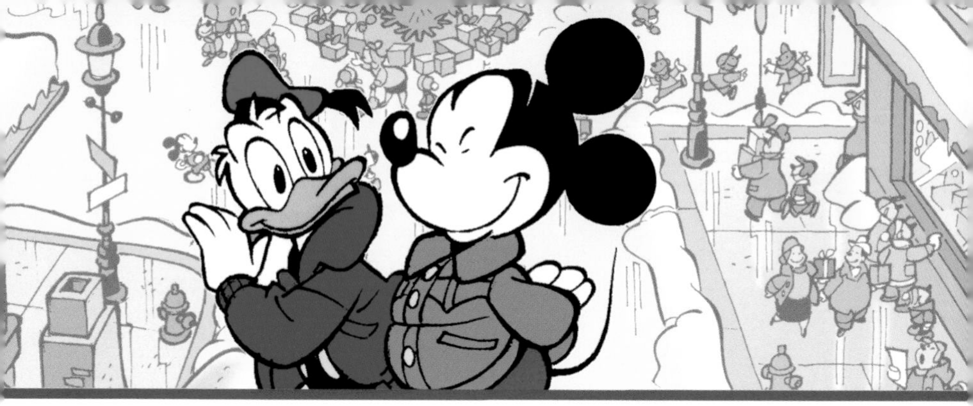

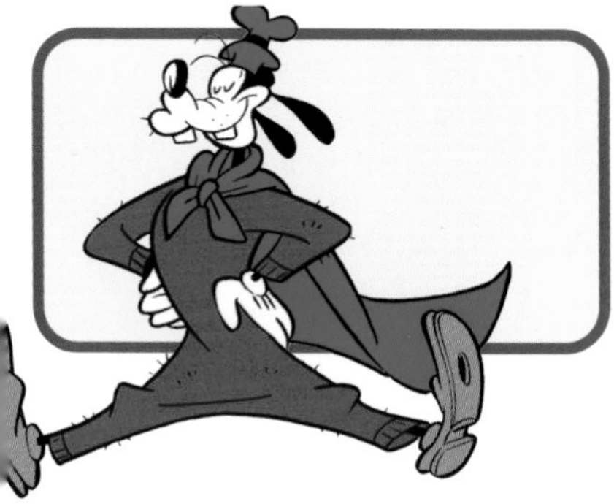

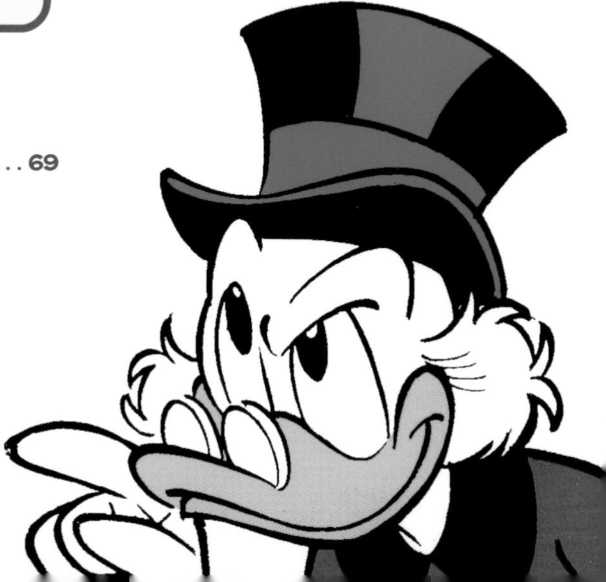

DISNEY COMICS

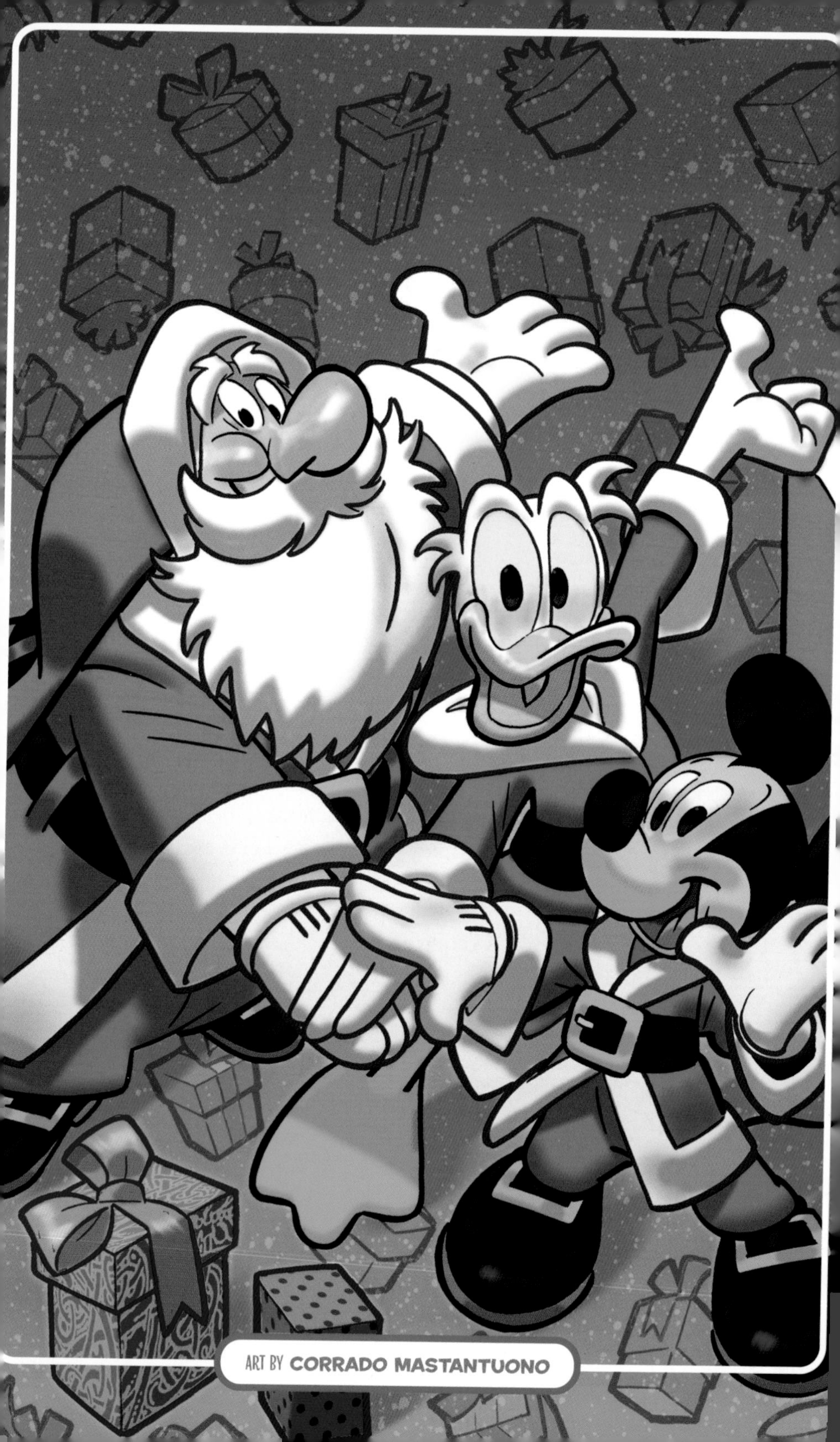
ART BY CORRADO MASTANTUONO

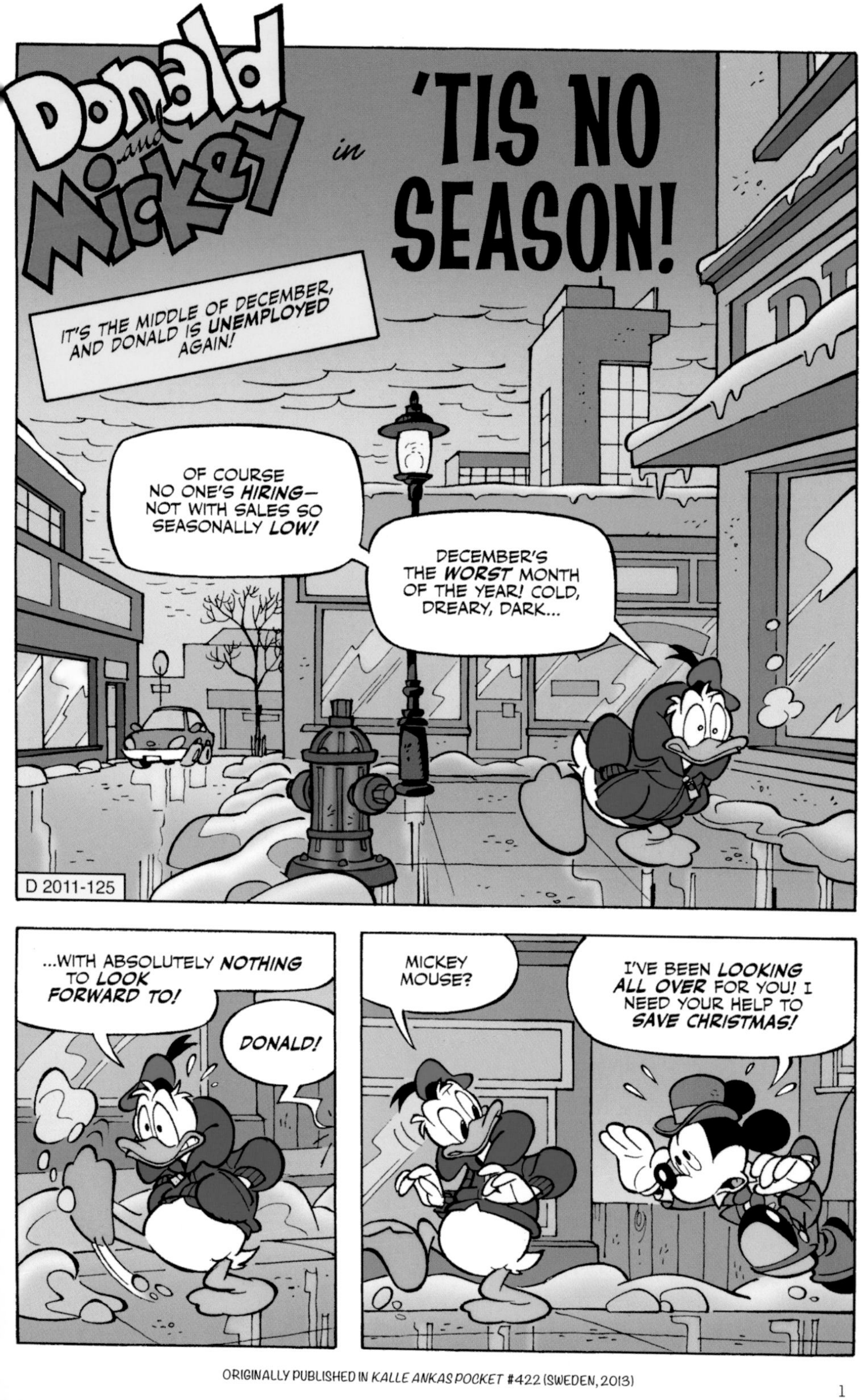
Donald and Mickey in
'TIS NO SEASON!
IT'S THE MIDDLE OF DECEMBER, AND DONALD IS UNEMPLOYED AGAIN!
OF COURSE NO ONE'S HIRING— NOT WITH SALES SO SEASONALLY LOW!
DECEMBER'S THE WORST MONTH OF THE YEAR! COLD, DREARY, DARK...
D 2011-125
...WITH ABSOLUTELY NOTHING TO LOOK FORWARD TO!
DONALD!
MICKEY MOUSE?
I'VE BEEN LOOKING ALL OVER FOR YOU! I NEED YOUR HELP TO SAVE CHRISTMAS!

ORIGINALLY PUBLISHED IN *KALLE ANKAS POCKET* #422 (SWEDEN, 2013)

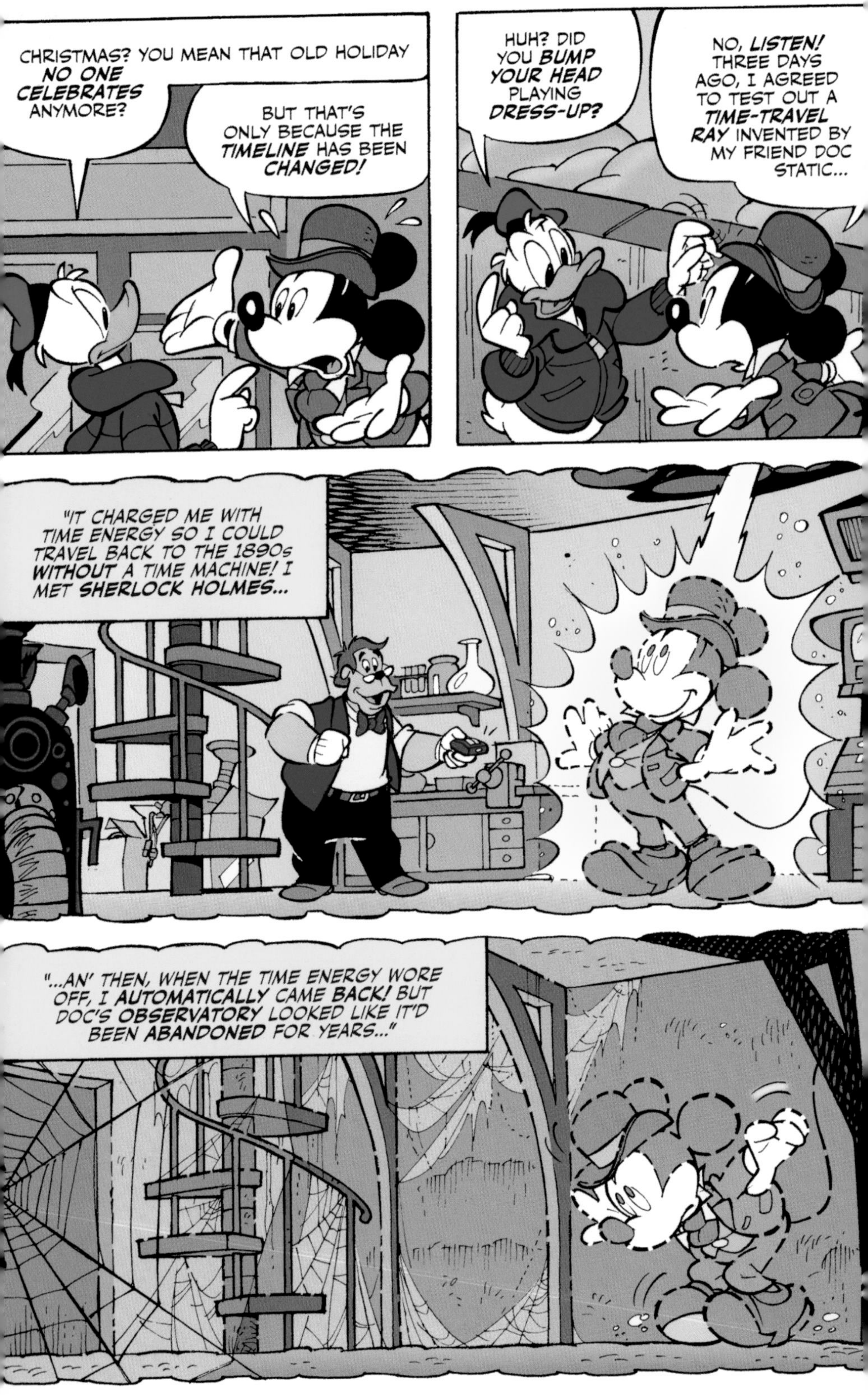
CHRISTMAS? YOU MEAN THAT OLD HOLIDAY NO ONE CELEBRATES ANYMORE?
BUT THAT'S ONLY BECAUSE THE TIMELINE HAS BEEN CHANGED!
HUH? DID YOU BUMP YOUR HEAD PLAYING DRESS-UP?
NO, LISTEN! THREE DAYS AGO, I AGREED TO TEST OUT A TIME-TRAVEL RAY INVENTED BY MY FRIEND DOC STATIC...
"IT CHARGED ME WITH TIME ENERGY SO I COULD TRAVEL BACK TO THE 1890s WITHOUT A TIME MACHINE! I MET SHERLOCK HOLMES...
"...AN' THEN, WHEN THE TIME ENERGY WORE OFF, I AUTOMATICALLY CAME BACK! BUT DOC'S OBSERVATORY LOOKED LIKE IT'D BEEN ABANDONED FOR YEARS..."

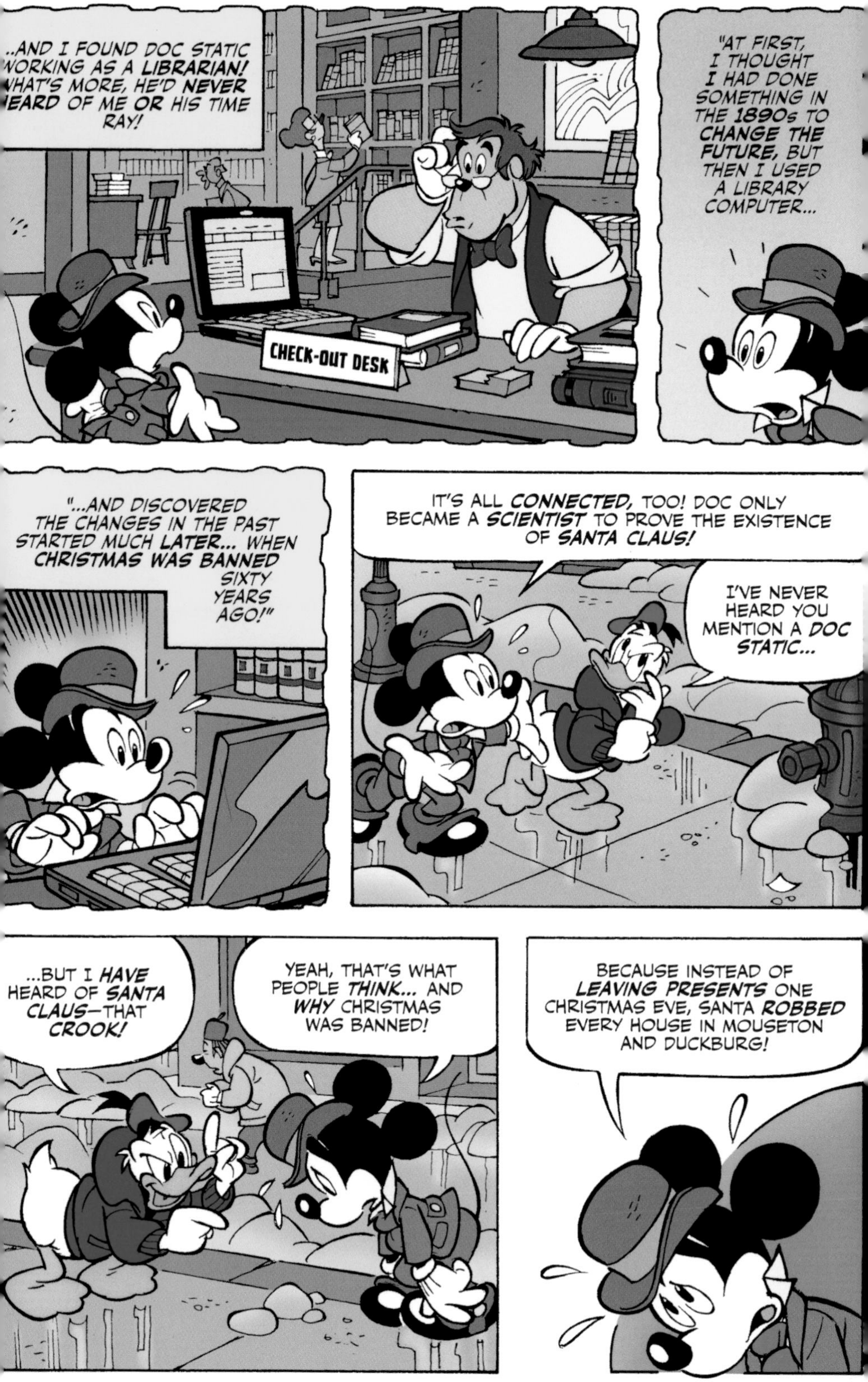
..AND I FOUND DOC STATIC WORKING AS A LIBRARIAN! WHAT'S MORE, HE'D NEVER HEARD OF ME OR HIS TIME RAY!
CHECK-OUT DESK
"AT FIRST, I THOUGHT I HAD DONE SOMETHING IN THE 1890s TO CHANGE THE FUTURE, BUT THEN I USED A LIBRARY COMPUTER...
"...AND DISCOVERED THE CHANGES IN THE PAST STARTED MUCH LATER... WHEN CHRISTMAS WAS BANNED SIXTY YEARS AGO!"
IT'S ALL CONNECTED, TOO! DOC ONLY BECAME A SCIENTIST TO PROVE THE EXISTENCE OF SANTA CLAUS!
I'VE NEVER HEARD YOU MENTION A DOC STATIC...
...BUT I HAVE HEARD OF SANTA CLAUS—THAT CROOK!
YEAH, THAT'S WHAT PEOPLE THINK... AND WHY CHRISTMAS WAS BANNED!
BECAUSE INSTEAD OF LEAVING PRESENTS ONE CHRISTMAS EVE, SANTA ROBBED EVERY HOUSE IN MOUSETON AND DUCKBURG!

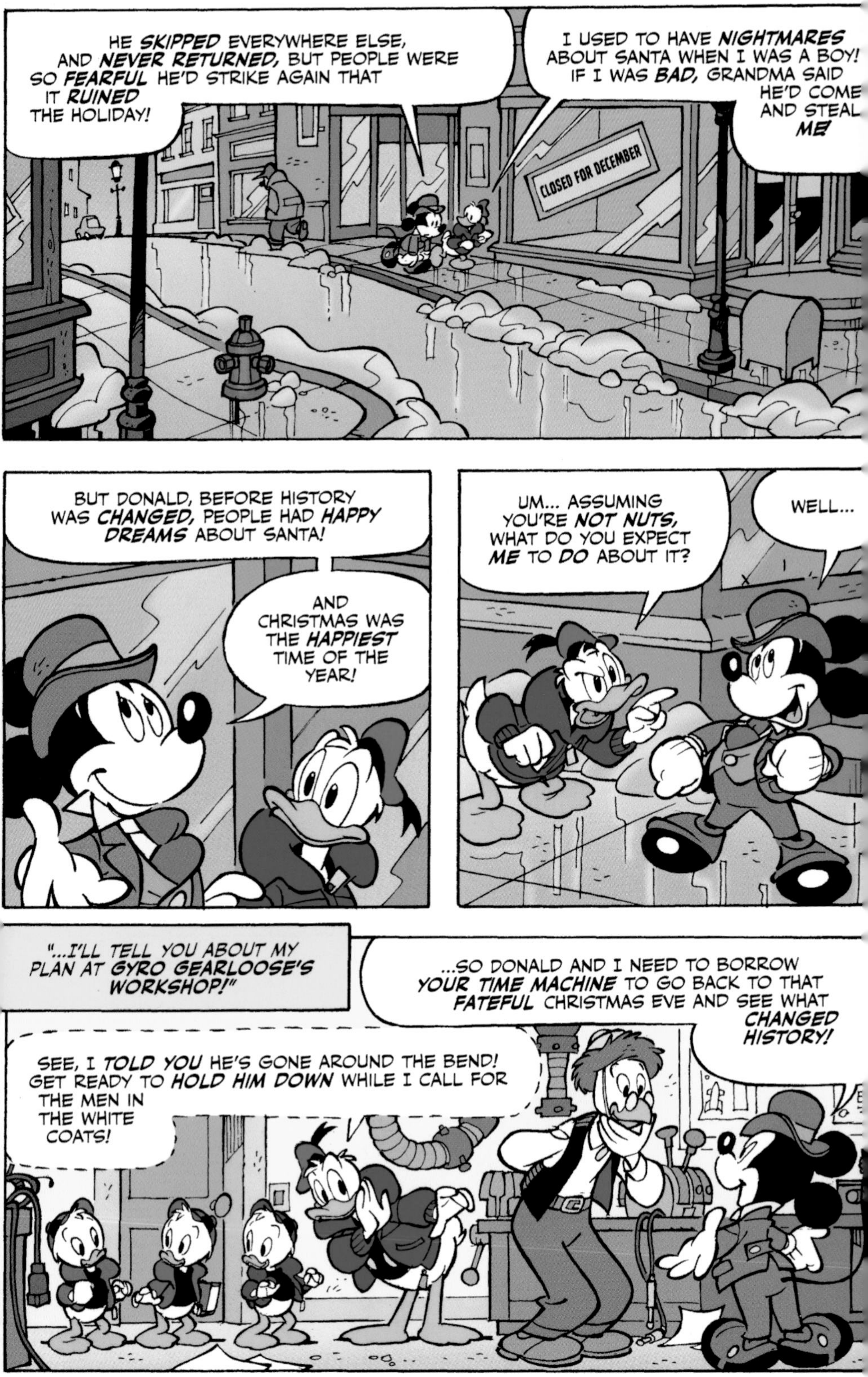
HE SKIPPED EVERYWHERE ELSE, AND NEVER RETURNED, BUT PEOPLE WERE SO FEARFUL HE'D STRIKE AGAIN THAT IT RUINED THE HOLIDAY!
I USED TO HAVE NIGHTMARES ABOUT SANTA WHEN I WAS A BOY! IF I WAS BAD, GRANDMA SAID HE'D COME AND STEAL ME!
CLOSED FOR DECEMBER
BUT DONALD, BEFORE HISTORY WAS CHANGED, PEOPLE HAD HAPPY DREAMS ABOUT SANTA!
AND CHRISTMAS WAS THE HAPPIEST TIME OF THE YEAR!
UM... ASSUMING YOU'RE NOT NUTS, WHAT DO YOU EXPECT ME TO DO ABOUT IT?
WELL...
"...I'LL TELL YOU ABOUT MY PLAN AT GYRO GEARLOOSE'S WORKSHOP!"
...SO DONALD AND I NEED TO BORROW YOUR TIME MACHINE TO GO BACK TO THAT FATEFUL CHRISTMAS EVE AND SEE WHAT CHANGED HISTORY!
SEE, I TOLD YOU HE'S GONE AROUND THE BEND! GET READY TO HOLD HIM DOWN WHILE I CALL FOR THE MEN IN THE WHITE COATS!

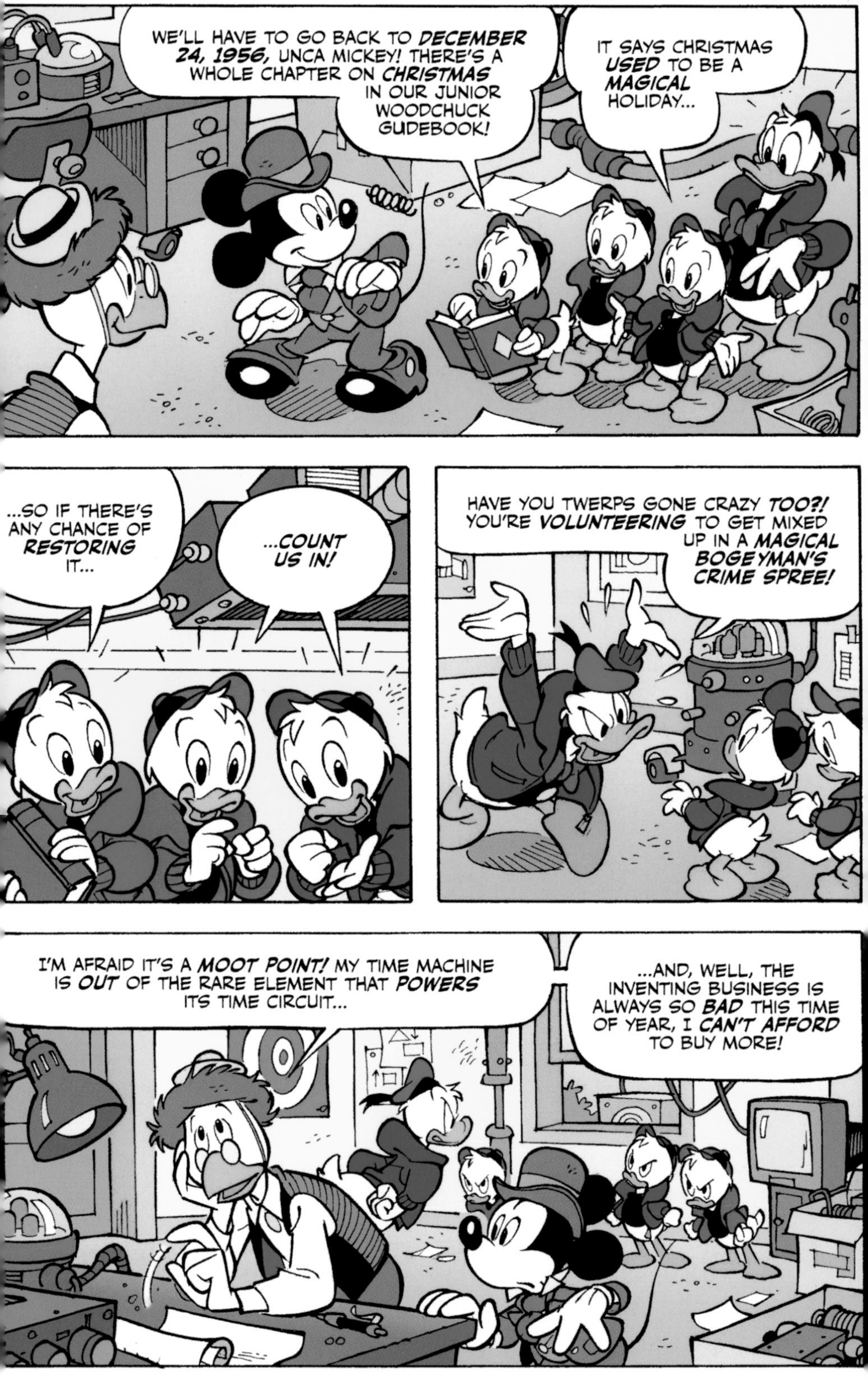
WE'LL HAVE TO GO BACK TO DECEMBER 24, 1956, UNCA MICKEY! THERE'S A WHOLE CHAPTER ON CHRISTMAS IN OUR JUNIOR WOODCHUCK GUDEBOOK!
IT SAYS CHRISTMAS USED TO BE A MAGICAL HOLIDAY...
...SO IF THERE'S ANY CHANCE OF RESTORING IT...
...COUNT US IN!
HAVE YOU TWERPS GONE CRAZY TOO?! YOU'RE VOLUNTEERING TO GET MIXED UP IN A MAGICAL BOGEYMAN'S CRIME SPREE!
I'M AFRAID IT'S A MOOT POINT! MY TIME MACHINE IS OUT OF THE RARE ELEMENT THAT POWERS ITS TIME CIRCUIT...
...AND, WELL, THE INVENTING BUSINESS IS ALWAYS SO BAD THIS TIME OF YEAR, I CAN'T AFFORD TO BUY MORE!

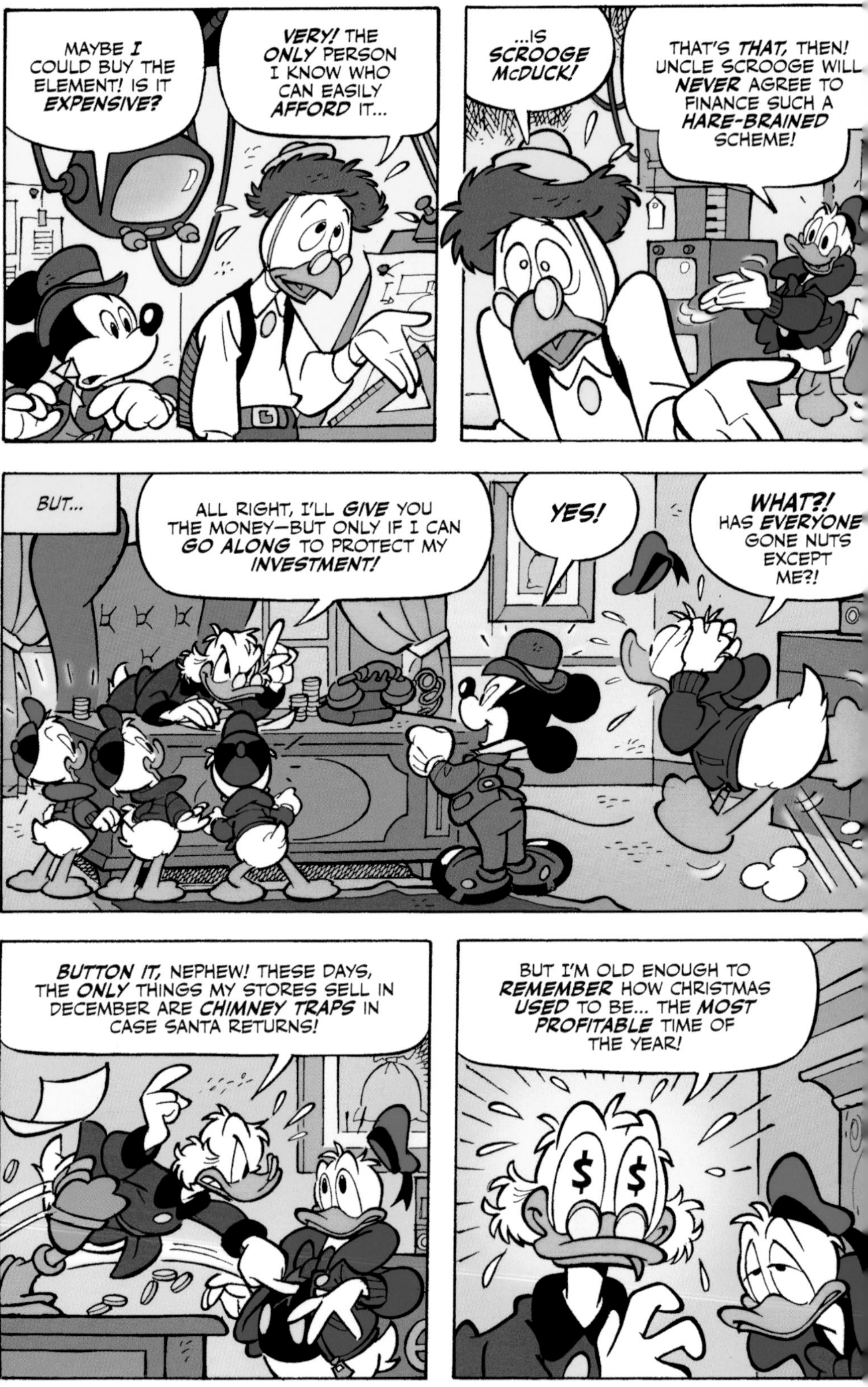
MAYBE I COULD BUY THE ELEMENT! IS IT EXPENSIVE?
VERY! THE ONLY PERSON I KNOW WHO CAN EASILY AFFORD IT...
...IS SCROOGE McDUCK!
THAT'S THAT, THEN! UNCLE SCROOGE WILL NEVER AGREE TO FINANCE SUCH A HARE-BRAINED SCHEME!
BUT...
ALL RIGHT, I'LL GIVE YOU THE MONEY—BUT ONLY IF I CAN GO ALONG TO PROTECT MY INVESTMENT!
YES!
WHAT?! HAS EVERYONE GONE NUTS EXCEPT ME?!
BUTTON IT, NEPHEW! THESE DAYS, THE ONLY THINGS MY STORES SELL IN DECEMBER ARE CHIMNEY TRAPS IN CASE SANTA RETURNS!
BUT I'M OLD ENOUGH TO REMEMBER HOW CHRISTMAS USED TO BE... THE MOST PROFITABLE TIME OF THE YEAR!

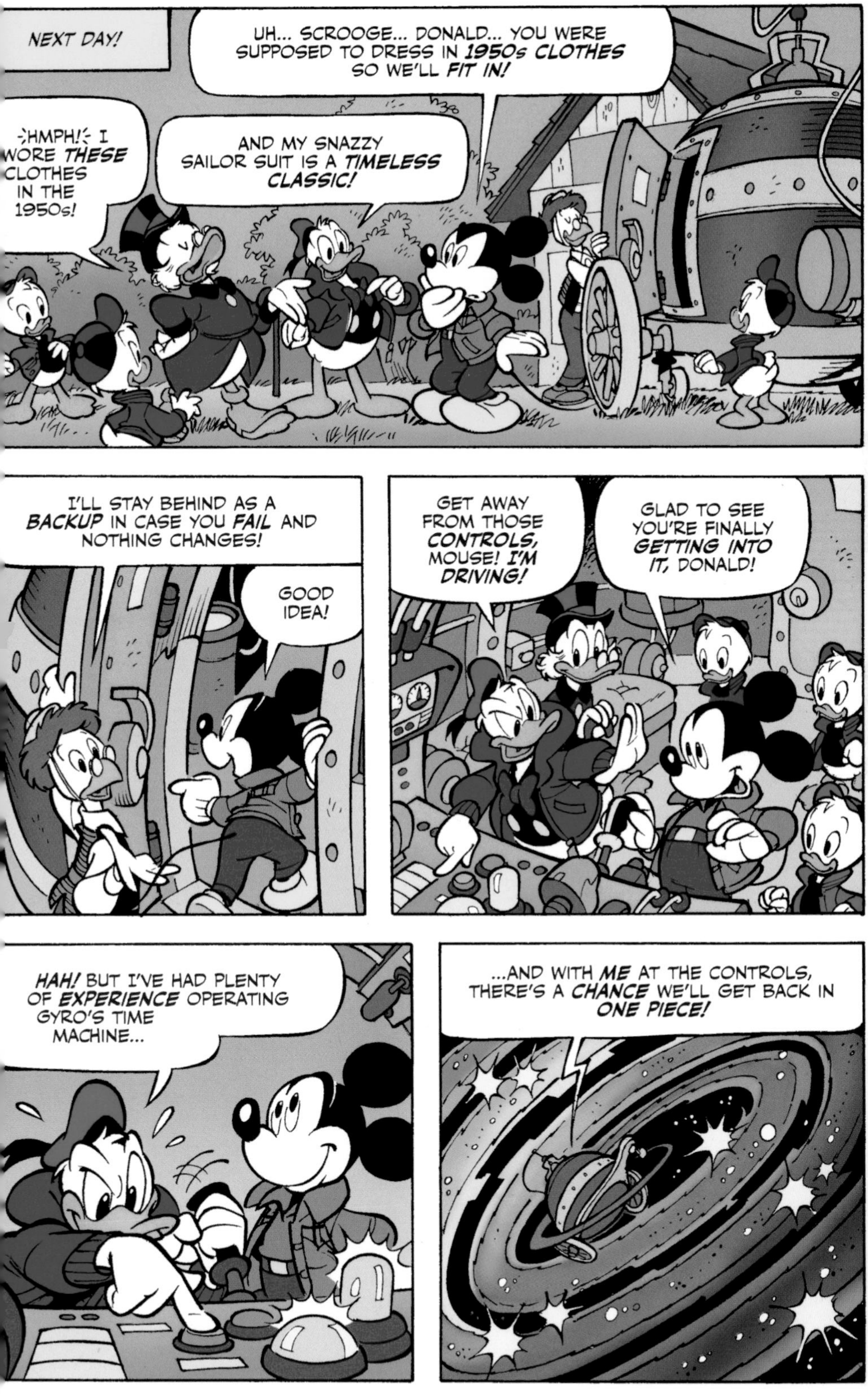

NEXT DAY!
UH... SCROOGE... DONALD... YOU WERE SUPPOSED TO DRESS IN 1950s CLOTHES SO WE'LL FIT IN!
HMPH! I WORE THESE CLOTHES IN THE 1950s!
AND MY SNAZZY SAILOR SUIT IS A TIMELESS CLASSIC!
I'LL STAY BEHIND AS A BACKUP IN CASE YOU FAIL AND NOTHING CHANGES!
GOOD IDEA!
GET AWAY FROM THOSE CONTROLS, MOUSE! I'M DRIVING!
GLAD TO SEE YOU'RE FINALLY GETTING INTO IT, DONALD!
HAH! BUT I'VE HAD PLENTY OF EXPERIENCE OPERATING GYRO'S TIME MACHINE...
...AND WITH ME AT THE CONTROLS, THERE'S A CHANCE WE'LL GET BACK IN ONE PIECE!

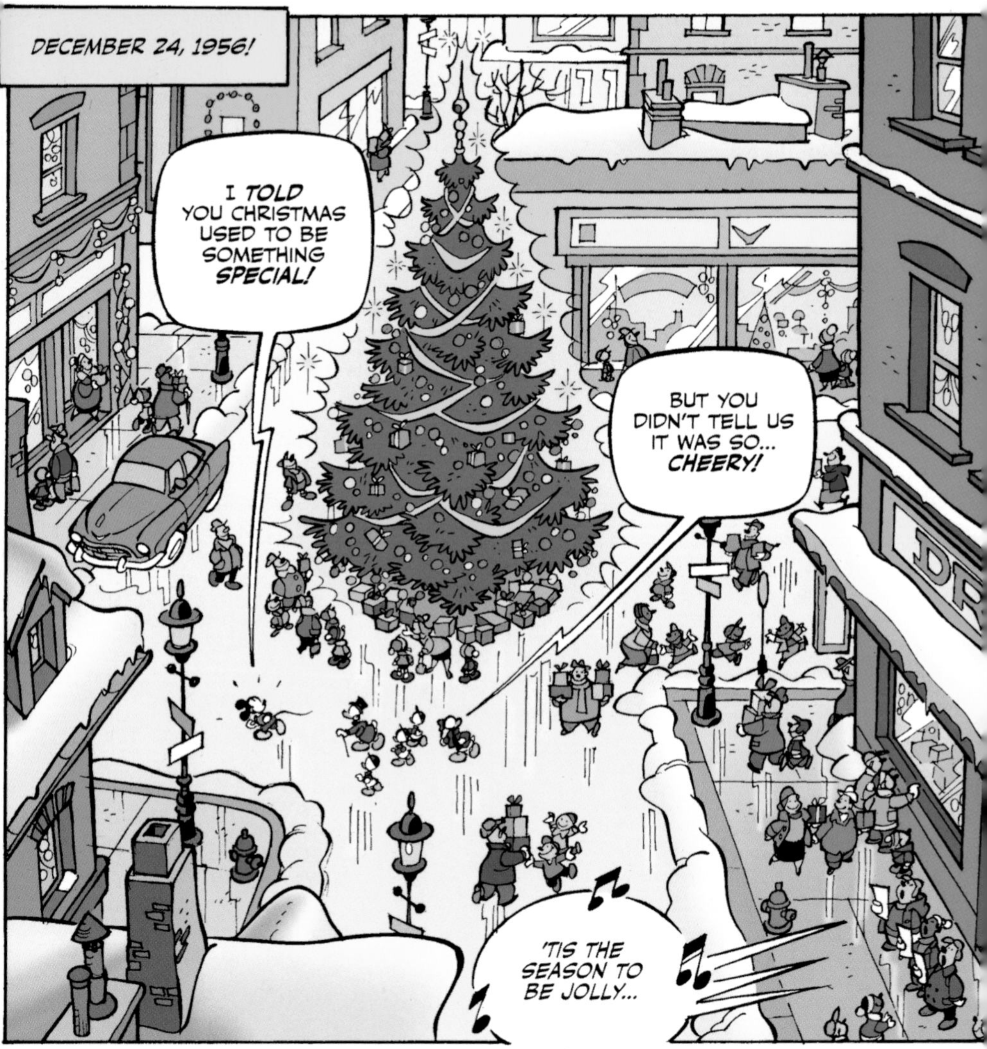
DECEMBER 24, 1956!
I TOLD YOU CHRISTMAS USED TO BE SOMETHING SPECIAL!
BUT YOU DIDN'T TELL US IT WAS SO... CHEERY!
'TIS THE SEASON TO BE JOLLY...

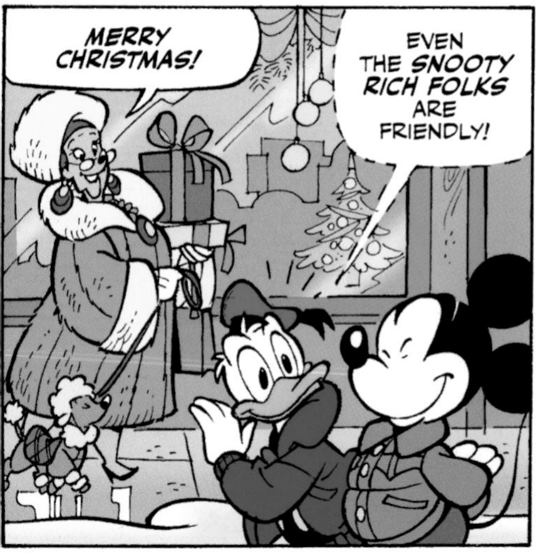
MERRY CHRISTMAS!
EVEN THE SNOOTY RICH FOLKS ARE FRIENDLY!

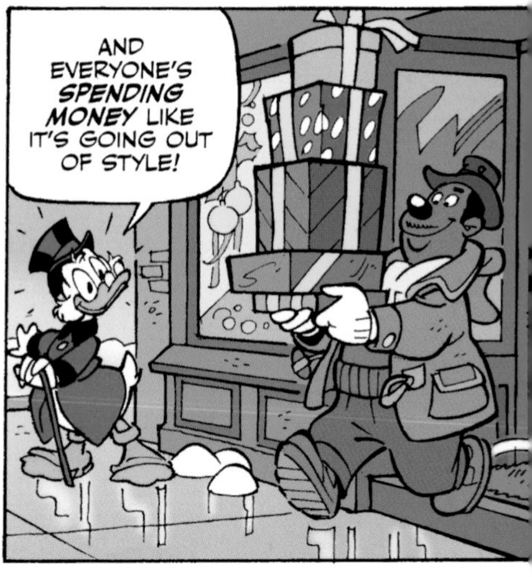
AND EVERYONE'S SPENDING MONEY LIKE IT'S GOING OUT OF STYLE!

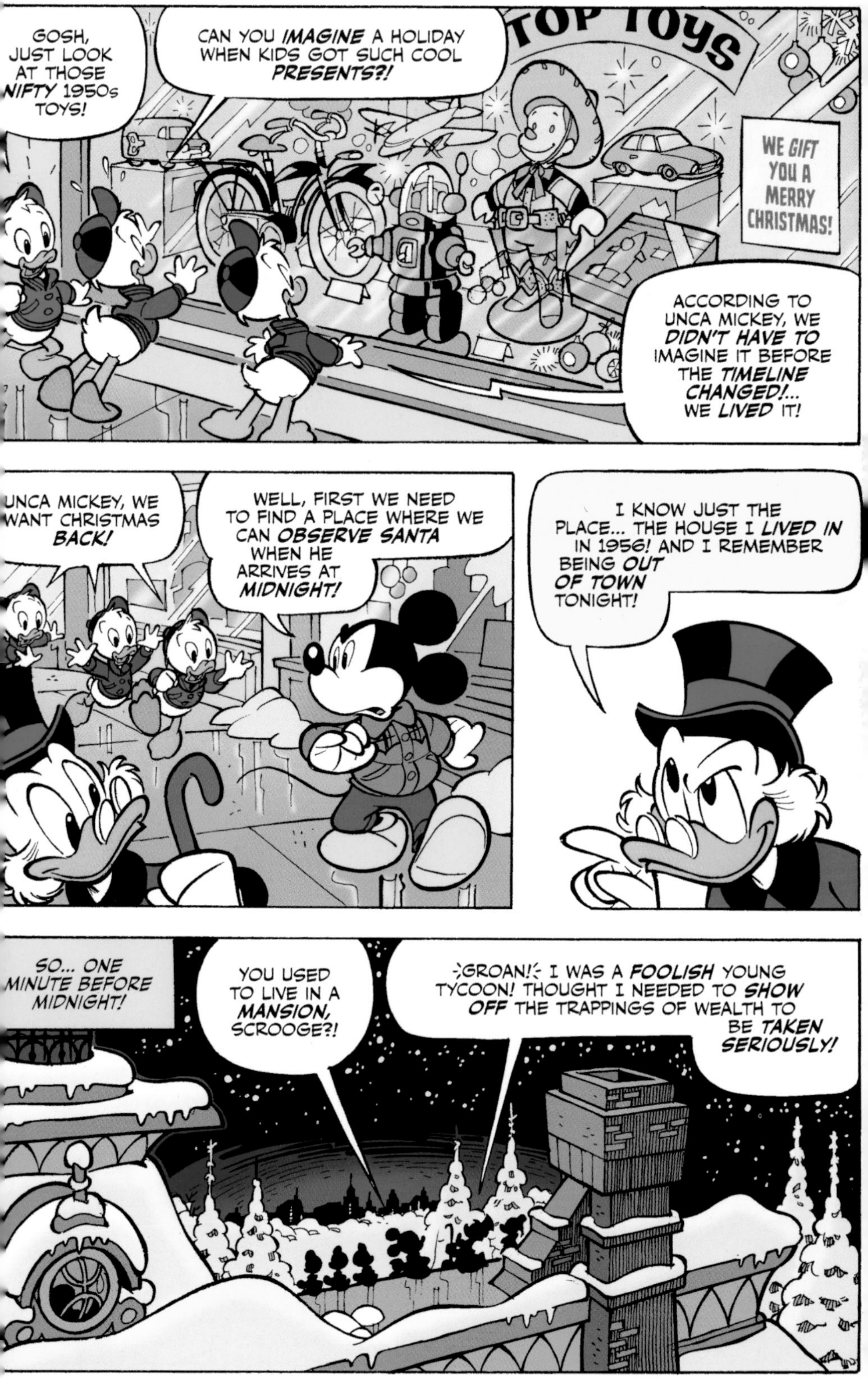
TOP TOYS
GOSH, JUST LOOK AT THOSE NIFTY 1950s TOYS!
CAN YOU IMAGINE A HOLIDAY WHEN KIDS GOT SUCH COOL PRESENTS?!
WE GIFT YOU A MERRY CHRISTMAS!
ACCORDING TO UNCA MICKEY, WE DIDN'T HAVE TO IMAGINE IT BEFORE THE TIMELINE CHANGED!... WE LIVED IT!
UNCA MICKEY, WE WANT CHRISTMAS BACK!
WELL, FIRST WE NEED TO FIND A PLACE WHERE WE CAN OBSERVE SANTA WHEN HE ARRIVES AT MIDNIGHT!
I KNOW JUST THE PLACE... THE HOUSE I LIVED IN IN 1956! AND I REMEMBER BEING OUT OF TOWN TONIGHT!
SO... ONE MINUTE BEFORE MIDNIGHT!
YOU USED TO LIVE IN A MANSION, SCROOGE?!
GROAN! I WAS A FOOLISH YOUNG TYCOON! THOUGHT I NEEDED TO SHOW OFF THE TRAPPINGS OF WEALTH TO BE TAKEN SERIOUSLY!

BAH! NOW I REALIZE IT'S BETTER TO **HAVE** IT THAN **SHOW** IT!

ESPECIALLY IF YOU CAN HAVE IT IN A **SHOWY** MONEY BIN!

⸆SHH!⸅ SOMETHING'S **HAPPENING!**

HUH? WHAT THE HECK'S **THAT?!** A **WORMHOLE** SPITTING OUT A SWARM OF **LOCUSTS** FROM **OUTER SPACE?!**

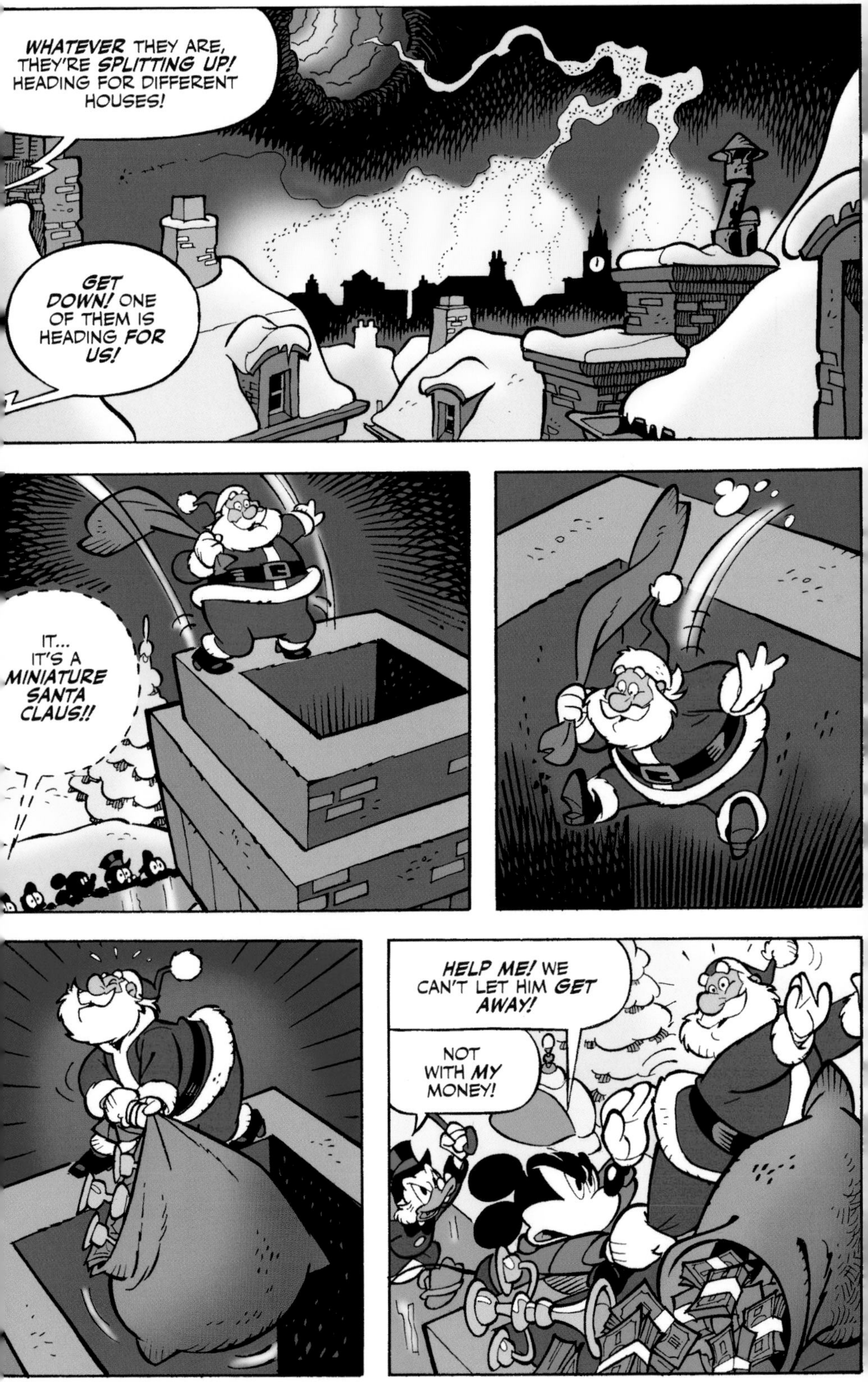
WHATEVER THEY ARE, THEY'RE SPLITTING UP! HEADING FOR DIFFERENT HOUSES!
GET DOWN! ONE OF THEM IS HEADING FOR US!
IT... IT'S A MINIATURE SANTA CLAUS!!
HELP ME! WE CAN'T LET HIM GET AWAY!
NOT WITH MY MONEY!

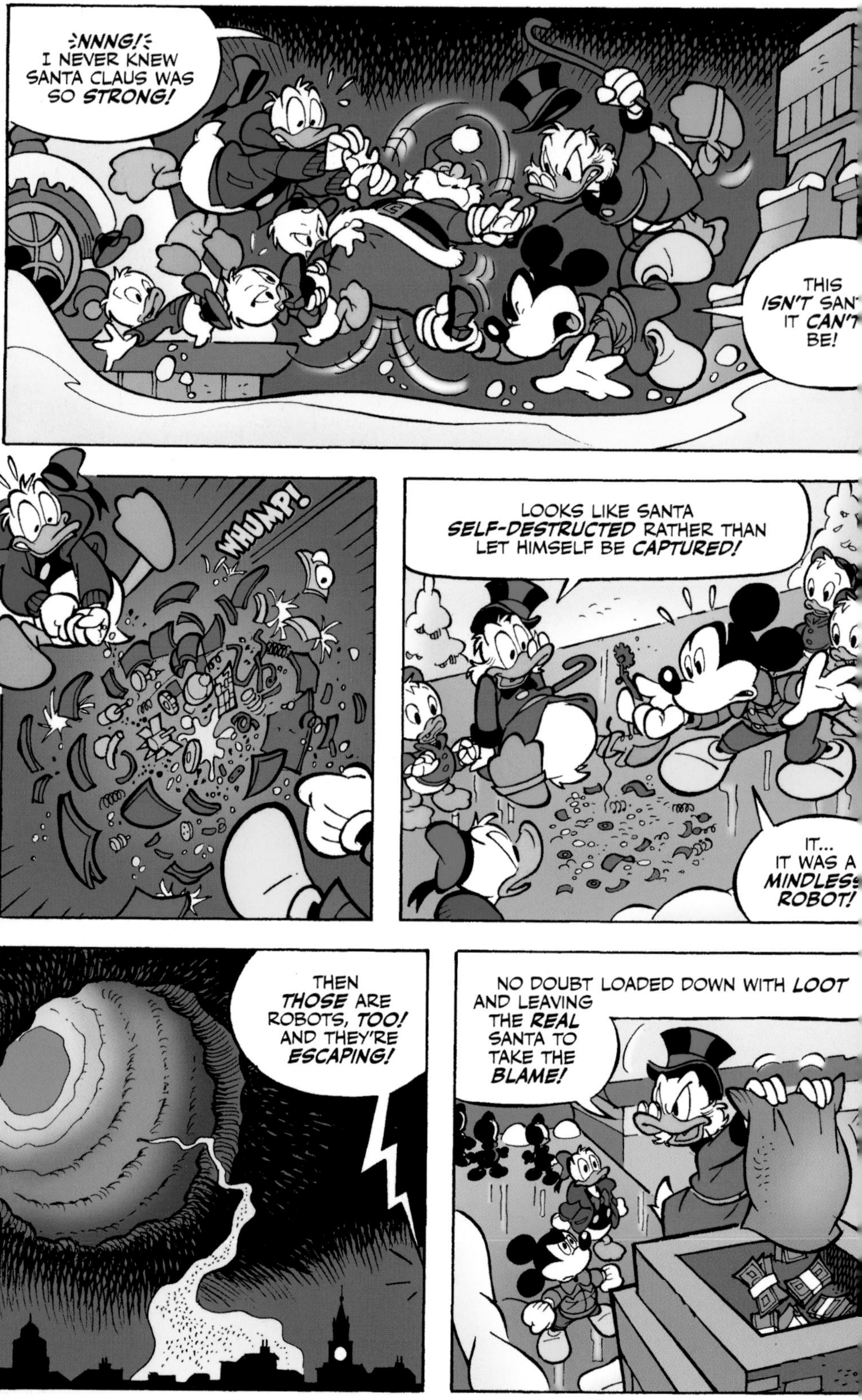

NNNG! I NEVER KNEW SANTA CLAUS WAS SO STRONG!
THIS ISN'T SAN IT CAN'T BE!
WHUMP!
LOOKS LIKE SANTA SELF-DESTRUCTED RATHER THAN LET HIMSELF BE CAPTURED!
IT... IT WAS A MINDLESS ROBOT!
THEN THOSE ARE ROBOTS, TOO! AND THEY'RE ESCAPING!
NO DOUBT LOADED DOWN WITH LOOT AND LEAVING THE REAL SANTA TO TAKE THE BLAME!

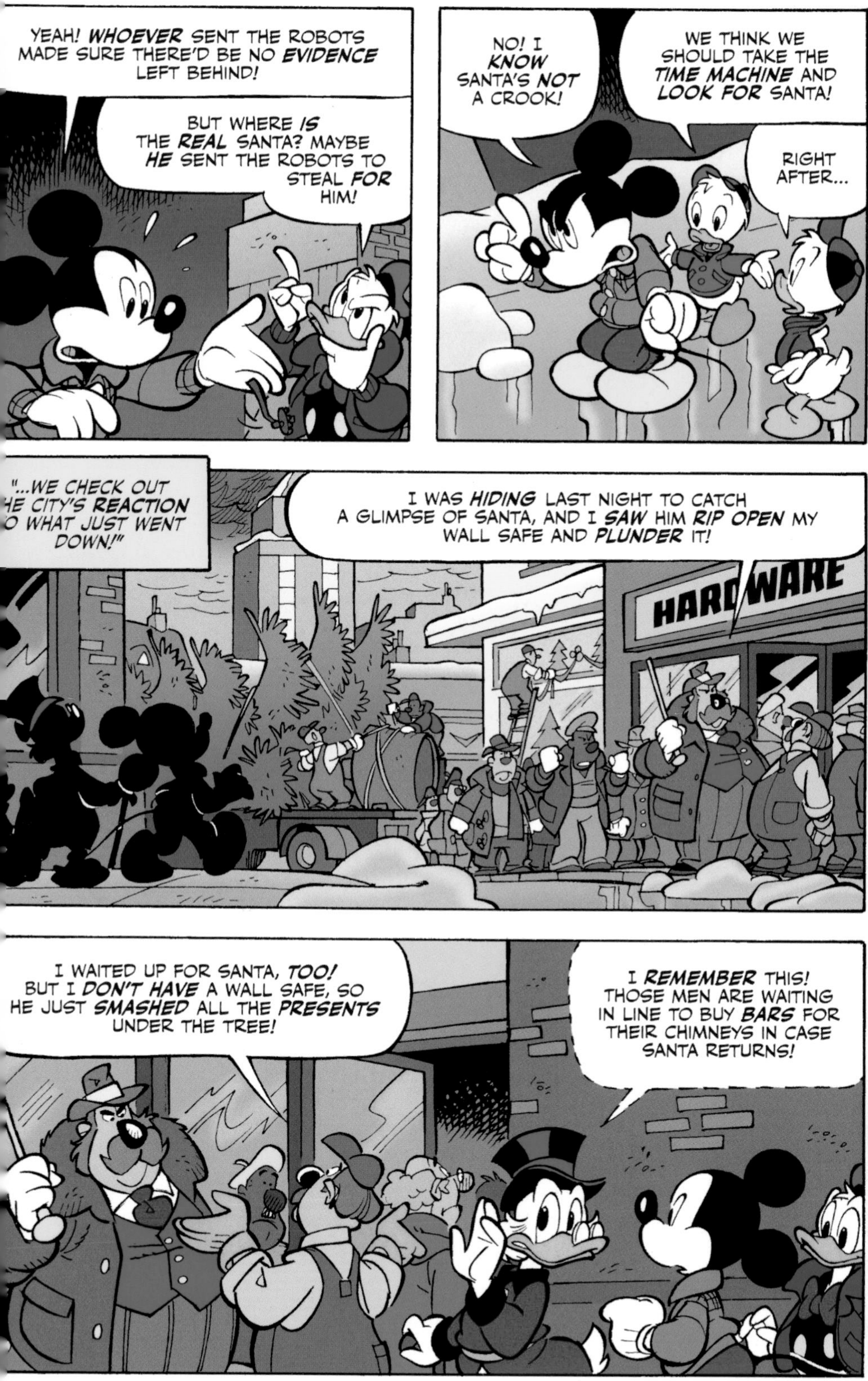
YEAH! WHOEVER SENT THE ROBOTS MADE SURE THERE'D BE NO EVIDENCE LEFT BEHIND!
BUT WHERE IS THE REAL SANTA? MAYBE HE SENT THE ROBOTS TO STEAL FOR HIM!
NO! I KNOW SANTA'S NOT A CROOK!
WE THINK WE SHOULD TAKE THE TIME MACHINE AND LOOK FOR SANTA!
RIGHT AFTER...
"...WE CHECK OUT HE CITY'S REACTION O WHAT JUST WENT DOWN!"
I WAS HIDING LAST NIGHT TO CATCH A GLIMPSE OF SANTA, AND I SAW HIM RIP OPEN MY WALL SAFE AND PLUNDER IT!
HARDWARE
I WAITED UP FOR SANTA, TOO! BUT I DON'T HAVE A WALL SAFE, SO HE JUST SMASHED ALL THE PRESENTS UNDER THE TREE!
I REMEMBER THIS! THOSE MEN ARE WAITING IN LINE TO BUY BARS FOR THEIR CHIMNEYS IN CASE SANTA RETURNS!

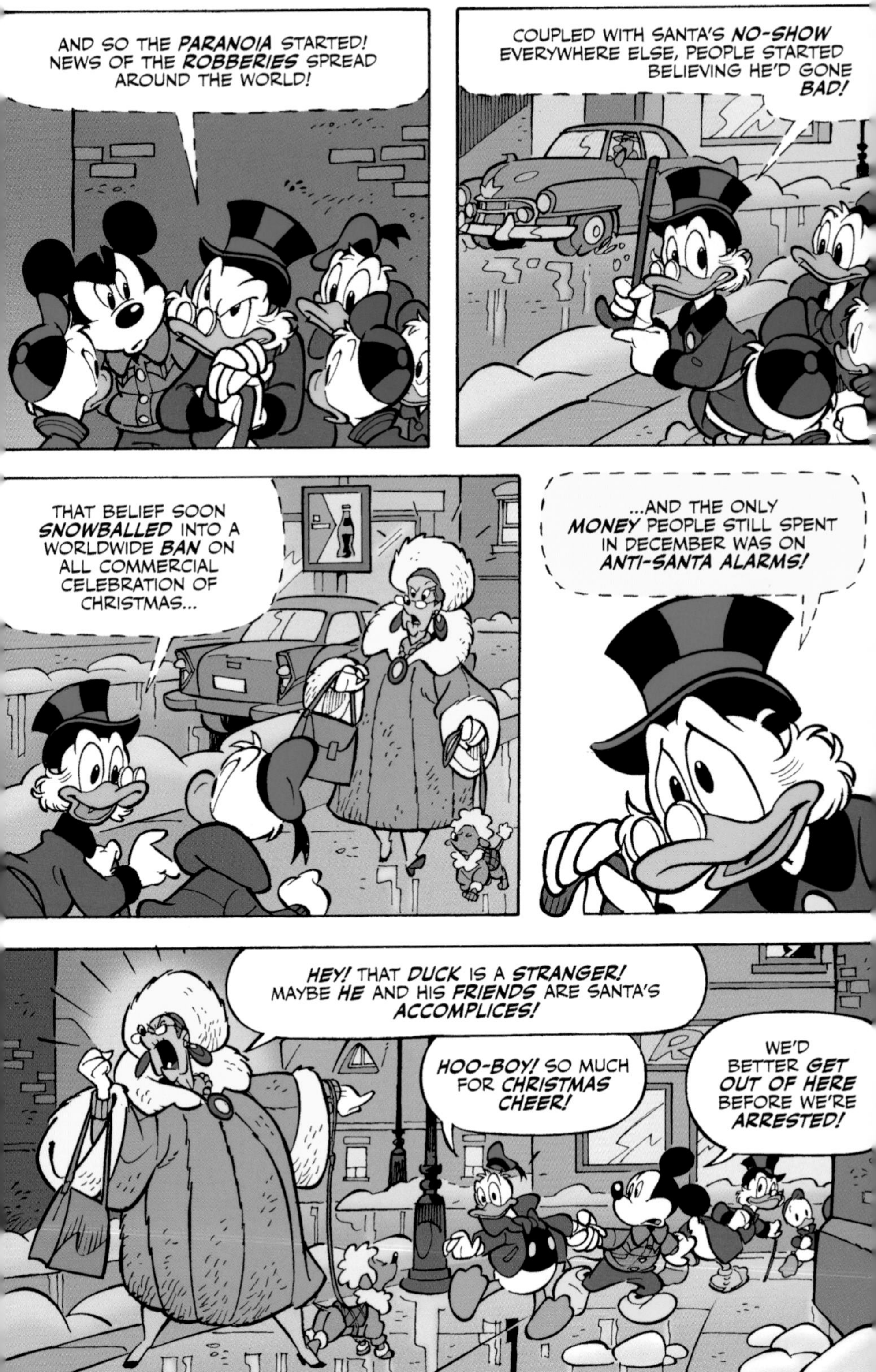
AND SO THE PARANOIA STARTED! NEWS OF THE ROBBERIES SPREAD AROUND THE WORLD!
COUPLED WITH SANTA'S NO-SHOW EVERYWHERE ELSE, PEOPLE STARTED BELIEVING HE'D GONE BAD!
THAT BELIEF SOON SNOWBALLED INTO A WORLDWIDE BAN ON ALL COMMERCIAL CELEBRATION OF CHRISTMAS...
...AND THE ONLY MONEY PEOPLE STILL SPENT IN DECEMBER WAS ON ANTI-SANTA ALARMS!
HEY! THAT DUCK IS A STRANGER! MAYBE HE AND HIS FRIENDS ARE SANTA'S ACCOMPLICES!
HOO-BOY! SO MUCH FOR CHRISTMAS CHEER!
WE'D BETTER GET OUT OF HERE BEFORE WE'RE ARRESTED!

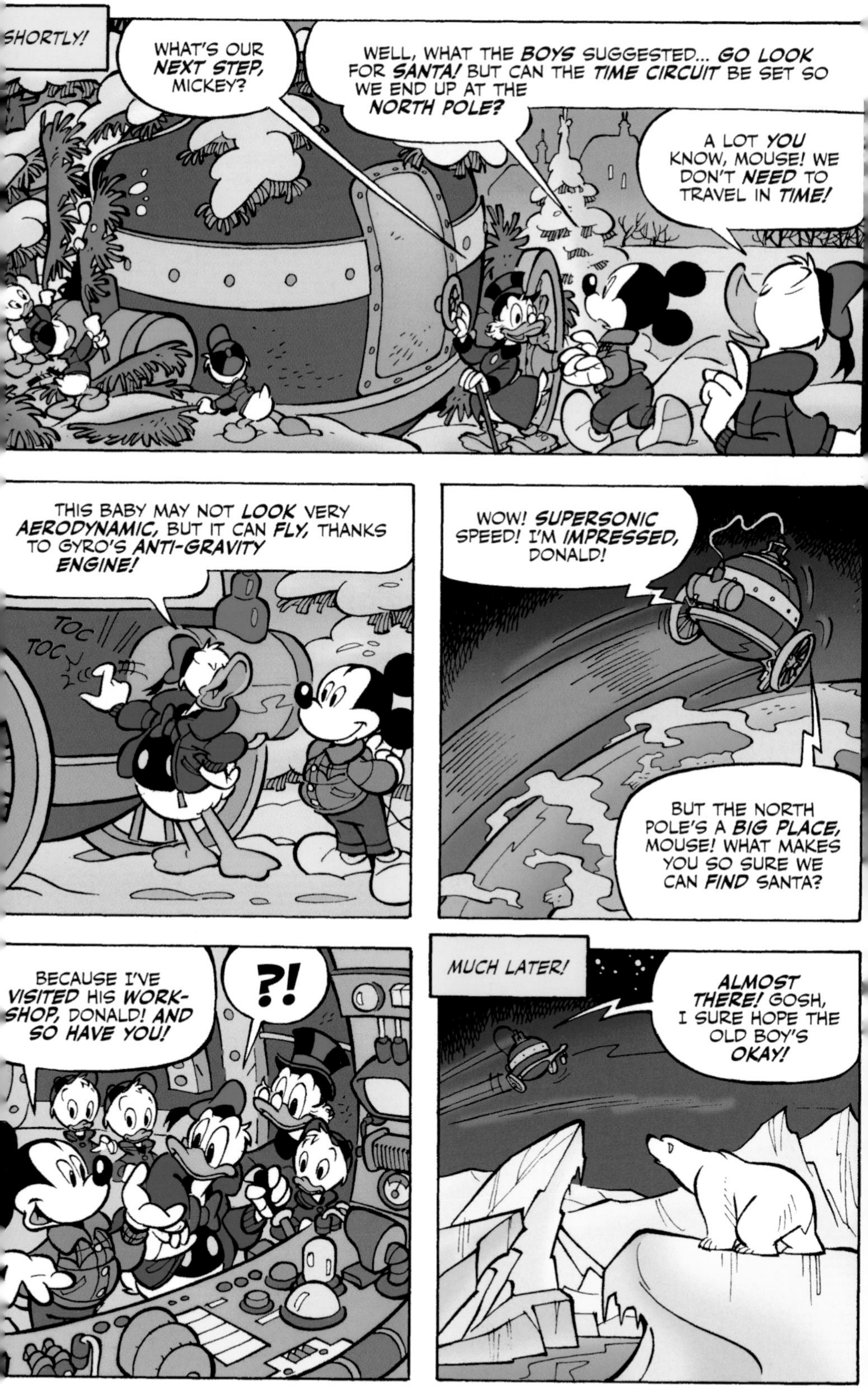
SHORTLY!
WHAT'S OUR NEXT STEP, MICKEY?
WELL, WHAT THE BOYS SUGGESTED... GO LOOK FOR SANTA! BUT CAN THE TIME CIRCUIT BE SET SO WE END UP AT THE NORTH POLE?
A LOT YOU KNOW, MOUSE! WE DON'T NEED TO TRAVEL IN TIME!
THIS BABY MAY NOT LOOK VERY AERODYNAMIC, BUT IT CAN FLY, THANKS TO GYRO'S ANTI-GRAVITY ENGINE!
TOC TOC
WOW! SUPERSONIC SPEED! I'M IMPRESSED, DONALD!
BUT THE NORTH POLE'S A BIG PLACE, MOUSE! WHAT MAKES YOU SO SURE WE CAN FIND SANTA?
BECAUSE I'VE VISITED HIS WORK-SHOP, DONALD! AND SO HAVE YOU!
?!
MUCH LATER!
ALMOST THERE! GOSH, I SURE HOPE THE OLD BOY'S OKAY!

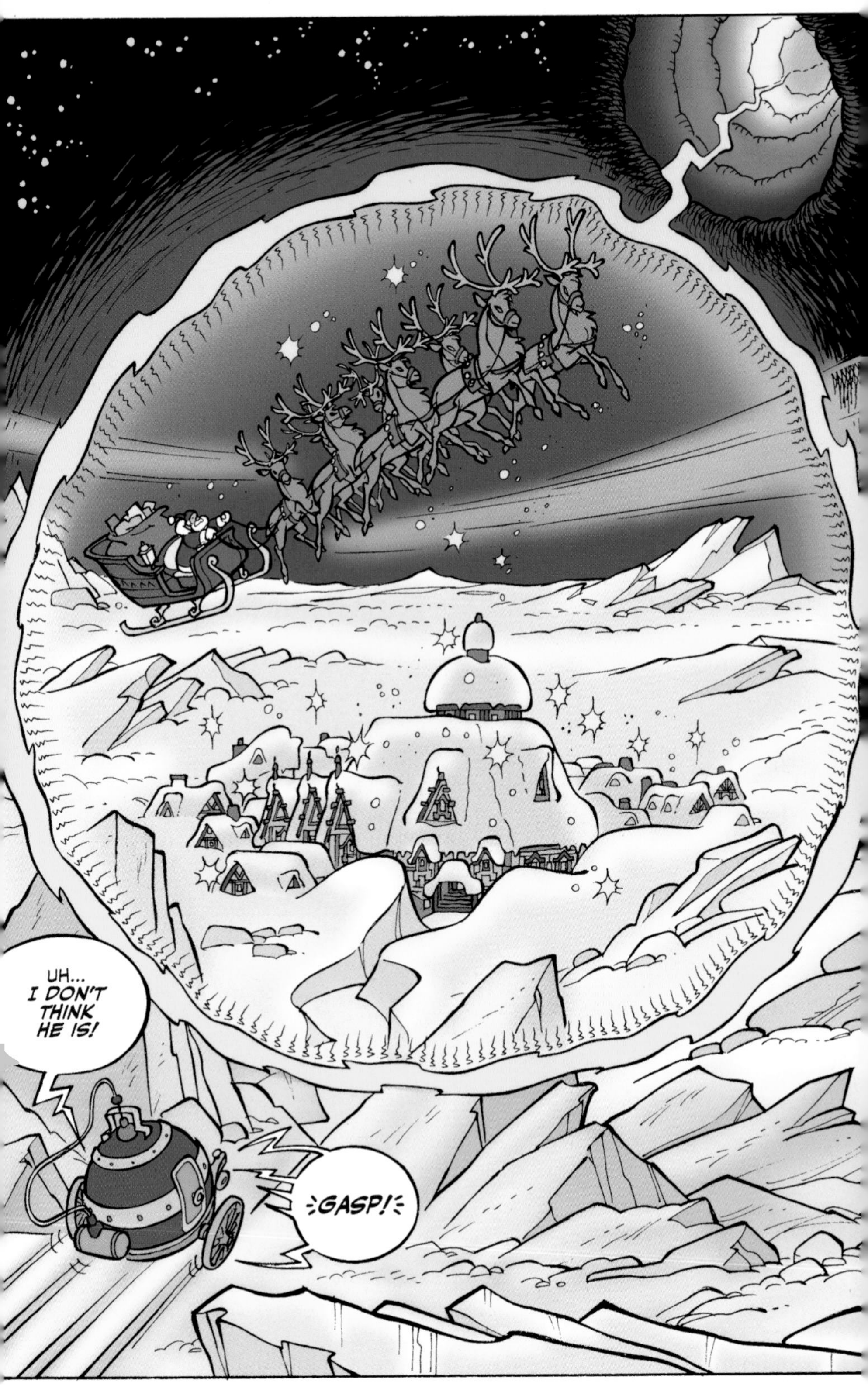
UH... I DON'T THINK HE IS!
GASP!

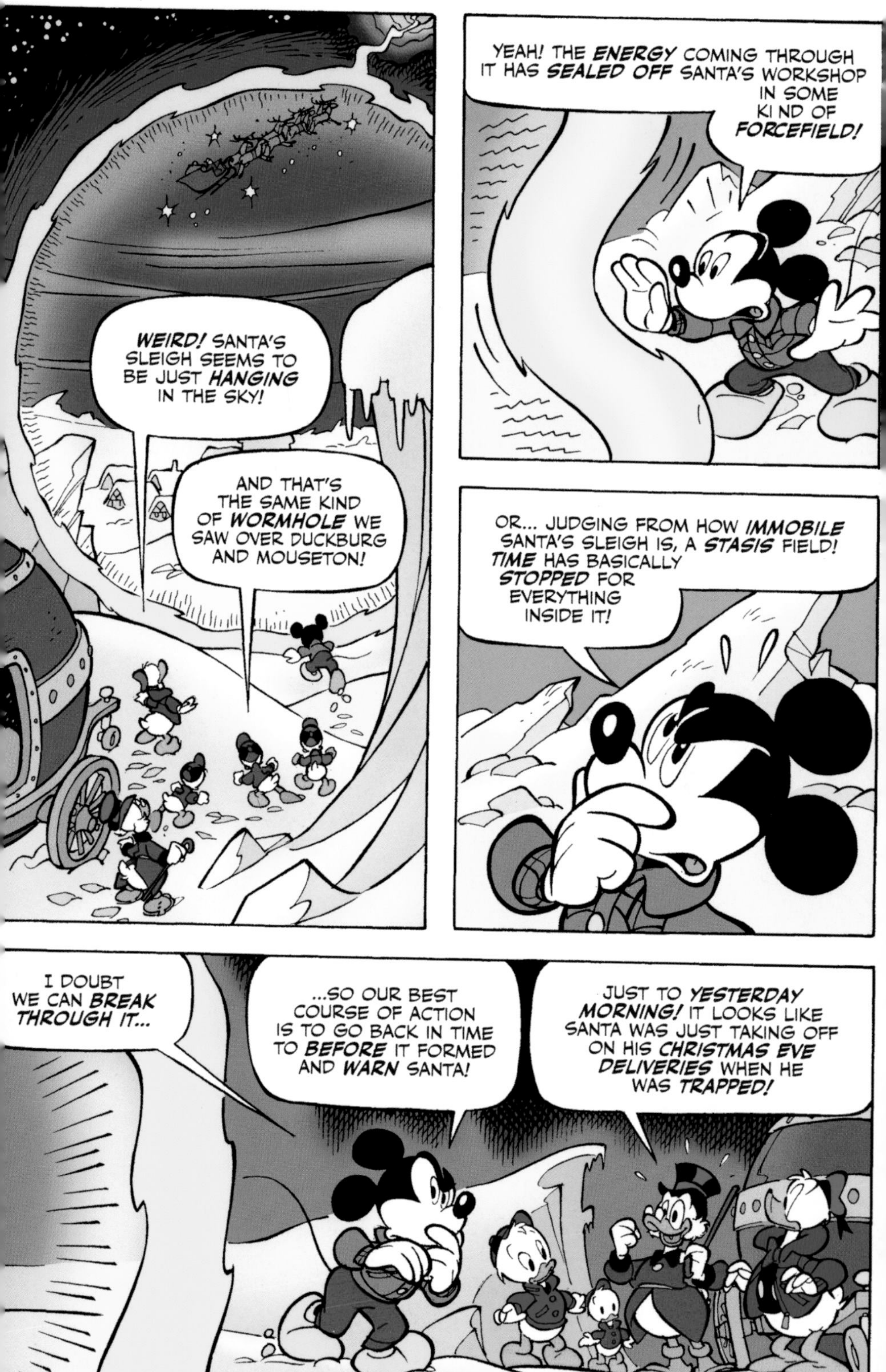
WEIRD! SANTA'S SLEIGH SEEMS TO BE JUST HANGING IN THE SKY!
AND THAT'S THE SAME KIND OF WORMHOLE WE SAW OVER DUCKBURG AND MOUSETON!
YEAH! THE ENERGY COMING THROUGH IT HAS SEALED OFF SANTA'S WORKSHOP IN SOME KIND OF FORCEFIELD!
OR... JUDGING FROM HOW IMMOBILE SANTA'S SLEIGH IS, A STASIS FIELD! TIME HAS BASICALLY STOPPED FOR EVERYTHING INSIDE IT!
I DOUBT WE CAN BREAK THROUGH IT...
...SO OUR BEST COURSE OF ACTION IS TO GO BACK IN TIME TO BEFORE IT FORMED AND WARN SANTA!
JUST TO YESTERDAY MORNING! IT LOOKS LIKE SANTA WAS JUST TAKING OFF ON HIS CHRISTMAS EVE DELIVERIES WHEN HE WAS TRAPPED!

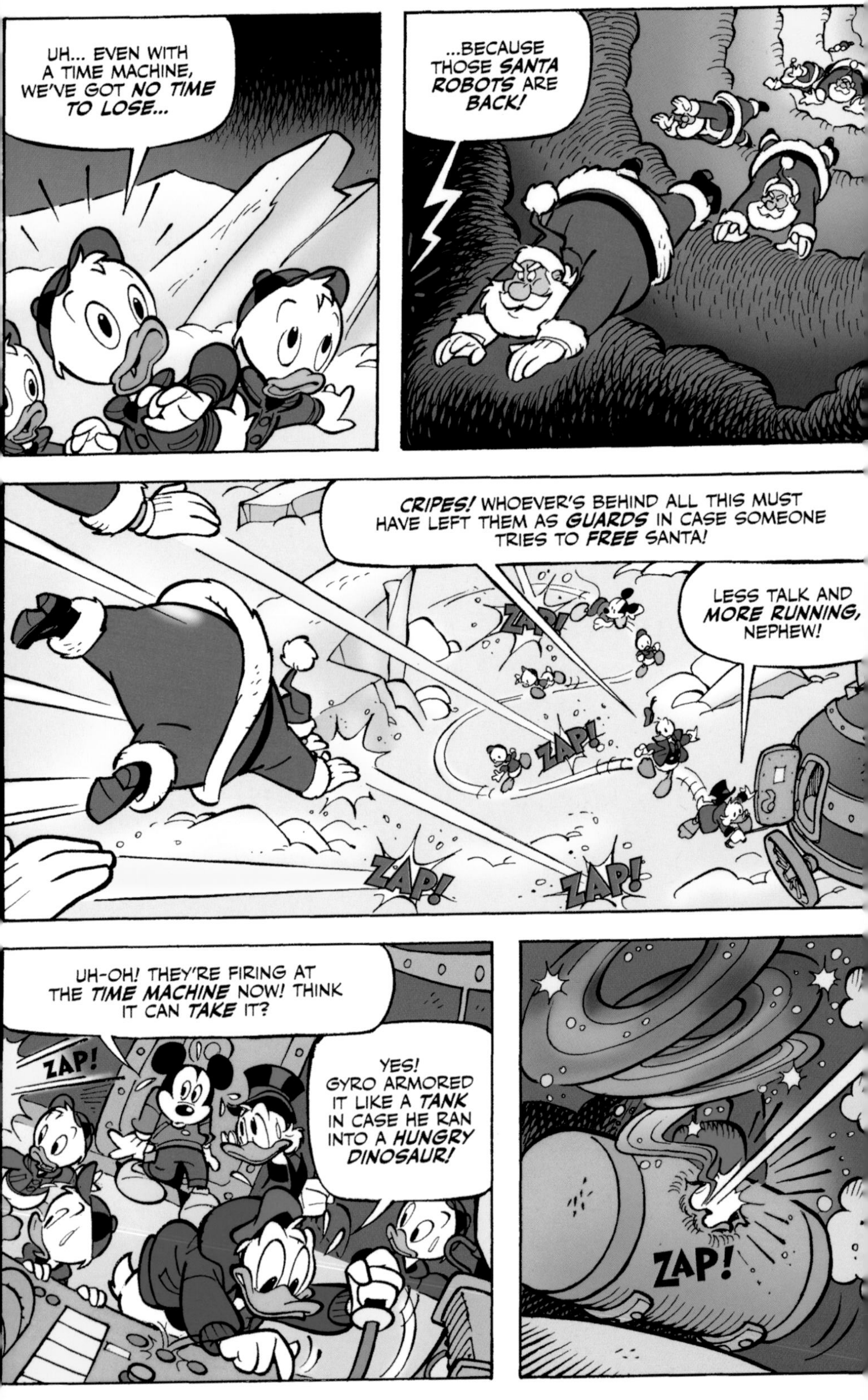
UH... EVEN WITH A TIME MACHINE, WE'VE GOT NO TIME TO LOSE...
...BECAUSE THOSE SANTA ROBOTS ARE BACK!
CRIPES! WHOEVER'S BEHIND ALL THIS MUST HAVE LEFT THEM AS GUARDS IN CASE SOMEONE TRIES TO FREE SANTA!
LESS TALK AND MORE RUNNING, NEPHEW!
ZAP!
ZAP!
ZAP!
ZAP!
UH-OH! THEY'RE FIRING AT THE TIME MACHINE NOW! THINK IT CAN TAKE IT?
ZAP!
YES! GYRO ARMORED IT LIKE A TANK IN CASE HE RAN INTO A HUNGRY DINOSAUR!
ZAP!

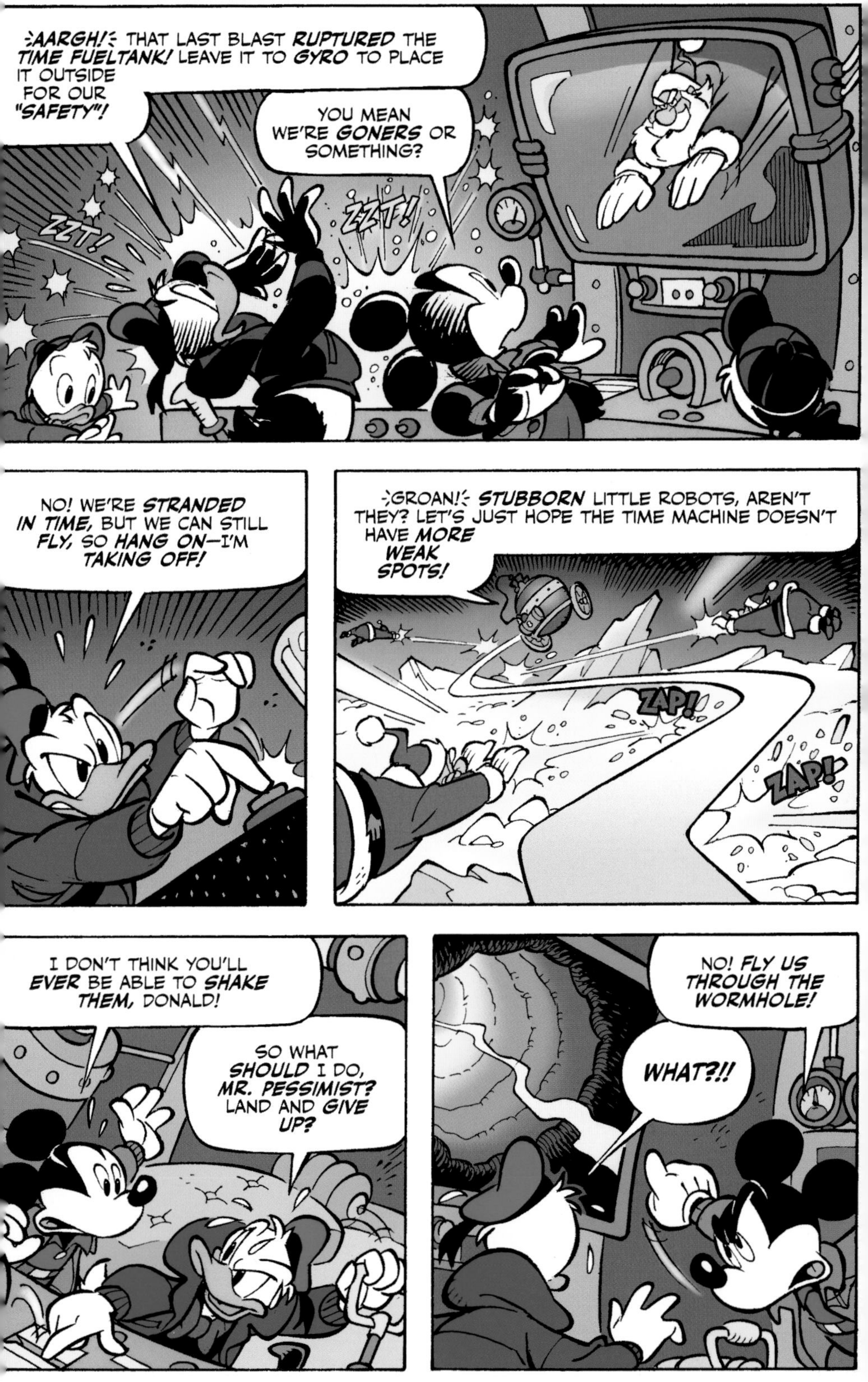

-AARGH!- THAT LAST BLAST RUPTURED THE TIME FUELTANK! LEAVE IT TO GYRO TO PLACE IT OUTSIDE FOR OUR "SAFETY"!
YOU MEAN WE'RE GONERS OR SOMETHING?
ZZT!
ZZT!
NO! WE'RE STRANDED IN TIME, BUT WE CAN STILL FLY, SO HANG ON—I'M TAKING OFF!
-GROAN!- STUBBORN LITTLE ROBOTS, AREN'T THEY? LET'S JUST HOPE THE TIME MACHINE DOESN'T HAVE MORE WEAK SPOTS!
ZAP!
ZAP!
I DON'T THINK YOU'LL EVER BE ABLE TO SHAKE THEM, DONALD!
SO WHAT SHOULD I DO, MR. PESSIMIST? LAND AND GIVE UP?
NO! FLY US THROUGH THE WORMHOLE!
WHAT?!!

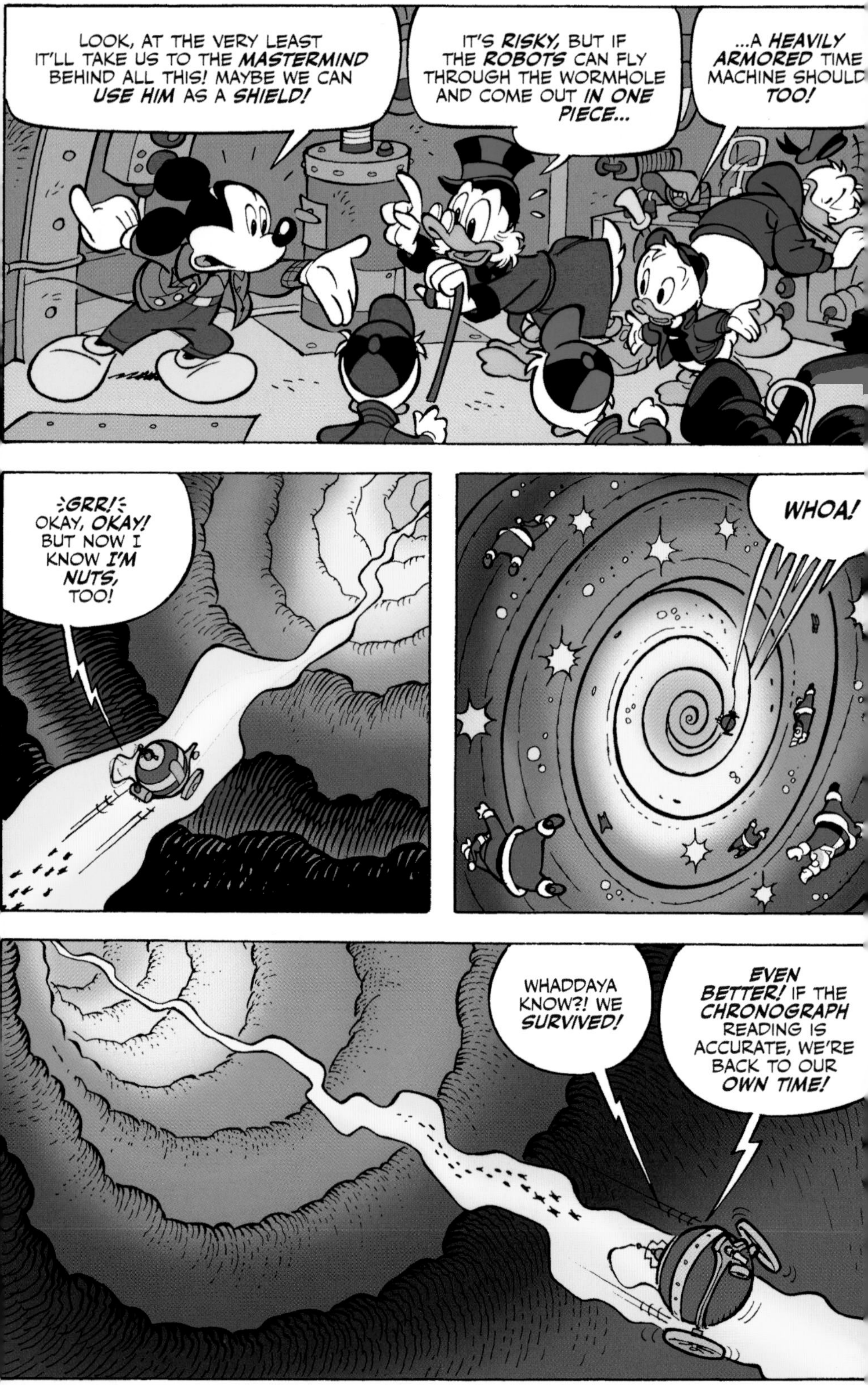
LOOK, AT THE VERY LEAST IT'LL TAKE US TO THE MASTERMIND BEHIND ALL THIS! MAYBE WE CAN USE HIM AS A SHIELD!
IT'S RISKY, BUT IF THE ROBOTS CAN FLY THROUGH THE WORMHOLE AND COME OUT IN ONE PIECE...
...A HEAVILY ARMORED TIME MACHINE SHOULD TOO!
GRR! OKAY, OKAY! BUT NOW I KNOW I'M NUTS, TOO!
WHOA!
WHADDAYA KNOW?! WE SURVIVED!
EVEN BETTER! IF THE CHRONOGRAPH READING IS ACCURATE, WE'RE BACK TO OUR OWN TIME!

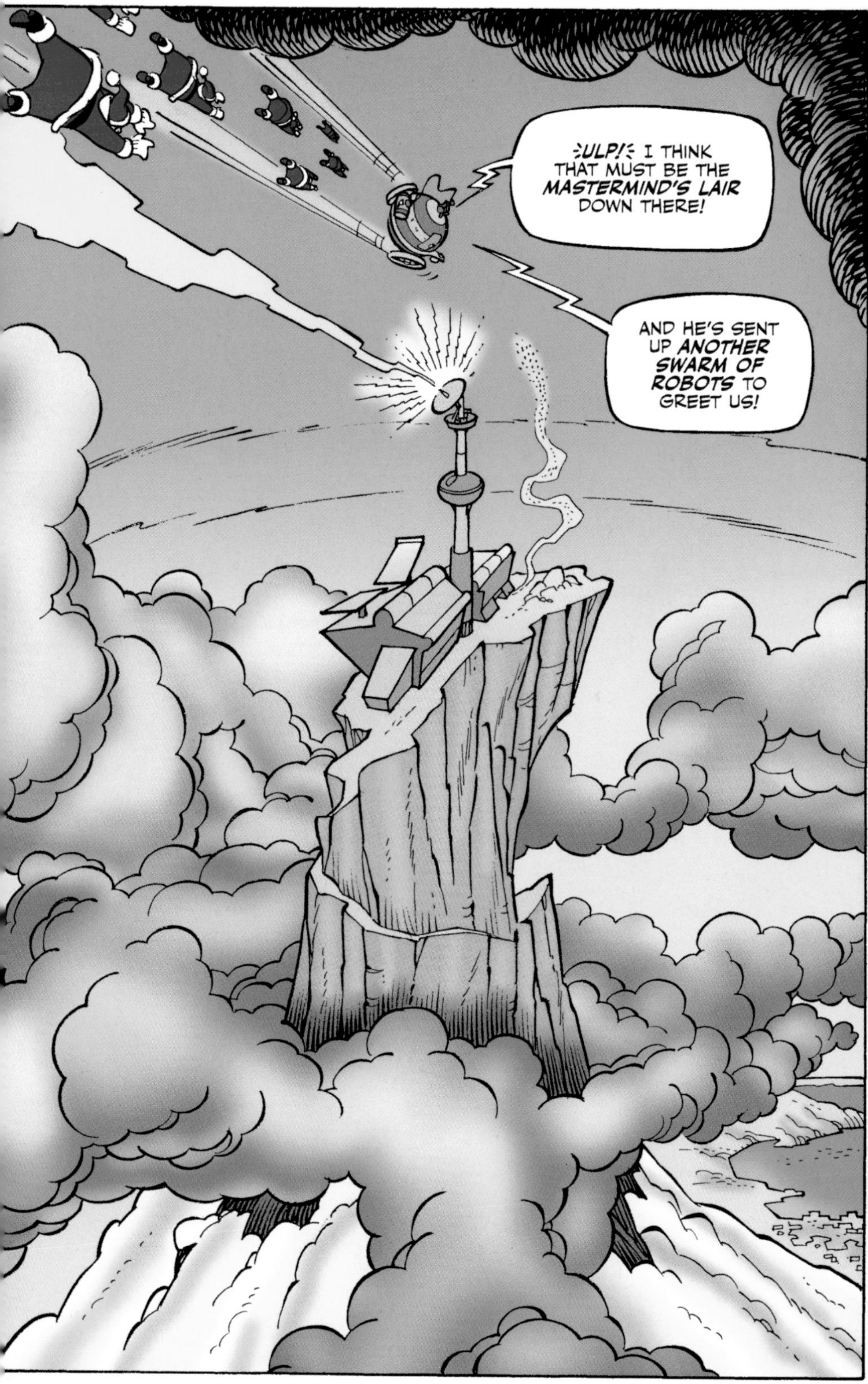

ULP! I THINK THAT MUST BE THE MASTERMIND'S LAIR DOWN THERE!
AND HE'S SENT UP ANOTHER SWARM OF ROBOTS TO GREET US!

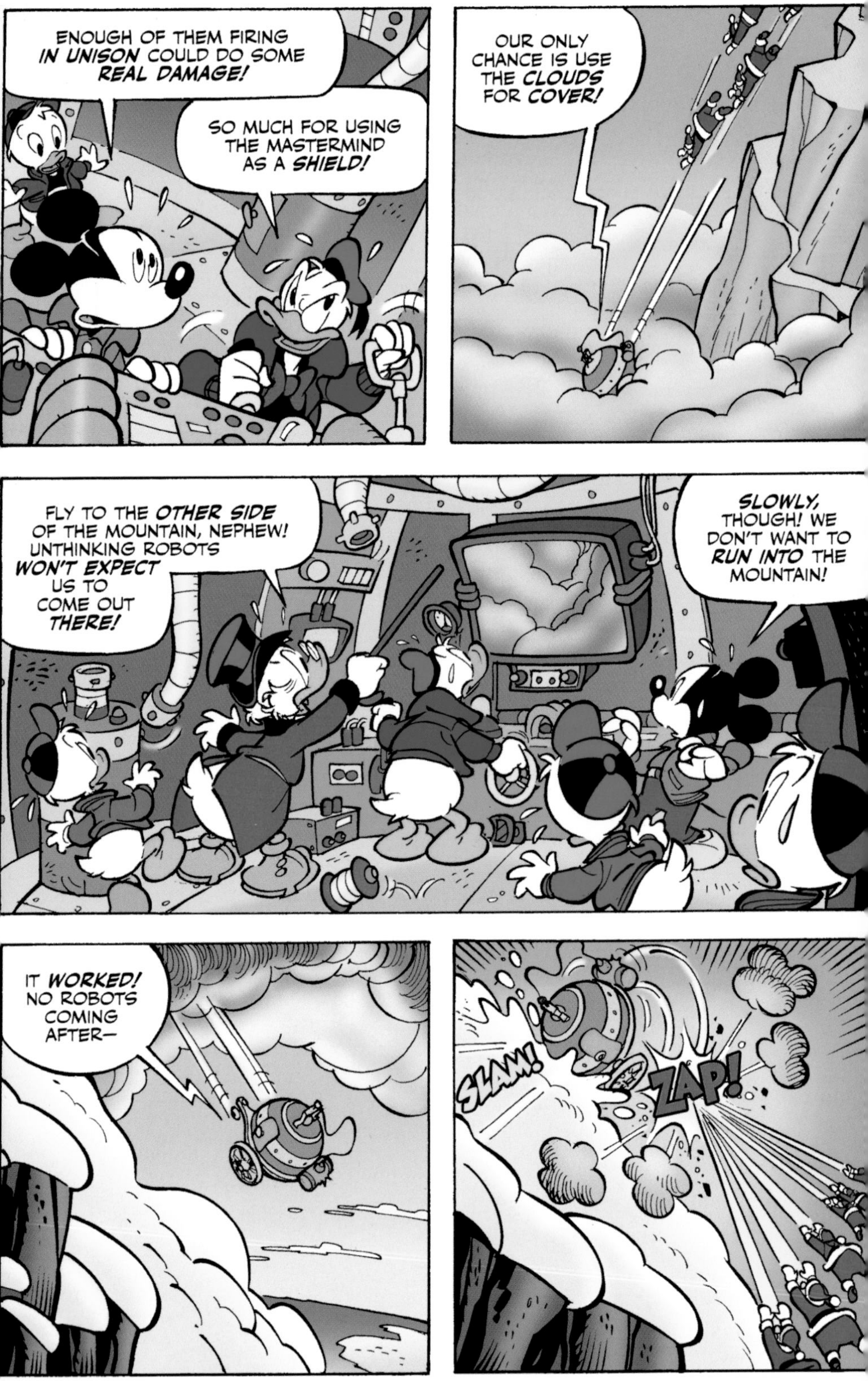
ENOUGH OF THEM FIRING IN UNISON COULD DO SOME REAL DAMAGE!
SO MUCH FOR USING THE MASTERMIND AS A SHIELD!
OUR ONLY CHANCE IS USE THE CLOUDS FOR COVER!
FLY TO THE OTHER SIDE OF THE MOUNTAIN, NEPHEW! UNTHINKING ROBOTS WON'T EXPECT US TO COME OUT THERE!
SLOWLY, THOUGH! WE DON'T WANT TO RUN INTO THE MOUNTAIN!
IT WORKED! NO ROBOTS COMING AFTER—
SLAM!
ZAP!

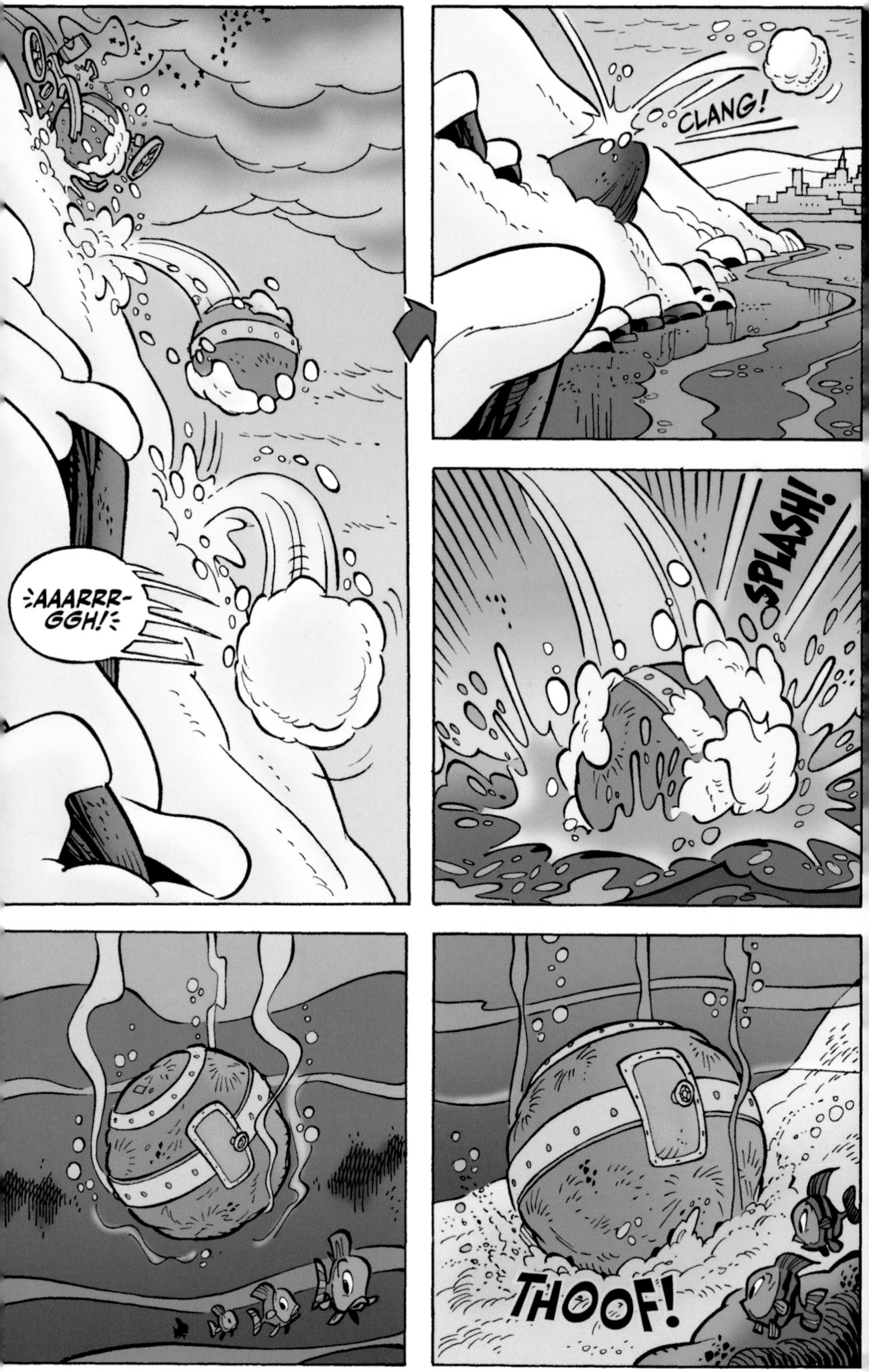

AAARRR-GGH!
CLANG!
SPLASH!
THOOF!

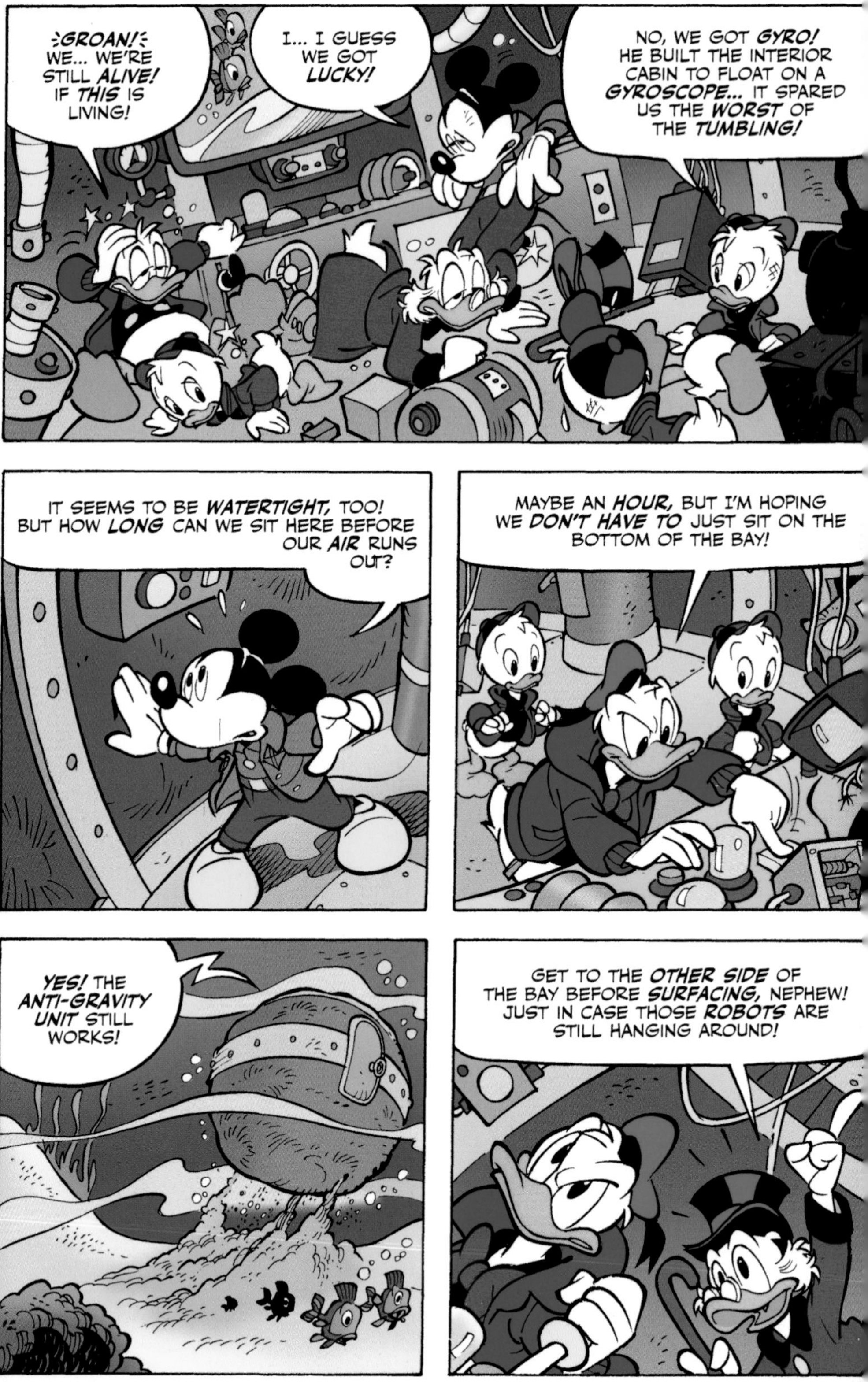

GROAN! WE... WE'RE STILL ALIVE! IF THIS IS LIVING!
I... I GUESS WE GOT LUCKY!
NO, WE GOT GYRO! HE BUILT THE INTERIOR CABIN TO FLOAT ON A GYROSCOPE... IT SPARED US THE WORST OF THE TUMBLING!
IT SEEMS TO BE WATERTIGHT, TOO! BUT HOW LONG CAN WE SIT HERE BEFORE OUR AIR RUNS OUT?
MAYBE AN HOUR, BUT I'M HOPING WE DON'T HAVE TO JUST SIT ON THE BOTTOM OF THE BAY!
YES! THE ANTI-GRAVITY UNIT STILL WORKS!
GET TO THE OTHER SIDE OF THE BAY BEFORE SURFACING, NEPHEW! JUST IN CASE THOSE ROBOTS ARE STILL HANGING AROUND!

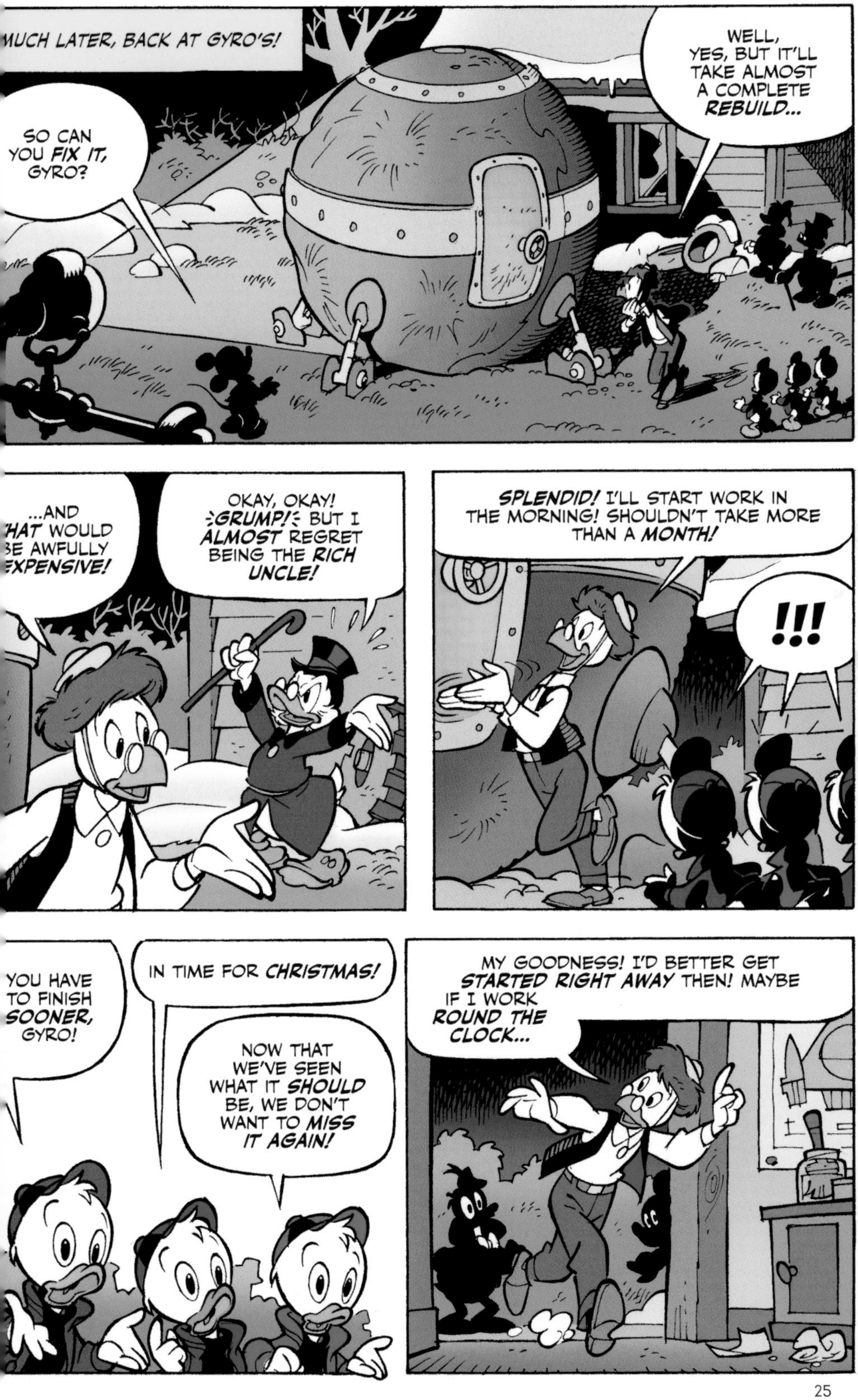
MUCH LATER, BACK AT GYRO'S!
SO CAN YOU FIX IT, GYRO?
WELL, YES, BUT IT'LL TAKE ALMOST A COMPLETE REBUILD...
...AND THAT WOULD BE AWFULLY EXPENSIVE!
OKAY, OKAY! GRUMP! BUT I ALMOST REGRET BEING THE RICH UNCLE!
SPLENDID! I'LL START WORK IN THE MORNING! SHOULDN'T TAKE MORE THAN A MONTH!
!!!
YOU HAVE TO FINISH SOONER, GYRO!
IN TIME FOR CHRISTMAS!
NOW THAT WE'VE SEEN WHAT IT SHOULD BE, WE DON'T WANT TO MISS IT AGAIN!
MY GOODNESS! I'D BETTER GET STARTED RIGHT AWAY THEN! MAYBE IF I WORK ROUND THE CLOCK...

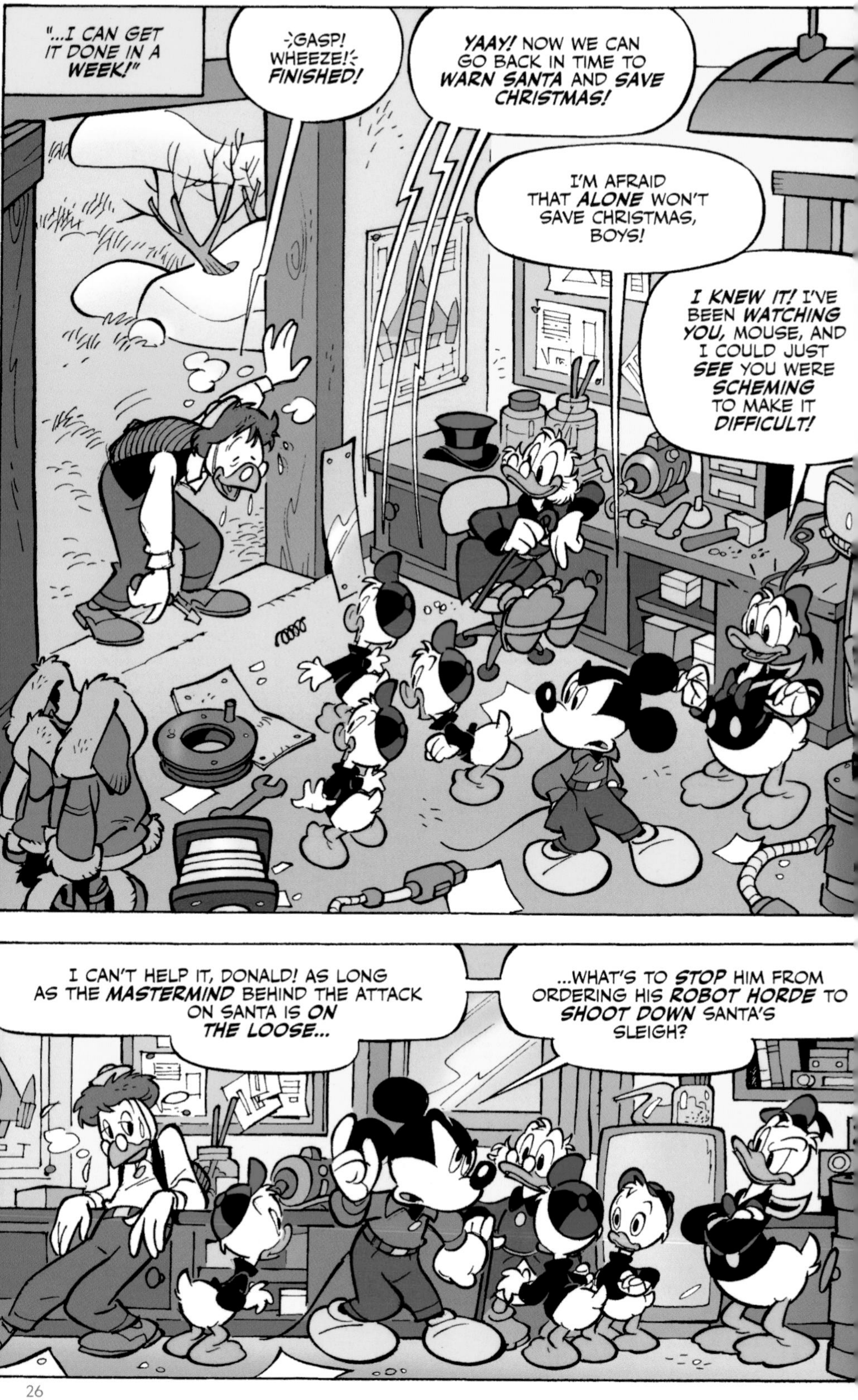
"...I CAN GET IT DONE IN A WEEK!"
GASP! WHEEZE! FINISHED!
YAAY! NOW WE CAN GO BACK IN TIME TO WARN SANTA AND SAVE CHRISTMAS!
I'M AFRAID THAT ALONE WON'T SAVE CHRISTMAS, BOYS!
I KNEW IT! I'VE BEEN WATCHING YOU, MOUSE, AND I COULD JUST SEE YOU WERE SCHEMING TO MAKE IT DIFFICULT!
I CAN'T HELP IT, DONALD! AS LONG AS THE MASTERMIND BEHIND THE ATTACK ON SANTA IS ON THE LOOSE...
...WHAT'S TO STOP HIM FROM ORDERING HIS ROBOT HORDE TO SHOOT DOWN SANTA'S SLEIGH?

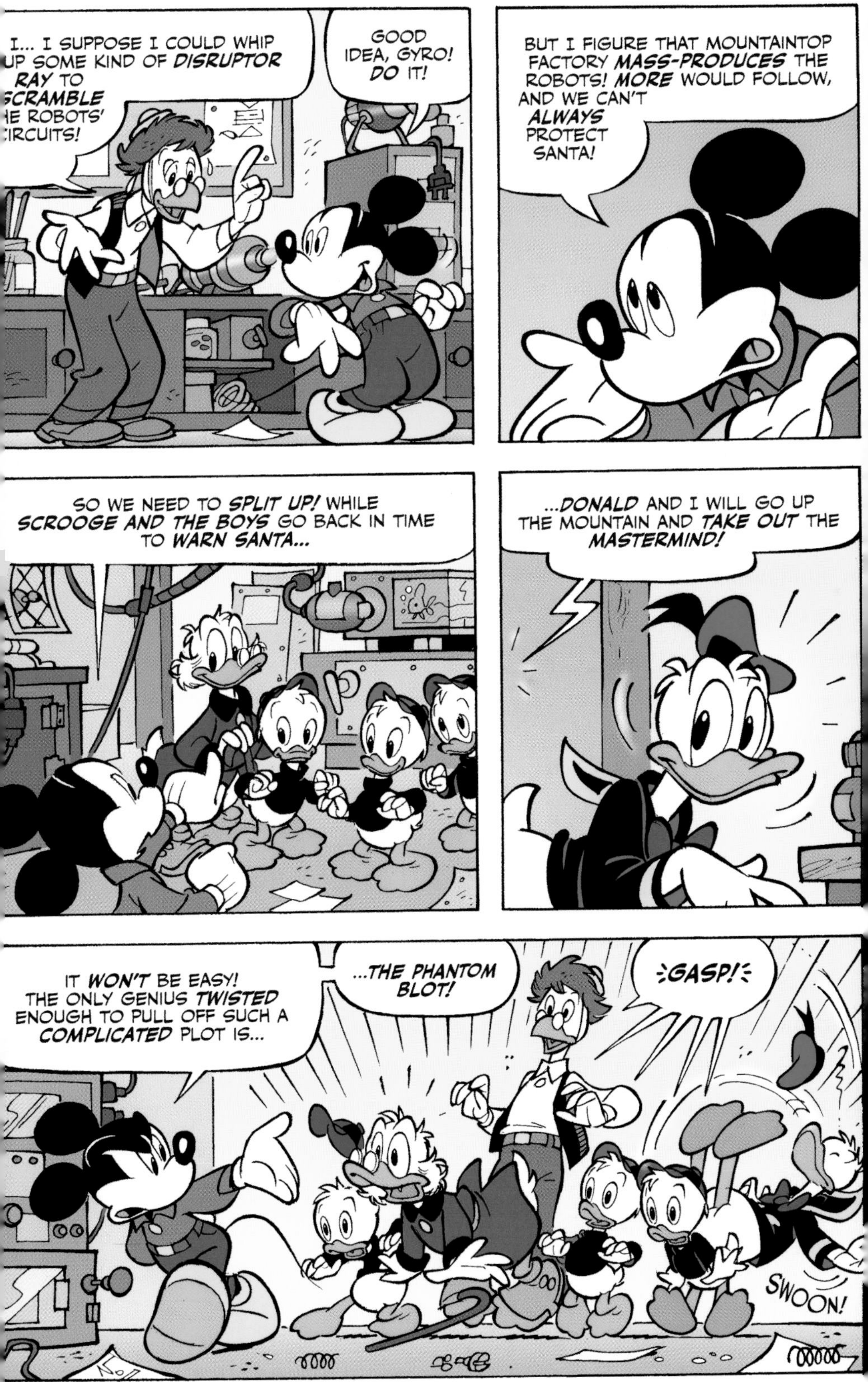

I... I SUPPOSE I COULD WHIP UP SOME KIND OF DISRUPTOR RAY TO SCRAMBLE THE ROBOTS' CIRCUITS!
GOOD IDEA, GYRO! DO IT!
BUT I FIGURE THAT MOUNTAINTOP FACTORY MASS-PRODUCES THE ROBOTS! MORE WOULD FOLLOW, AND WE CAN'T ALWAYS PROTECT SANTA!
SO WE NEED TO SPLIT UP! WHILE SCROOGE AND THE BOYS GO BACK IN TIME TO WARN SANTA...
...DONALD AND I WILL GO UP THE MOUNTAIN AND TAKE OUT THE MASTERMIND!
IT WON'T BE EASY! THE ONLY GENIUS TWISTED ENOUGH TO PULL OFF SUCH A COMPLICATED PLOT IS...
...THE PHANTOM BLOT!
GASP!
SWOON!

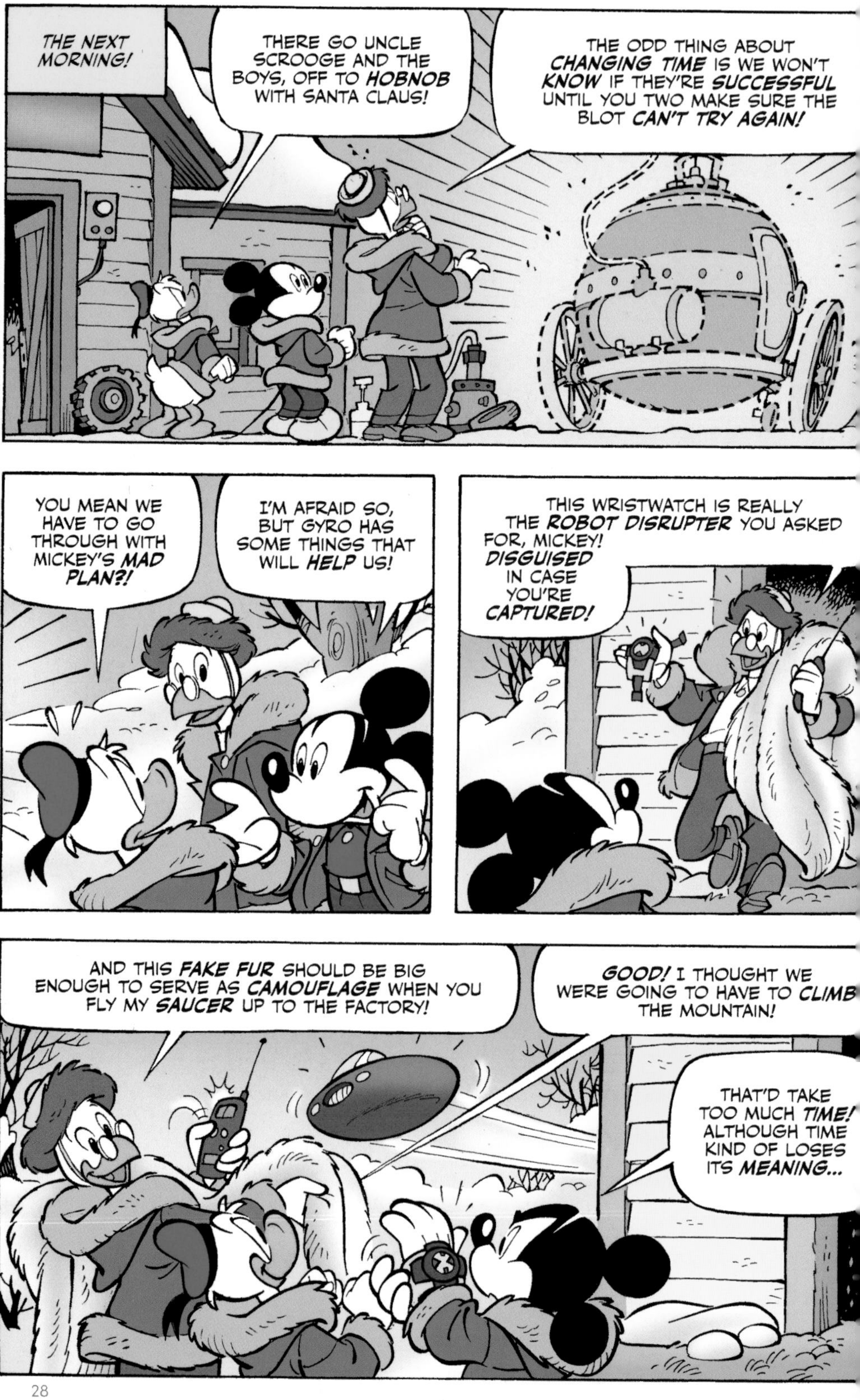
THE NEXT MORNING!
THERE GO UNCLE SCROOGE AND THE BOYS, OFF TO HOBNOB WITH SANTA CLAUS!
THE ODD THING ABOUT CHANGING TIME IS WE WON'T KNOW IF THEY'RE SUCCESSFUL UNTIL YOU TWO MAKE SURE THE BLOT CAN'T TRY AGAIN!
YOU MEAN WE HAVE TO GO THROUGH WITH MICKEY'S MAD PLAN?!
I'M AFRAID SO, BUT GYRO HAS SOME THINGS THAT WILL HELP US!
THIS WRISTWATCH IS REALLY THE ROBOT DISRUPTER YOU ASKED FOR, MICKEY! DISGUISED IN CASE YOU'RE CAPTURED!
AND THIS FAKE FUR SHOULD BE BIG ENOUGH TO SERVE AS CAMOUFLAGE WHEN YOU FLY MY SAUCER UP TO THE FACTORY!
GOOD! I THOUGHT WE WERE GOING TO HAVE TO CLIMB THE MOUNTAIN!
THAT'D TAKE TOO MUCH TIME! ALTHOUGH TIME KIND OF LOSES ITS MEANING...

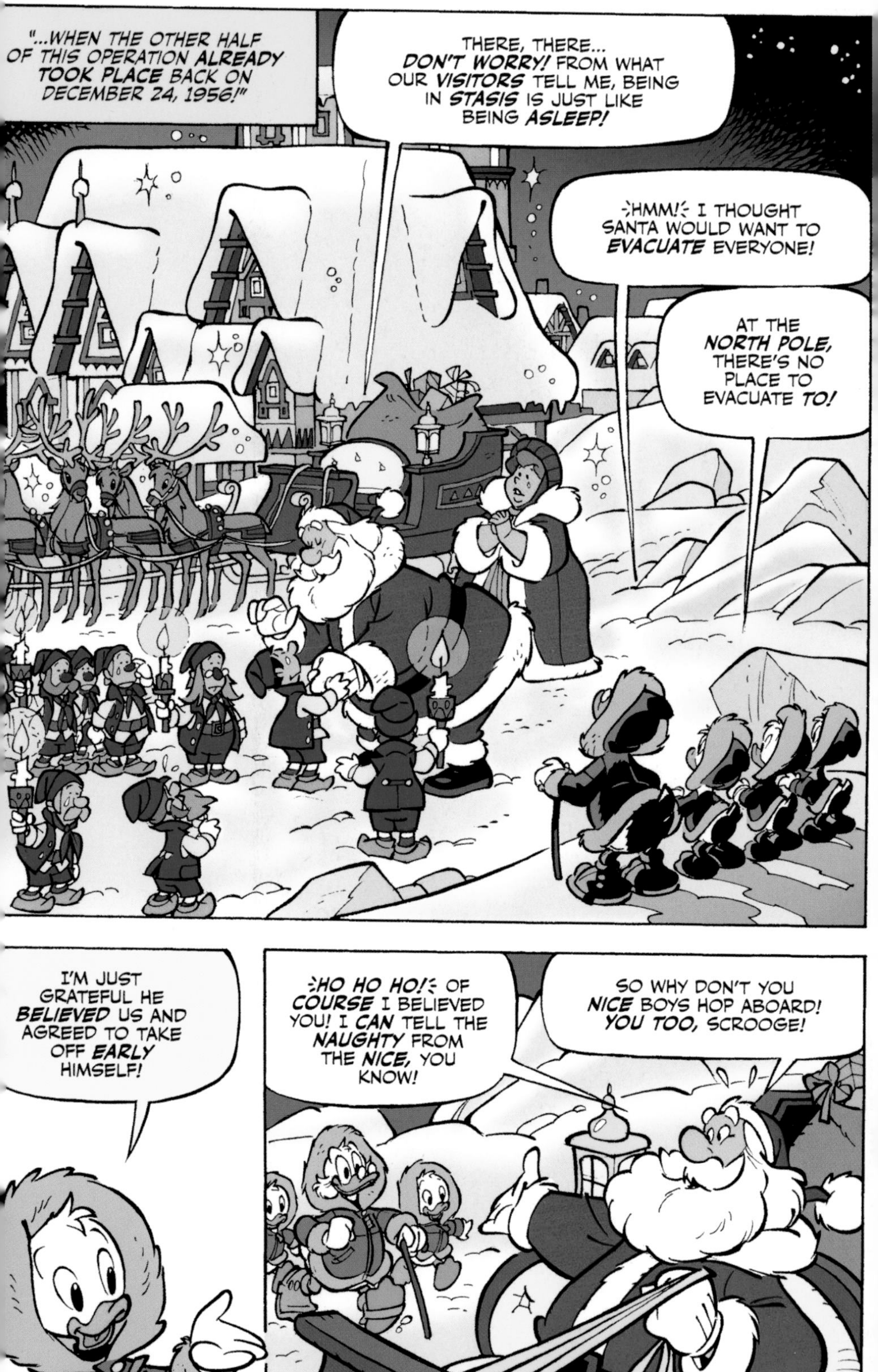

"...WHEN THE OTHER HALF OF THIS OPERATION ALREADY TOOK PLACE BACK ON DECEMBER 24, 1956!"
THERE, THERE... DON'T WORRY! FROM WHAT OUR VISITORS TELL ME, BEING IN STASIS IS JUST LIKE BEING ASLEEP!
HMM! I THOUGHT SANTA WOULD WANT TO EVACUATE EVERYONE!
AT THE NORTH POLE, THERE'S NO PLACE TO EVACUATE TO!
I'M JUST GRATEFUL HE BELIEVED US AND AGREED TO TAKE OFF EARLY HIMSELF!
HO HO HO! OF COURSE I BELIEVED YOU! I CAN TELL THE NAUGHTY FROM THE NICE, YOU KNOW!
SO WHY DON'T YOU NICE BOYS HOP ABOARD! YOU TOO, SCROOGE!

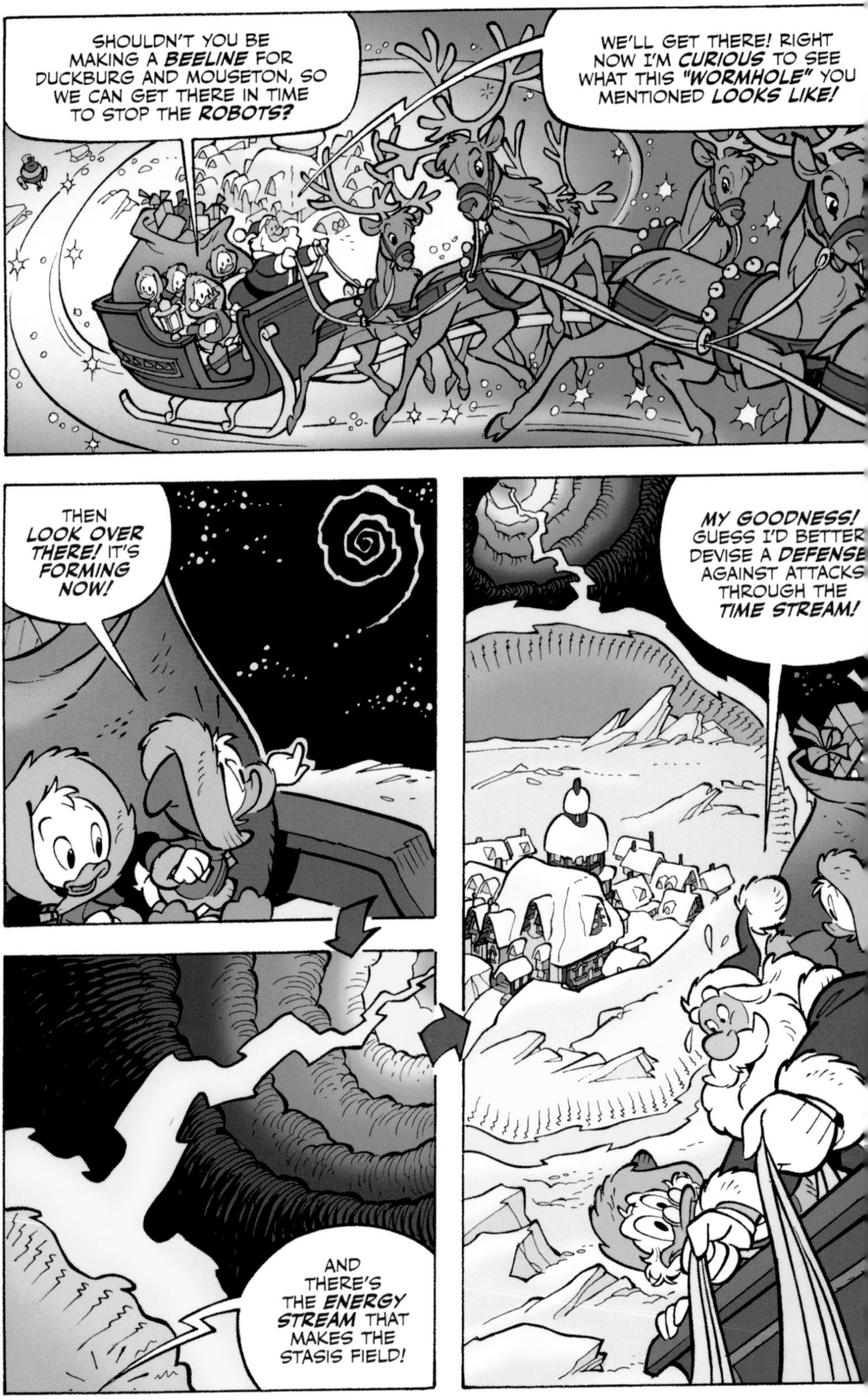
SHOULDN'T YOU BE MAKING A BEELINE FOR DUCKBURG AND MOUSETON, SO WE CAN GET THERE IN TIME TO STOP THE ROBOTS?
WE'LL GET THERE! RIGHT NOW I'M CURIOUS TO SEE WHAT THIS "WORMHOLE" YOU MENTIONED LOOKS LIKE!
THEN LOOK OVER THERE! IT'S FORMING NOW!
AND THERE'S THE ENERGY STREAM THAT MAKES THE STASIS FIELD!
MY GOODNESS! GUESS I'D BETTER DEVISE A DEFENSE AGAINST ATTACKS THROUGH THE TIME STREAM!

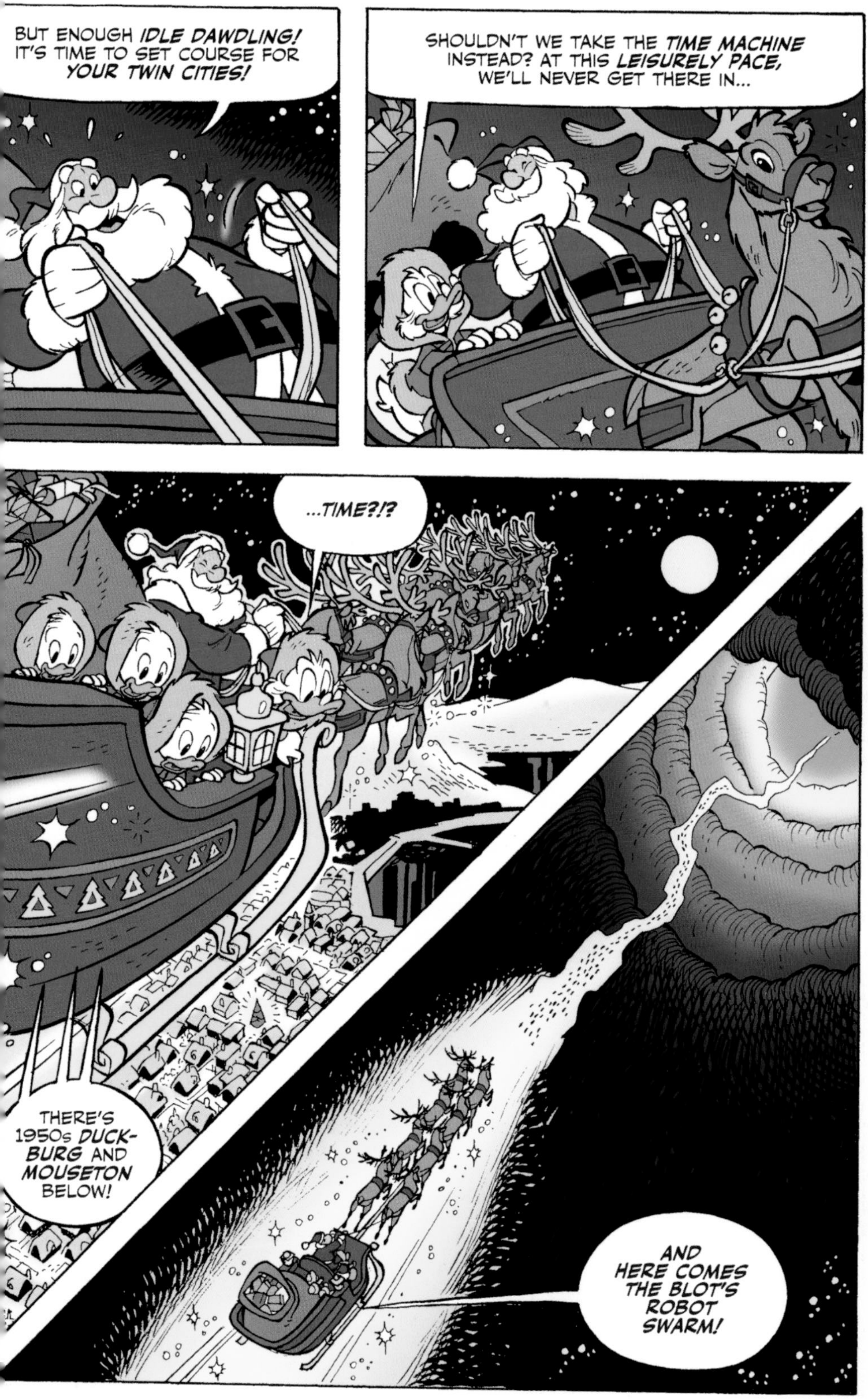
BUT ENOUGH IDLE DAWDLING! IT'S TIME TO SET COURSE FOR YOUR TWIN CITIES!
SHOULDN'T WE TAKE THE TIME MACHINE INSTEAD? AT THIS LEISURELY PACE, WE'LL NEVER GET THERE IN...
...TIME?!?
THERE'S 1950s DUCKBURG AND MOUSETON BELOW!
AND HERE COMES THE BLOT'S ROBOT SWARM!

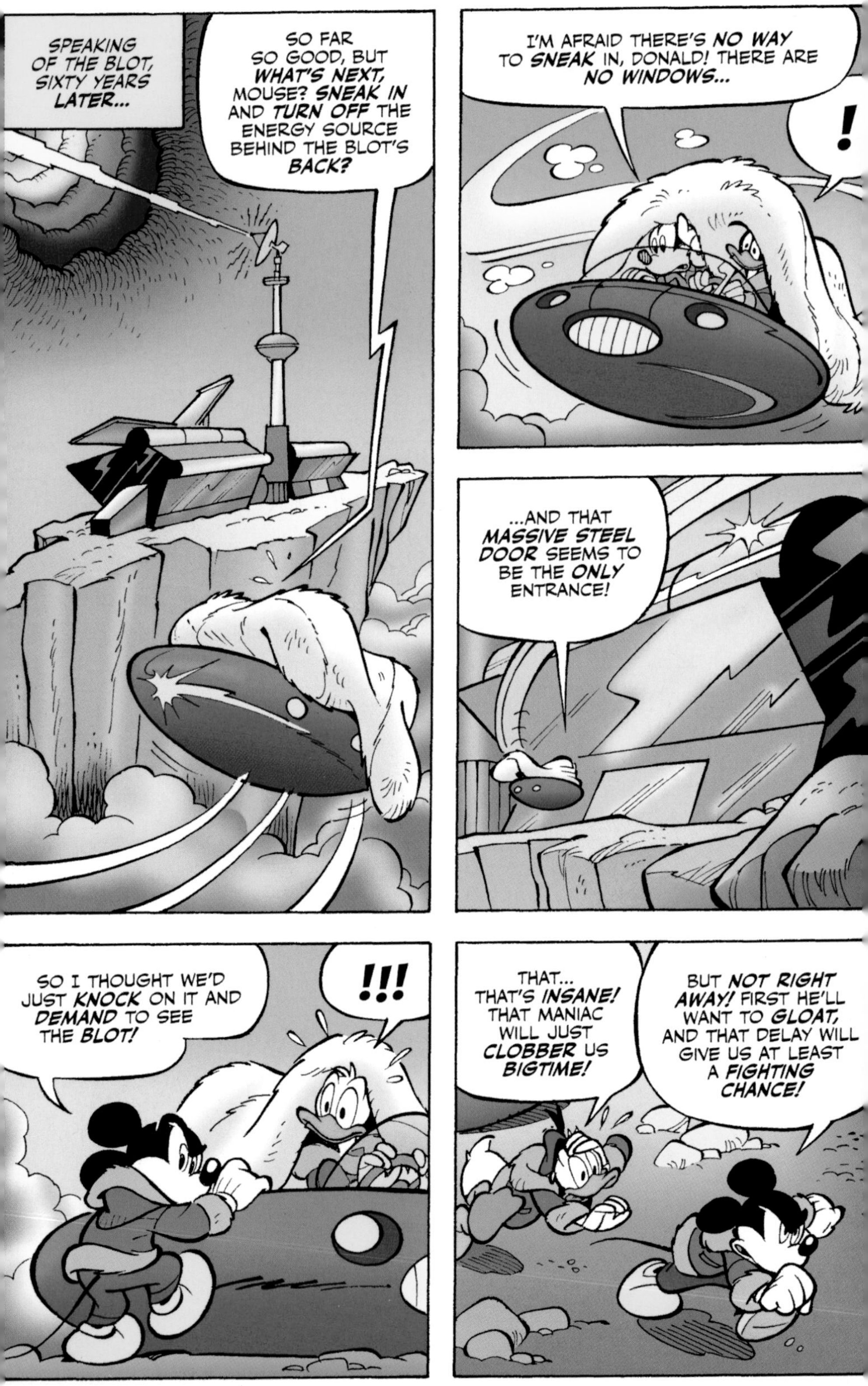
SPEAKING OF THE BLOT, SIXTY YEARS LATER...
SO FAR SO GOOD, BUT WHAT'S NEXT, MOUSE? SNEAK IN AND TURN OFF THE ENERGY SOURCE BEHIND THE BLOT'S BACK?
I'M AFRAID THERE'S NO WAY TO SNEAK IN, DONALD! THERE ARE NO WINDOWS...
!
...AND THAT MASSIVE STEEL DOOR SEEMS TO BE THE ONLY ENTRANCE!
SO I THOUGHT WE'D JUST KNOCK ON IT AND DEMAND TO SEE THE BLOT!
!!!
THAT... THAT'S INSANE! THAT MANIAC WILL JUST CLOBBER US BIGTIME!
BUT NOT RIGHT AWAY! FIRST HE'LL WANT TO GLOAT, AND THAT DELAY WILL GIVE US AT LEAST A FIGHTING CHANCE!

I'D LIKE YOU *WITH* ME, DONALD, BUT YOU *DON'T HAVE TO COME!* YOU CAN ALWAYS *ESCAPE* ON GYRO'S SAUCER!

YOU BET I—

I... I *CAN'T!*

THE TRUTH IS, I *LIKED* WHAT I SAW OF *CHRISTMAS...* ENOUGH TO *RISK ANYTHING* TO RESTORE IT!

NOT JUST FOR *ME,* EITHER! THE *BOYS...* THE BOYS *DESERVE* THE *HAPPINESS* IT BRINGS!

POUND! POUND! POUND! POUND!

BUT IF THIS *DOESN'T WORK,* I'M GONNA COME BACK AND *HAUNT* YOU!

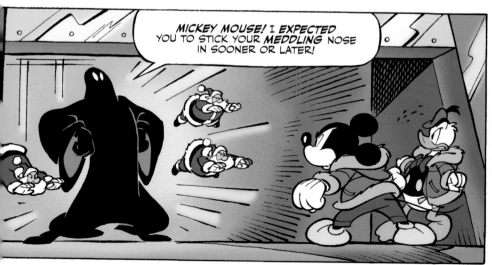

MICKEY MOUSE! I EXPECTED YOU TO STICK YOUR *MEDDLING* NOSE IN SOONER OR LATER!

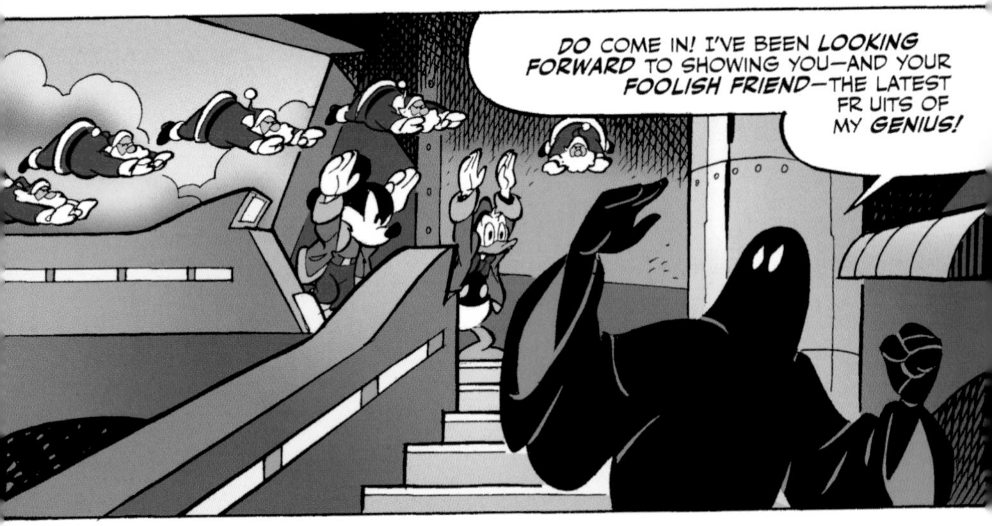
DO COME IN! I'VE BEEN LOOKING FORWARD TO SHOWING YOU—AND YOUR FOOLISH FRIEND—THE LATEST FR UITS OF MY GENIUS!

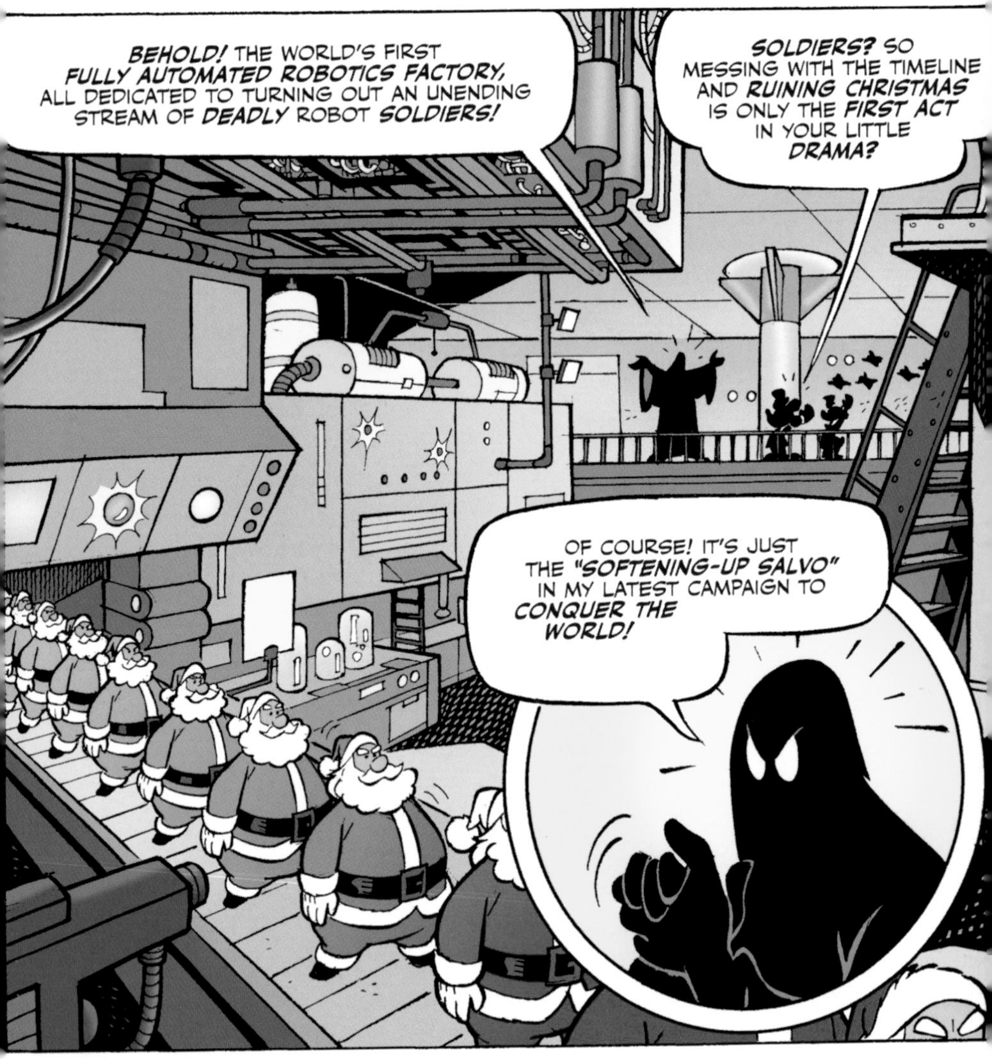
BEHOLD! THE WORLD'S FIRST FULLY AUTOMATED ROBOTICS FACTORY, ALL DEDICATED TO TURNING OUT AN UNENDING STREAM OF DEADLY ROBOT SOLDIERS!
SOLDIERS? SO MESSING WITH THE TIMELINE AND RUINING CHRISTMAS IS ONLY THE FIRST ACT IN YOUR LITTLE DRAMA?
OF COURSE! IT'S JUST THE "SOFTENING-UP SALVO" IN MY LATEST CAMPAIGN TO CONQUER THE WORLD!

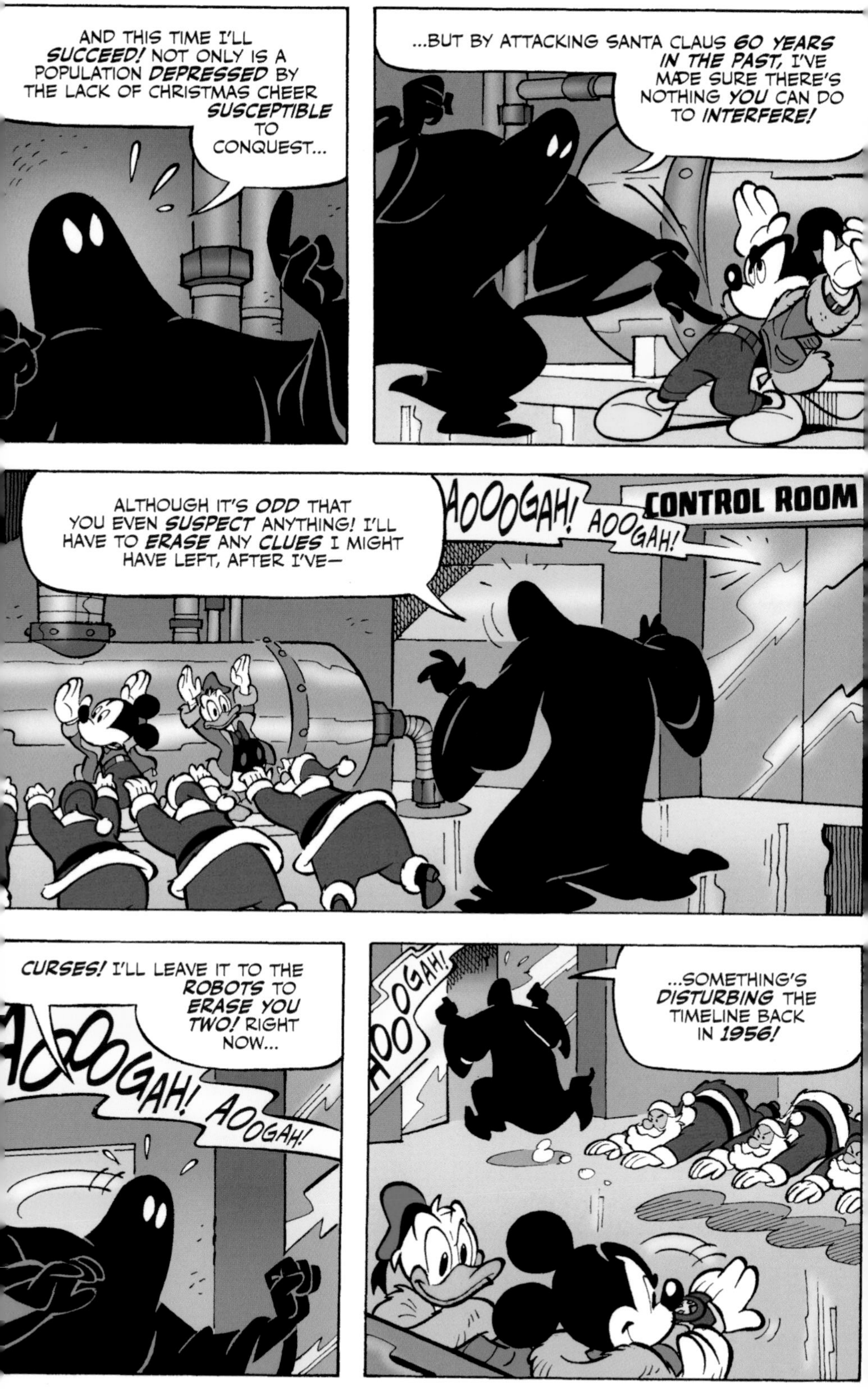
AND THIS TIME I'LL SUCCEED! NOT ONLY IS A POPULATION DEPRESSED BY THE LACK OF CHRISTMAS CHEER SUSCEPTIBLE TO CONQUEST...
...BUT BY ATTACKING SANTA CLAUS 60 YEARS IN THE PAST, I'VE MADE SURE THERE'S NOTHING YOU CAN DO TO INTERFERE!
ALTHOUGH IT'S ODD THAT YOU EVEN SUSPECT ANYTHING! I'LL HAVE TO ERASE ANY CLUES I MIGHT HAVE LEFT, AFTER I'VE—
AOOOGAH! AOOGAH!
CONTROL ROOM
CURSES! I'LL LEAVE IT TO THE ROBOTS TO ERASE YOU TWO! RIGHT NOW...
AOOOOGAH! AOOGAH!
AOOOGAH!
...SOMETHING'S DISTURBING THE TIMELINE BACK IN 1956!

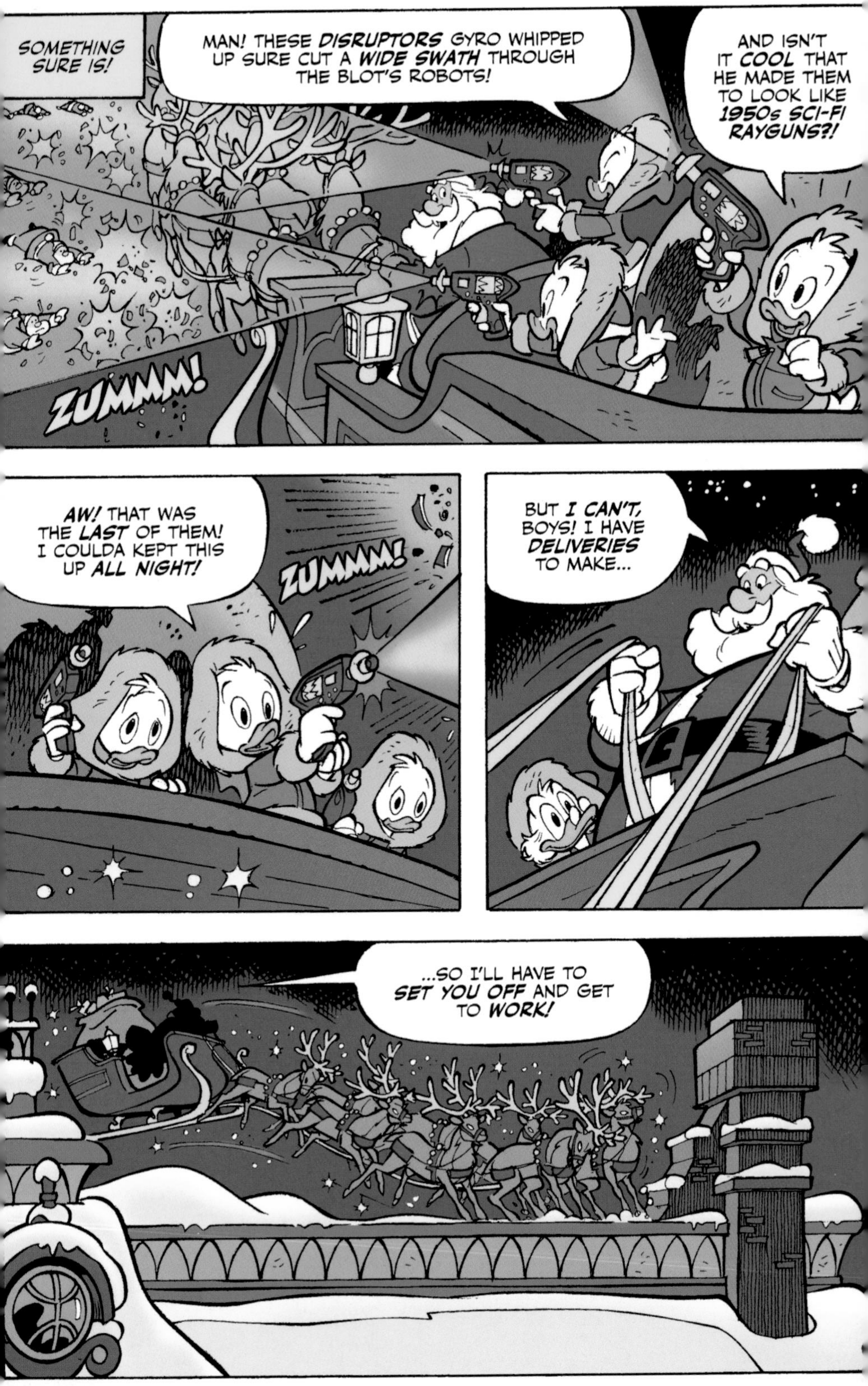
SOMETHING SURE IS!
MAN! THESE DISRUPTORS GYRO WHIPPED UP SURE CUT A WIDE SWATH THROUGH THE BLOT'S ROBOTS!
AND ISN'T IT COOL THAT HE MADE THEM TO LOOK LIKE 1950s SCI-FI RAYGUNS?!
ZUMMM!
AW! THAT WAS THE LAST OF THEM! I COULDA KEPT THIS UP ALL NIGHT!
ZUMMM!
BUT I CAN'T, BOYS! I HAVE DELIVERIES TO MAKE...
...SO I'LL HAVE TO SET YOU OFF AND GET TO WORK!

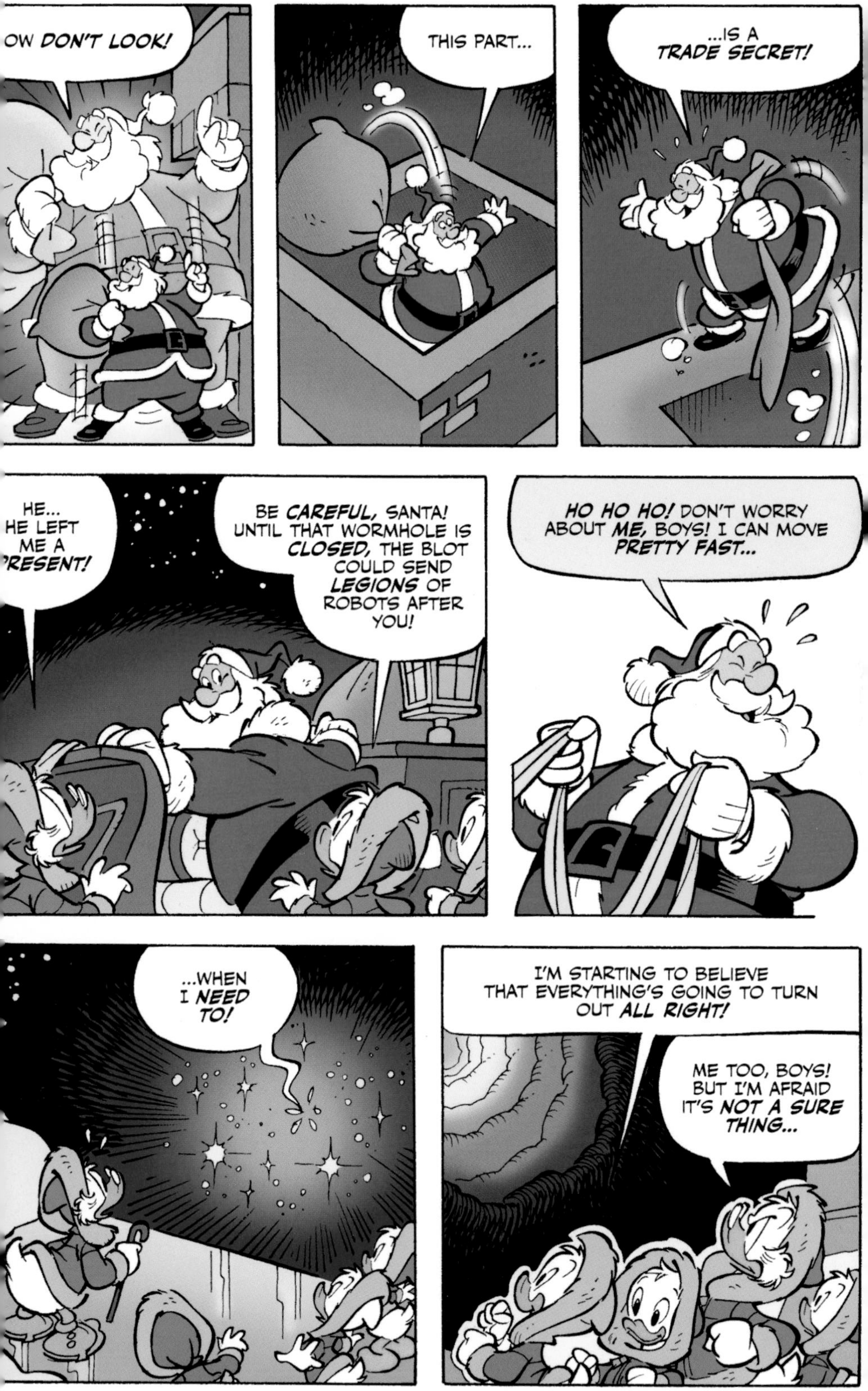
OW DON'T LOOK!
THIS PART...
...IS A TRADE SECRET!
HE... HE LEFT ME A PRESENT!
BE CAREFUL, SANTA! UNTIL THAT WORMHOLE IS CLOSED, THE BLOT COULD SEND LEGIONS OF ROBOTS AFTER YOU!
HO HO HO! DON'T WORRY ABOUT ME, BOYS! I CAN MOVE PRETTY FAST...
...WHEN I NEED TO!
I'M STARTING TO BELIEVE THAT EVERYTHING'S GOING TO TURN OUT ALL RIGHT!
ME TOO, BOYS! BUT I'M AFRAID IT'S NOT A SURE THING...

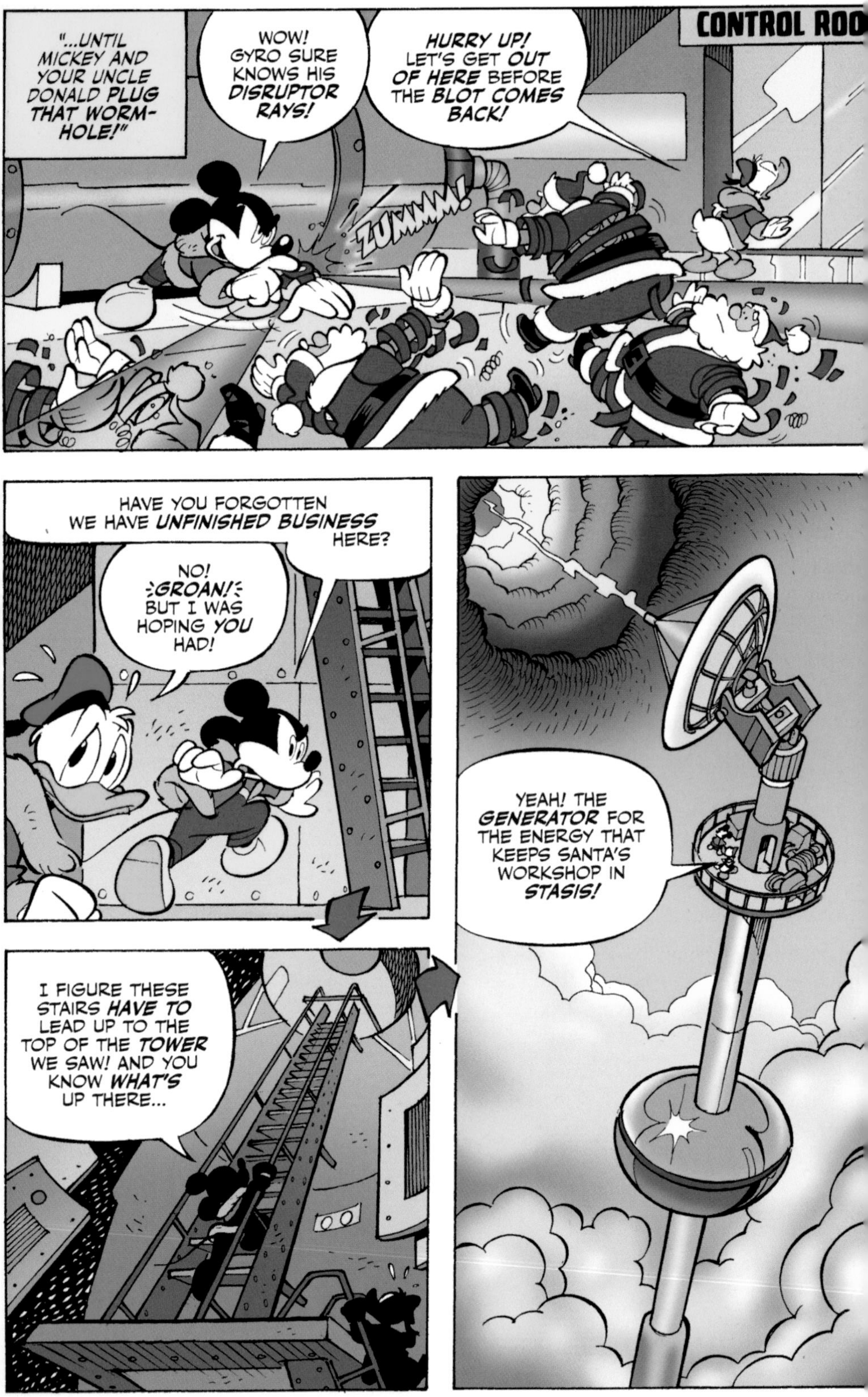
CONTROL ROO
"...UNTIL MICKEY AND YOUR UNCLE DONALD PLUG THAT WORM-HOLE!"
WOW! GYRO SURE KNOWS HIS DISRUPTOR RAYS!
HURRY UP! LET'S GET OUT OF HERE BEFORE THE BLOT COMES BACK!
ZUMMM!
HAVE YOU FORGOTTEN WE HAVE UNFINISHED BUSINESS HERE?
NO! GROAN! BUT I WAS HOPING YOU HAD!
I FIGURE THESE STAIRS HAVE TO LEAD UP TO THE TOP OF THE TOWER WE SAW! AND YOU KNOW WHAT'S UP THERE...
YEAH! THE GENERATOR FOR THE ENERGY THAT KEEPS SANTA'S WORKSHOP IN STASIS!

...O IS THERE AN *OFF SWITCH* ON ALL THAT MACHINERY?

DON'T SEE ONE! BUT THIS MACHINERY IS ALL *ELECTRONIC*...

...SO LET'S SEE IF *GYRO'S DISRUPTOR RAY* CAN DISRUPT *ITS CIRCUITS,* TOO!

WELL, I'LL BE! A *SIMPLE SOLUTION!*

ZUMMM!

ZZT! CRACKLE!!

IT'S *WORKING,* MICKEY! WE'VE *CUT OFF THE POWER* TO THE STASIS FIELD AROUND SANTA'S WORKSHOP!

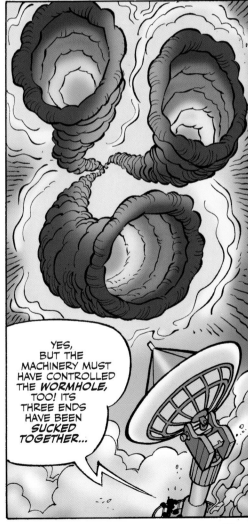

YES, BUT THE MACHINERY MUST HAVE CONTROLLED THE *WORMHOLE,* TOO! ITS THREE ENDS HAVE BEEN *SUCKED TOGETHER*...

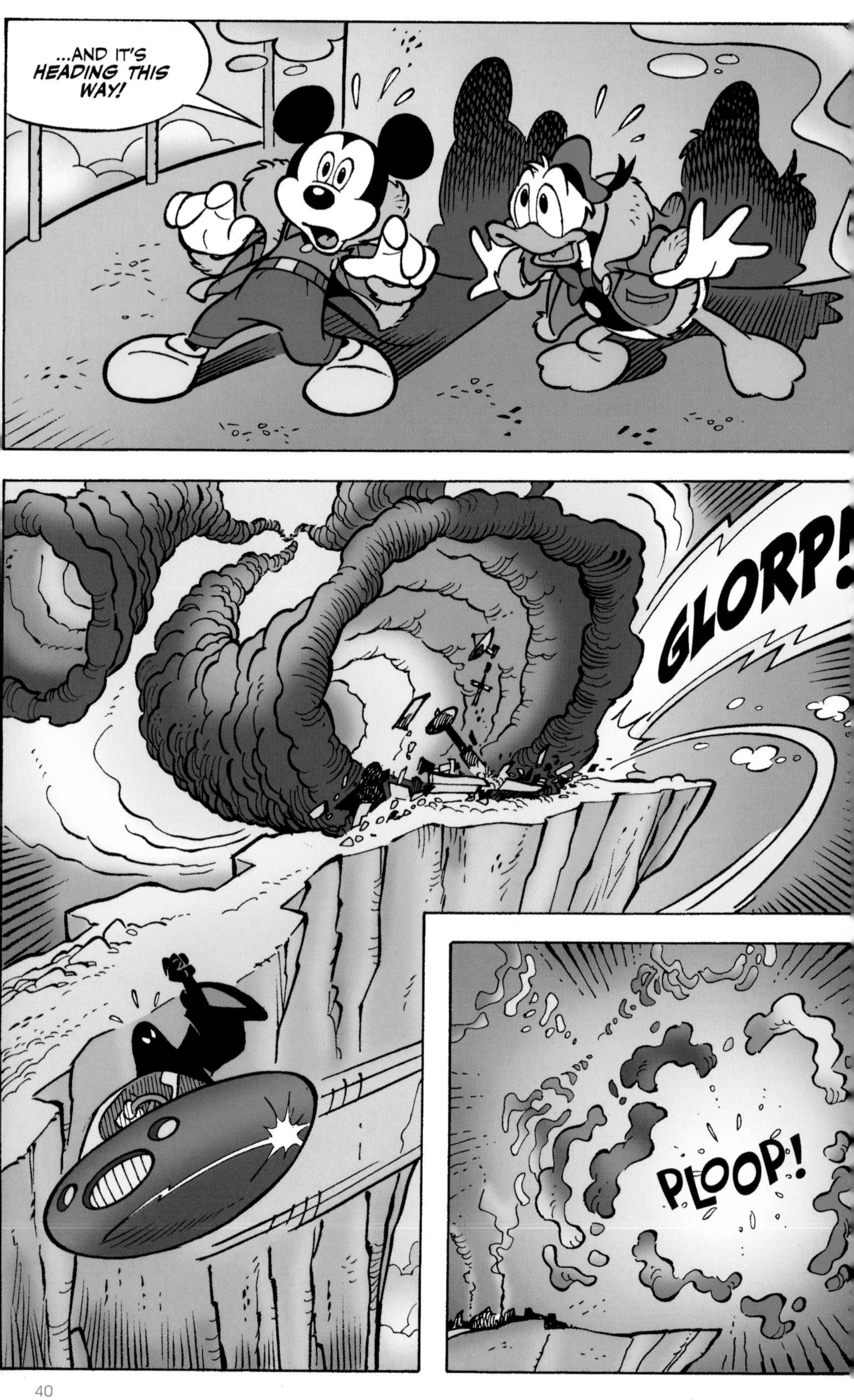
...AND IT'S HEADING THIS WAY!
GLORP!
PLOOP!

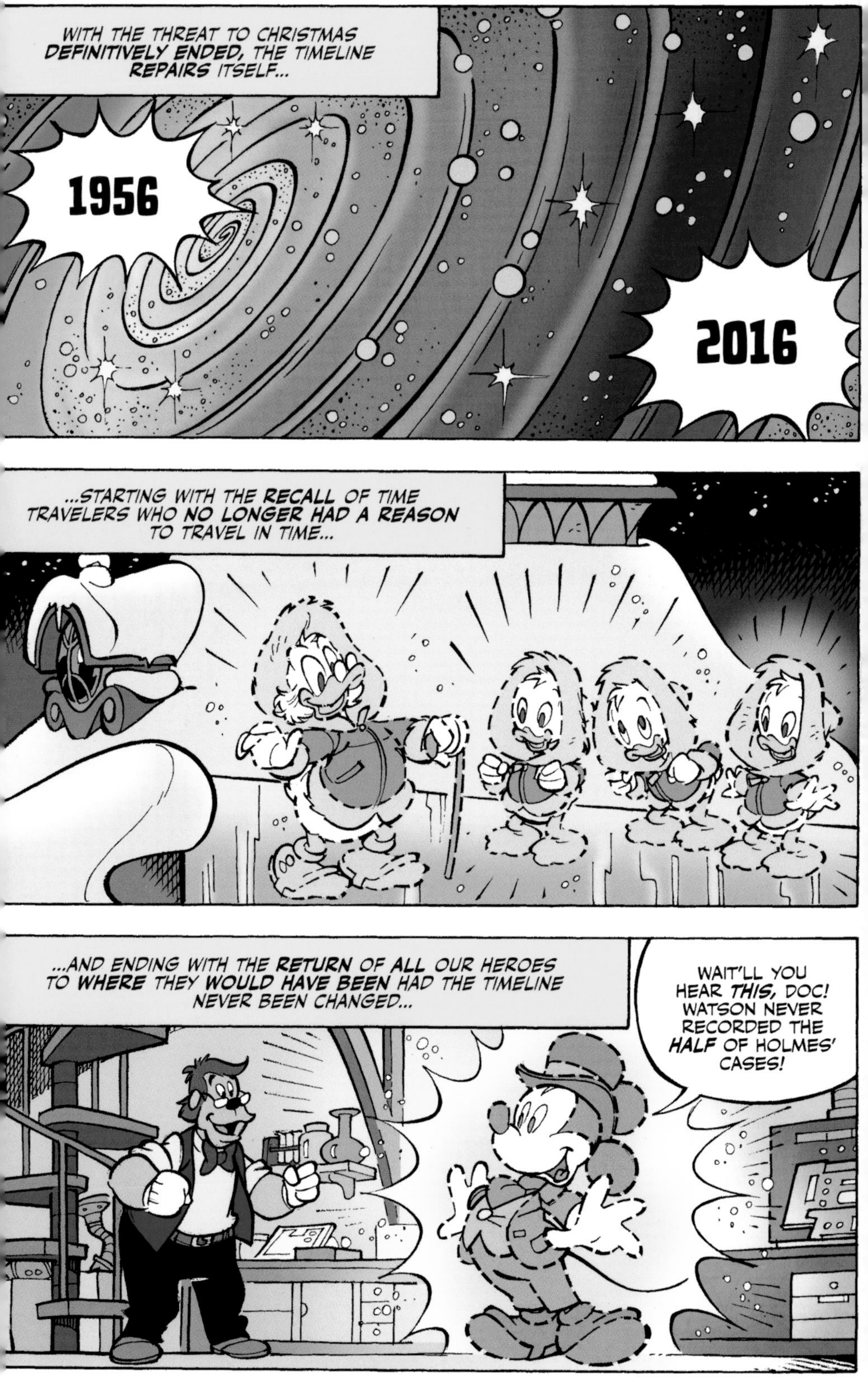
WITH THE THREAT TO CHRISTMAS DEFINITIVELY ENDED, THE TIMELINE REPAIRS ITSELF...
1956
2016
...STARTING WITH THE RECALL OF TIME TRAVELERS WHO NO LONGER HAD A REASON TO TRAVEL IN TIME...
...AND ENDING WITH THE RETURN OF ALL OUR HEROES TO WHERE THEY WOULD HAVE BEEN HAD THE TIMELINE NEVER BEEN CHANGED...
WAIT'LL YOU HEAR THIS, DOC! WATSON NEVER RECORDED THE HALF OF HOLMES' CASES!

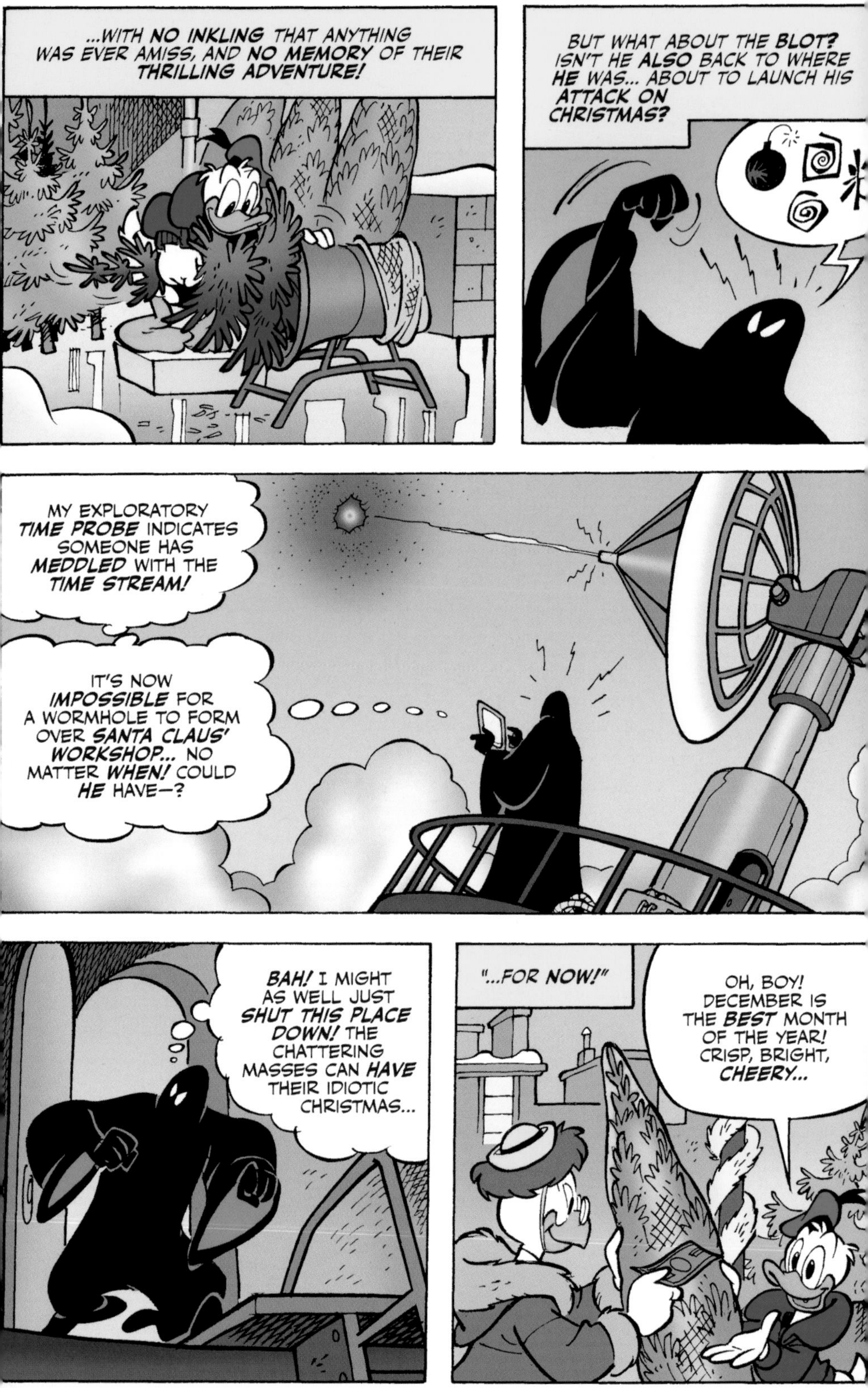

...WITH NO INKLING THAT ANYTHING WAS EVER AMISS, AND NO MEMORY OF THEIR THRILLING ADVENTURE!
BUT WHAT ABOUT THE BLOT? ISN'T HE ALSO BACK TO WHERE HE WAS... ABOUT TO LAUNCH HIS ATTACK ON CHRISTMAS?
MY EXPLORATORY TIME PROBE INDICATES SOMEONE HAS MEDDLED WITH THE TIME STREAM!
IT'S NOW IMPOSSIBLE FOR A WORMHOLE TO FORM OVER SANTA CLAUS' WORKSHOP... NO MATTER WHEN! COULD HE HAVE—?
BAH! I MIGHT AS WELL JUST SHUT THIS PLACE DOWN! THE CHATTERING MASSES CAN HAVE THEIR IDIOTIC CHRISTMAS...
"...FOR NOW!"
OH, BOY! DECEMBER IS THE BEST MONTH OF THE YEAR! CRISP, BRIGHT, CHEERY...

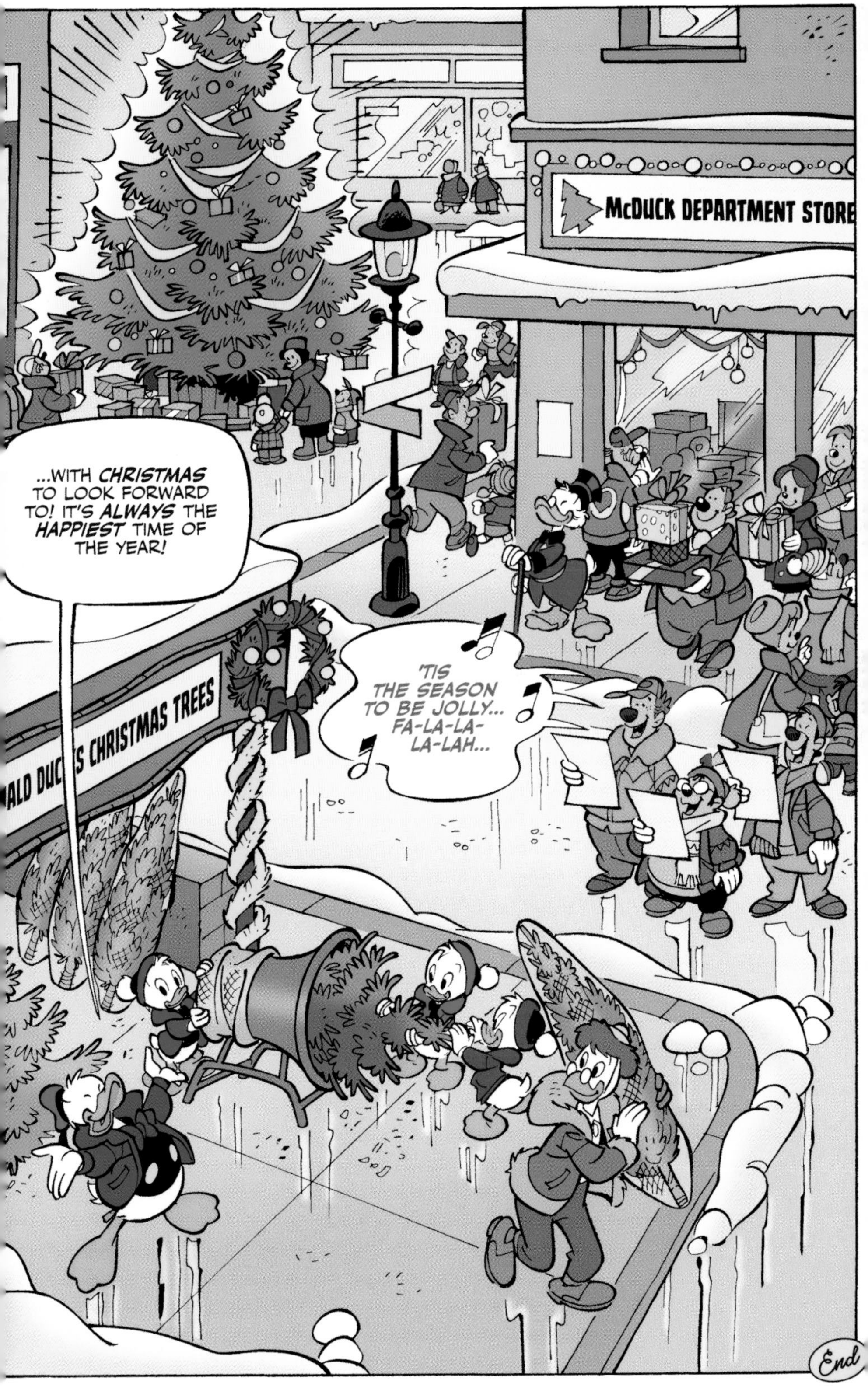
McDUCK DEPARTMENT STORE
...WITH CHRISTMAS TO LOOK FORWARD TO! IT'S ALWAYS THE HAPPIEST TIME OF THE YEAR!
'TIS THE SEASON TO BE JOLLY... FA-LA-LA-LA-LAH...
ALD DUC S CHRISTMAS TREES
End

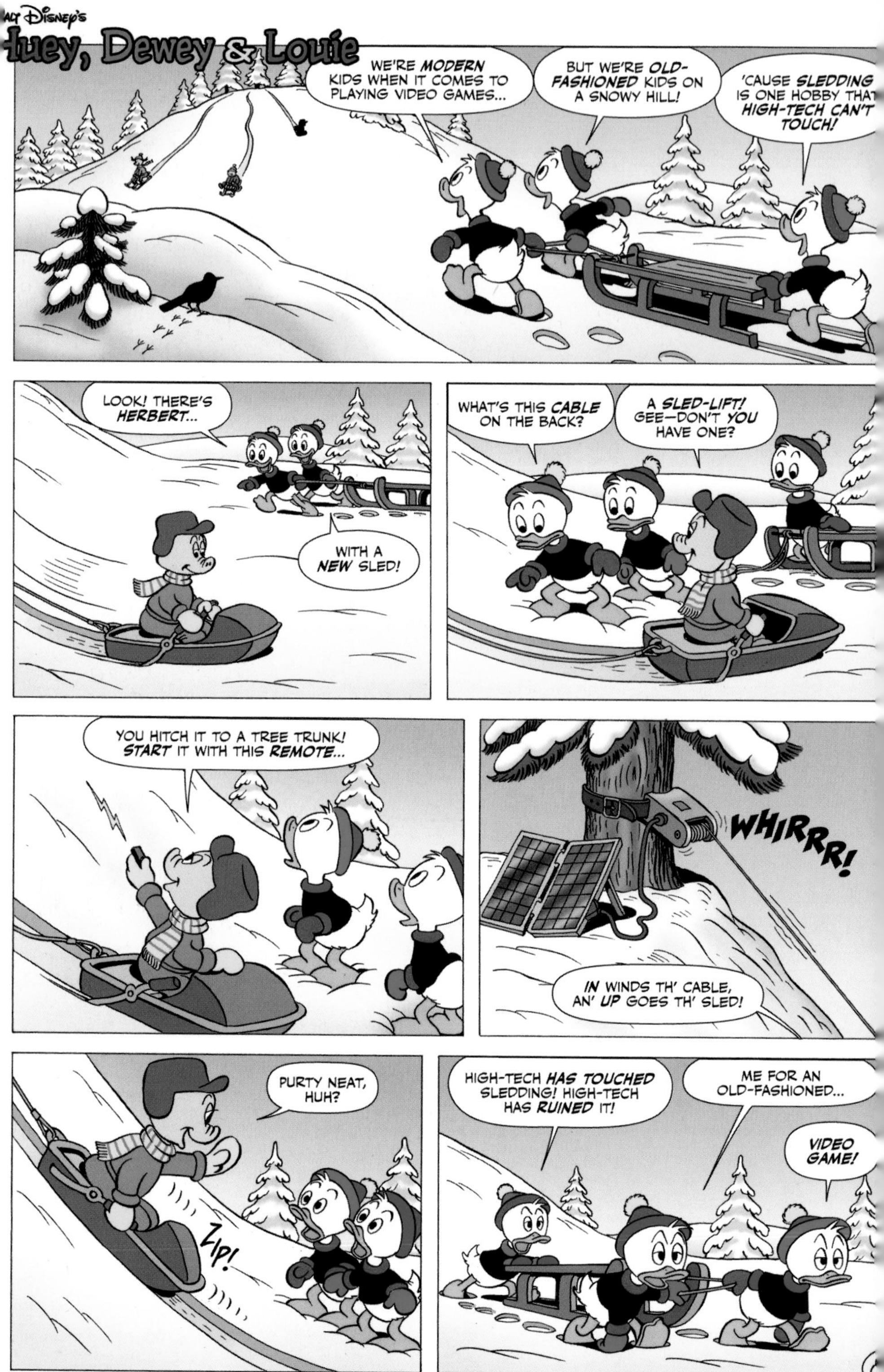
Walt Disney's
Huey, Dewey & Louie
WE'RE MODERN KIDS WHEN IT COMES TO PLAYING VIDEO GAMES...
BUT WE'RE OLD-FASHIONED KIDS ON A SNOWY HILL!
'CAUSE SLEDDING IS ONE HOBBY THAT HIGH-TECH CAN'T TOUCH!
LOOK! THERE'S HERBERT...
WITH A NEW SLED!
WHAT'S THIS CABLE ON THE BACK?
A SLED-LIFT! GEE—DON'T YOU HAVE ONE?
YOU HITCH IT TO A TREE TRUNK! START IT WITH THIS REMOTE...
WHIRRR!
IN WINDS TH' CABLE, AN' UP GOES TH' SLED!
PURTY NEAT, HUH?
ZIP!
HIGH-TECH HAS TOUCHED SLEDDING! HIGH-TECH HAS RUINED IT!
ME FOR AN OLD-FASHIONED...
VIDEO GAME!

ORIGINALLY PUBLISHED IN *DONALD DUCK* #1/2013 (NETHERLANDS, 2013)

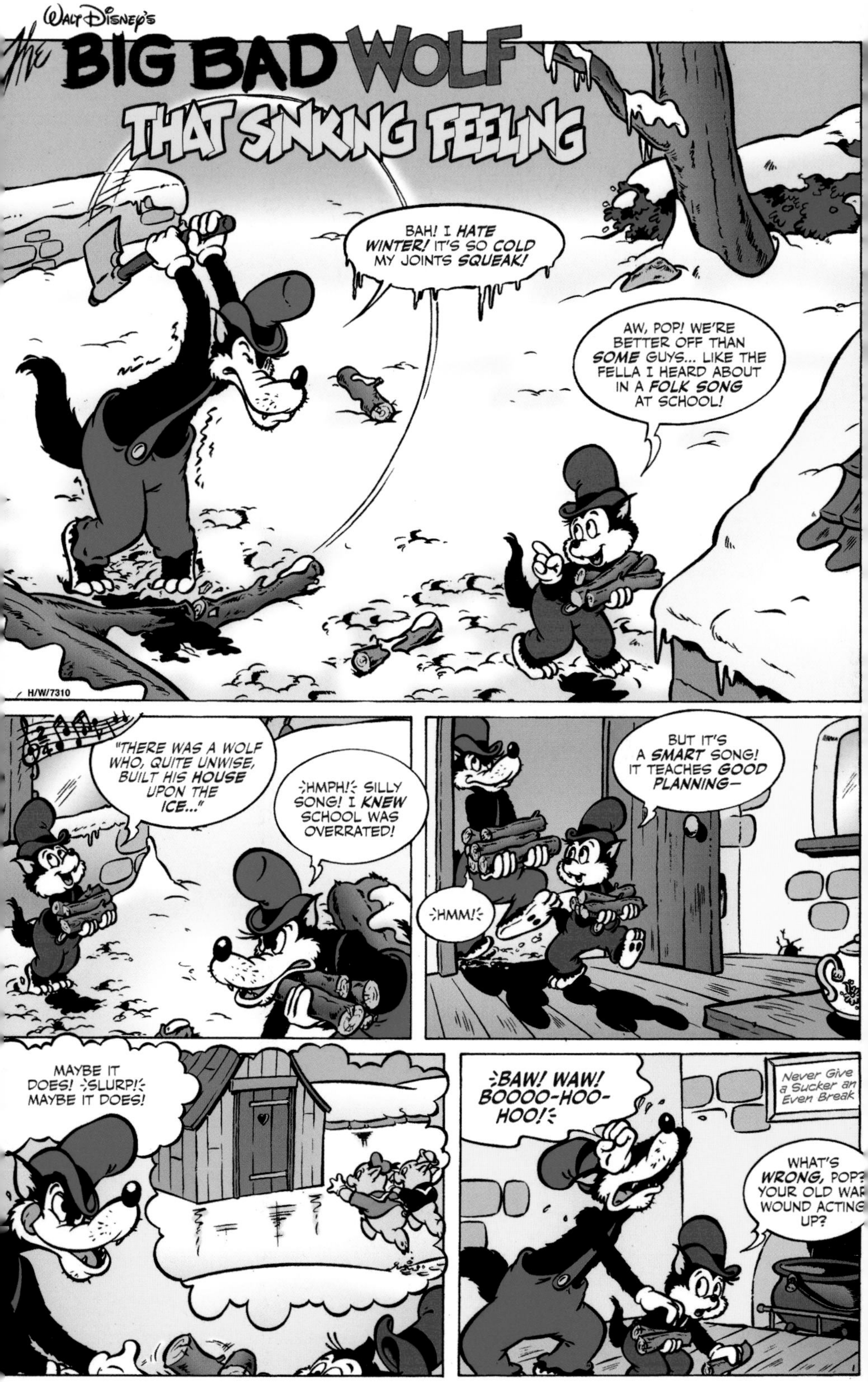
Walt Disney's
The Big Bad Wolf
That Sinking Feeling
BAH! I HATE WINTER! IT'S SO COLD MY JOINTS SQUEAK!
AW, POP! WE'RE BETTER OFF THAN SOME GUYS... LIKE THE FELLA I HEARD ABOUT IN A FOLK SONG AT SCHOOL!
H/W/7310
"THERE WAS A WOLF WHO, QUITE UNWISE, BUILT HIS HOUSE UPON THE ICE..."
HMPH! SILLY SONG! I KNEW SCHOOL WAS OVERRATED!
BUT IT'S A SMART SONG! IT TEACHES GOOD PLANNING—
HMM!
MAYBE IT DOES! SLURP! MAYBE IT DOES!
BAW! WAW! BOOOO-HOO-HOO!
Never Give a Sucker an Even Break
WHAT'S WRONG, POP? YOUR OLD WAR WOUND ACTING UP?

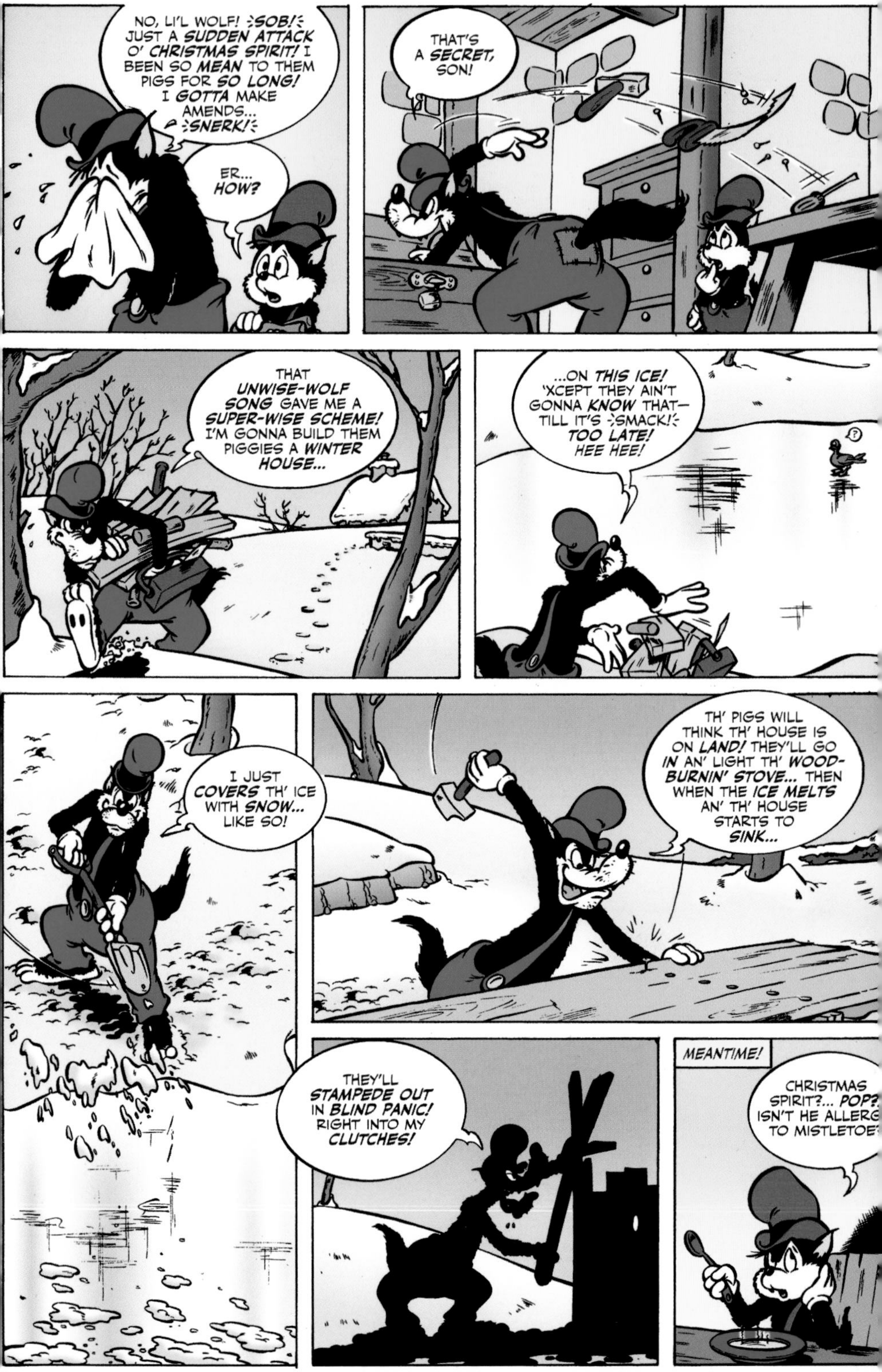
NO, LI'L WOLF! SOB! JUST A SUDDEN ATTACK O' CHRISTMAS SPIRIT! I BEEN SO MEAN TO THEM PIGS FOR SO LONG! I GOTTA MAKE AMENDS... SNERK!
ER... HOW?
THAT'S A SECRET, SON!
THAT UNWISE-WOLF SONG GAVE ME A SUPER-WISE SCHEME! I'M GONNA BUILD THEM PIGGIES A WINTER HOUSE...
...ON THIS ICE! 'XCEPT THEY AIN'T GONNA KNOW THAT— TILL IT'S SMACK! TOO LATE! HEE HEE!
?
I JUST COVERS TH' ICE WITH SNOW... LIKE SO!
TH' PIGS WILL THINK TH' HOUSE IS ON LAND! THEY'LL GO IN AN' LIGHT TH' WOOD-BURNIN' STOVE... THEN WHEN THE ICE MELTS AN' TH' HOUSE STARTS TO SINK...
THEY'LL STAMPEDE OUT IN BLIND PANIC! RIGHT INTO MY CLUTCHES!
MEANTIME!
CHRISTMAS SPIRIT?... POP? ISN'T HE ALLERG TO MISTLETOE

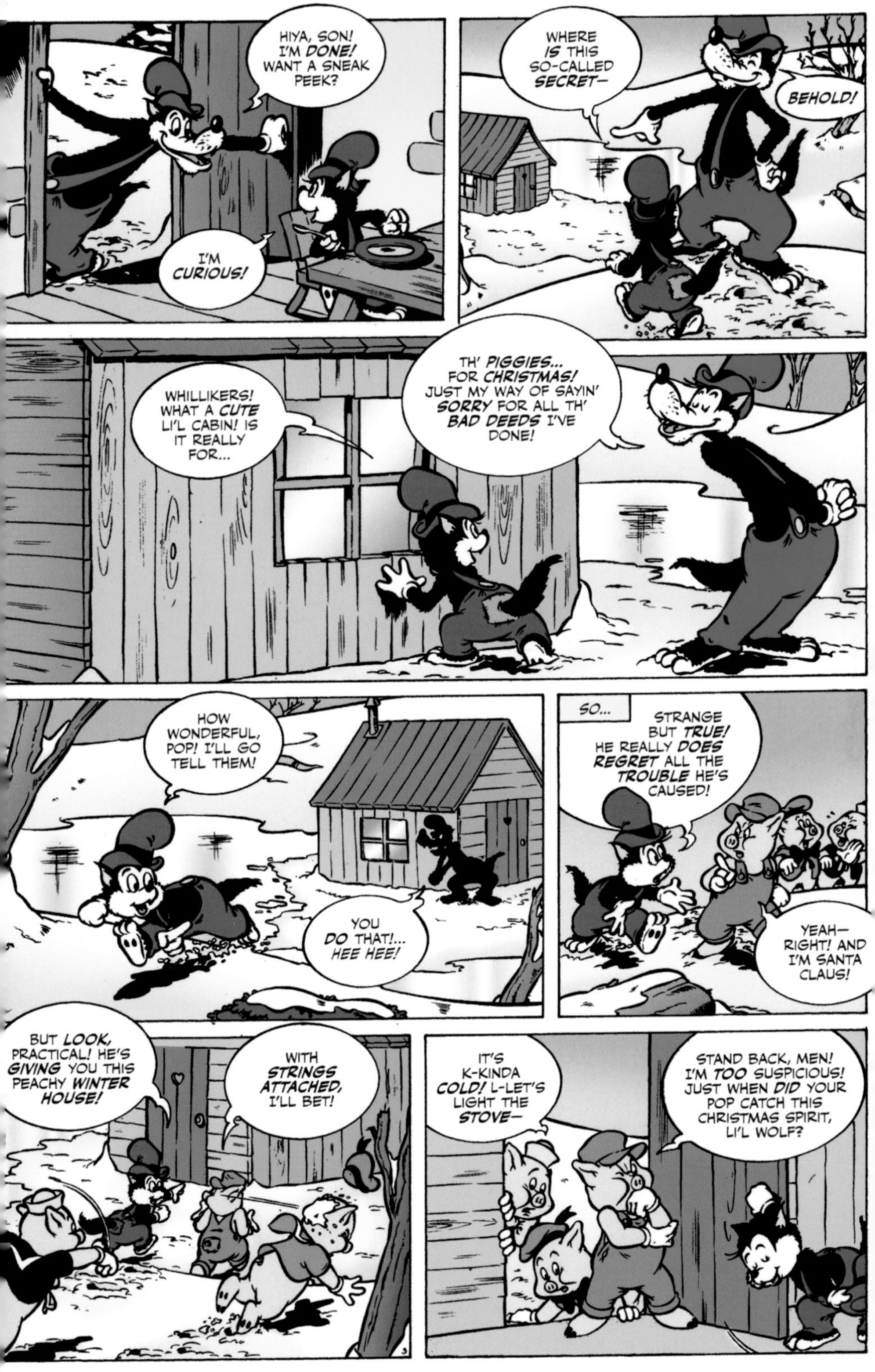
HIYA, SON! I'M DONE! WANT A SNEAK PEEK?
I'M CURIOUS!
WHERE IS THIS SO-CALLED SECRET—
BEHOLD!
WHILLIKERS! WHAT A CUTE LI'L CABIN! IS IT REALLY FOR...
TH' PIGGIES... FOR CHRISTMAS! JUST MY WAY OF SAYIN' SORRY FOR ALL TH' BAD DEEDS I'VE DONE!
HOW WONDERFUL, POP! I'LL GO TELL THEM!
YOU DO THAT!... HEE HEE!
SO...
STRANGE BUT TRUE! HE REALLY DOES REGRET ALL THE TROUBLE HE'S CAUSED!
YEAH— RIGHT! AND I'M SANTA CLAUS!
BUT LOOK, PRACTICAL! HE'S GIVING YOU THIS PEACHY WINTER HOUSE!
WITH STRINGS ATTACHED, I'LL BET!
IT'S K-KINDA COLD! L-LET'S LIGHT THE STOVE—
STAND BACK, MEN! I'M TOO SUSPICIOUS! JUST WHEN DID YOUR POP CATCH THIS CHRISTMAS SPIRIT, LI'L WOLF?

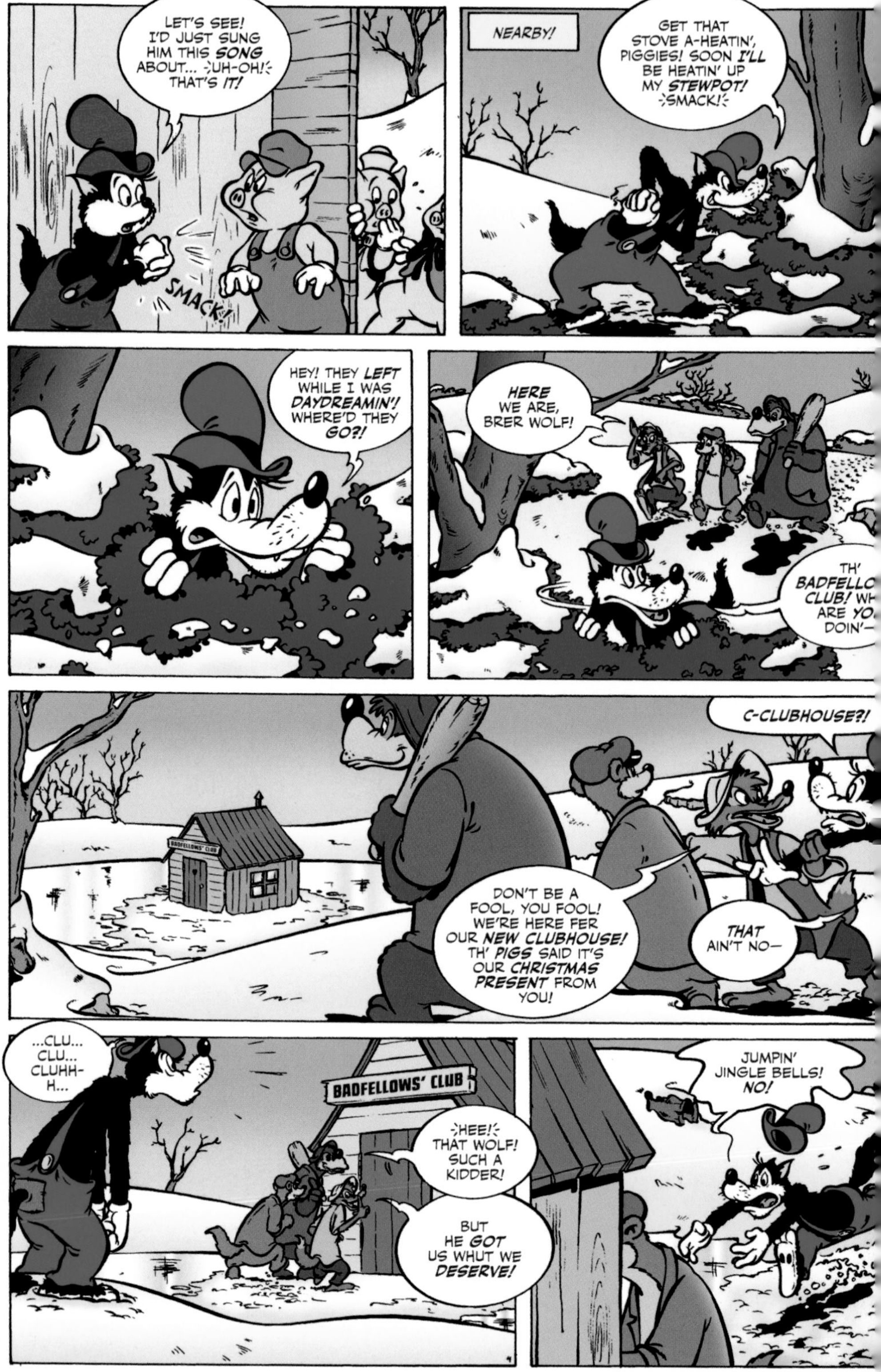

LET'S SEE! I'D JUST SUNG HIM THIS SONG ABOUT... UH-OH! THAT'S IT!
SMACK!
NEARBY!
GET THAT STOVE A-HEATIN', PIGGIES! SOON I'LL BE HEATIN' UP MY STEWPOT! SMACK!
HEY! THEY LEFT WHILE I WAS DAYDREAMIN'! WHERE'D THEY GO?!
HERE WE ARE, BRER WOLF!
TH' BADFELLO CLUB! WH ARE YO DOIN'—
C-CLUBHOUSE?!
BADFELLOWS' CLUB
DON'T BE A FOOL, YOU FOOL! WE'RE HERE FER OUR NEW CLUBHOUSE! TH' PIGS SAID IT'S OUR CHRISTMAS PRESENT FROM YOU!
THAT AIN'T NO—
...CLU... CLU... CLUHH-H...
BADFELLOWS' CLUB
HEE! THAT WOLF! SUCH A KIDDER!
BUT HE GOT US WHUT WE DESERVE!
JUMPIN' JINGLE BELLS! NO!

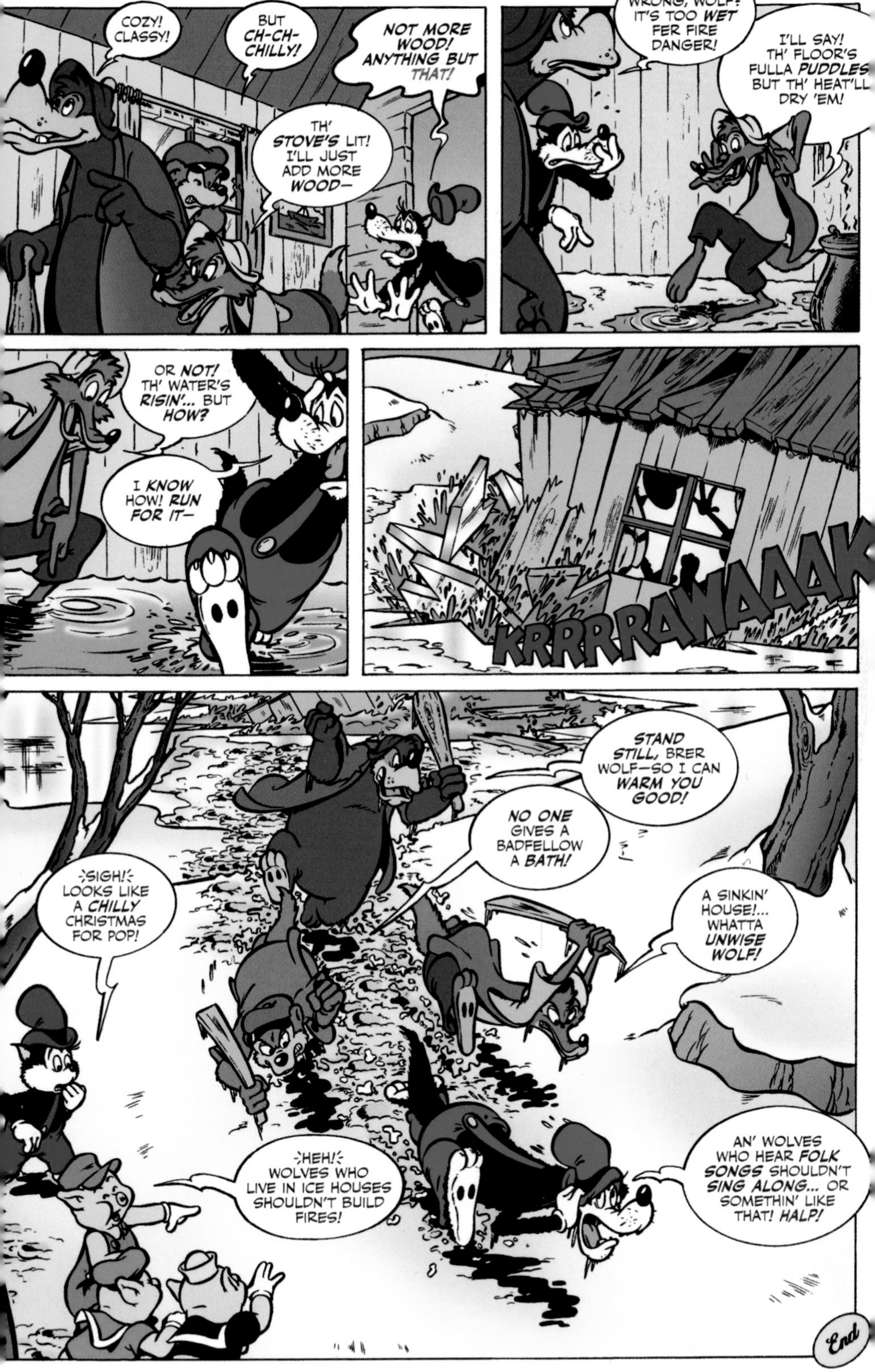

COZY! CLASSY!
BUT CH-CH-CHILLY!
TH' STOVE'S LIT! I'LL JUST ADD MORE WOOD—
NOT MORE WOOD! ANYTHING BUT THAT!
WHAT'S WRONG, WOLF? IT'S TOO WET FER FIRE DANGER!
I'LL SAY! TH' FLOOR'S FULLA PUDDLES. BUT TH' HEAT'LL DRY 'EM!
OR NOT! TH' WATER'S RISIN'... BUT HOW?
I KNOW HOW! RUN FOR IT—
KRRRRAAAAAK
STAND STILL, BRER WOLF—SO I CAN WARM YOU GOOD!
NO ONE GIVES A BADFELLOW A BATH!
A SINKIN' HOUSE!... WHATTA UNWISE WOLF!
-SIGH!- LOOKS LIKE A CHILLY CHRISTMAS FOR POP!
-HEH!- WOLVES WHO LIVE IN ICE HOUSES SHOULDN'T BUILD FIRES!
AN' WOLVES WHO HEAR FOLK SONGS SHOULDN'T SING ALONG... OR SOMETHIN' LIKE THAT! HALP!
End

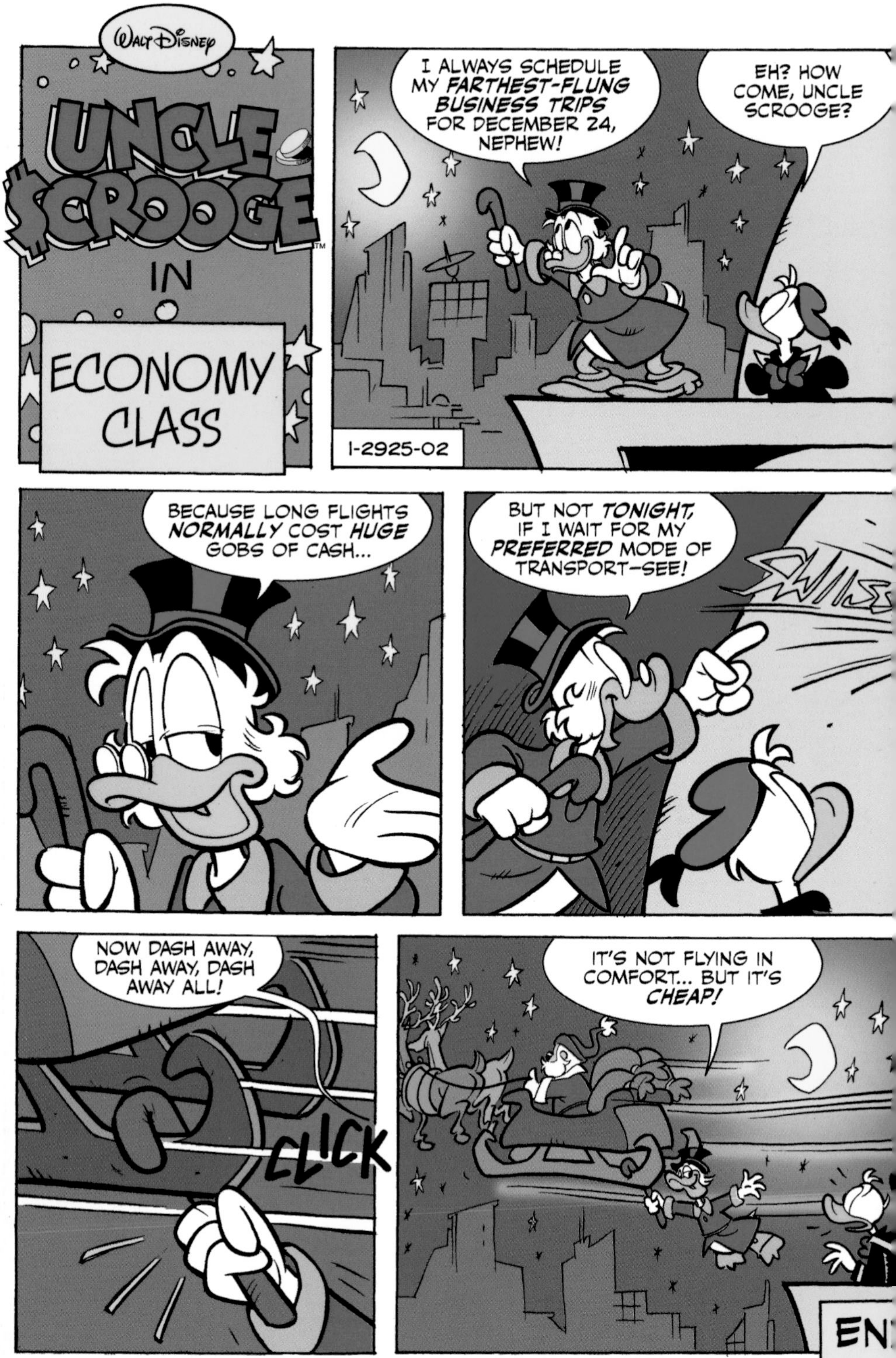
WALT DISNEY
UNCLE $CROOGE IN
ECONOMY CLASS
I-2925-02
I ALWAYS SCHEDULE MY FARTHEST-FLUNG BUSINESS TRIPS FOR DECEMBER 24, NEPHEW!
EH? HOW COME, UNCLE SCROOGE?
BECAUSE LONG FLIGHTS NORMALLY COST HUGE GOBS OF CASH...
BUT NOT TONIGHT, IF I WAIT FOR MY PREFERRED MODE OF TRANSPORT—SEE!
NOW DASH AWAY, DASH AWAY, DASH AWAY ALL!
CLICK
IT'S NOT FLYING IN COMFORT... BUT IT'S CHEAP!

ORIGINALLY PUBLISHED IN *TOPOLINO* #2925 (ITALY, 2011)

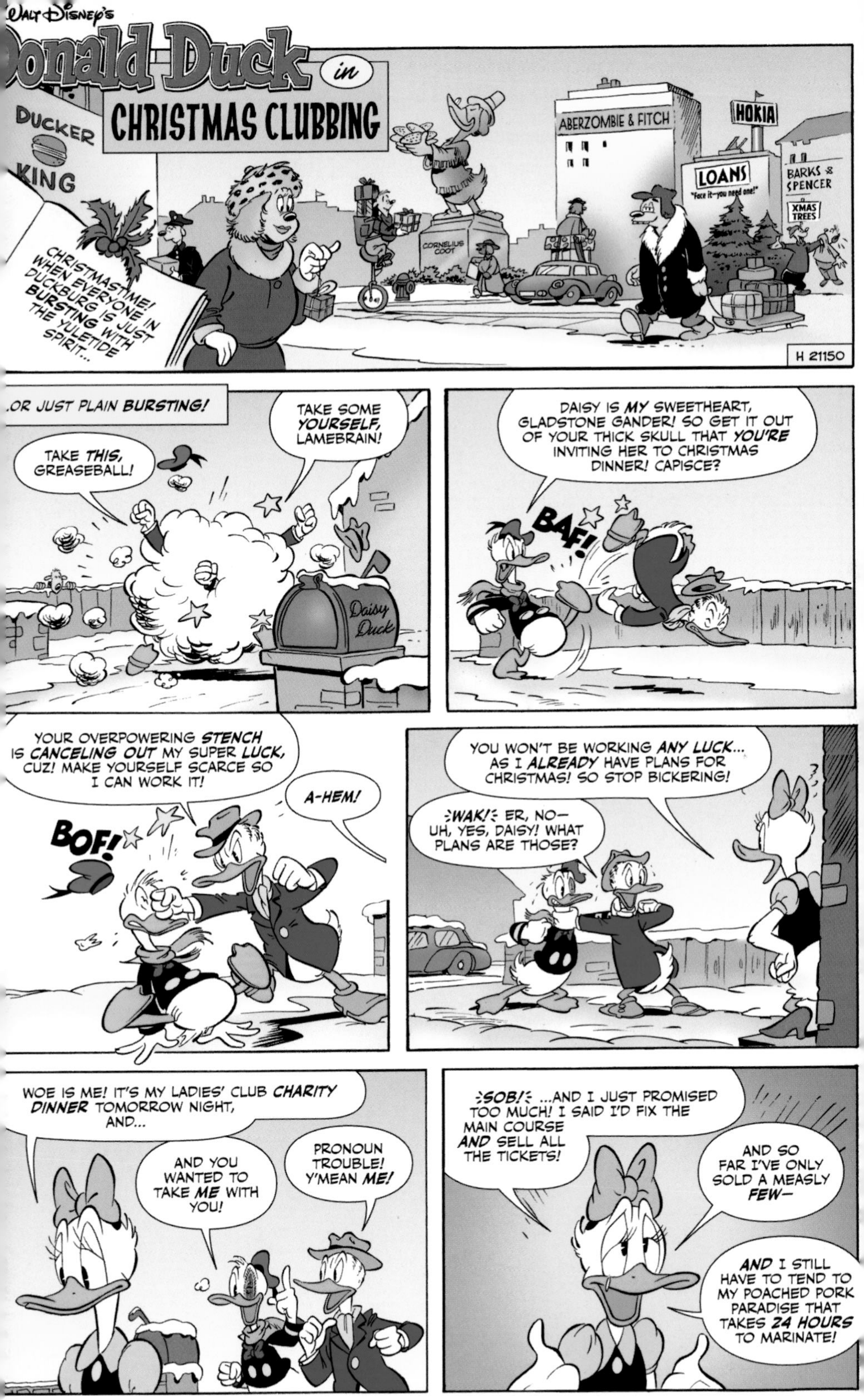
Walt Disney's
Donald Duck in
CHRISTMAS CLUBBING
DUCKER KING
ABERZOMBIE & FITCH
HOKIA
LOANS
"Face it—you need one!"
BARKS & SPENCER
XMAS TREES
CORNELIUS COOT
CHRISTMASTIME! WHEN EVERYONE IN DUCKBURG IS JUST BURSTING WITH THE YULETIDE SPIRIT...
H 21150
...OR JUST PLAIN BURSTING!
TAKE THIS, GREASEBALL!
TAKE SOME YOURSELF, LAMEBRAIN!
Daisy Duck
DAISY IS MY SWEETHEART, GLADSTONE GANDER! SO GET IT OUT OF YOUR THICK SKULL THAT YOU'RE INVITING HER TO CHRISTMAS DINNER! CAPISCE?
BAF!
YOUR OVERPOWERING STENCH IS CANCELING OUT MY SUPER LUCK, CUZ! MAKE YOURSELF SCARCE SO I CAN WORK IT!
A-HEM!
BOF!
YOU WON'T BE WORKING ANY LUCK... AS I ALREADY HAVE PLANS FOR CHRISTMAS! SO STOP BICKERING!
WAK! ER, NO— UH, YES, DAISY! WHAT PLANS ARE THOSE?
WOE IS ME! IT'S MY LADIES' CLUB CHARITY DINNER TOMORROW NIGHT, AND...
AND YOU WANTED TO TAKE ME WITH YOU!
PRONOUN TROUBLE! Y'MEAN ME!
SOB! ...AND I JUST PROMISED TOO MUCH! I SAID I'D FIX THE MAIN COURSE AND SELL ALL THE TICKETS!
AND SO FAR I'VE ONLY SOLD A MEASLY FEW—
AND I STILL HAVE TO TEND TO MY POACHED PORK PARADISE THAT TAKES 24 HOURS TO MARINATE!

ORIGINALLY PUBLISHED IN *DONALD DUCK* #52/2002 (NETHERLANDS, 2002)

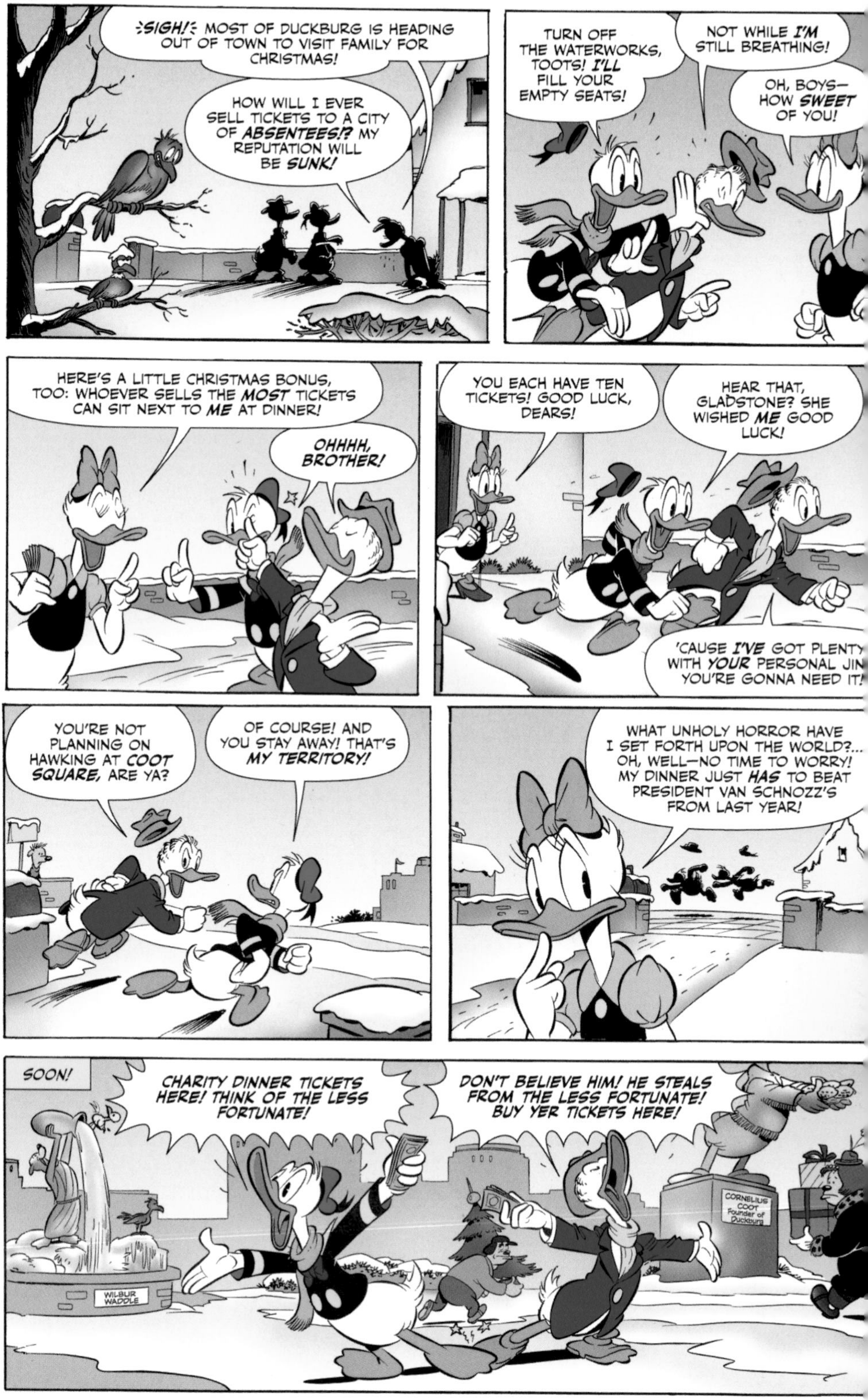
:SIGH!: MOST OF DUCKBURG IS HEADING OUT OF TOWN TO VISIT FAMILY FOR CHRISTMAS!
HOW WILL I EVER SELL TICKETS TO A CITY OF ABSENTEES!? MY REPUTATION WILL BE SUNK!
TURN OFF THE WATERWORKS, TOOTS! I'LL FILL YOUR EMPTY SEATS!
NOT WHILE I'M STILL BREATHING!
OH, BOYS— HOW SWEET OF YOU!
HERE'S A LITTLE CHRISTMAS BONUS, TOO: WHOEVER SELLS THE MOST TICKETS CAN SIT NEXT TO ME AT DINNER!
OHHHH, BROTHER!
YOU EACH HAVE TEN TICKETS! GOOD LUCK, DEARS!
HEAR THAT, GLADSTONE? SHE WISHED ME GOOD LUCK!
'CAUSE I'VE GOT PLENTY WITH YOUR PERSONAL JIN YOU'RE GONNA NEED IT!
YOU'RE NOT PLANNING ON HAWKING AT COOT SQUARE, ARE YA?
OF COURSE! AND YOU STAY AWAY! THAT'S MY TERRITORY!
WHAT UNHOLY HORROR HAVE I SET FORTH UPON THE WORLD?... OH, WELL—NO TIME TO WORRY! MY DINNER JUST HAS TO BEAT PRESIDENT VAN SCHNOZZ'S FROM LAST YEAR!
SOON!
CHARITY DINNER TICKETS HERE! THINK OF THE LESS FORTUNATE!
DON'T BELIEVE HIM! HE STEALS FROM THE LESS FORTUNATE! BUY YER TICKETS HERE!
WILBUR WADDLE
CORNELIUS COOT Founder of Duckburg

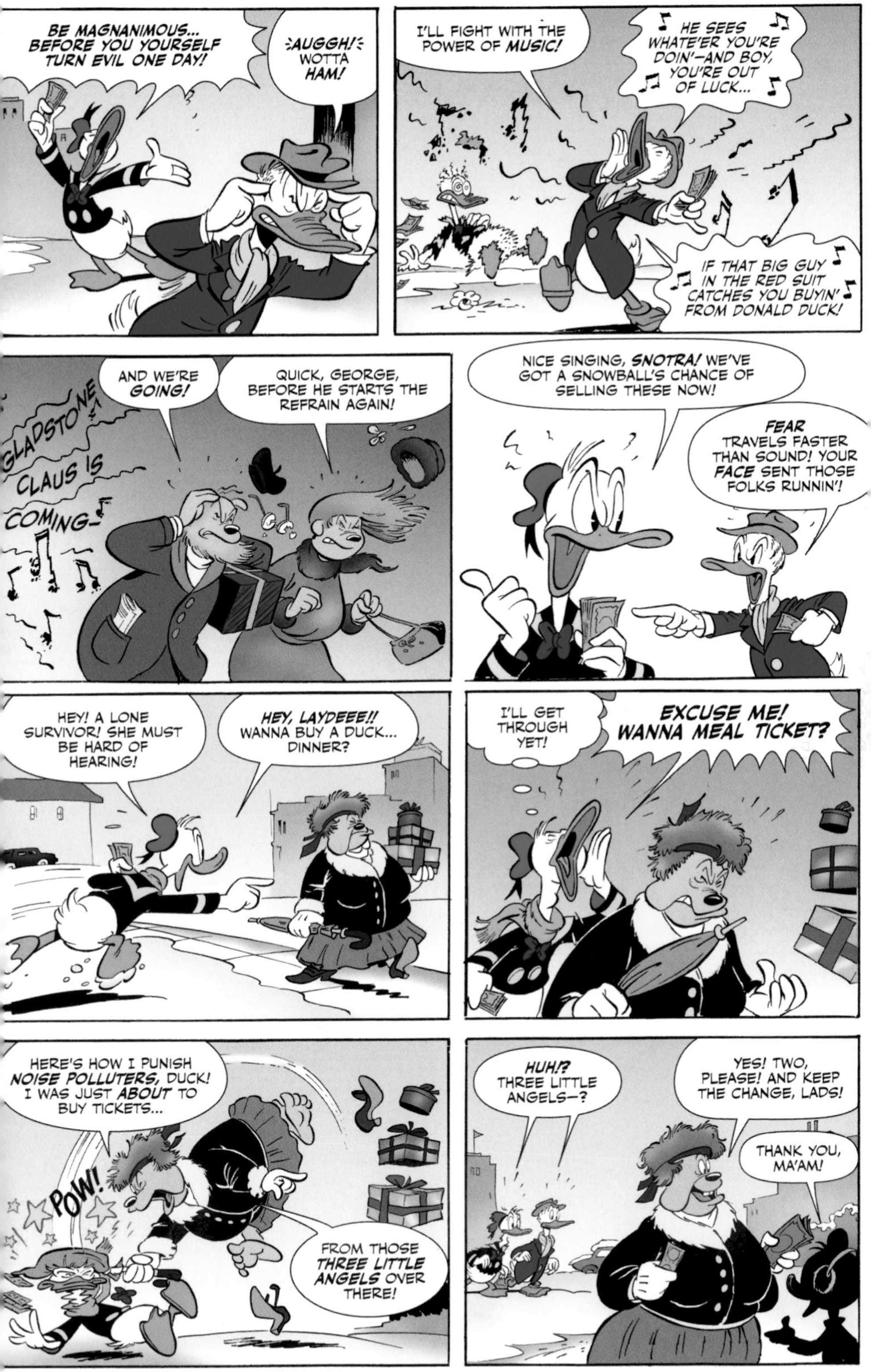
BE MAGNANIMOUS... BEFORE YOU YOURSELF TURN EVIL ONE DAY!
AUGGH! WOTTA HAM!
I'LL FIGHT WITH THE POWER OF MUSIC!
HE SEES WHATE'ER YOU'RE DOIN'—AND BOY, YOU'RE OUT OF LUCK...
IF THAT BIG GUY IN THE RED SUIT CATCHES YOU BUYIN' FROM DONALD DUCK!
GLADSTONE CLAUS IS COMING
AND WE'RE GOING!
QUICK, GEORGE, BEFORE HE STARTS THE REFRAIN AGAIN!
NICE SINGING, SNOTRA! WE'VE GOT A SNOWBALL'S CHANCE OF SELLING THESE NOW!
FEAR TRAVELS FASTER THAN SOUND! YOUR FACE SENT THOSE FOLKS RUNNIN'!
HEY! A LONE SURVIVOR! SHE MUST BE HARD OF HEARING!
HEY, LAYDEEE!! WANNA BUY A DUCK... DINNER?
I'LL GET THROUGH YET!
EXCUSE ME! WANNA MEAL TICKET?
HERE'S HOW I PUNISH NOISE POLLUTERS, DUCK! I WAS JUST ABOUT TO BUY TICKETS...
POW!
FROM THOSE THREE LITTLE ANGELS OVER THERE!
HUH!? THREE LITTLE ANGELS—?
YES! TWO, PLEASE! AND KEEP THE CHANGE, LADS!
THANK YOU, MA'AM!

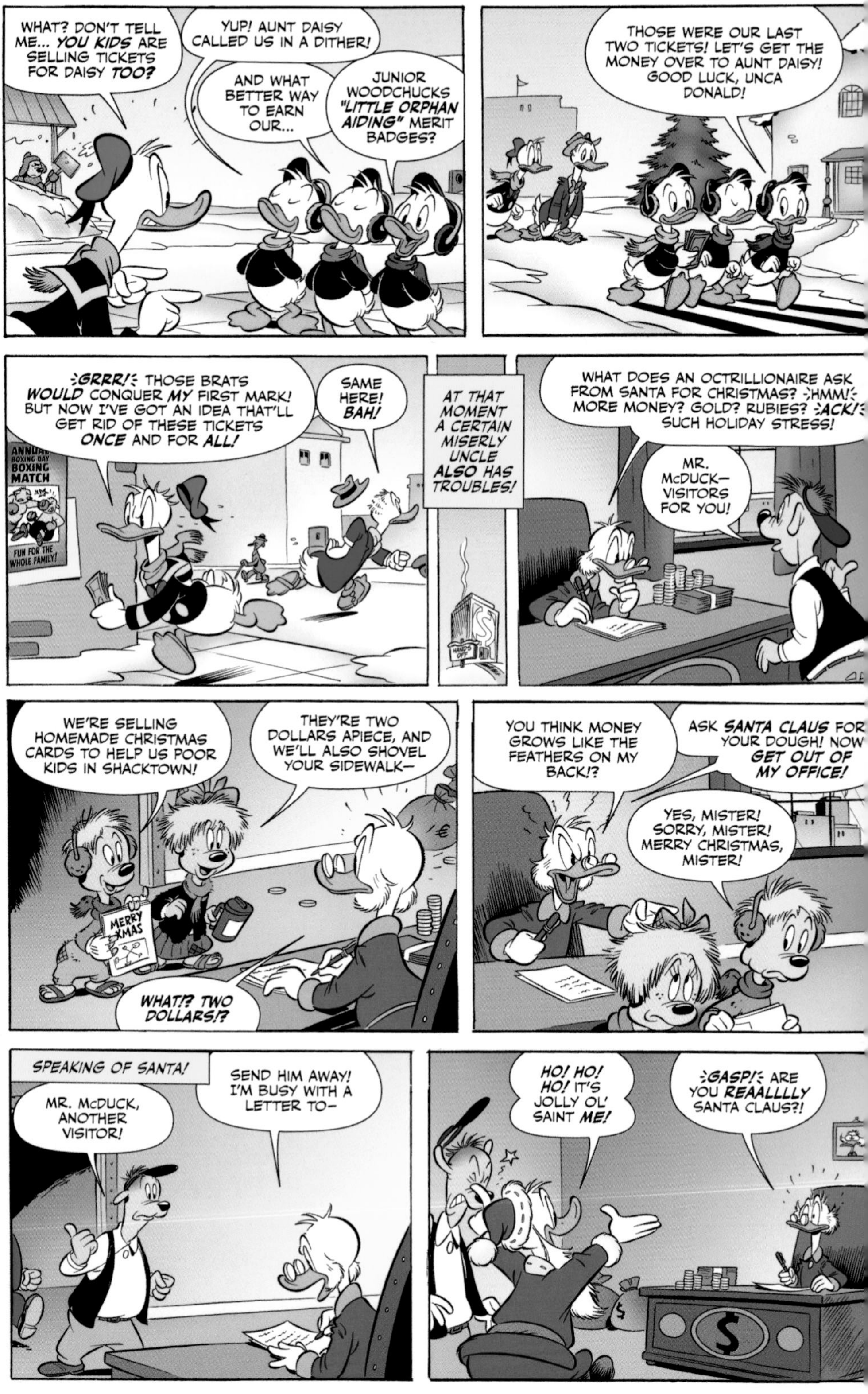
WHAT? DON'T TELL ME... YOU KIDS ARE SELLING TICKETS FOR DAISY TOO?
YUP! AUNT DAISY CALLED US IN A DITHER!
AND WHAT BETTER WAY TO EARN OUR...
JUNIOR WOODCHUCKS "LITTLE ORPHAN AIDING" MERIT BADGES?
THOSE WERE OUR LAST TWO TICKETS! LET'S GET THE MONEY OVER TO AUNT DAISY! GOOD LUCK, UNCA DONALD!
GRRR! THOSE BRATS WOULD CONQUER MY FIRST MARK! BUT NOW I'VE GOT AN IDEA THAT'LL GET RID OF THESE TICKETS ONCE AND FOR ALL!
SAME HERE! BAH!
ANNUAL BOXING DAY BOXING MATCH
FUN FOR THE WHOLE FAMILY!
AT THAT MOMENT A CERTAIN MISERLY UNCLE ALSO HAS TROUBLES!
WHAT DOES AN OCTRILLIONAIRE ASK FROM SANTA FOR CHRISTMAS? HMM! MORE MONEY? GOLD? RUBIES? ACK! SUCH HOLIDAY STRESS!
MR. McDUCK— VISITORS FOR YOU!
WE'RE SELLING HOMEMADE CHRISTMAS CARDS TO HELP US POOR KIDS IN SHACKTOWN!
THEY'RE TWO DOLLARS APIECE, AND WE'LL ALSO SHOVEL YOUR SIDEWALK—
MERRY XMAS
WHAT!? TWO DOLLARS!?
YOU THINK MONEY GROWS LIKE THE FEATHERS ON MY BACK!?
ASK SANTA CLAUS FOR YOUR DOUGH! NOW GET OUT OF MY OFFICE!
YES, MISTER! SORRY, MISTER! MERRY CHRISTMAS, MISTER!
SPEAKING OF SANTA!
MR. McDUCK, ANOTHER VISITOR!
SEND HIM AWAY! I'M BUSY WITH A LETTER TO—
HO! HO! HO! IT'S JOLLY OL' SAINT ME!
GASP! ARE YOU REAALLLLY SANTA CLAUS?!

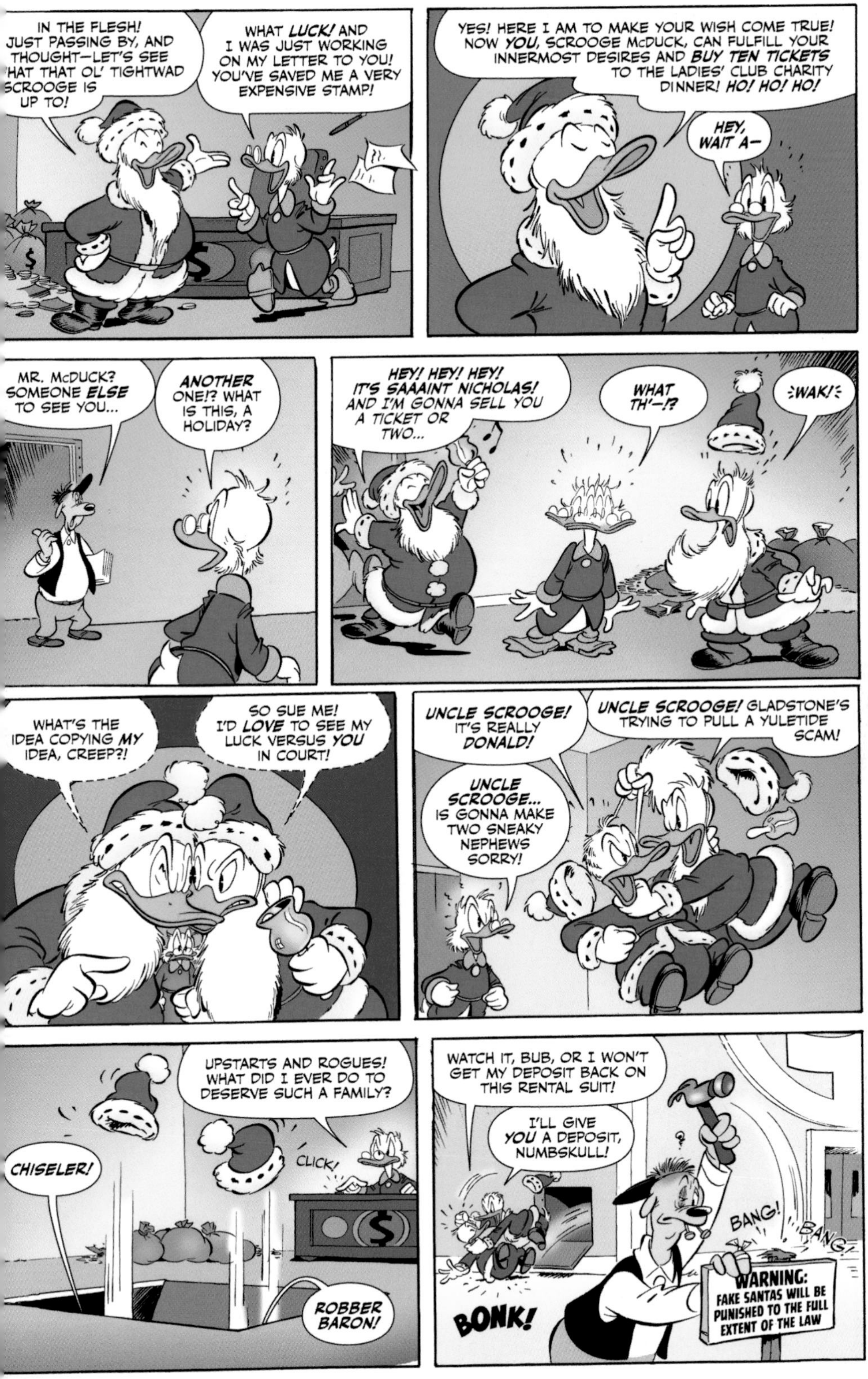

IN THE FLESH! JUST PASSING BY, AND THOUGHT—LET'S SEE 'HAT THAT OL' TIGHTWAD SCROOGE IS UP TO!
WHAT LUCK! AND I WAS JUST WORKING ON MY LETTER TO YOU! YOU'VE SAVED ME A VERY EXPENSIVE STAMP!
YES! HERE I AM TO MAKE YOUR WISH COME TRUE! NOW YOU, SCROOGE McDUCK, CAN FULFILL YOUR INNERMOST DESIRES AND BUY TEN TICKETS TO THE LADIES' CLUB CHARITY DINNER! HO! HO! HO!
HEY, WAIT A—
MR. McDUCK? SOMEONE ELSE TO SEE YOU...
ANOTHER ONE!? WHAT IS THIS, A HOLIDAY?
HEY! HEY! HEY! IT'S SAAAINT NICHOLAS! AND I'M GONNA SELL YOU A TICKET OR TWO...
WHAT TH'—!?
WAK!
WHAT'S THE IDEA COPYING MY IDEA, CREEP?!
SO SUE ME! I'D LOVE TO SEE MY LUCK VERSUS YOU IN COURT!
UNCLE SCROOGE! IT'S REALLY DONALD!
UNCLE SCROOGE! GLADSTONE'S TRYING TO PULL A YULETIDE SCAM!
UNCLE SCROOGE... IS GONNA MAKE TWO SNEAKY NEPHEWS SORRY!
CHISELER!
UPSTARTS AND ROGUES! WHAT DID I EVER DO TO DESERVE SUCH A FAMILY?
CLICK!
ROBBER BARON!
WATCH IT, BUB, OR I WON'T GET MY DEPOSIT BACK ON THIS RENTAL SUIT!
I'LL GIVE YOU A DEPOSIT, NUMBSKULL!
BANG!
BANG!
BONK!
WARNING: FAKE SANTAS WILL BE PUNISHED TO THE FULL EXTENT OF THE LAW

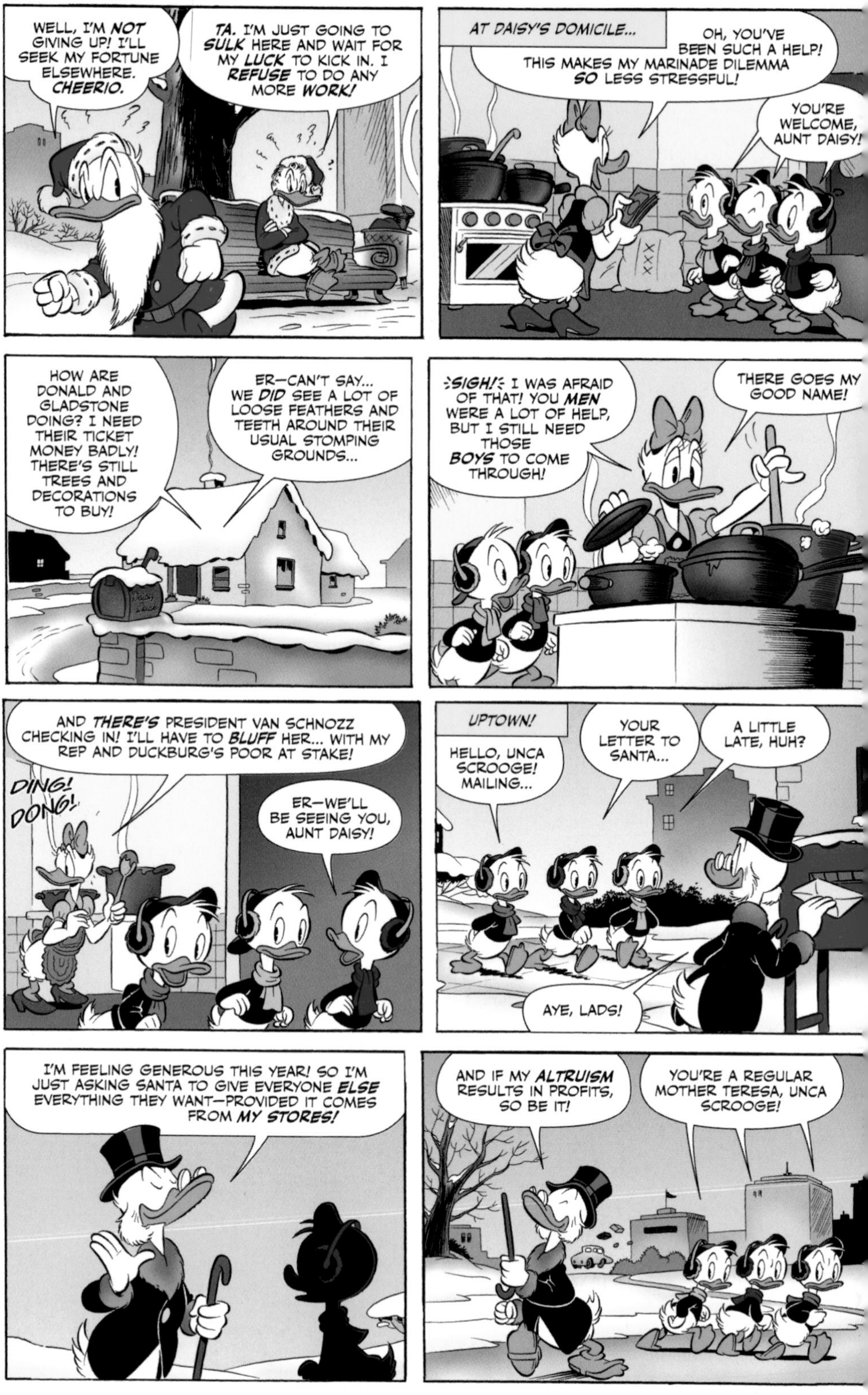
WELL, I'M NOT GIVING UP! I'LL SEEK MY FORTUNE ELSEWHERE. CHEERIO.
TA. I'M JUST GOING TO SULK HERE AND WAIT FOR MY LUCK TO KICK IN. I REFUSE TO DO ANY MORE WORK!
AT DAISY'S DOMICILE...
OH, YOU'VE BEEN SUCH A HELP! THIS MAKES MY MARINADE DILEMMA SO LESS STRESSFUL!
YOU'RE WELCOME, AUNT DAISY!
HOW ARE DONALD AND GLADSTONE DOING? I NEED THEIR TICKET MONEY BADLY! THERE'S STILL TREES AND DECORATIONS TO BUY!
ER—CAN'T SAY... WE DID SEE A LOT OF LOOSE FEATHERS AND TEETH AROUND THEIR USUAL STOMPING GROUNDS...
SIGH! I WAS AFRAID OF THAT! YOU MEN WERE A LOT OF HELP, BUT I STILL NEED THOSE BOYS TO COME THROUGH!
THERE GOES MY GOOD NAME!
AND THERE'S PRESIDENT VAN SCHNOZZ CHECKING IN! I'LL HAVE TO BLUFF HER... WITH MY REP AND DUCKBURG'S POOR AT STAKE!
DING! DONG!
ER—WE'LL BE SEEING YOU, AUNT DAISY!
UPTOWN!
HELLO, UNCA SCROOGE! MAILING...
YOUR LETTER TO SANTA...
A LITTLE LATE, HUH?
AYE, LADS!
I'M FEELING GENEROUS THIS YEAR! SO I'M JUST ASKING SANTA TO GIVE EVERYONE ELSE EVERYTHING THEY WANT—PROVIDED IT COMES FROM MY STORES!
AND IF MY ALTRUISM RESULTS IN PROFITS, SO BE IT!
YOU'RE A REGULAR MOTHER TERESA, UNCA SCROOGE!

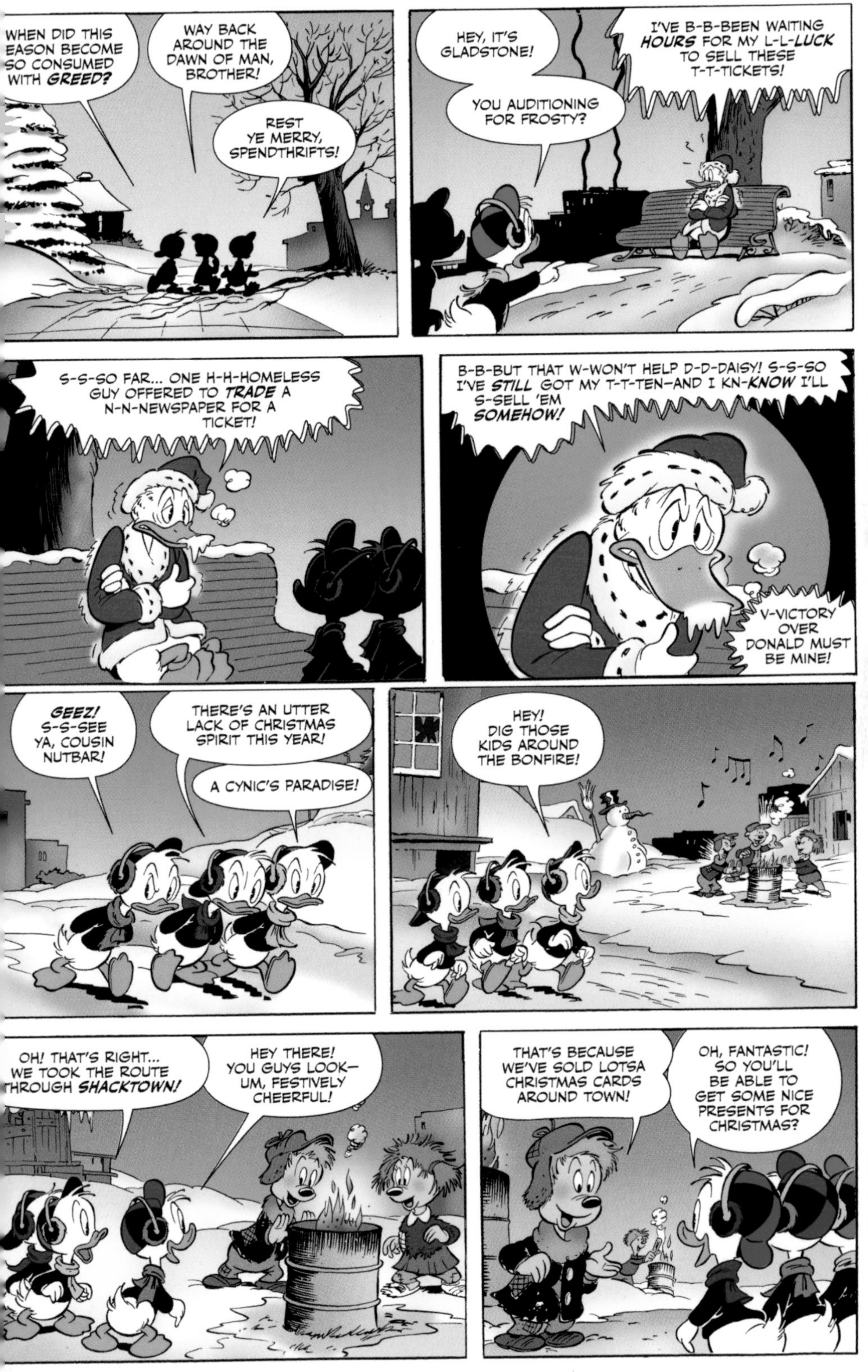
WHEN DID THIS EASON BECOME SO CONSUMED WITH *GREED?*
WAY BACK AROUND THE DAWN OF MAN, BROTHER!
REST YE MERRY, SPENDTHRIFTS!
HEY, IT'S GLADSTONE!
YOU AUDITIONING FOR FROSTY?
I'VE B-B-BEEN WAITING *HOURS* FOR MY L-L-*LUCK* TO SELL THESE T-T-TICKETS!
S-S-SO FAR... ONE H-H-HOMELESS GUY OFFERED TO *TRADE* A N-N-NEWSPAPER FOR A TICKET!
B-B-BUT THAT W-WON'T HELP D-D-DAISY! S-S-SO I'VE *STILL* GOT MY T-T-TEN—AND I KN-*KNOW* I'LL S-SELL 'EM *SOMEHOW!*
V-VICTORY OVER DONALD MUST BE MINE!
GEEZ! S-S-SEE YA, COUSIN NUTBAR!
THERE'S AN UTTER LACK OF CHRISTMAS SPIRIT THIS YEAR!
A CYNIC'S PARADISE!
HEY! DIG THOSE KIDS AROUND THE BONFIRE!
OH! THAT'S RIGHT... WE TOOK THE ROUTE THROUGH *SHACKTOWN!*
HEY THERE! YOU GUYS LOOK—UM, FESTIVELY CHEERFUL!
THAT'S BECAUSE WE'VE SOLD LOTSA CHRISTMAS CARDS AROUND TOWN!
OH, FANTASTIC! SO YOU'LL BE ABLE TO GET SOME NICE PRESENTS FOR CHRISTMAS?

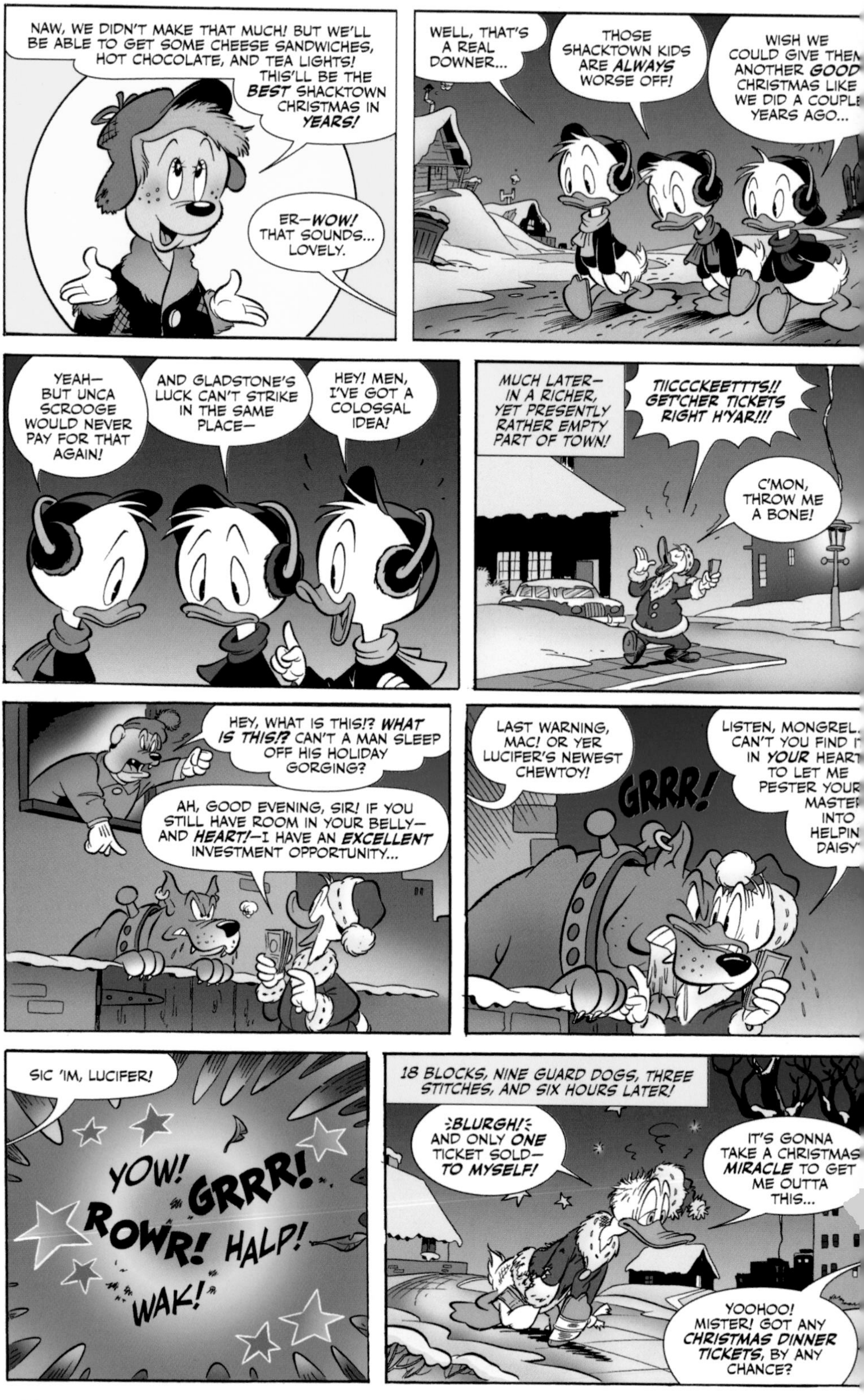
NAW, WE DIDN'T MAKE THAT MUCH! BUT WE'LL BE ABLE TO GET SOME CHEESE SANDWICHES, HOT CHOCOLATE, AND TEA LIGHTS! THIS'LL BE THE BEST SHACKTOWN CHRISTMAS IN YEARS!
ER—WOW! THAT SOUNDS... LOVELY.
WELL, THAT'S A REAL DOWNER...
THOSE SHACKTOWN KIDS ARE ALWAYS WORSE OFF!
WISH WE COULD GIVE THEM ANOTHER GOOD CHRISTMAS LIKE WE DID A COUPLE YEARS AGO...
YEAH— BUT UNCA SCROOGE WOULD NEVER PAY FOR THAT AGAIN!
AND GLADSTONE'S LUCK CAN'T STRIKE IN THE SAME PLACE—
HEY! MEN, I'VE GOT A COLOSSAL IDEA!
MUCH LATER— IN A RICHER, YET PRESENTLY RATHER EMPTY PART OF TOWN!
TIICCCKEETTTS!! GET'CHER TICKETS RIGHT H'YAR!!!
C'MON, THROW ME A BONE!
HEY, WHAT IS THIS!? WHAT IS THIS!? CAN'T A MAN SLEEP OFF HIS HOLIDAY GORGING?
AH, GOOD EVENING, SIR! IF YOU STILL HAVE ROOM IN YOUR BELLY— AND HEART!—I HAVE AN EXCELLENT INVESTMENT OPPORTUNITY...
LAST WARNING, MAC! OR YER LUCIFER'S NEWEST CHEWTOY!
GRRR!
LISTEN, MONGREL... CAN'T YOU FIND IT IN YOUR HEART TO LET ME PESTER YOUR MASTER INTO HELPIN' DAISY
SIC 'IM, LUCIFER!
YOW! GRRR! ROWR! HALP! WAK!
18 BLOCKS, NINE GUARD DOGS, THREE STITCHES, AND SIX HOURS LATER!
BLURGH! AND ONLY ONE TICKET SOLD— TO MYSELF!
IT'S GONNA TAKE A CHRISTMAS MIRACLE TO GET ME OUTTA THIS...
YOOHOO! MISTER! GOT ANY CHRISTMAS DINNER TICKETS, BY ANY CHANCE?

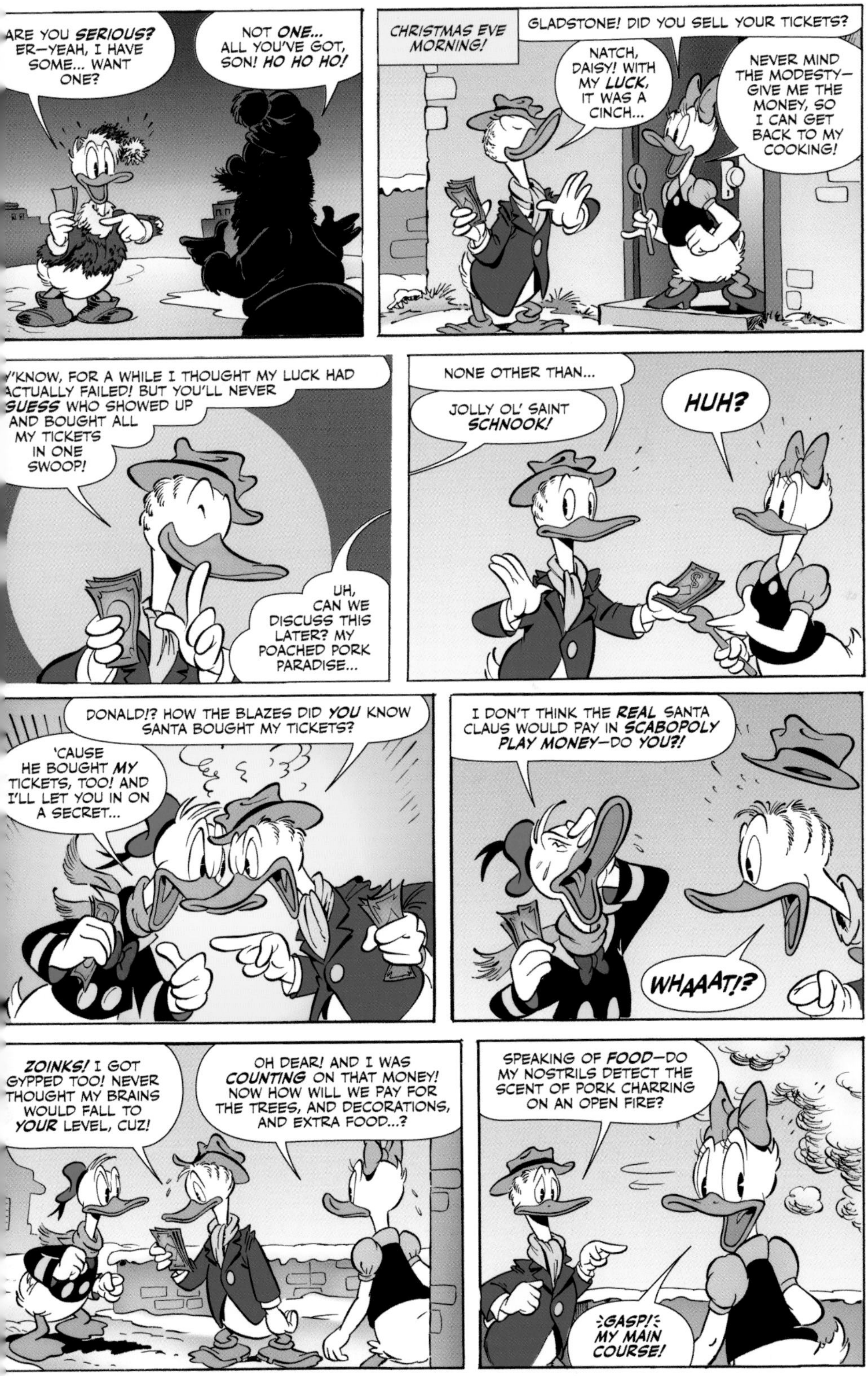
ARE YOU SERIOUS? ER—YEAH, I HAVE SOME... WANT ONE?
NOT ONE... ALL YOU'VE GOT, SON! HO HO HO!
CHRISTMAS EVE MORNING!
GLADSTONE! DID YOU SELL YOUR TICKETS?
NATCH, DAISY! WITH MY LUCK, IT WAS A CINCH...
NEVER MIND THE MODESTY—GIVE ME THE MONEY, SO I CAN GET BACK TO MY COOKING!
Y'KNOW, FOR A WHILE I THOUGHT MY LUCK HAD ACTUALLY FAILED! BUT YOU'LL NEVER GUESS WHO SHOWED UP AND BOUGHT ALL MY TICKETS IN ONE SWOOP!
UH, CAN WE DISCUSS THIS LATER? MY POACHED PORK PARADISE...
NONE OTHER THAN...
JOLLY OL' SAINT SCHNOOK!
HUH?
DONALD!? HOW THE BLAZES DID YOU KNOW SANTA BOUGHT MY TICKETS?
'CAUSE HE BOUGHT MY TICKETS, TOO! AND I'LL LET YOU IN ON A SECRET...
I DON'T THINK THE REAL SANTA CLAUS WOULD PAY IN SCABOPOLY PLAY MONEY—DO YOU?!
WHAAAT!?
ZOINKS! I GOT GYPPED TOO! NEVER THOUGHT MY BRAINS WOULD FALL TO YOUR LEVEL, CUZ!
OH DEAR! AND I WAS COUNTING ON THAT MONEY! NOW HOW WILL WE PAY FOR THE TREES, AND DECORATIONS, AND EXTRA FOOD...?
SPEAKING OF FOOD—DO MY NOSTRILS DETECT THE SCENT OF PORK CHARRING ON AN OPEN FIRE?
GASP! MY MAIN COURSE!

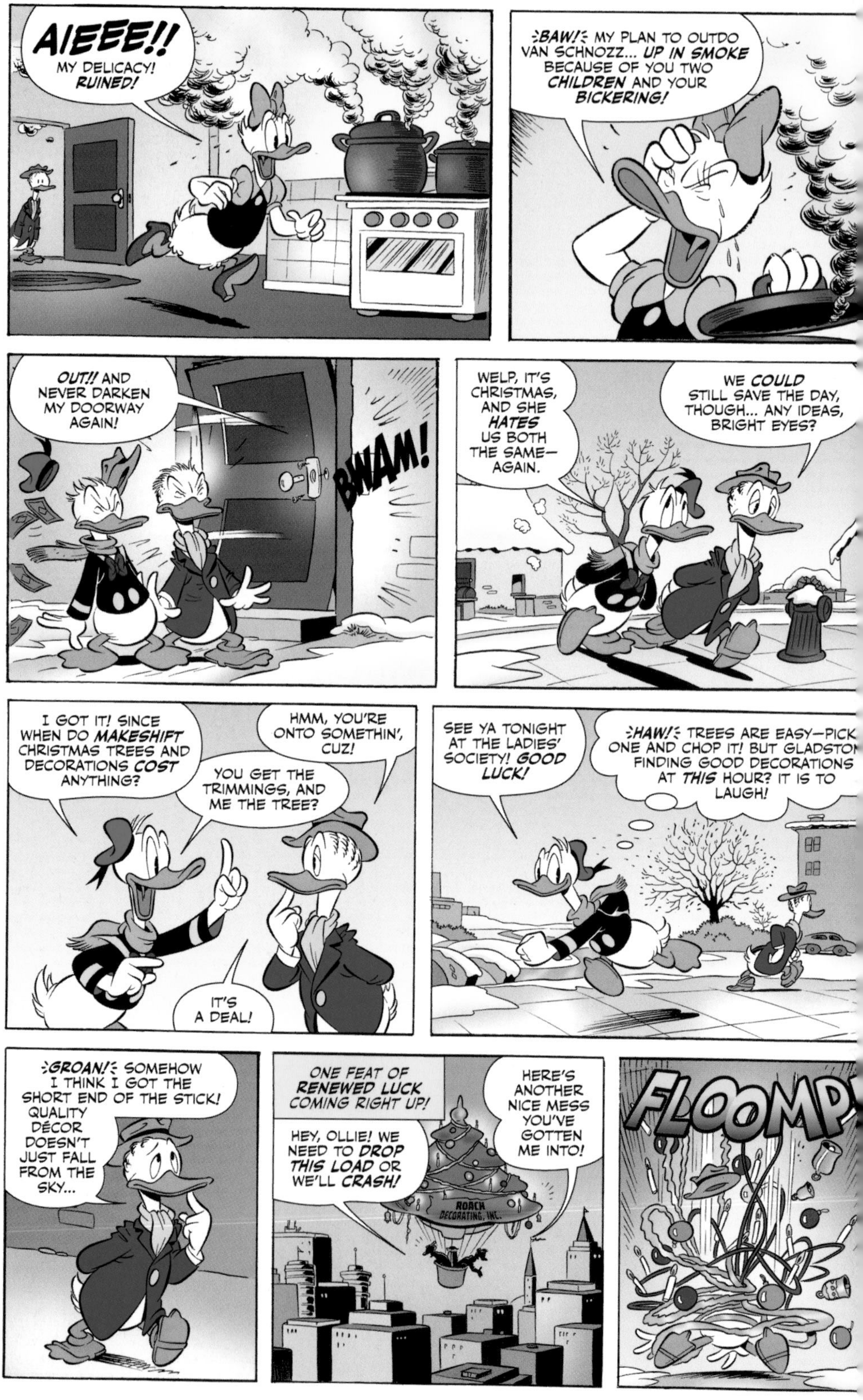

AIEEE!! MY DELICACY! RUINED!
:BAW!: MY PLAN TO OUTDO VAN SCHNOZZ... UP IN SMOKE BECAUSE OF YOU TWO CHILDREN AND YOUR BICKERING!
OUT!! AND NEVER DARKEN MY DOORWAY AGAIN!
BWAM!
WELP, IT'S CHRISTMAS, AND SHE HATES US BOTH THE SAME— AGAIN.
WE COULD STILL SAVE THE DAY, THOUGH... ANY IDEAS, BRIGHT EYES?
I GOT IT! SINCE WHEN DO MAKESHIFT CHRISTMAS TREES AND DECORATIONS COST ANYTHING?
HMM, YOU'RE ONTO SOMETHIN', CUZ!
YOU GET THE TRIMMINGS, AND ME THE TREE?
IT'S A DEAL!
SEE YA TONIGHT AT THE LADIES' SOCIETY! GOOD LUCK!
:HAW!: TREES ARE EASY—PICK ONE AND CHOP IT! BUT GLADSTO FINDING GOOD DECORATIONS AT THIS HOUR? IT IS TO LAUGH!
:GROAN!: SOMEHOW I THINK I GOT THE SHORT END OF THE STICK!
QUALITY DÉCOR DOESN'T JUST FALL FROM THE SKY...
ONE FEAT OF RENEWED LUCK COMING RIGHT UP!
HEY, OLLIE! WE NEED TO DROP THIS LOAD OR WE'LL CRASH!
HERE'S ANOTHER NICE MESS YOU'VE GOTTEN ME INTO!
ROACH DECORATING, INC.
FLOOMP

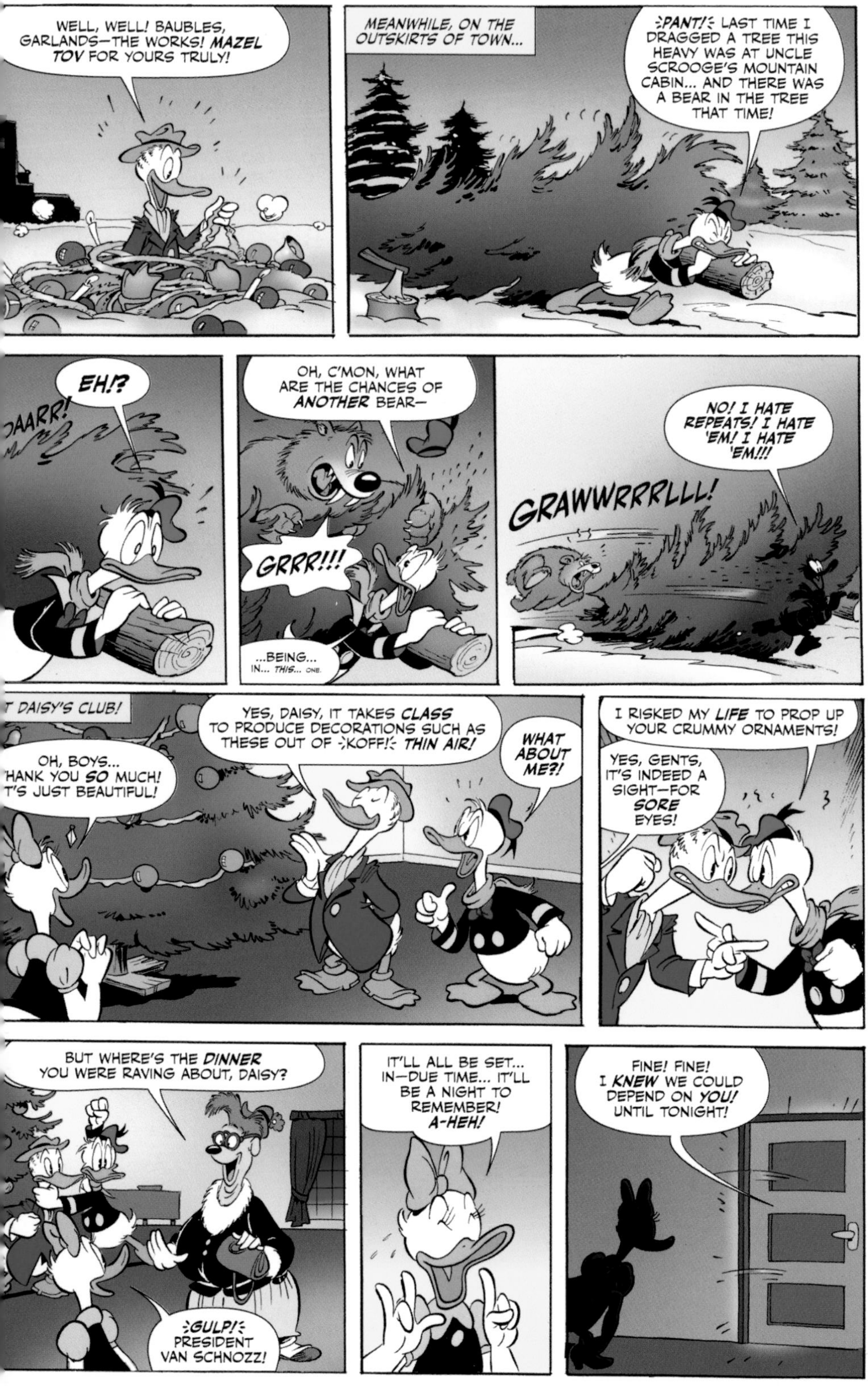
WELL, WELL! BAUBLES, GARLANDS—THE WORKS! MAZEL TOV FOR YOURS TRULY!
MEANWHILE, ON THE OUTSKIRTS OF TOWN...
PANT! LAST TIME I DRAGGED A TREE THIS HEAVY WAS AT UNCLE SCROOGE'S MOUNTAIN CABIN... AND THERE WAS A BEAR IN THE TREE THAT TIME!
DAARR!
EH!?
OH, C'MON, WHAT ARE THE CHANCES OF ANOTHER BEAR—
GRRR!!!
...BEING... IN... THIS... ONE.
NO! I HATE REPEATS! I HATE 'EM! I HATE 'EM!!!
GRAWWRRRLLL!
T DAISY'S CLUB!
OH, BOYS... HANK YOU SO MUCH! T'S JUST BEAUTIFUL!
YES, DAISY, IT TAKES CLASS TO PRODUCE DECORATIONS SUCH AS THESE OUT OF KOFF! THIN AIR!
WHAT ABOUT ME?!
I RISKED MY LIFE TO PROP UP YOUR CRUMMY ORNAMENTS!
YES, GENTS, IT'S INDEED A SIGHT—FOR SORE EYES!
BUT WHERE'S THE DINNER YOU WERE RAVING ABOUT, DAISY?
GULP! PRESIDENT VAN SCHNOZZ!
IT'LL ALL BE SET... IN—DUE TIME... IT'LL BE A NIGHT TO REMEMBER! A-HEH!
FINE! FINE! I KNEW WE COULD DEPEND ON YOU! UNTIL TONIGHT!

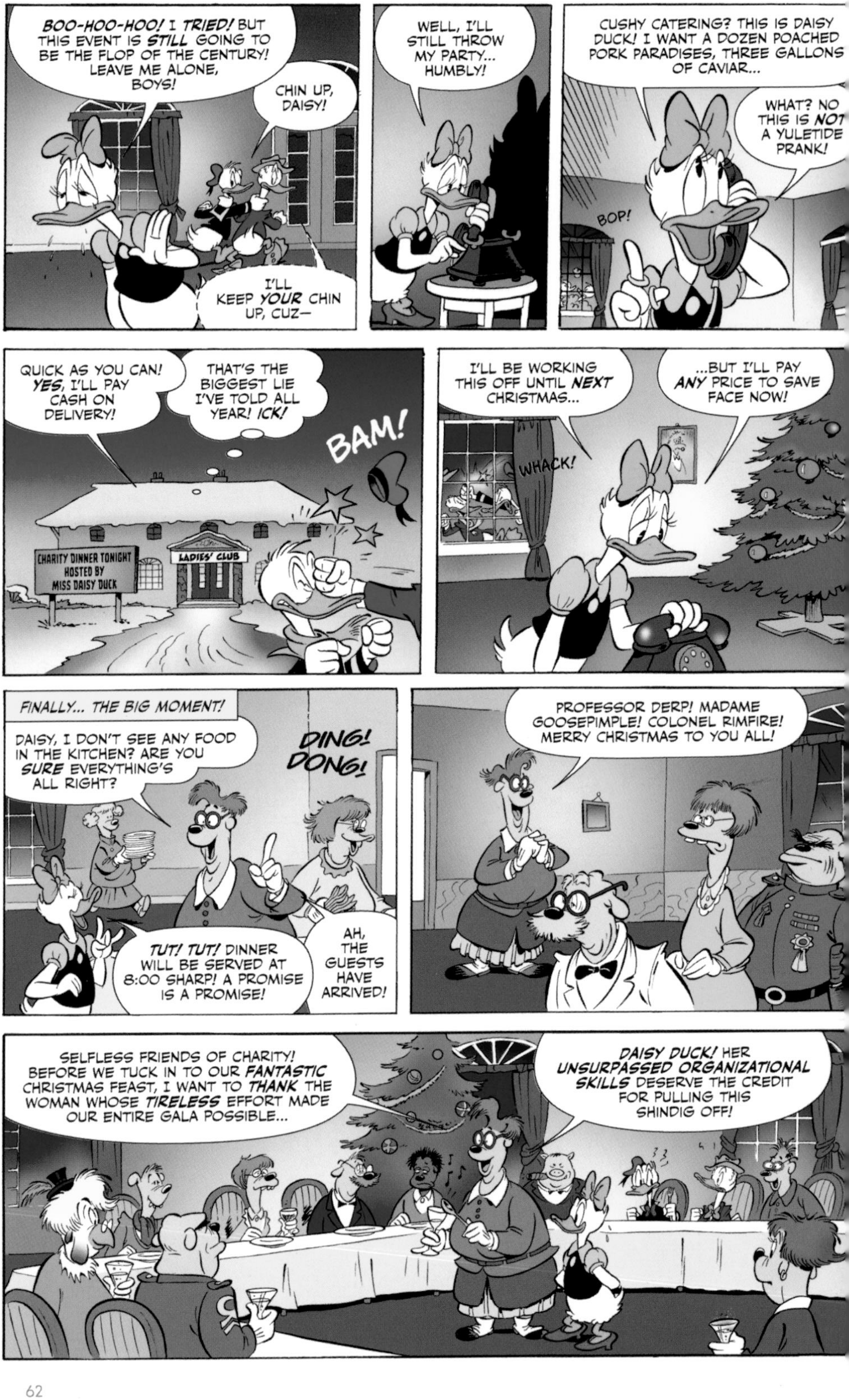
BOO-HOO-HOO! I TRIED! BUT THIS EVENT IS STILL GOING TO BE THE FLOP OF THE CENTURY! LEAVE ME ALONE, BOYS!
CHIN UP, DAISY!
I'LL KEEP YOUR CHIN UP, CUZ—
WELL, I'LL STILL THROW MY PARTY... HUMBLY!
CUSHY CATERING? THIS IS DAISY DUCK! I WANT A DOZEN POACHED PORK PARADISES, THREE GALLONS OF CAVIAR...
BOP!
WHAT? NO THIS IS NOT A YULETIDE PRANK!
QUICK AS YOU CAN! YES, I'LL PAY CASH ON DELIVERY!
THAT'S THE BIGGEST LIE I'VE TOLD ALL YEAR! ICK!
BAM!
CHARITY DINNER TONIGHT HOSTED BY MISS DAISY DUCK
LADIES' CLUB
I'LL BE WORKING THIS OFF UNTIL NEXT CHRISTMAS...
...BUT I'LL PAY ANY PRICE TO SAVE FACE NOW!
WHACK!
FINALLY... THE BIG MOMENT!
DAISY, I DON'T SEE ANY FOOD IN THE KITCHEN? ARE YOU SURE EVERYTHING'S ALL RIGHT?
DING! DONG!
TUT! TUT! DINNER WILL BE SERVED AT 8:00 SHARP! A PROMISE IS A PROMISE!
AH, THE GUESTS HAVE ARRIVED!
PROFESSOR DERP! MADAME GOOSEPIMPLE! COLONEL RIMFIRE! MERRY CHRISTMAS TO YOU ALL!
SELFLESS FRIENDS OF CHARITY! BEFORE WE TUCK IN TO OUR FANTASTIC CHRISTMAS FEAST, I WANT TO THANK THE WOMAN WHOSE TIRELESS EFFORT MADE OUR ENTIRE GALA POSSIBLE...
DAISY DUCK! HER UNSURPASSED ORGANIZATIONAL SKILLS DESERVE THE CREDIT FOR PULLING THIS SHINDIG OFF!

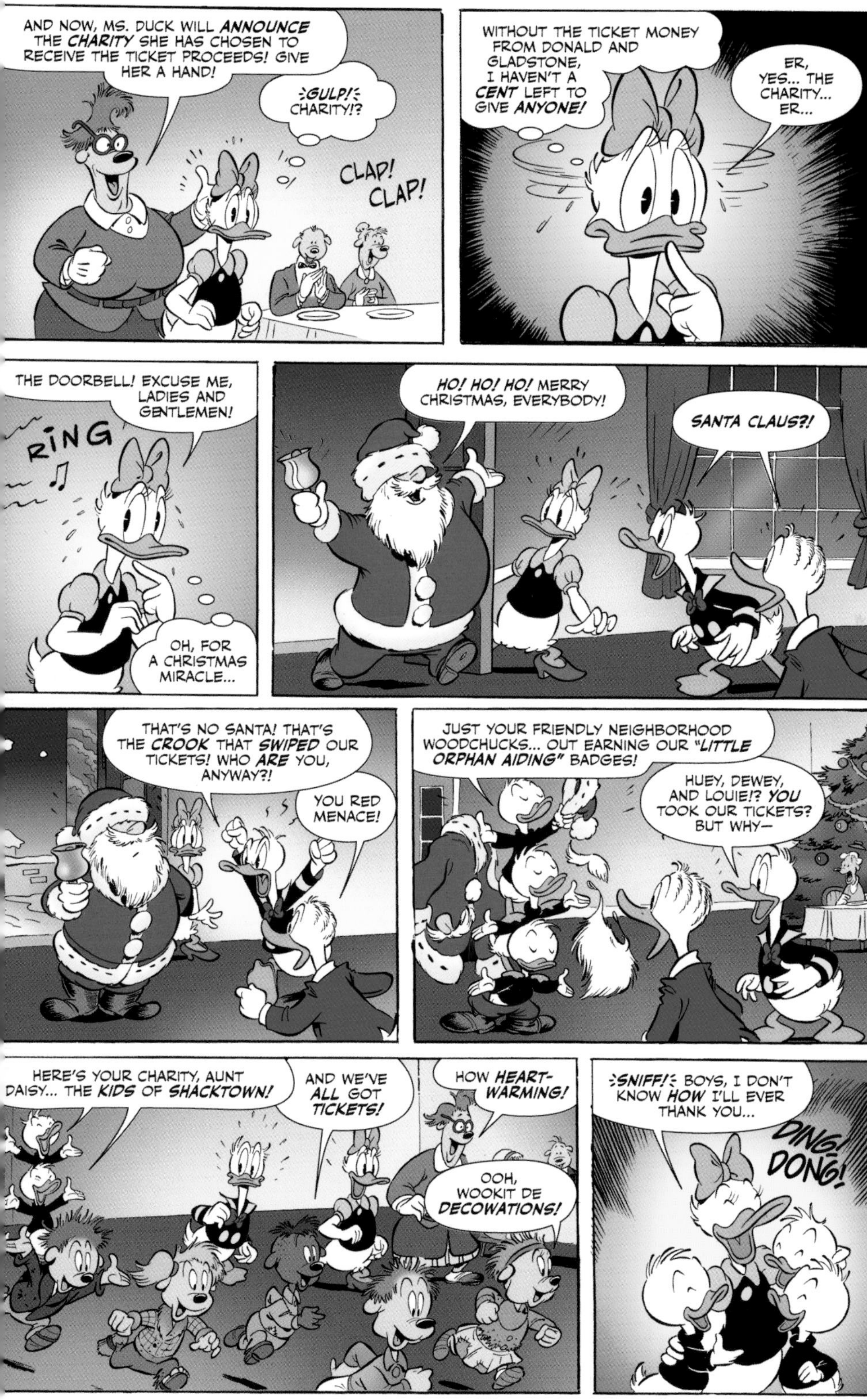
AND NOW, MS. DUCK WILL ANNOUNCE THE CHARITY SHE HAS CHOSEN TO RECEIVE THE TICKET PROCEEDS! GIVE HER A HAND!
GULP! CHARITY!?
CLAP! CLAP!
WITHOUT THE TICKET MONEY FROM DONALD AND GLADSTONE, I HAVEN'T A CENT LEFT TO GIVE ANYONE!
ER, YES... THE CHARITY... ER...
THE DOORBELL! EXCUSE ME, LADIES AND GENTLEMEN!
RING
OH, FOR A CHRISTMAS MIRACLE...
HO! HO! HO! MERRY CHRISTMAS, EVERYBODY!
SANTA CLAUS?!
THAT'S NO SANTA! THAT'S THE CROOK THAT SWIPED OUR TICKETS! WHO ARE YOU, ANYWAY?!
YOU RED MENACE!
JUST YOUR FRIENDLY NEIGHBORHOOD WOODCHUCKS... OUT EARNING OUR "LITTLE ORPHAN AIDING" BADGES!
HUEY, DEWEY, AND LOUIE!? YOU TOOK OUR TICKETS? BUT WHY—
HERE'S YOUR CHARITY, AUNT DAISY... THE KIDS OF SHACKTOWN!
AND WE'VE ALL GOT TICKETS!
HOW HEART-WARMING!
OOH, WOOKIT DE DECOWATIONS!
SNIFF! BOYS, I DON'T KNOW HOW I'LL EVER THANK YOU...
DING! DONG!

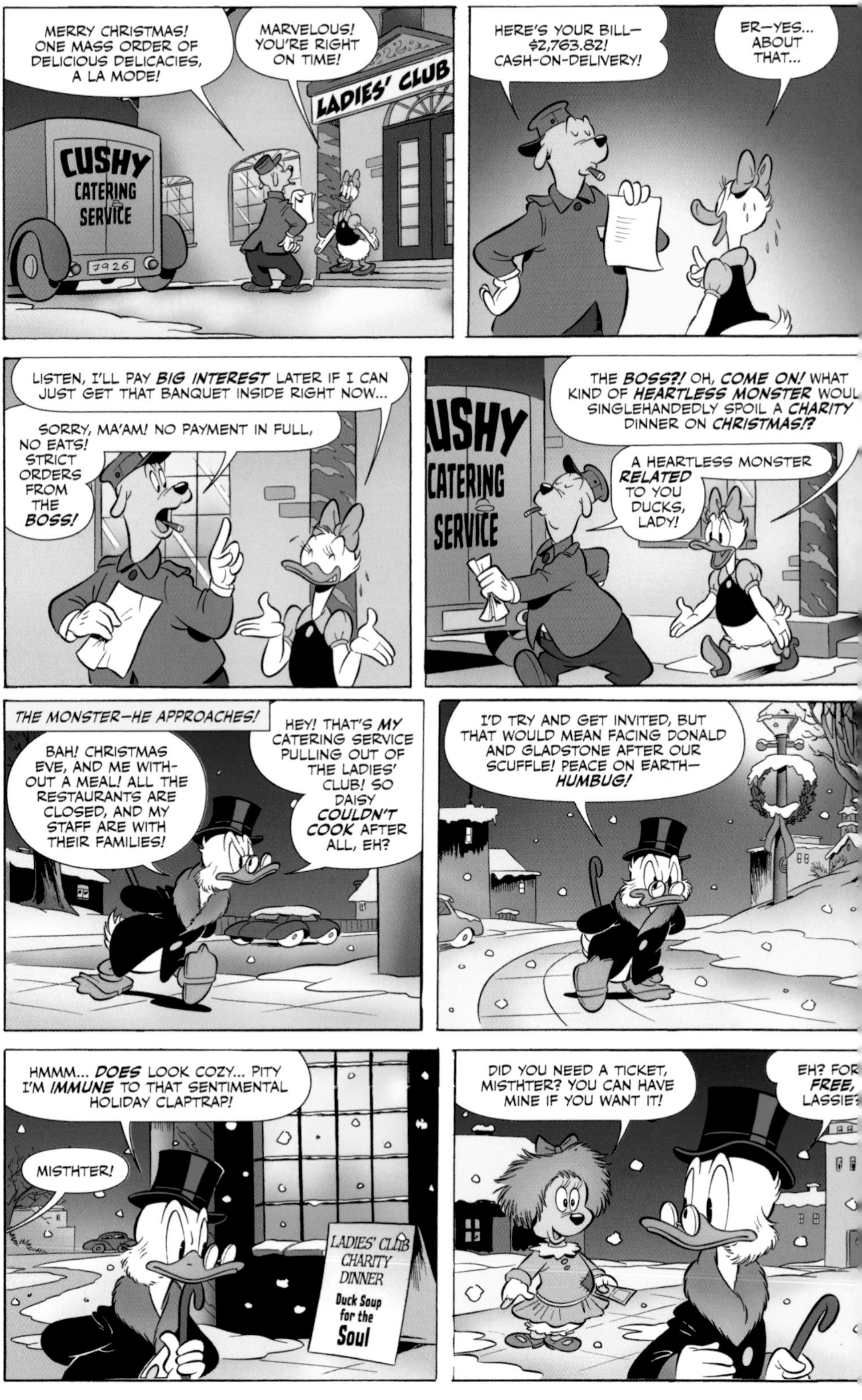
MERRY CHRISTMAS! ONE MASS ORDER OF DELICIOUS DELICACIES, A LA MODE!
MARVELOUS! YOU'RE RIGHT ON TIME!
LADIES' CLUB
CUSHY CATERING SERVICE
7926
HERE'S YOUR BILL— $2,763.82! CASH-ON-DELIVERY!
ER—YES... ABOUT THAT...
LISTEN, I'LL PAY BIG INTEREST LATER IF I CAN JUST GET THAT BANQUET INSIDE RIGHT NOW...
SORRY, MA'AM! NO PAYMENT IN FULL, NO EATS! STRICT ORDERS FROM THE BOSS!
THE BOSS?! OH, COME ON! WHAT KIND OF HEARTLESS MONSTER WOUL SINGLEHANDEDLY SPOIL A CHARITY DINNER ON CHRISTMAS!?
USHY CATERING SERVICE
A HEARTLESS MONSTER RELATED TO YOU DUCKS, LADY!
THE MONSTER—HE APPROACHES!
BAH! CHRISTMAS EVE, AND ME WITH-OUT A MEAL! ALL THE RESTAURANTS ARE CLOSED, AND MY STAFF ARE WITH THEIR FAMILIES!
HEY! THAT'S MY CATERING SERVICE PULLING OUT OF THE LADIES' CLUB! SO DAISY COULDN'T COOK AFTER ALL, EH?
I'D TRY AND GET INVITED, BUT THAT WOULD MEAN FACING DONALD AND GLADSTONE AFTER OUR SCUFFLE! PEACE ON EARTH— HUMBUG!
HMMM... DOES LOOK COZY... PITY I'M IMMUNE TO THAT SENTIMENTAL HOLIDAY CLAPTRAP!
MISTHTER!
LADIES' CLUB CHARITY DINNER Duck Soup for the Soul
DID YOU NEED A TICKET, MISTHTER? YOU CAN HAVE MINE IF YOU WANT IT!
EH? FOR FREE, LASSIE?

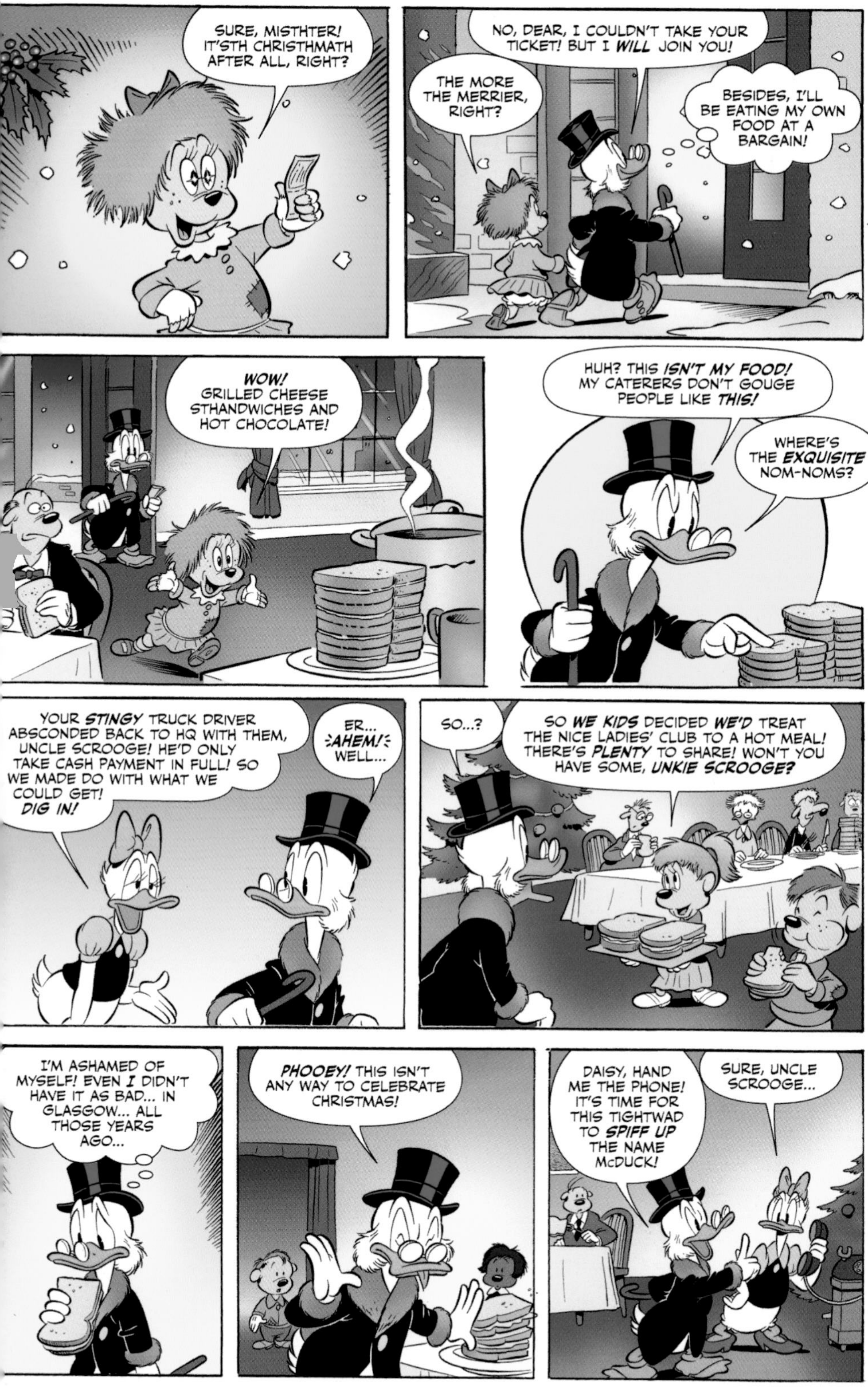
SURE, MISTHTER! IT'STH CHRISTHMATH AFTER ALL, RIGHT?
NO, DEAR, I COULDN'T TAKE YOUR TICKET! BUT I WILL JOIN YOU!
THE MORE THE MERRIER, RIGHT?
BESIDES, I'LL BE EATING MY OWN FOOD AT A BARGAIN!
WOW! GRILLED CHEESE STHANDWICHES AND HOT CHOCOLATE!
HUH? THIS ISN'T MY FOOD! MY CATERERS DON'T GOUGE PEOPLE LIKE THIS!
WHERE'S THE EXQUISITE NOM-NOMS?
YOUR STINGY TRUCK DRIVER ABSCONDED BACK TO HQ WITH THEM, UNCLE SCROOGE! HE'D ONLY TAKE CASH PAYMENT IN FULL! SO WE MADE DO WITH WHAT WE COULD GET! DIG IN!
ER... AHEM! WELL...
SO...?
SO WE KIDS DECIDED WE'D TREAT THE NICE LADIES' CLUB TO A HOT MEAL! THERE'S PLENTY TO SHARE! WON'T YOU HAVE SOME, UNKIE SCROOGE?
I'M ASHAMED OF MYSELF! EVEN I DIDN'T HAVE IT AS BAD... IN GLASGOW... ALL THOSE YEARS AGO...
PHOOEY! THIS ISN'T ANY WAY TO CELEBRATE CHRISTMAS!
DAISY, HAND ME THE PHONE! IT'S TIME FOR THIS TIGHTWAD TO SPIFF UP THE NAME McDUCK!
SURE, UNCLE SCROOGE...

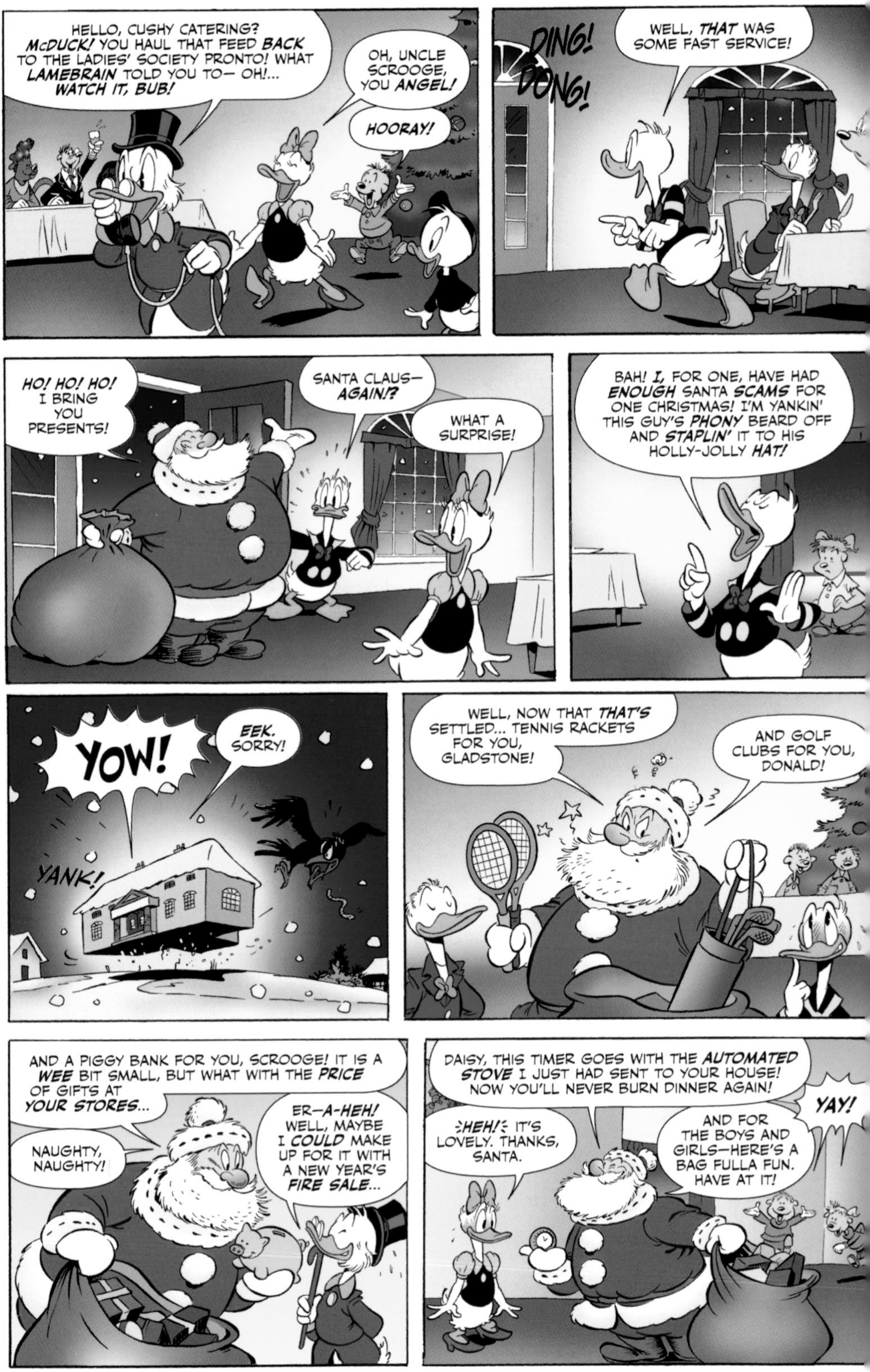

HELLO, CUSHY CATERING? McDUCK! YOU HAUL THAT FEED BACK TO THE LADIES' SOCIETY PRONTO! WHAT LAMEBRAIN TOLD YOU TO— OH!... WATCH IT, BUB!
OH, UNCLE SCROOGE, YOU ANGEL!
HOORAY!
DING! DONG!
WELL, THAT WAS SOME FAST SERVICE!
HO! HO! HO! I BRING YOU PRESENTS!
SANTA CLAUS— AGAIN!?
WHAT A SURPRISE!
BAH! I, FOR ONE, HAVE HAD ENOUGH SANTA SCAMS FOR ONE CHRISTMAS! I'M YANKIN' THIS GUY'S PHONY BEARD OFF AND STAPLIN' IT TO HIS HOLLY-JOLLY HAT!
YOW!
EEK. SORRY!
YANK!
WELL, NOW THAT THAT'S SETTLED... TENNIS RACKETS FOR YOU, GLADSTONE!
AND GOLF CLUBS FOR YOU, DONALD!
AND A PIGGY BANK FOR YOU, SCROOGE! IT IS A WEE BIT SMALL, BUT WHAT WITH THE PRICE OF GIFTS AT YOUR STORES...
NAUGHTY, NAUGHTY!
ER—A-HEH! WELL, MAYBE I COULD MAKE UP FOR IT WITH A NEW YEAR'S FIRE SALE...
DAISY, THIS TIMER GOES WITH THE AUTOMATED STOVE I JUST HAD SENT TO YOUR HOUSE! NOW YOU'LL NEVER BURN DINNER AGAIN!
HEH! IT'S LOVELY. THANKS, SANTA.
AND FOR THE BOYS AND GIRLS—HERE'S A BAG FULLA FUN. HAVE AT IT!
YAY!

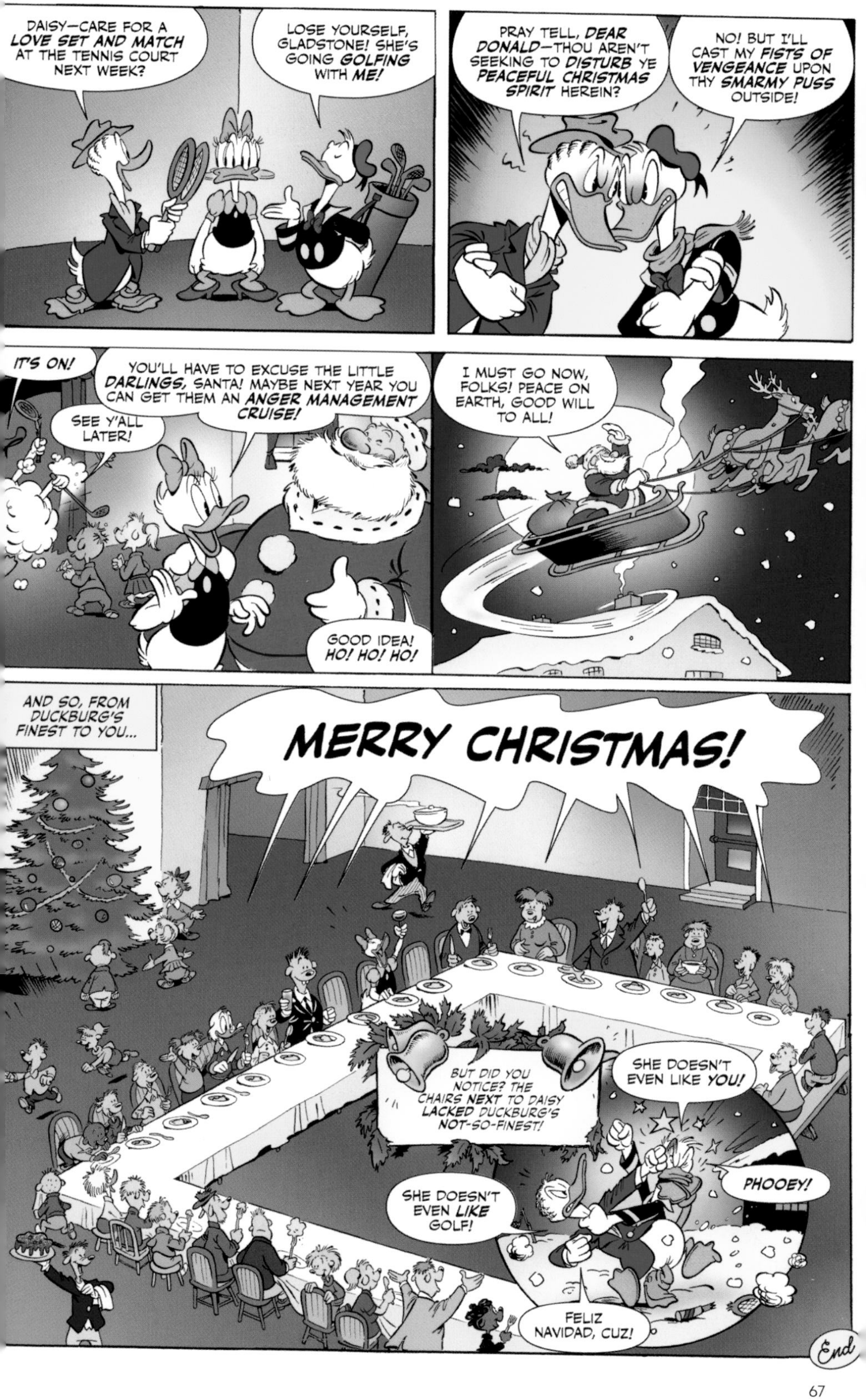

DAISY—CARE FOR A LOVE SET AND MATCH AT THE TENNIS COURT NEXT WEEK?
LOSE YOURSELF, GLADSTONE! SHE'S GOING GOLFING WITH ME!
PRAY TELL, DEAR DONALD—THOU AREN'T SEEKING TO DISTURB YE PEACEFUL CHRISTMAS SPIRIT HEREIN?
NO! BUT I'LL CAST MY FISTS OF VENGEANCE UPON THY SMARMY PUSS OUTSIDE!
IT'S ON!
YOU'LL HAVE TO EXCUSE THE LITTLE DARLINGS, SANTA! MAYBE NEXT YEAR YOU CAN GET THEM AN ANGER MANAGEMENT CRUISE!
SEE Y'ALL LATER!
GOOD IDEA! HO! HO! HO!
I MUST GO NOW, FOLKS! PEACE ON EARTH, GOOD WILL TO ALL!
AND SO, FROM DUCKBURG'S FINEST TO YOU...
MERRY CHRISTMAS!
BUT DID YOU NOTICE? THE CHAIRS NEXT TO DAISY LACKED DUCKBURG'S NOT-SO-FINEST!
SHE DOESN'T EVEN LIKE YOU!
PHOOEY!
SHE DOESN'T EVEN LIKE GOLF!
FELIZ NAVIDAD, CUZ!
End

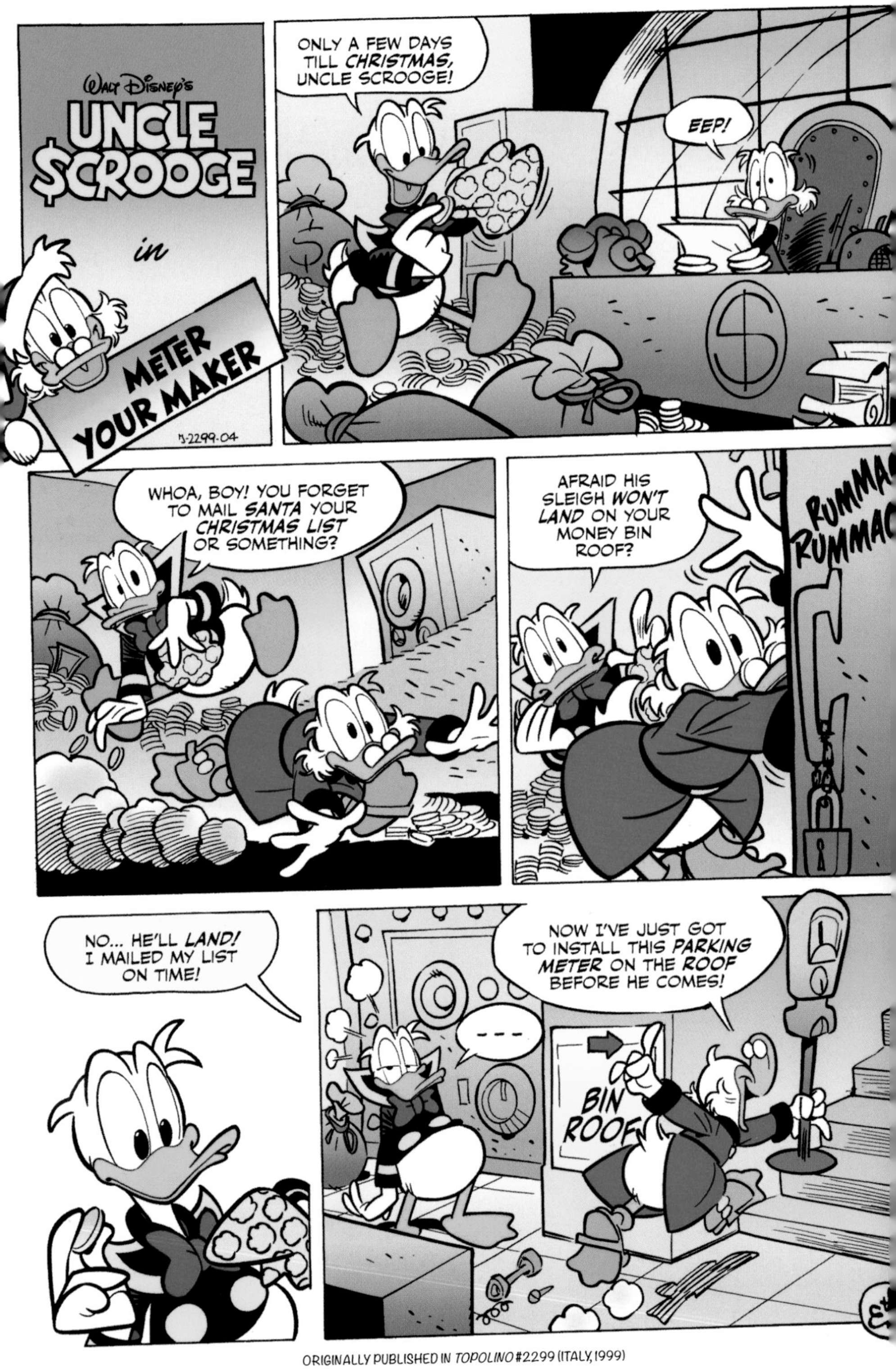

WALT DISNEY'S
UNCLE $CROOGE
in
METER YOUR MAKER
ONLY A FEW DAYS TILL CHRISTMAS, UNCLE SCROOGE!
EEP!
WHOA, BOY! YOU FORGET TO MAIL SANTA YOUR CHRISTMAS LIST OR SOMETHING?
AFRAID HIS SLEIGH WON'T LAND ON YOUR MONEY BIN ROOF?
NO... HE'LL LAND! I MAILED MY LIST ON TIME!
NOW I'VE JUST GOT TO INSTALL THIS PARKING METER ON THE ROOF BEFORE HE COMES!
- - -
BIN ROOF

ORIGINALLY PUBLISHED IN *TOPOLINO* #2299 (ITALY, 1999)

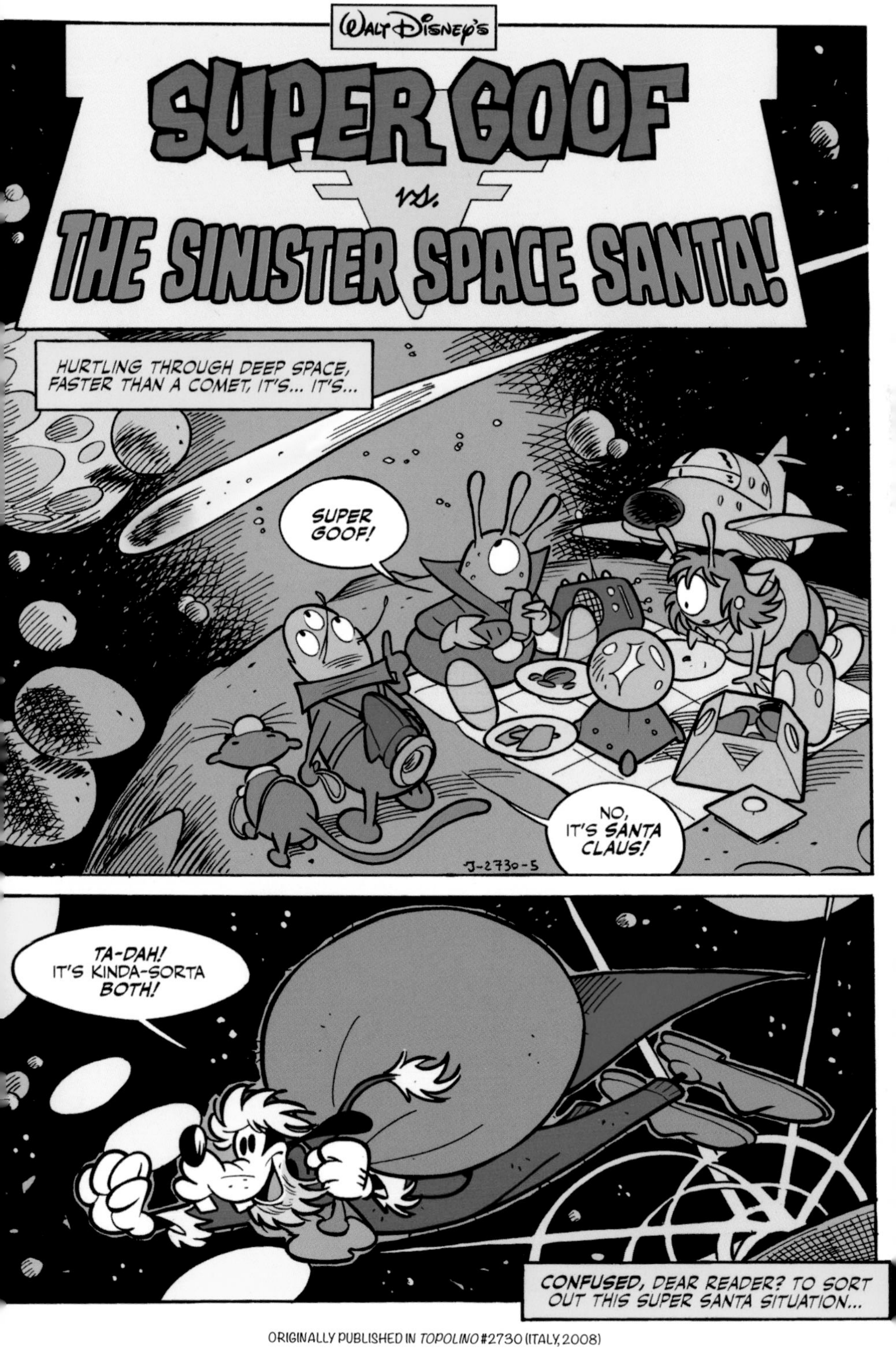
WALT DISNEY'S
SUPER GOOF
VS.
THE SINISTER SPACE SANTA!
HURTLING THROUGH DEEP SPACE, FASTER THAN A COMET, IT'S... IT'S...
SUPER GOOF!
NO, IT'S SANTA CLAUS!
J-2730-5
TA-DAH! IT'S KINDA-SORTA BOTH!
CONFUSED, DEAR READER? TO SORT OUT THIS SUPER SANTA SITUATION...

ORIGINALLY PUBLISHED IN *TOPOLINO* #2730 (ITALY, 2008)

...LET'S TURN BACK TIME A DAY OR SO— AND TURN BACK *SPACE* A FEW MILLION MILES!

MUH *SUPER-HEARIN'* IS HEARIN' A CRY FOR *HELP!*

YUP! CONFIRMED BY MUH *SUPER-SIGHT!*

"TAKE THE *SARCONIAN SPACEWAY,* JORJ," I SAID! "WE'LL MAKE *BETTER TIME,*" I SAID! BUT *NOOOO!*

JAAN—I TELL YOU THAT ASTEROID *WASN'T THERE* A CHRONO-TICK AGO!... *S.O.S.! S.O.S.!*

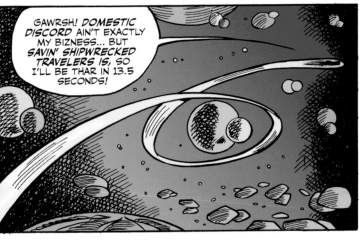

GAWRSH! *DOMESTIC DISCORD* AIN'T EXACTLY MY BIZNESS... BUT *SAVIN' SHIPWRECKED TRAVELERS IS,* SO I'LL BE THAR IN 13.5 SECONDS!

SORRY! IT SEEMS WE'VE CONFUSED MATTERS EVEN *MORE* THAN BEFORE. LET'S ROLL THE TIME AND DISTANCE BACK A BIT *FURTHER,* SHALL WE?

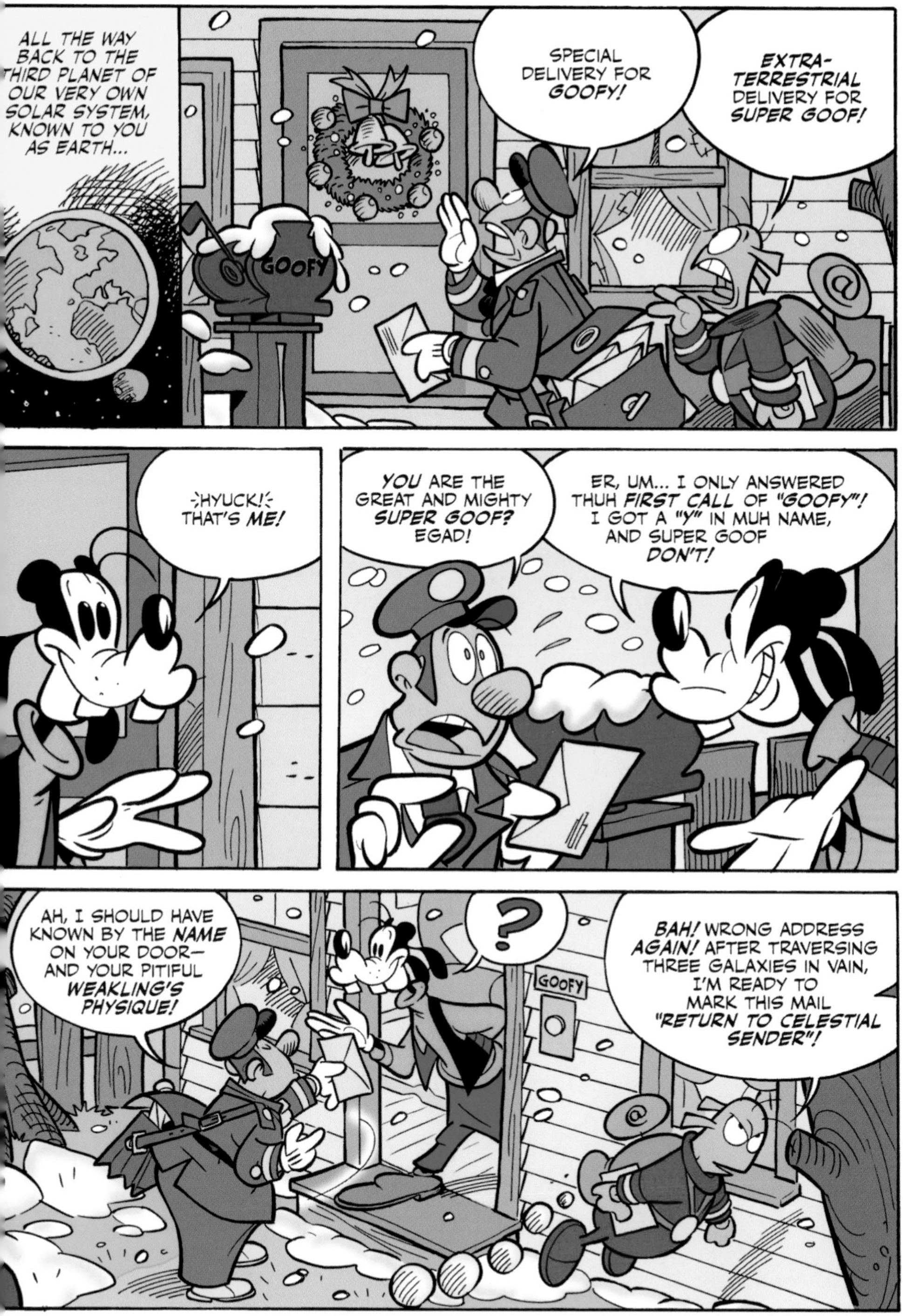

ALL THE WAY BACK TO THE THIRD PLANET OF OUR VERY OWN SOLAR SYSTEM, KNOWN TO YOU AS EARTH...
SPECIAL DELIVERY FOR GOOFY!
EXTRA-TERRESTRIAL DELIVERY FOR SUPER GOOF!
GOOFY
HYUCK! THAT'S ME!
YOU ARE THE GREAT AND MIGHTY SUPER GOOF? EGAD!
ER, UM... I ONLY ANSWERED THUH FIRST CALL OF "GOOFY"! I GOT A "Y" IN MUH NAME, AND SUPER GOOF DON'T!
AH, I SHOULD HAVE KNOWN BY THE NAME ON YOUR DOOR— AND YOUR PITIFUL WEAKLING'S PHYSIQUE!
?
GOOFY
BAH! WRONG ADDRESS AGAIN! AFTER TRAVERSING THREE GALAXIES IN VAIN, I'M READY TO MARK THIS MAIL "RETURN TO CELESTIAL SENDER"!

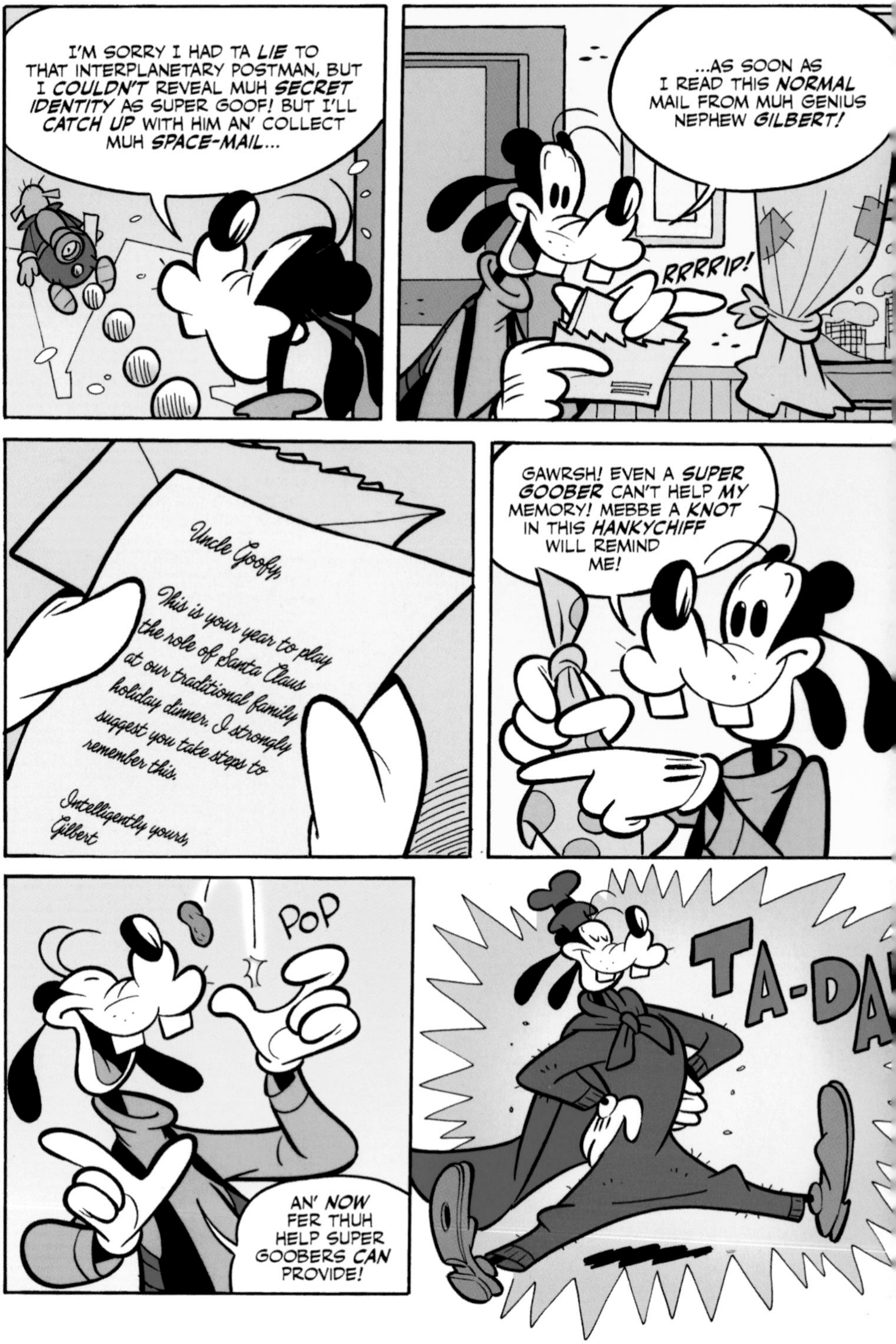
I'M SORRY I HAD TA LIE TO THAT INTERPLANETARY POSTMAN, BUT I COULDN'T REVEAL MUH SECRET IDENTITY AS SUPER GOOF! BUT I'LL CATCH UP WITH HIM AN' COLLECT MUH SPACE-MAIL...
...AS SOON AS I READ THIS NORMAL MAIL FROM MUH GENIUS NEPHEW GILBERT!
RRRRIP!
Uncle Goofy,
This is your year to play the role of Santa Claus at our traditional family holiday dinner. I strongly suggest you take steps to remember this.
Intelligently yours,
Gilbert
GAWRSH! EVEN A SUPER GOOBER CAN'T HELP MY MEMORY! MEBBE A KNOT IN THIS HANKYCHIFF WILL REMIND ME!
POP
AN' NOW FER THUH HELP SUPER GOOBERS CAN PROVIDE!
TA-DA

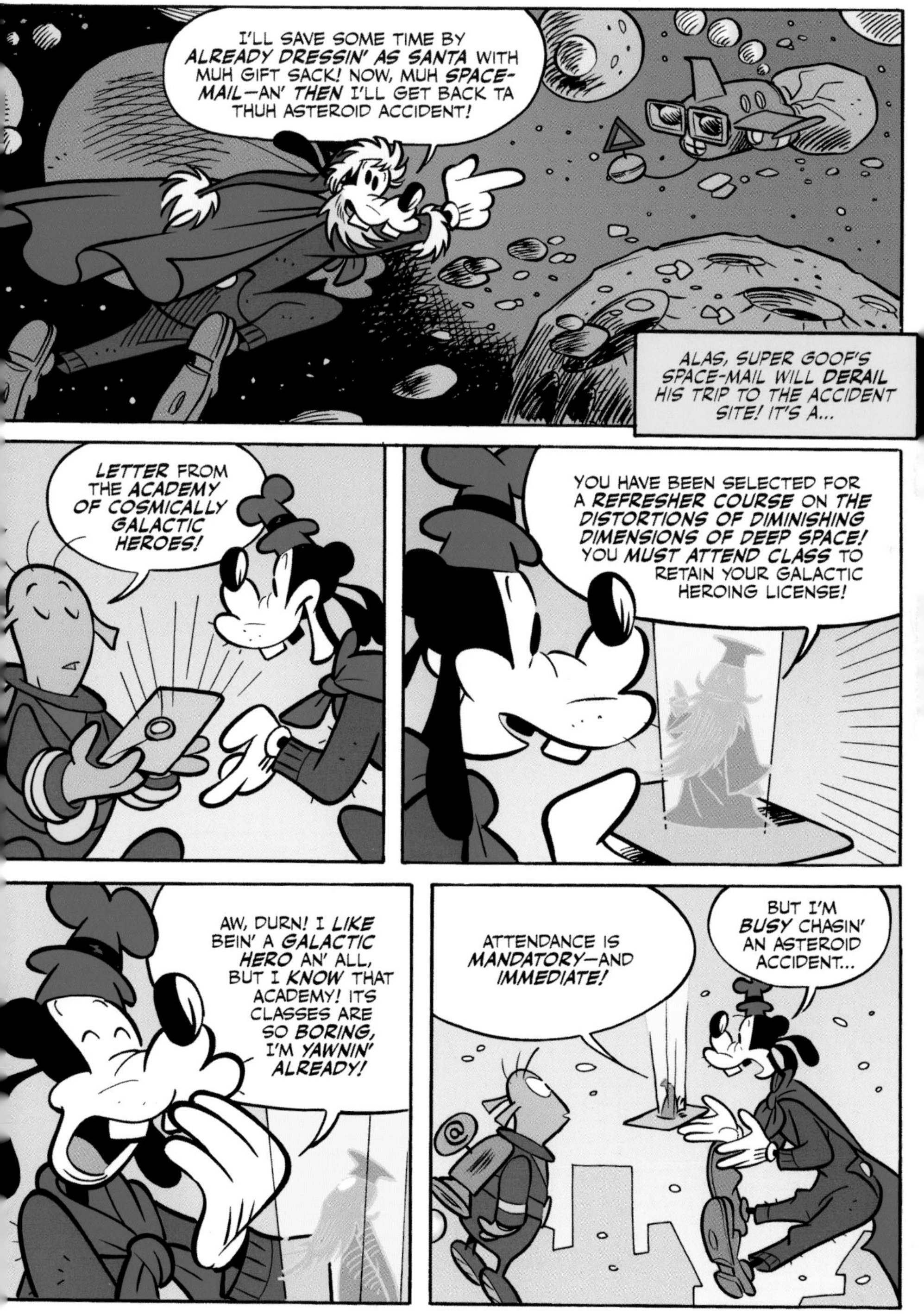
I'LL SAVE SOME TIME BY ALREADY DRESSIN' AS SANTA WITH MUH GIFT SACK! NOW, MUH SPACE-MAIL—AN' THEN I'LL GET BACK TA THUH ASTEROID ACCIDENT!
ALAS, SUPER GOOF'S SPACE-MAIL WILL DERAIL HIS TRIP TO THE ACCIDENT SITE! IT'S A...
LETTER FROM THE ACADEMY OF COSMICALLY GALACTIC HEROES!
YOU HAVE BEEN SELECTED FOR A REFRESHER COURSE ON THE DISTORTIONS OF DIMINISHING DIMENSIONS OF DEEP SPACE! YOU MUST ATTEND CLASS TO RETAIN YOUR GALACTIC HEROING LICENSE!
AW, DURN! I LIKE BEIN' A GALACTIC HERO AN' ALL, BUT I KNOW THAT ACADEMY! ITS CLASSES ARE SO BORING, I'M YAWNIN' ALREADY!
ATTENDANCE IS MANDATORY—AND IMMEDIATE!
BUT I'M BUSY CHASIN' AN ASTEROID ACCIDENT...

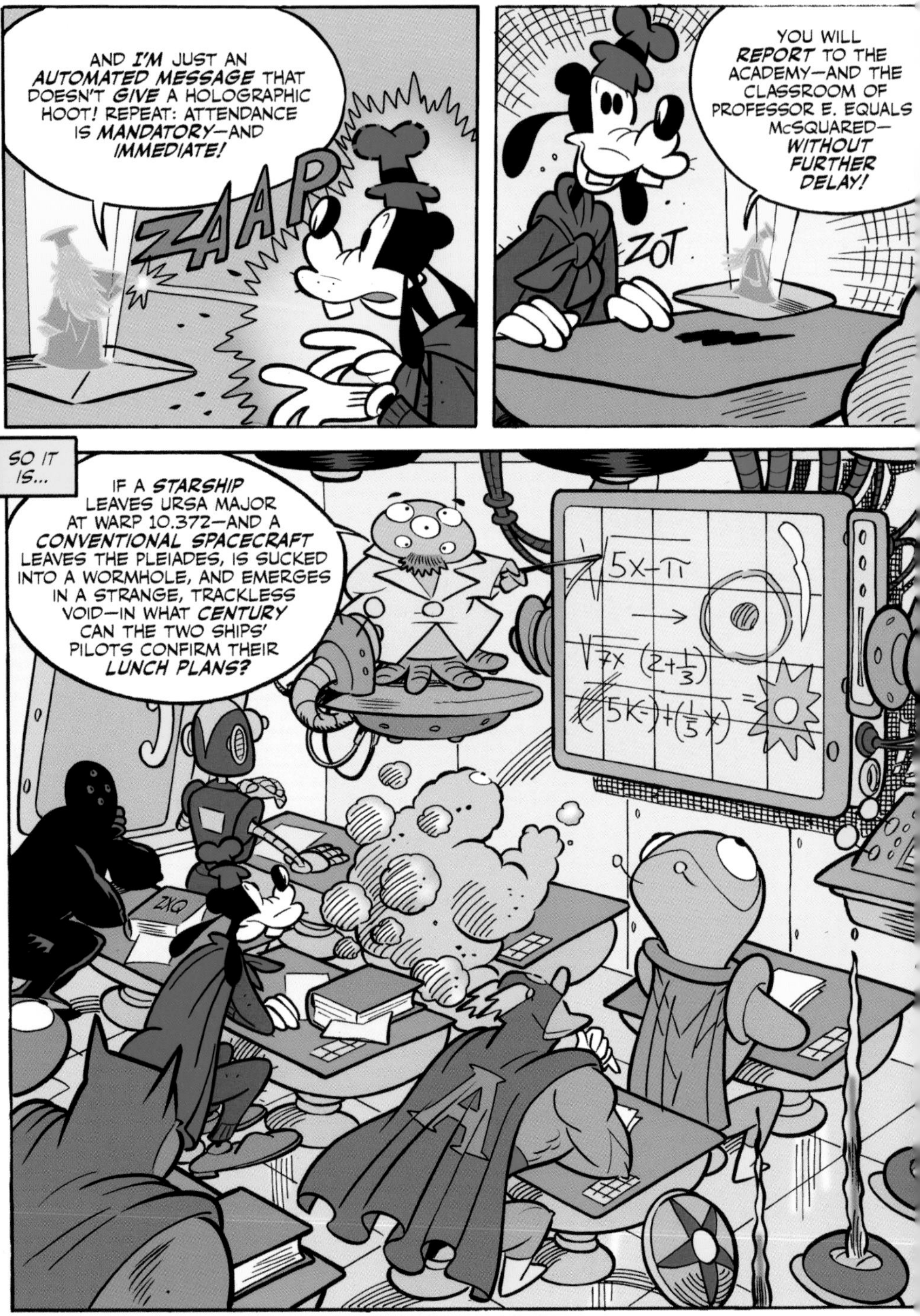
AND I'M JUST AN AUTOMATED MESSAGE THAT DOESN'T GIVE A HOLOGRAPHIC HOOT! REPEAT: ATTENDANCE IS MANDATORY—AND IMMEDIATE!
ZAAP
YOU WILL REPORT TO THE ACADEMY—AND THE CLASSROOM OF PROFESSOR E. EQUALS McSQUARED—WITHOUT FURTHER DELAY!
ZOT
SO IT IS...
IF A STARSHIP LEAVES URSA MAJOR AT WARP 10.372—AND A CONVENTIONAL SPACECRAFT LEAVES THE PLEIADES, IS SUCKED INTO A WORMHOLE, AND EMERGES IN A STRANGE, TRACKLESS VOID—IN WHAT CENTURY CAN THE TWO SHIPS' PILOTS CONFIRM THEIR LUNCH PLANS?
ZXQ

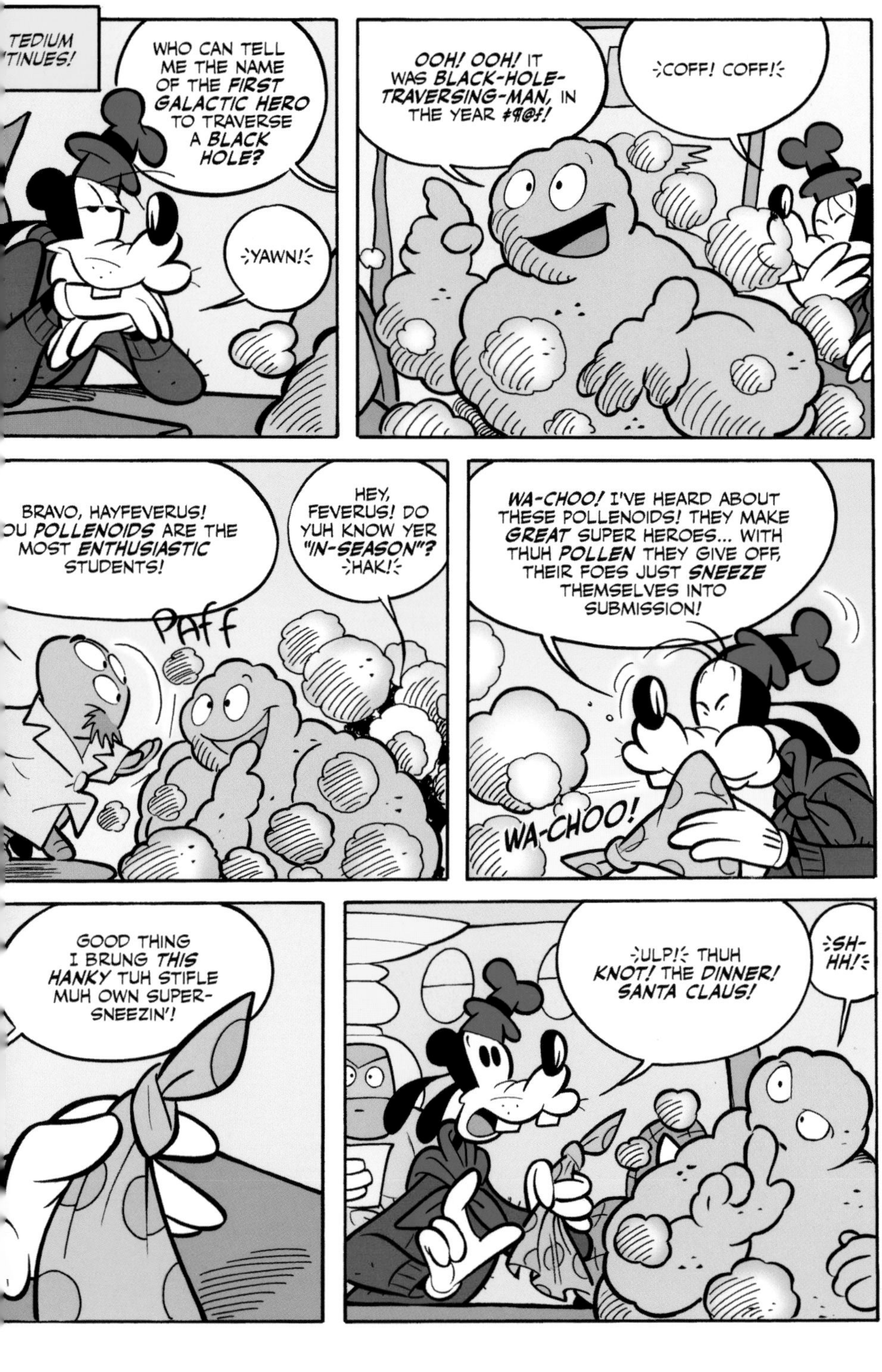

TEDIUM
TINUES!
WHO CAN TELL ME THE NAME OF THE FIRST GALACTIC HERO TO TRAVERSE A BLACK HOLE?
YAWN!
OOH! OOH! IT WAS BLACK-HOLE-TRAVERSING-MAN, IN THE YEAR #¶@$!
COFF! COFF!
BRAVO, HAYFEVERUS! OU POLLENOIDS ARE THE MOST ENTHUSIASTIC STUDENTS!
HEY, FEVERUS! DO YUH KNOW YER "IN-SEASON"? HAK!
PAFF
WA-CHOO! I'VE HEARD ABOUT THESE POLLENOIDS! THEY MAKE GREAT SUPER HEROES... WITH THUH POLLEN THEY GIVE OFF, THEIR FOES JUST SNEEZE THEMSELVES INTO SUBMISSION!
WA-CHOO!
GOOD THING I BRUNG THIS HANKY TUH STIFLE MUH OWN SUPER-SNEEZIN'!
ULP! THUH KNOT! THE DINNER! SANTA CLAUS!
SH-HH!

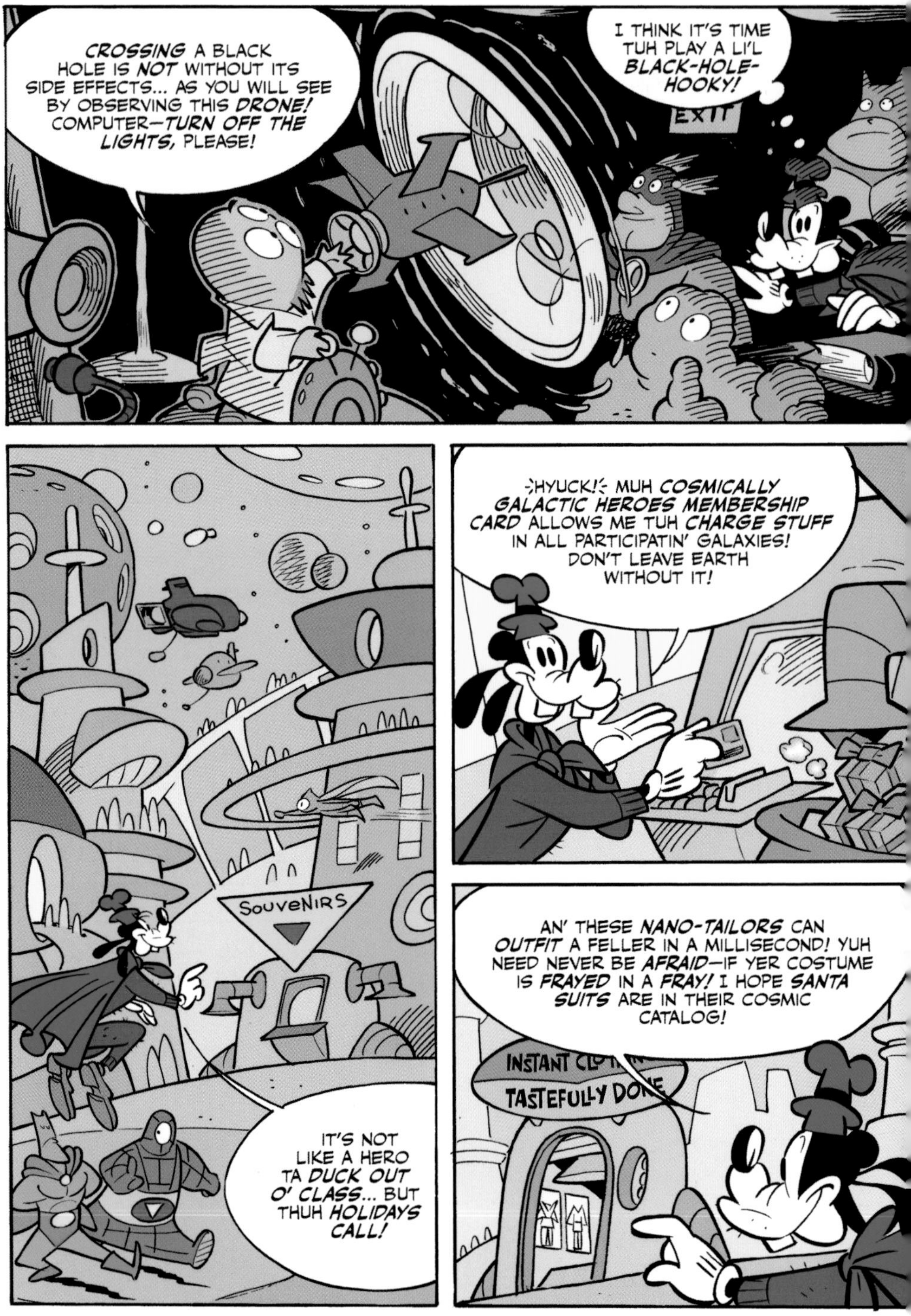
CROSSING A BLACK HOLE IS NOT WITHOUT ITS SIDE EFFECTS... AS YOU WILL SEE BY OBSERVING THIS DRONE! COMPUTER—TURN OFF THE LIGHTS, PLEASE!
I THINK IT'S TIME TUH PLAY A LI'L BLACK-HOLE-HOOKY!
EXIT
SOUVENIRS
IT'S NOT LIKE A HERO TA DUCK OUT O' CLASS... BUT THUH HOLIDAYS CALL!
HYUCK! MUH COSMICALLY GALACTIC HEROES MEMBERSHIP CARD ALLOWS ME TUH CHARGE STUFF IN ALL PARTICIPATIN' GALAXIES! DON'T LEAVE EARTH WITHOUT IT!
AN' THESE NANO-TAILORS CAN OUTFIT A FELLER IN A MILLISECOND! YUH NEED NEVER BE AFRAID—IF YER COSTUME IS FRAYED IN A FRAY! I HOPE SANTA SUITS ARE IN THEIR COSMIC CATALOG!
TASTEFULLY DONE

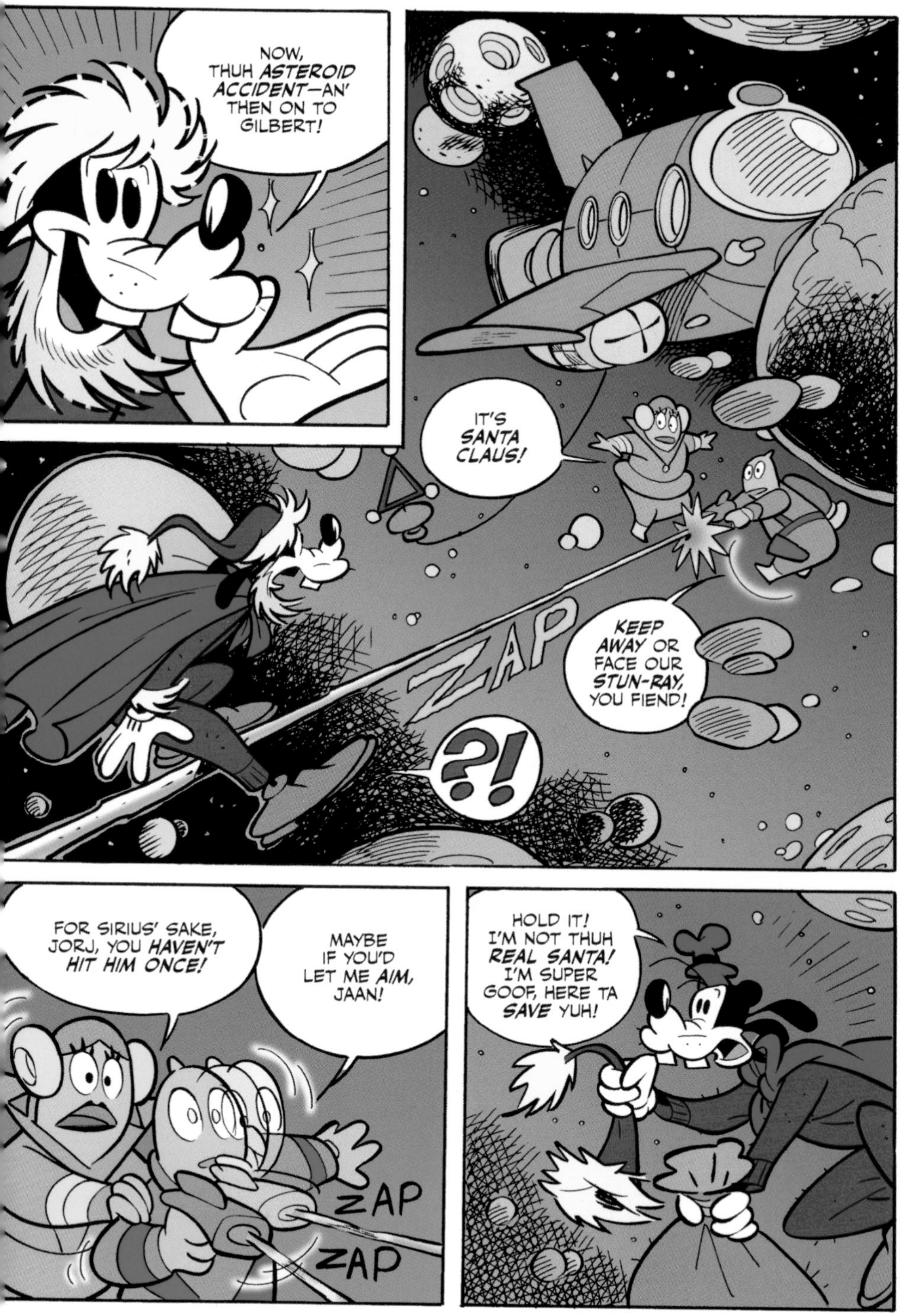
NOW, THUH ASTEROID ACCIDENT—AN' THEN ON TO GILBERT!
IT'S SANTA CLAUS!
ZAP
KEEP AWAY OR FACE OUR STUN-RAY, YOU FIEND!
?!
FOR SIRIUS' SAKE, JORJ, YOU HAVEN'T HIT HIM ONCE!
MAYBE IF YOU'D LET ME AIM, JAAN!
ZAP
ZAP
HOLD IT! I'M NOT THUH REAL SANTA! I'M SUPER GOOF, HERE TA SAVE YUH!

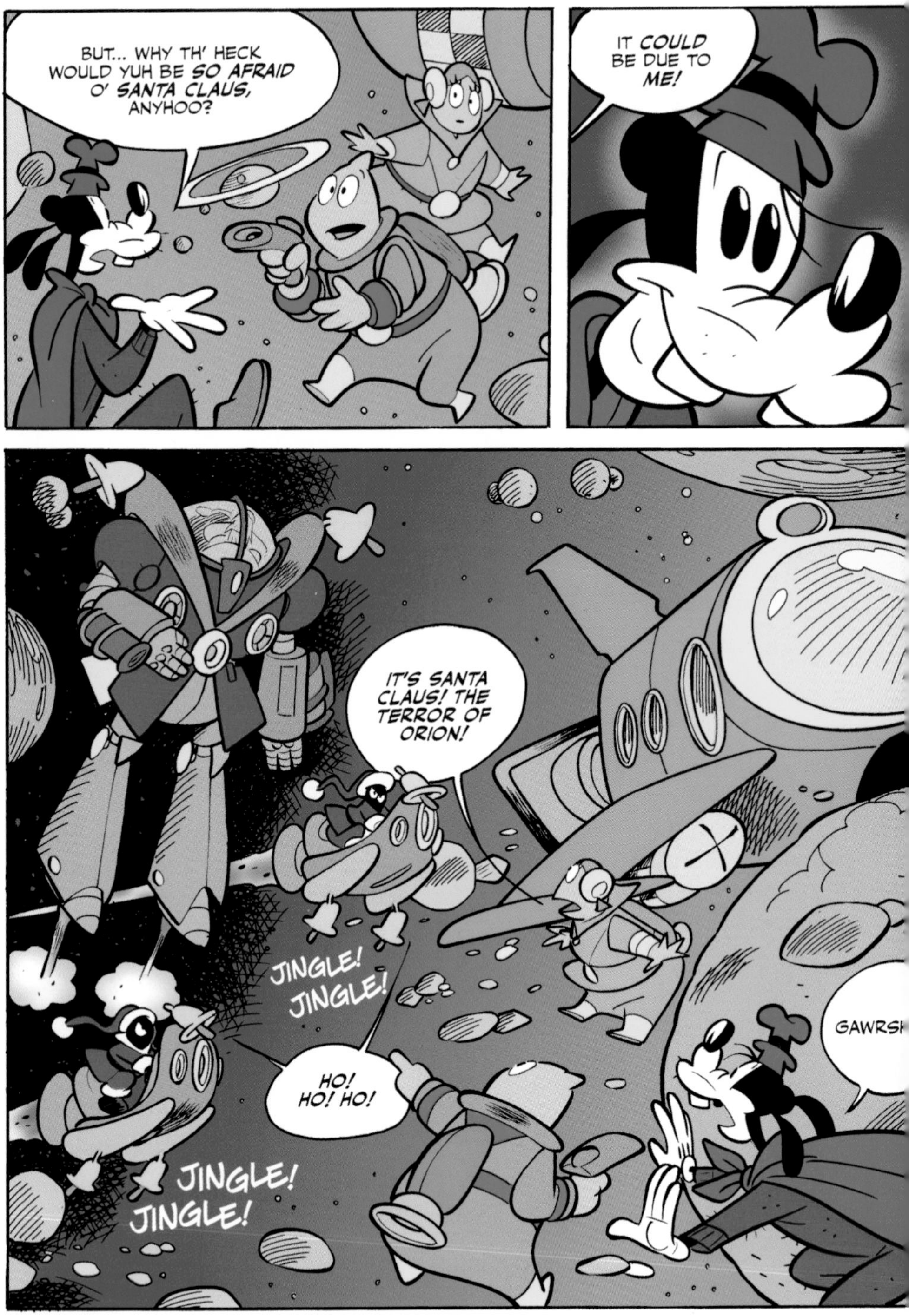

BUT... WHY TH' HECK WOULD YUH BE SO AFRAID O' SANTA CLAUS, ANYHOO?
IT COULD BE DUE TO ME!
IT'S SANTA CLAUS! THE TERROR OF ORION!
JINGLE! JINGLE!
HO! HO! HO!
JINGLE! JINGLE!
GAWRSH

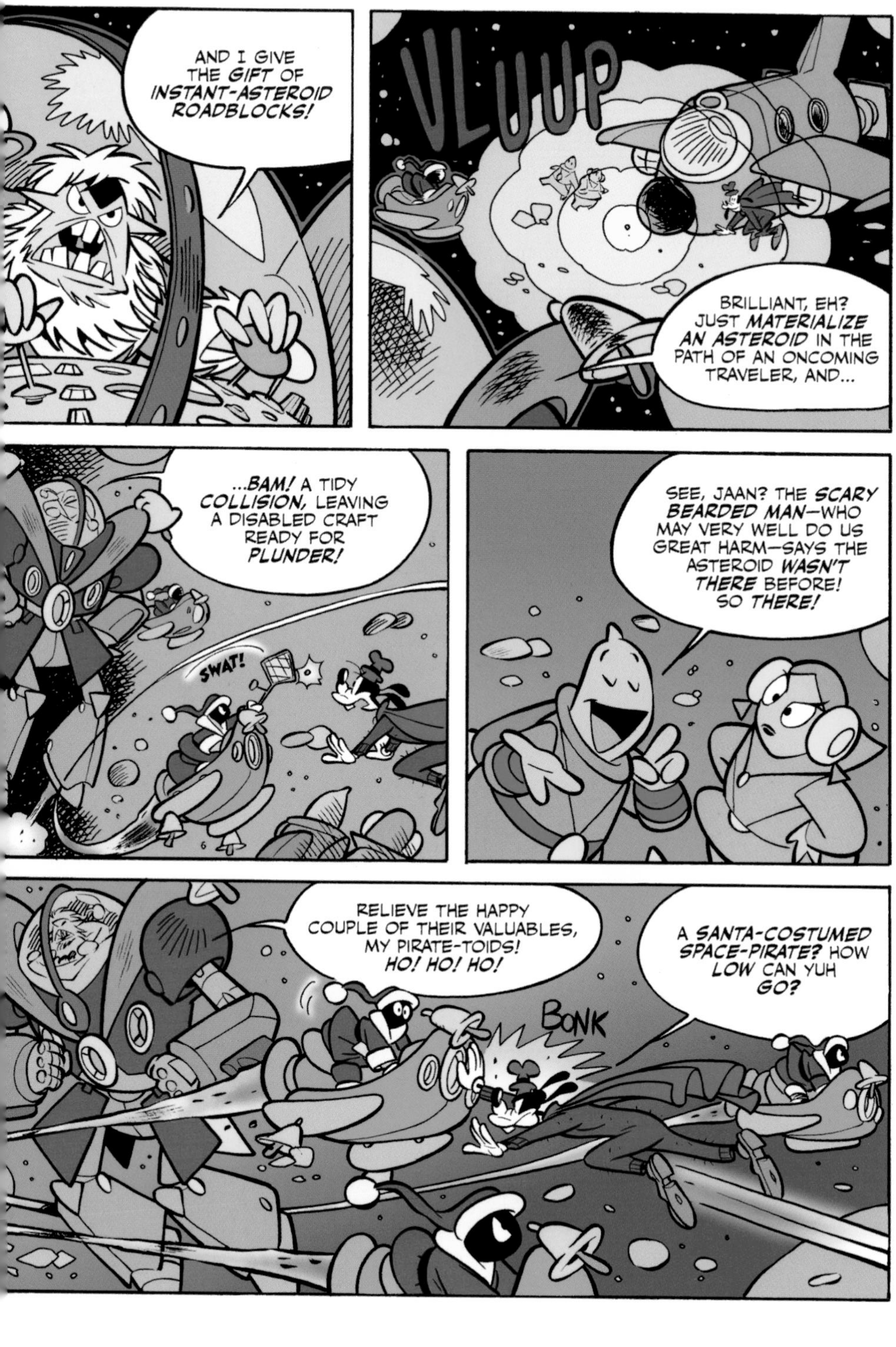
AND I GIVE THE GIFT OF INSTANT-ASTEROID ROADBLOCKS!
VLUUP
BRILLIANT, EH? JUST MATERIALIZE AN ASTEROID IN THE PATH OF AN ONCOMING TRAVELER, AND...
...BAM! A TIDY COLLISION, LEAVING A DISABLED CRAFT READY FOR PLUNDER!
SWAT!
SEE, JAAN? THE SCARY BEARDED MAN—WHO MAY VERY WELL DO US GREAT HARM—SAYS THE ASTEROID WASN'T THERE BEFORE! SO THERE!
RELIEVE THE HAPPY COUPLE OF THEIR VALUABLES, MY PIRATE-TOIDS! HO! HO! HO!
A SANTA-COSTUMED SPACE-PIRATE? HOW LOW CAN YUH GO?
BONK

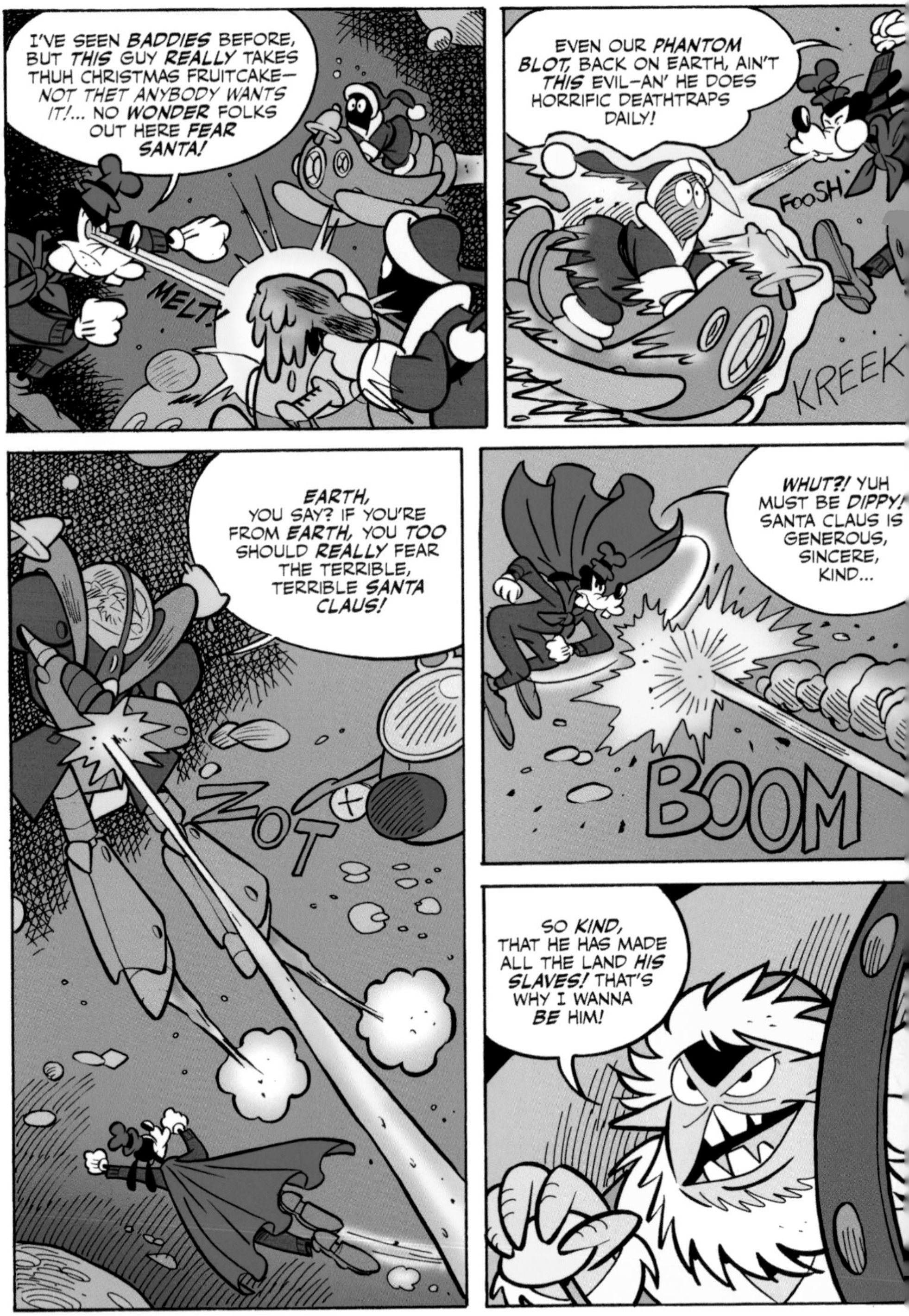
I'VE SEEN BADDIES BEFORE, BUT THIS GUY REALLY TAKES THUH CHRISTMAS FRUITCAKE—NOT THET ANYBODY WANTS IT!... NO WONDER FOLKS OUT HERE FEAR SANTA!
MELT!
EVEN OUR PHANTOM BLOT, BACK ON EARTH, AIN'T THIS EVIL—AN' HE DOES HORRIFIC DEATHTRAPS DAILY!
FOOSH
KREEK
EARTH, YOU SAY? IF YOU'RE FROM EARTH, YOU TOO SHOULD REALLY FEAR THE TERRIBLE, TERRIBLE SANTA CLAUS!
ZOT
WHUT?! YUH MUST BE DIPPY! SANTA CLAUS IS GENEROUS, SINCERE, KIND...
BOOM
SO KIND, THAT HE HAS MADE ALL THE LAND HIS SLAVES! THAT'S WHY I WANNA BE HIM!

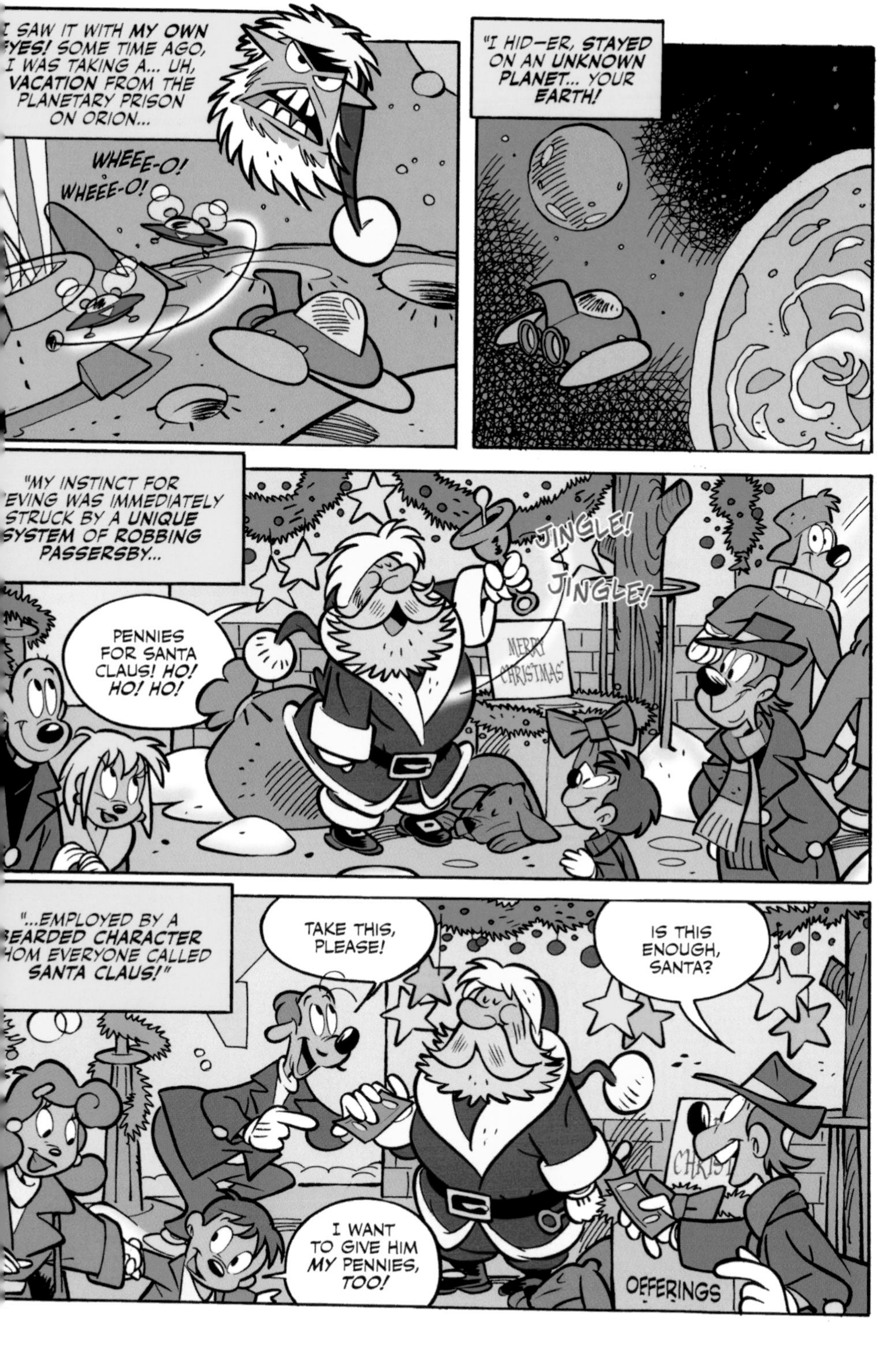
I SAW IT WITH MY OWN EYES! SOME TIME AGO, I WAS TAKING A... UH, VACATION FROM THE PLANETARY PRISON ON ORION...
WHEEE-O!
WHEEE-O!
"I HID—ER, STAYED ON AN UNKNOWN PLANET... YOUR EARTH!
"MY INSTINCT FOR THIEVING WAS IMMEDIATELY STRUCK BY A UNIQUE SYSTEM OF ROBBING PASSERSBY...
PENNIES FOR SANTA CLAUS! HO! HO! HO!
JINGLE! & JINGLE!
MERRY CHRISTMAS
"...EMPLOYED BY A BEARDED CHARACTER WHOM EVERYONE CALLED SANTA CLAUS!"
TAKE THIS, PLEASE!
IS THIS ENOUGH, SANTA?
I WANT TO GIVE HIM MY PENNIES, TOO!
OFFERINGS

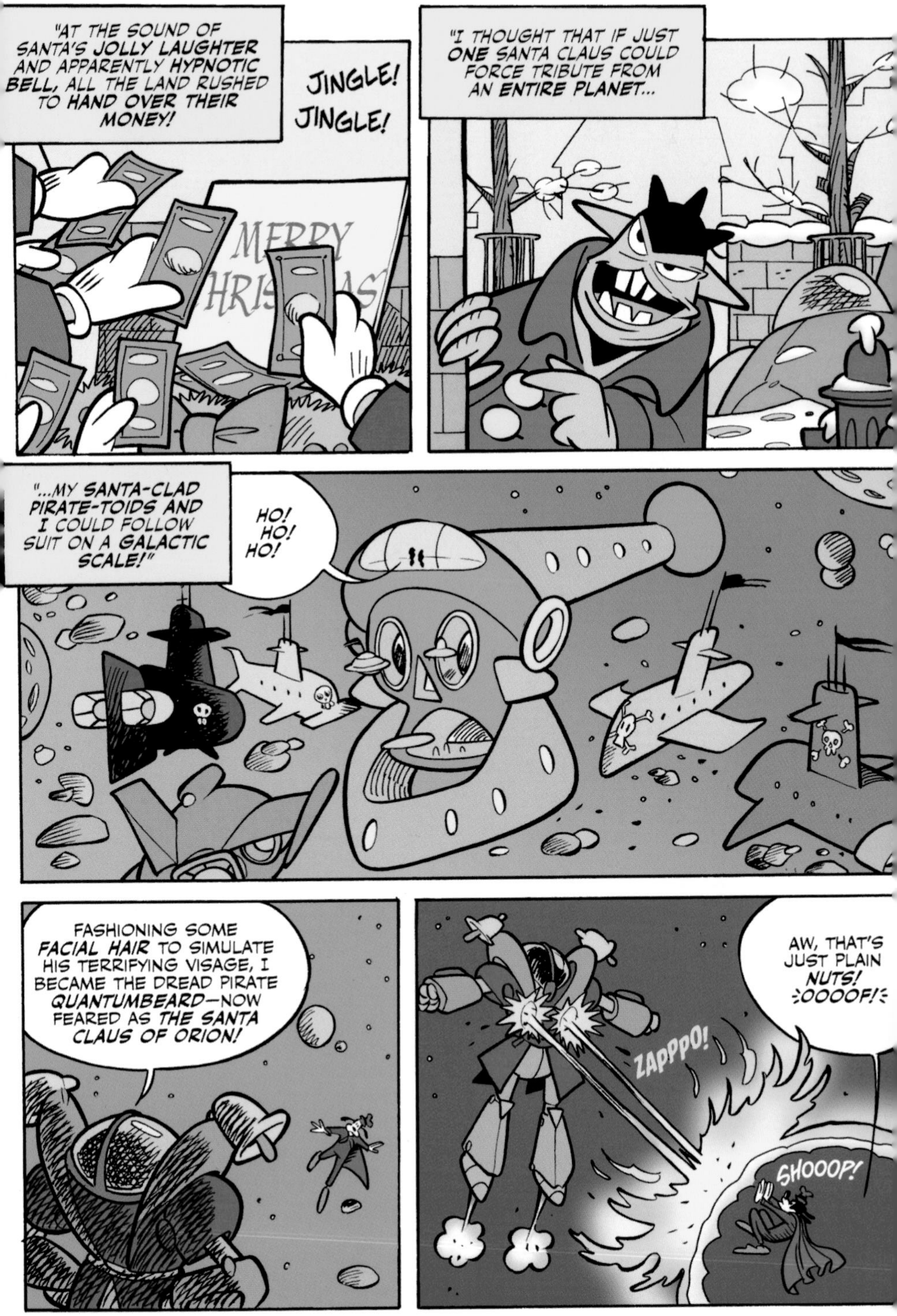
"AT THE SOUND OF SANTA'S JOLLY LAUGHTER AND APPARENTLY HYPNOTIC BELL, ALL THE LAND RUSHED TO HAND OVER THEIR MONEY!
JINGLE! JINGLE!
MERRY CHRISTMAS
"I THOUGHT THAT IF JUST ONE SANTA CLAUS COULD FORCE TRIBUTE FROM AN ENTIRE PLANET...
"...MY SANTA-CLAD PIRATE-TOIDS AND I COULD FOLLOW SUIT ON A GALACTIC SCALE!"
HO! HO! HO!
FASHIONING SOME FACIAL HAIR TO SIMULATE HIS TERRIFYING VISAGE, I BECAME THE DREAD PIRATE QUANTUMBEARD—NOW FEARED AS THE SANTA CLAUS OF ORION!
ZAPPPO!
AW, THAT'S JUST PLAIN NUTS! OOOOF!
SHOOOP!

THAT WAS NO *THIEF* YOU SAW, MISTER! IT WAS A WORLDWIDE CUSTOM OF *GENEROSITY, SHARIN', AN' GIVIN'* TO THUH *POOR!*...
÷OUCH!÷ THAT BLOCKBUSTER STINGS!

FOLKS ARE *EXTRA* GEN'ROUS AT *CHRISTMAS TIME!* THEY WERE RUNNIN' TA SANTA WITH *DONATIONS,* NOT *TRIBUTE!*

WHOOOOSH!

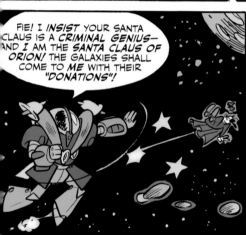

FIE! I *INSIST* YOUR SANTA CLAUS IS A *CRIMINAL GENIUS*—AND *I* AM THE *SANTA CLAUS OF ORION!* THE GALAXIES SHALL COME TO *ME* WITH THEIR *"DONATIONS"!*

NO! I WON'T LET YOU *TARNISH* THUH *REPUTATION* OF SANTA CLAUS!

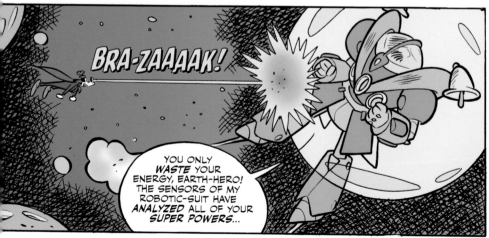

BRA-ZAAAAK!

YOU ONLY *WASTE* YOUR ENERGY, EARTH-HERO! THE SENSORS OF MY ROBOTIC-SUIT HAVE *ANALYZED* ALL OF YOUR *SUPER POWERS*...

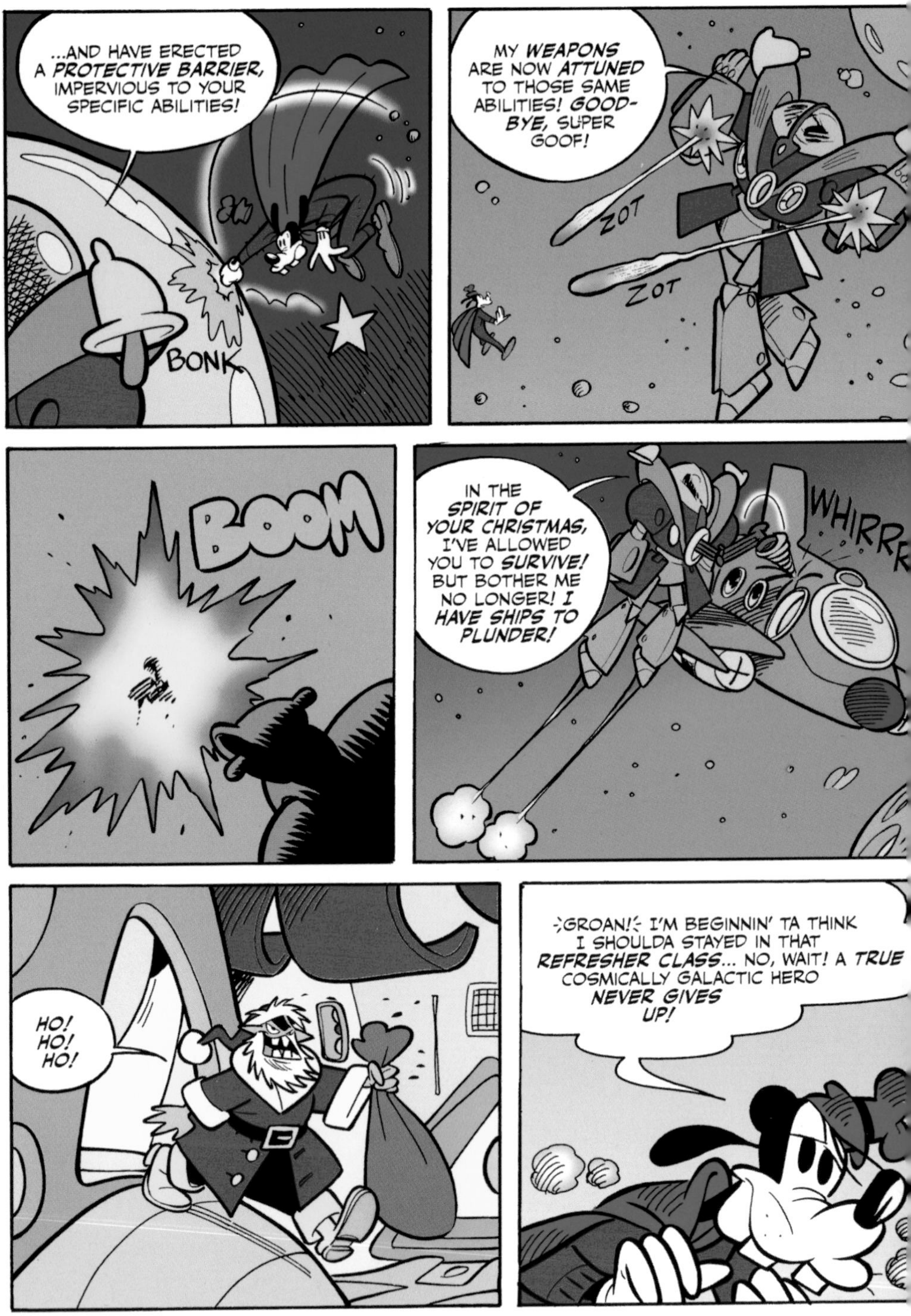
...AND HAVE ERECTED A PROTECTIVE BARRIER, IMPERVIOUS TO YOUR SPECIFIC ABILITIES!
BONK
MY WEAPONS ARE NOW ATTUNED TO THOSE SAME ABILITIES! GOOD-BYE, SUPER GOOF!
ZOT
ZOT
BOOM
IN THE SPIRIT OF YOUR CHRISTMAS, I'VE ALLOWED YOU TO SURVIVE! BUT BOTHER ME NO LONGER! I HAVE SHIPS TO PLUNDER!
WHIRRR
HO! HO! HO!
GROAN! I'M BEGINNIN' TA THINK I SHOULDA STAYED IN THAT REFRESHER CLASS... NO, WAIT! A TRUE COSMICALLY GALACTIC HERO NEVER GIVES UP!

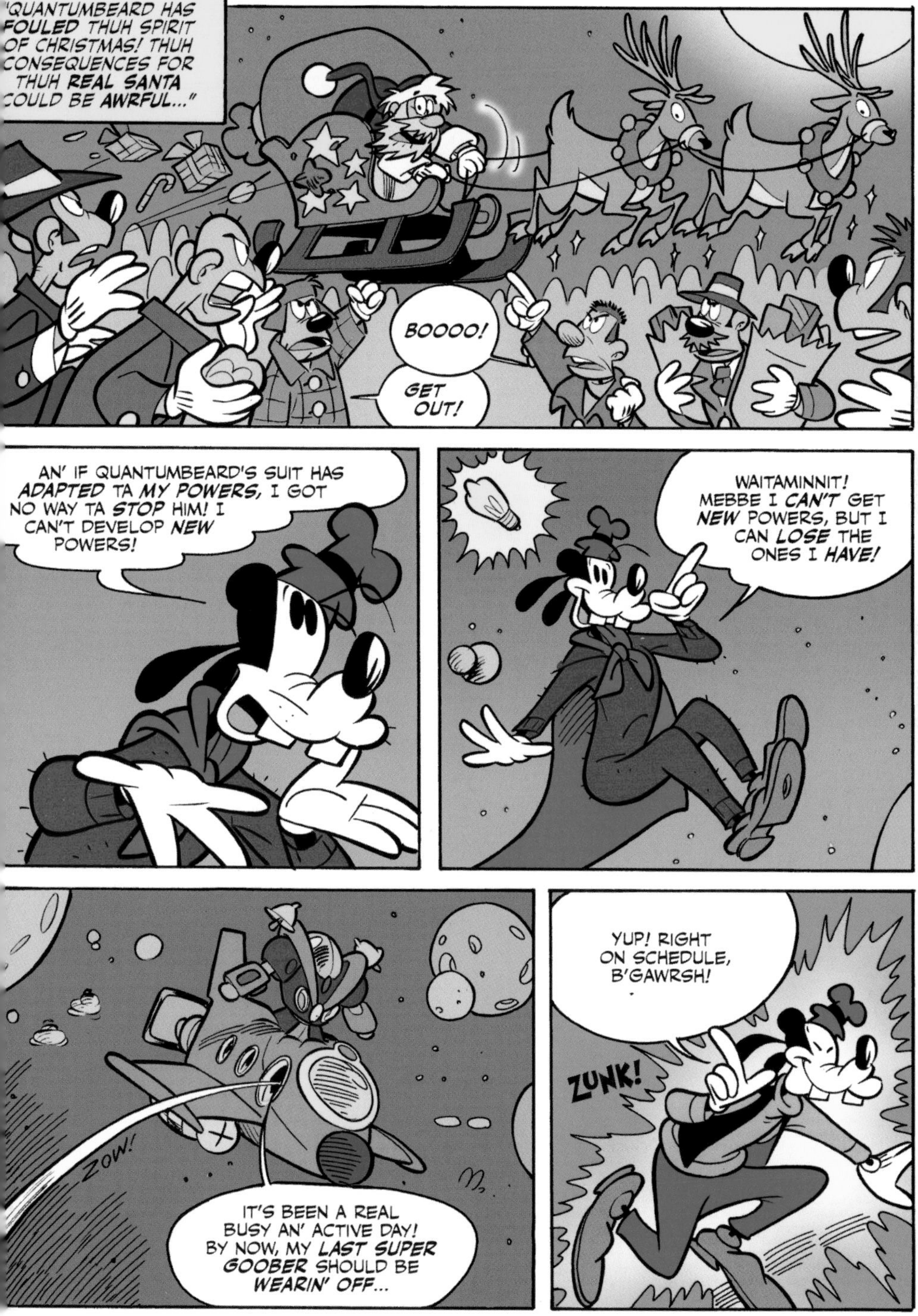
"QUANTUMBEARD HAS FOULED THUH SPIRIT OF CHRISTMAS! THUH CONSEQUENCES FOR THUH REAL SANTA COULD BE AWRFUL..."
BOOOO!
GET OUT!
AN' IF QUANTUMBEARD'S SUIT HAS ADAPTED TA MY POWERS, I GOT NO WAY TA STOP HIM! I CAN'T DEVELOP NEW POWERS!
WAITAMINNIT! MEBBE I CAN'T GET NEW POWERS, BUT I CAN LOSE THE ONES I HAVE!
ZOW!
IT'S BEEN A REAL BUSY AN' ACTIVE DAY! BY NOW, MY LAST SUPER GOOBER SHOULD BE WEARIN' OFF...
YUP! RIGHT ON SCHEDULE, B'GAWRSH!
ZUNK!

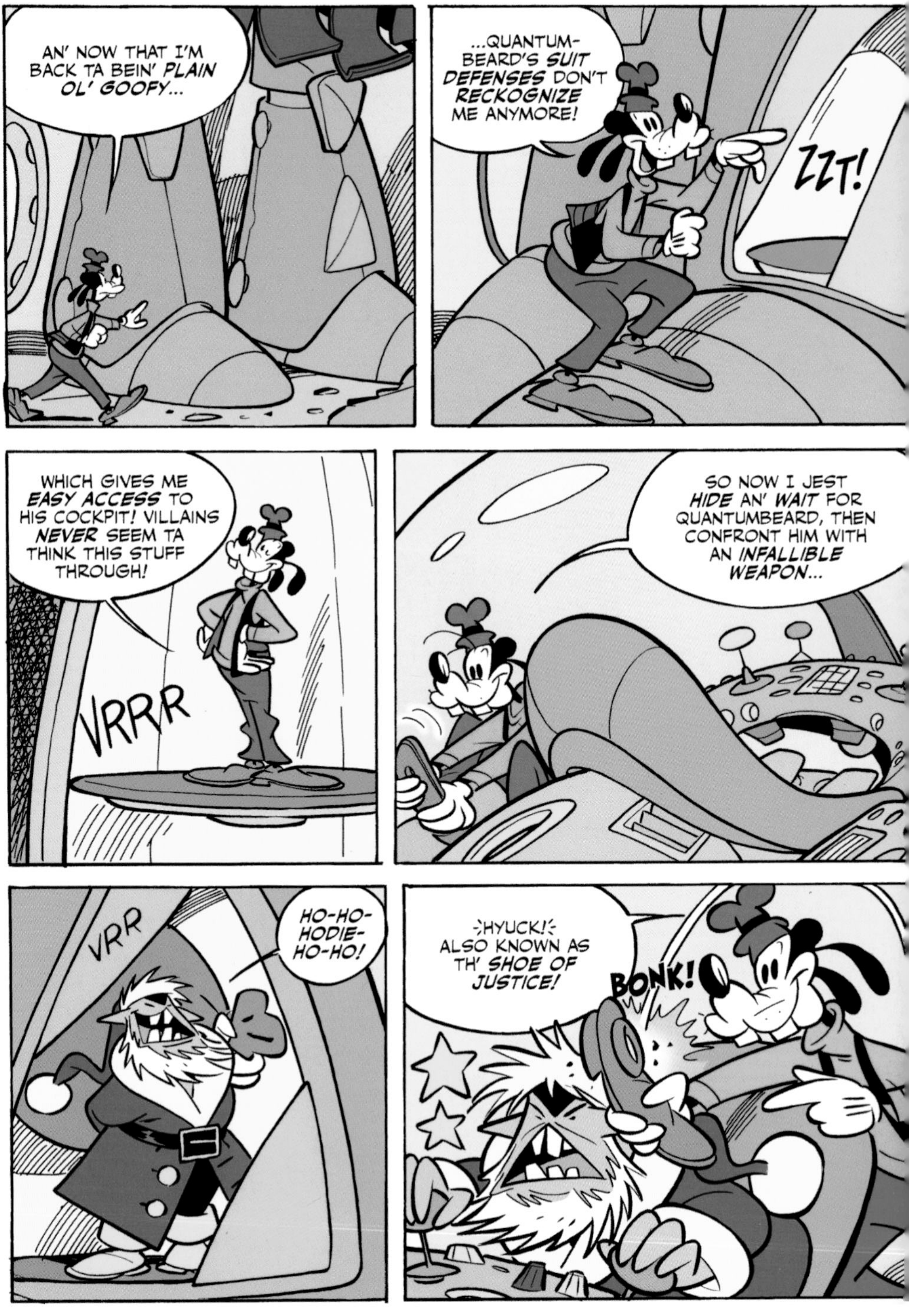
AN' NOW THAT I'M BACK TA BEIN' *PLAIN OL' GOOFY*...
...QUANTUM-BEARD'S *SUIT DEFENSES* DON'T *RECKOGNIZE* ME ANYMORE!
ZZT!
WHICH GIVES ME *EASY ACCESS* TO HIS COCKPIT! VILLAINS *NEVER* SEEM TA THINK THIS STUFF THROUGH!
VRRR
SO NOW I JEST *HIDE* AN' *WAIT* FOR QUANTUMBEARD, THEN CONFRONT HIM WITH AN *INFALLIBLE WEAPON*...
VRR
HO-HO-HODIE-HO-HO!
HYUCK! ALSO KNOWN AS TH' *SHOE OF JUSTICE!*
BONK!

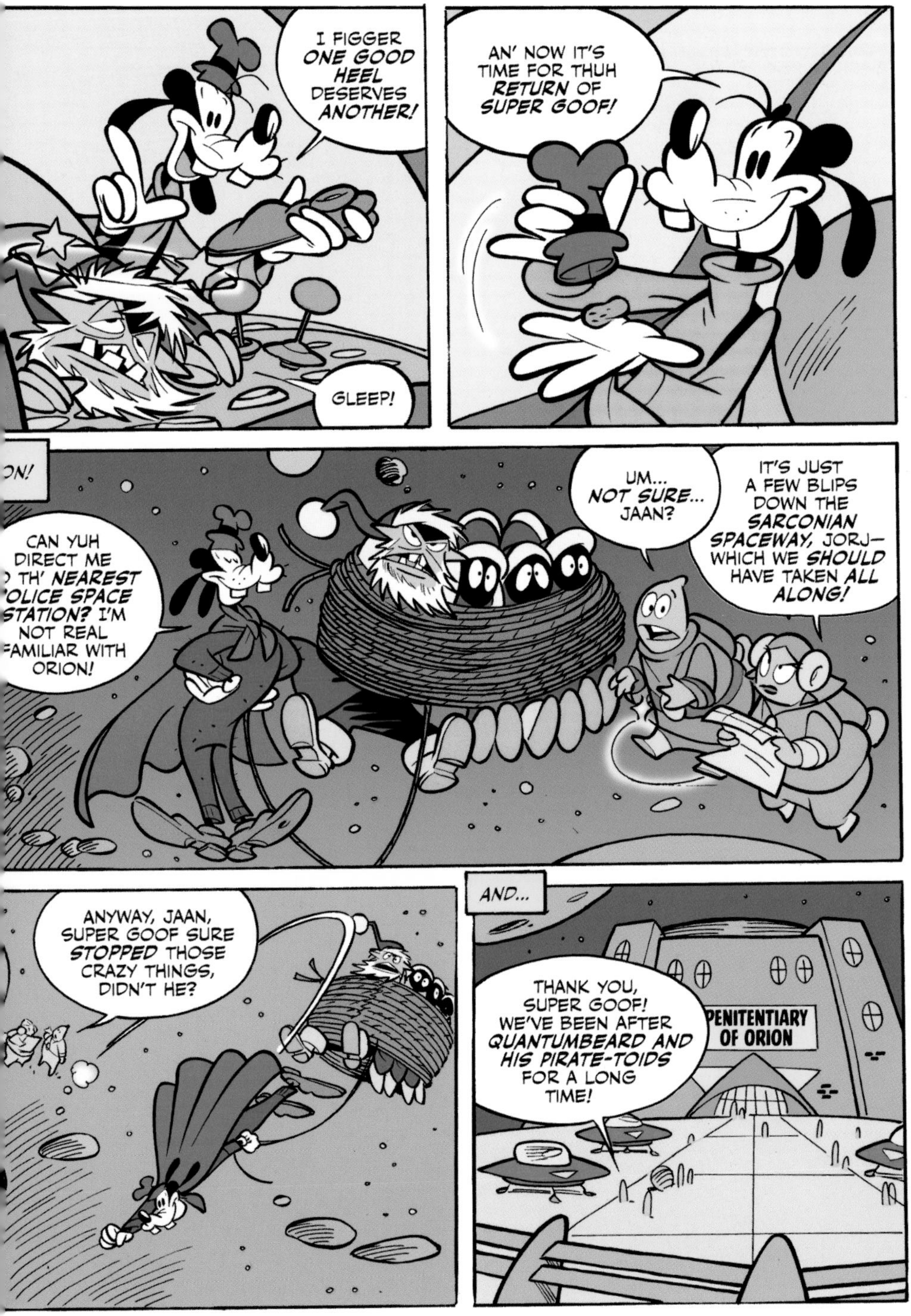
I FIGGER ONE GOOD HEEL DESERVES ANOTHER!
GLEEP!
AN' NOW IT'S TIME FOR THUH RETURN OF SUPER GOOF!
ON!
CAN YUH DIRECT ME TO TH' NEAREST POLICE SPACE STATION? I'M NOT REAL FAMILIAR WITH ORION!
UM... NOT SURE... JAAN?
IT'S JUST A FEW BLIPS DOWN THE SARCONIAN SPACEWAY, JORJ— WHICH WE SHOULD HAVE TAKEN ALL ALONG!
ANYWAY, JAAN, SUPER GOOF SURE STOPPED THOSE CRAZY THINGS, DIDN'T HE?
AND...
PENITENTIARY OF ORION
THANK YOU, SUPER GOOF! WE'VE BEEN AFTER QUANTUMBEARD AND HIS PIRATE-TOIDS FOR A LONG TIME!

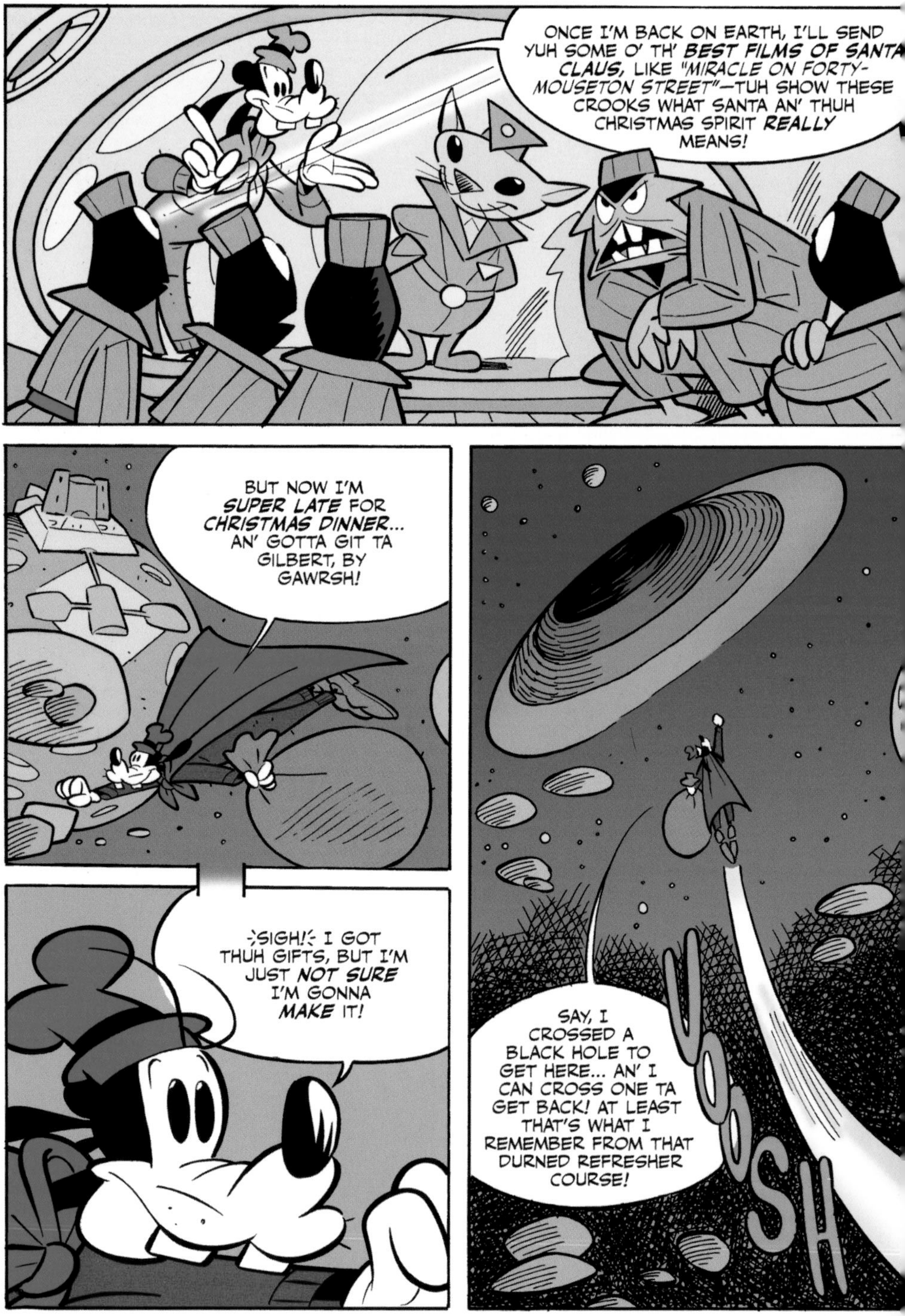
ONCE I'M BACK ON EARTH, I'LL SEND YUH SOME O' TH' BEST FILMS OF SANTA CLAUS, LIKE "MIRACLE ON FORTY-MOUSETON STREET"—TUH SHOW THESE CROOKS WHAT SANTA AN' THUH CHRISTMAS SPIRIT REALLY MEANS!
BUT NOW I'M SUPER LATE FOR CHRISTMAS DINNER... AN' GOTTA GIT TA GILBERT, BY GAWRSH!
-SIGH!- I GOT THUH GIFTS, BUT I'M JUST NOT SURE I'M GONNA MAKE IT!
SAY, I CROSSED A BLACK HOLE TO GET HERE... AN' I CAN CROSS ONE TA GET BACK! AT LEAST THAT'S WHAT I REMEMBER FROM THAT DURNED REFRESHER COURSE!
VOOOOSH

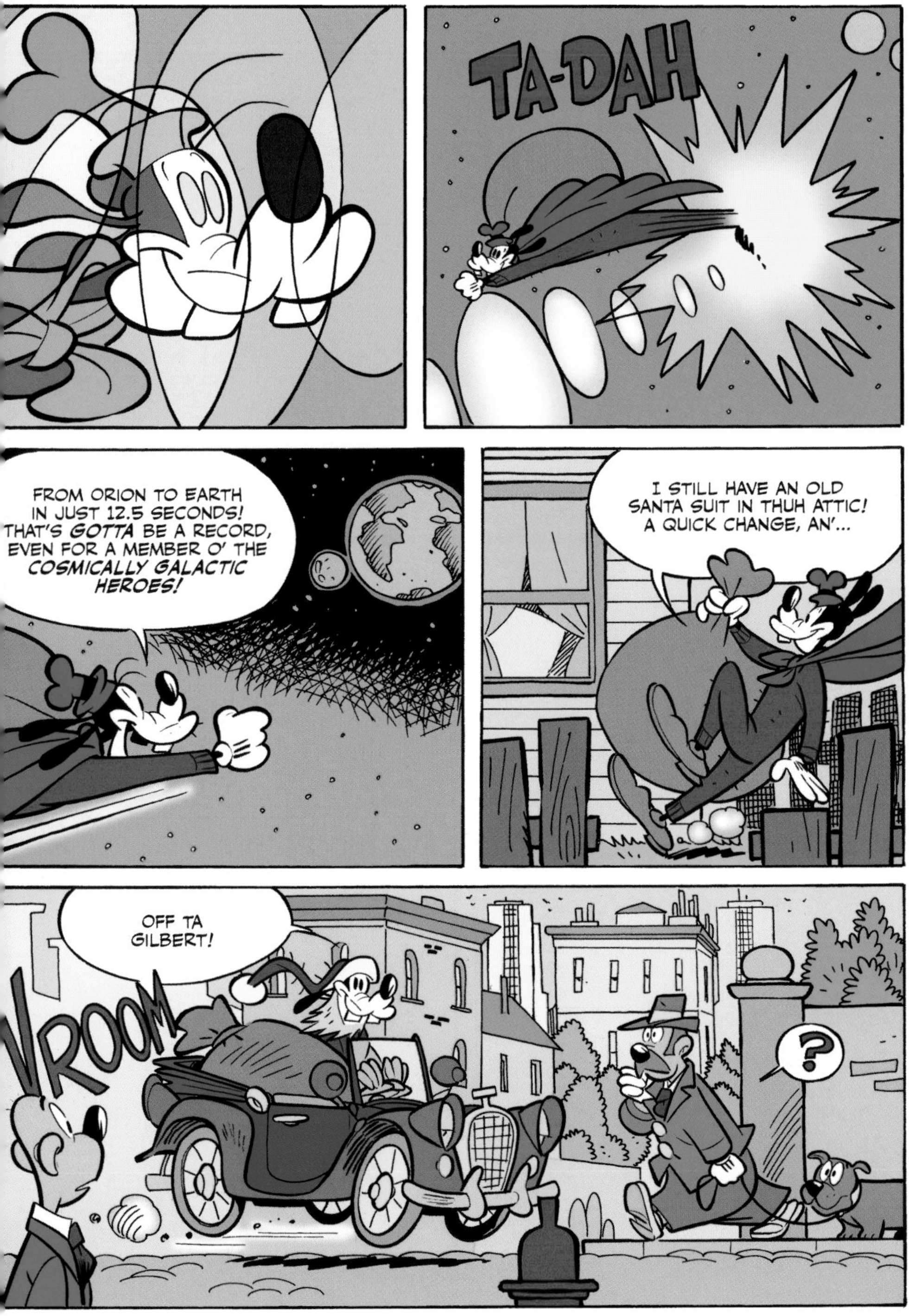
TA-DAH
FROM ORION TO EARTH IN JUST 12.5 SECONDS! THAT'S *GOTTA* BE A RECORD, EVEN FOR A MEMBER O' THE *COSMICALLY GALACTIC HEROES!*
I STILL HAVE AN OLD SANTA SUIT IN THUH ATTIC! A QUICK CHANGE, AN'...
OFF TA GILBERT!
VROOM
?

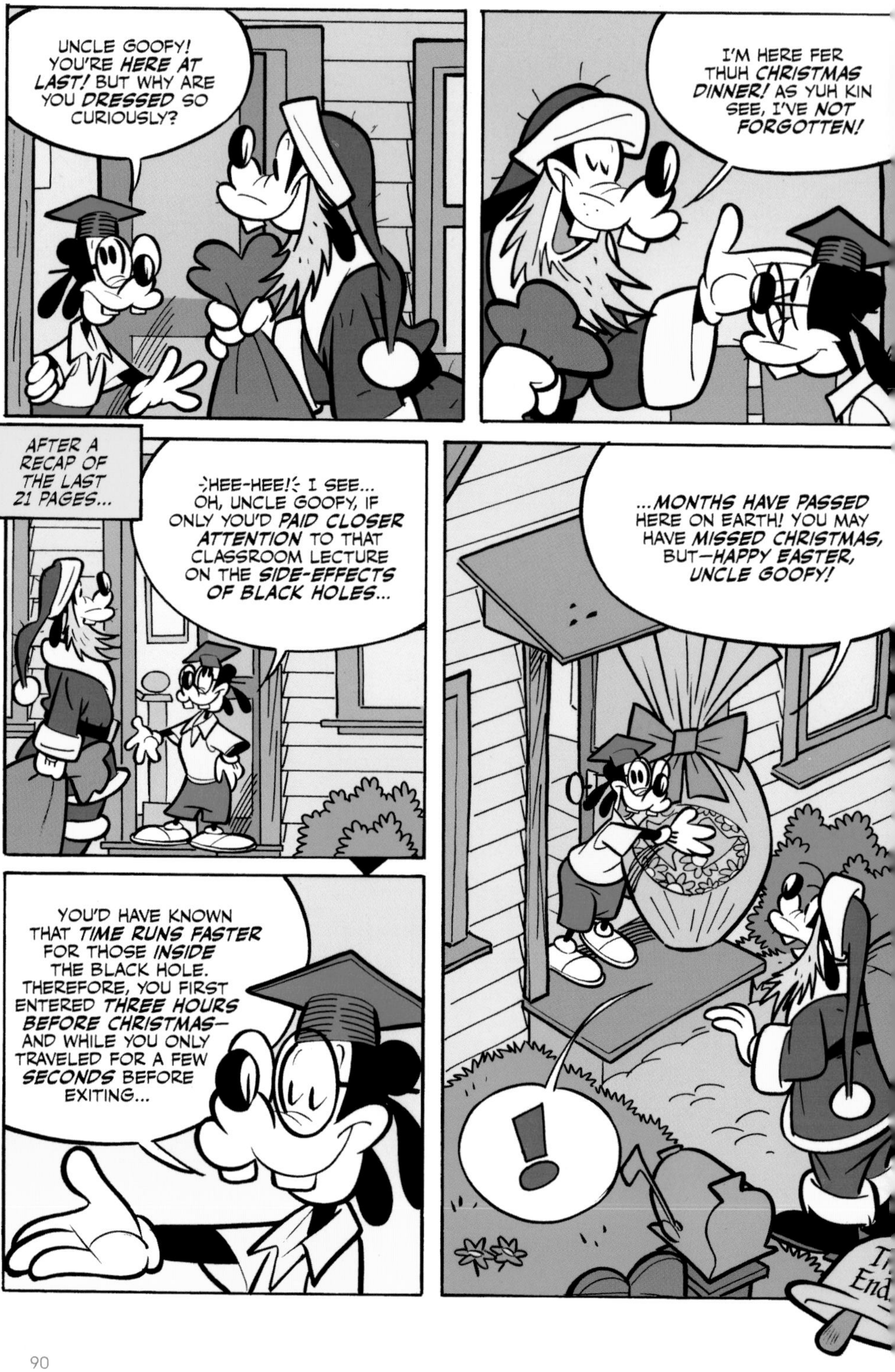
UNCLE GOOFY! YOU'RE HERE AT LAST! BUT WHY ARE YOU DRESSED SO CURIOUSLY?
I'M HERE FER THUH CHRISTMAS DINNER! AS YUH KIN SEE, I'VE NOT FORGOTTEN!
AFTER A RECAP OF THE LAST 21 PAGES...
HEE-HEE! I SEE... OH, UNCLE GOOFY, IF ONLY YOU'D PAID CLOSER ATTENTION TO THAT CLASSROOM LECTURE ON THE SIDE-EFFECTS OF BLACK HOLES...
YOU'D HAVE KNOWN THAT TIME RUNS FASTER FOR THOSE INSIDE THE BLACK HOLE. THEREFORE, YOU FIRST ENTERED THREE HOURS BEFORE CHRISTMAS— AND WHILE YOU ONLY TRAVELED FOR A FEW SECONDS BEFORE EXITING...
...MONTHS HAVE PASSED HERE ON EARTH! YOU MAY HAVE MISSED CHRISTMAS, BUT—HAPPY EASTER, UNCLE GOOFY!
!
The End

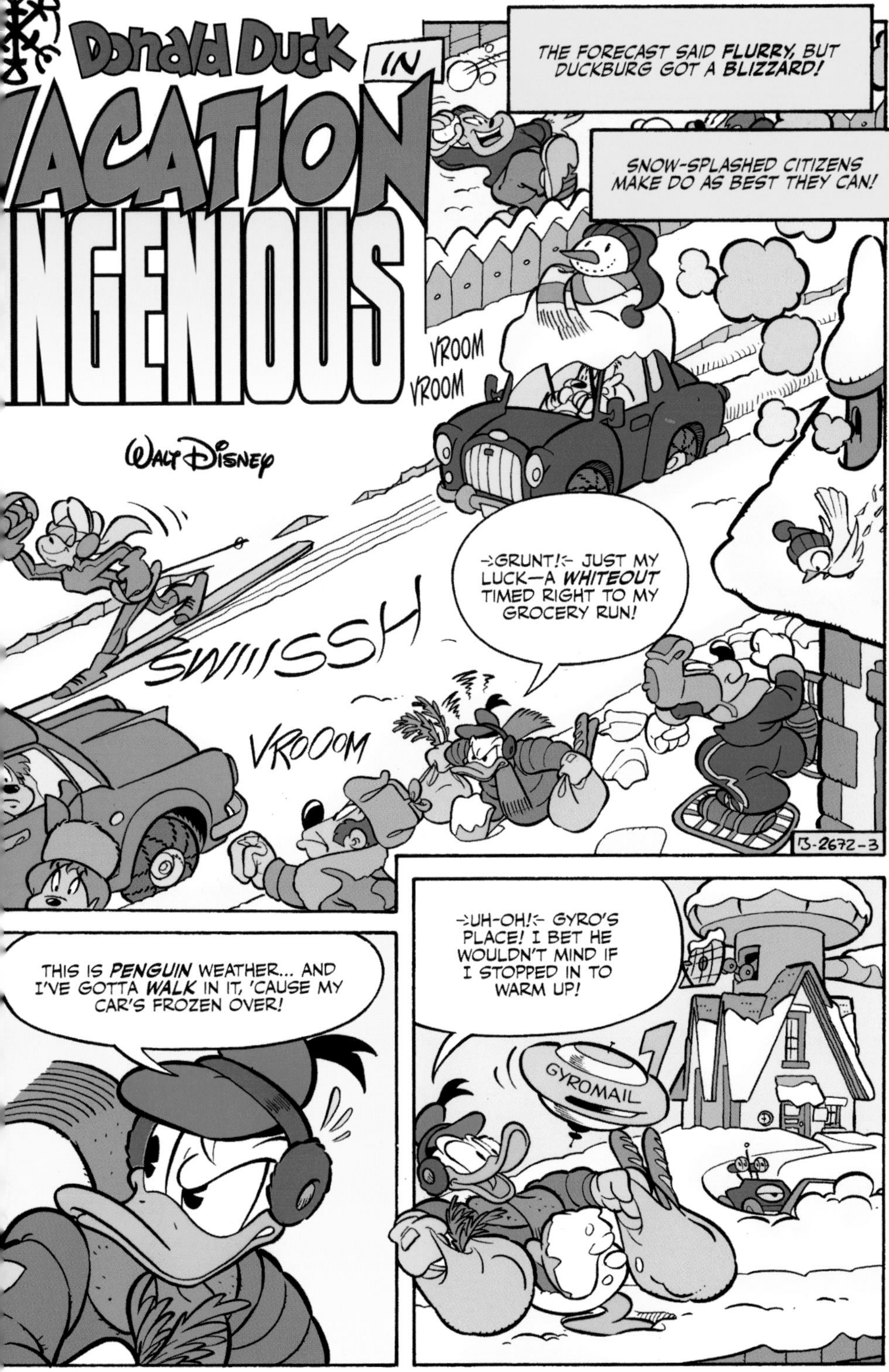
Donald Duck
IN
VACATION INGENIOUS
WALT DISNEY
THE FORECAST SAID FLURRY, BUT DUCKBURG GOT A BLIZZARD!
SNOW-SPLASHED CITIZENS MAKE DO AS BEST THEY CAN!
VROOM
VROOM
SWIIISSH
VROOOM
-GRUNT!- JUST MY LUCK—A WHITEOUT TIMED RIGHT TO MY GROCERY RUN!
B-2672-3
THIS IS PENGUIN WEATHER... AND I'VE GOTTA WALK IN IT, 'CAUSE MY CAR'S FROZEN OVER!
-UH-OH!- GYRO'S PLACE! I BET HE WOULDN'T MIND IF I STOPPED IN TO WARM UP!
GYROMAIL

ORIGINALLY PUBLISHED IN *TOPOLINO* #2672 (ITALY, 2007)

YOO-HOO! GYRO! ANYBODY HOME?

GENIUS AT WORK — COME ON IN!

-=WAK!=- DID THIS HOUSE GET HIT BY A *TORNADO?!*

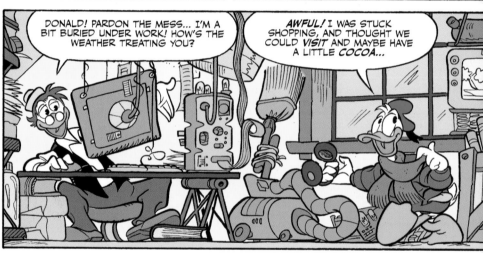

DONALD! PARDON THE MESS... I'M A BIT BURIED UNDER WORK! HOW'S THE WEATHER TREATING YOU?

AWFUL! I WAS STUCK SHOPPING, AND THOUGHT WE COULD *VISIT* AND MAYBE HAVE A LITTLE *COCOA...*

I'D LOVE TO, BUT I'M SWAMPED. WITH LOTS OF FOLKS STUCK AT HOME, THEY'RE FINDING NEW PROBLEMS FOR ME TO FIX!

I SEE!

AND TO MAKE MATTERS WORSE...

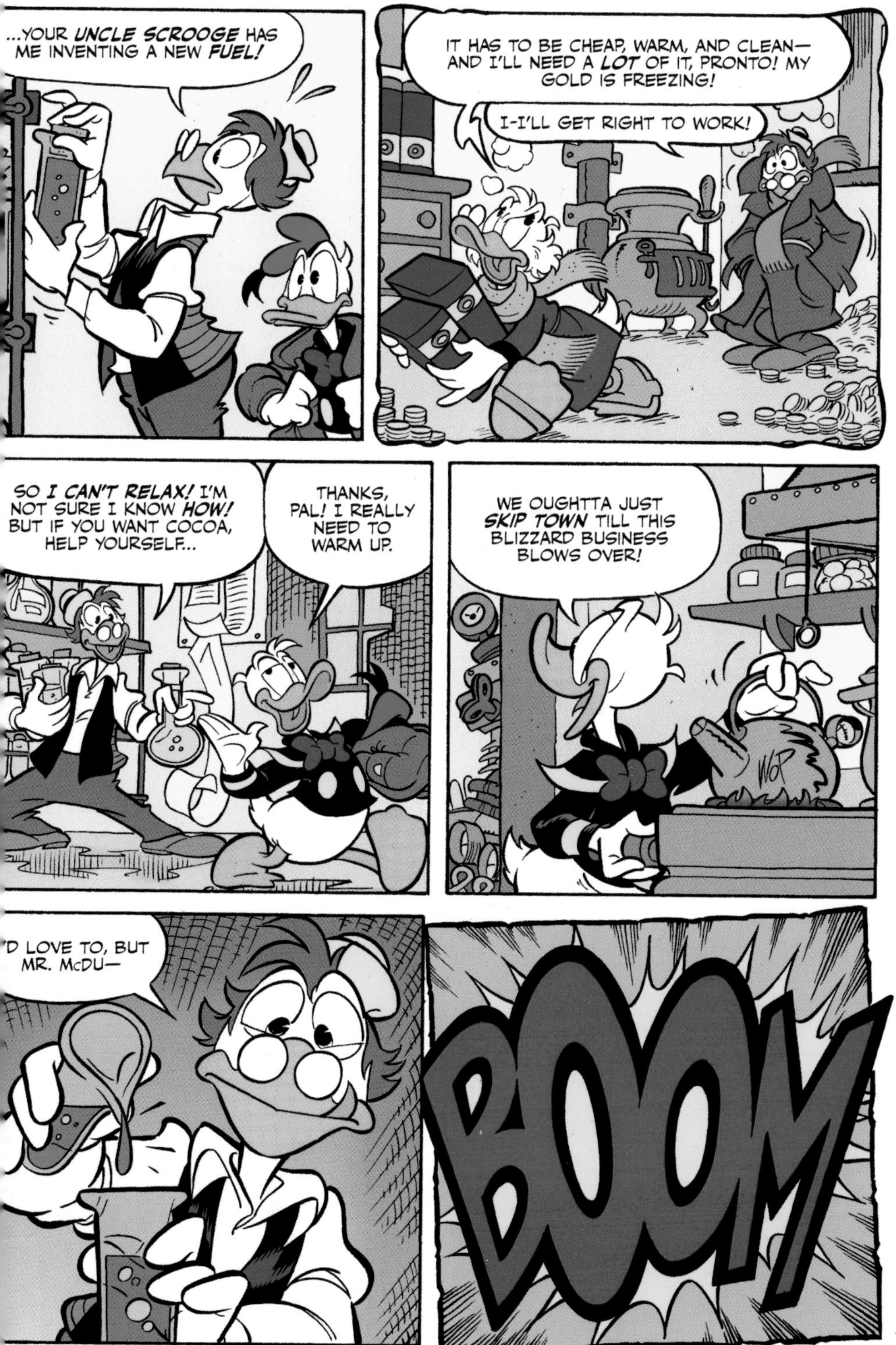

...YOUR UNCLE SCROOGE HAS ME INVENTING A NEW FUEL!
IT HAS TO BE CHEAP, WARM, AND CLEAN—AND I'LL NEED A LOT OF IT, PRONTO! MY GOLD IS FREEZING!
I-I'LL GET RIGHT TO WORK!
SO I CAN'T RELAX! I'M NOT SURE I KNOW HOW! BUT IF YOU WANT COCOA, HELP YOURSELF...
THANKS, PAL! I REALLY NEED TO WARM UP.
WE OUGHTTA JUST SKIP TOWN TILL THIS BLIZZARD BUSINESS BLOWS OVER!
'D LOVE TO, BUT MR. McDU—
BOOM

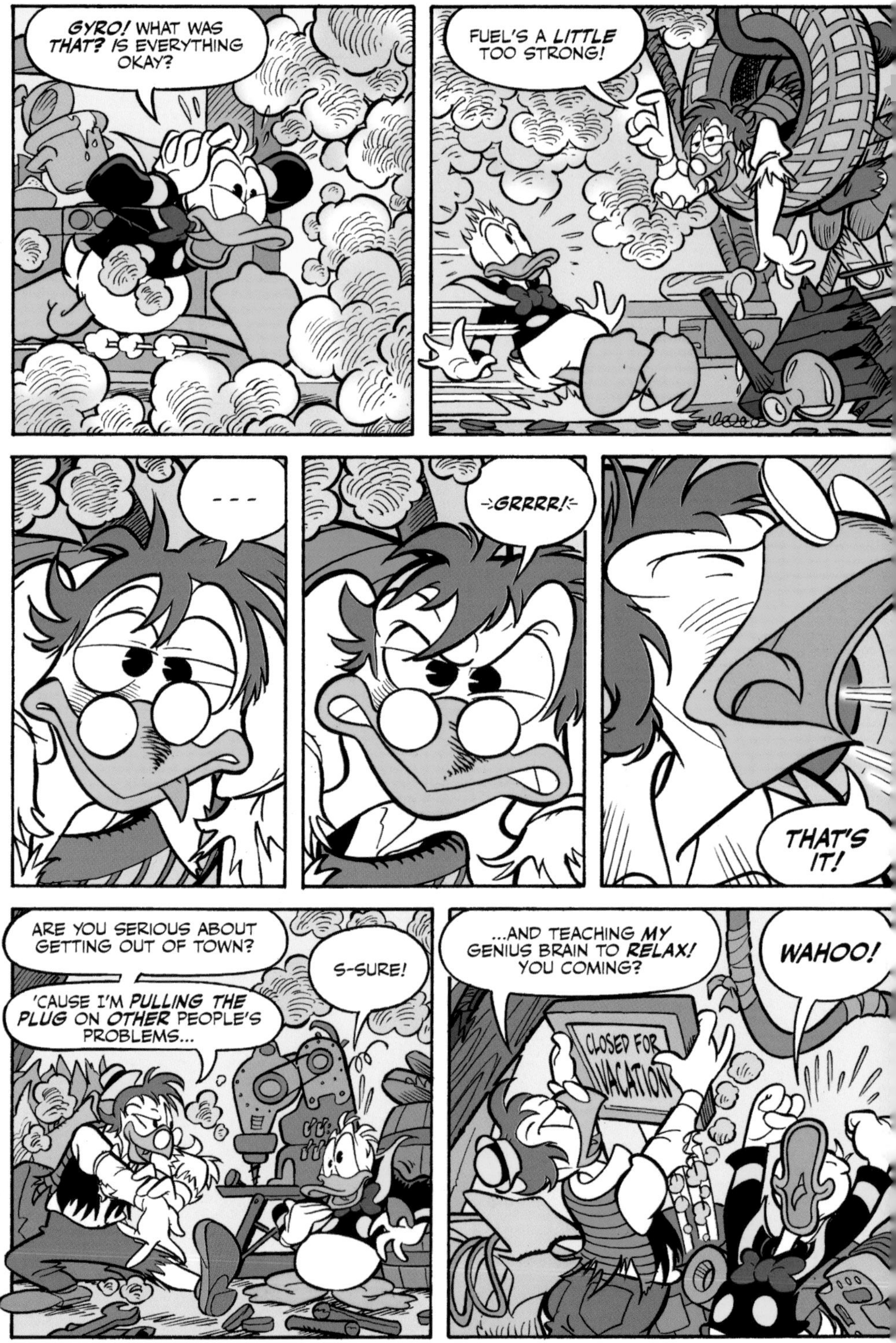
GYRO! WHAT WAS THAT? IS EVERYTHING OKAY?
FUEL'S A LITTLE TOO STRONG!
- - -
GRRRR!
THAT'S IT!
ARE YOU SERIOUS ABOUT GETTING OUT OF TOWN?
'CAUSE I'M PULLING THE PLUG ON OTHER PEOPLE'S PROBLEMS...
S-SURE!
...AND TEACHING MY GENIUS BRAIN TO RELAX! YOU COMING?
CLOSED FOR VACATION
WAHOO!

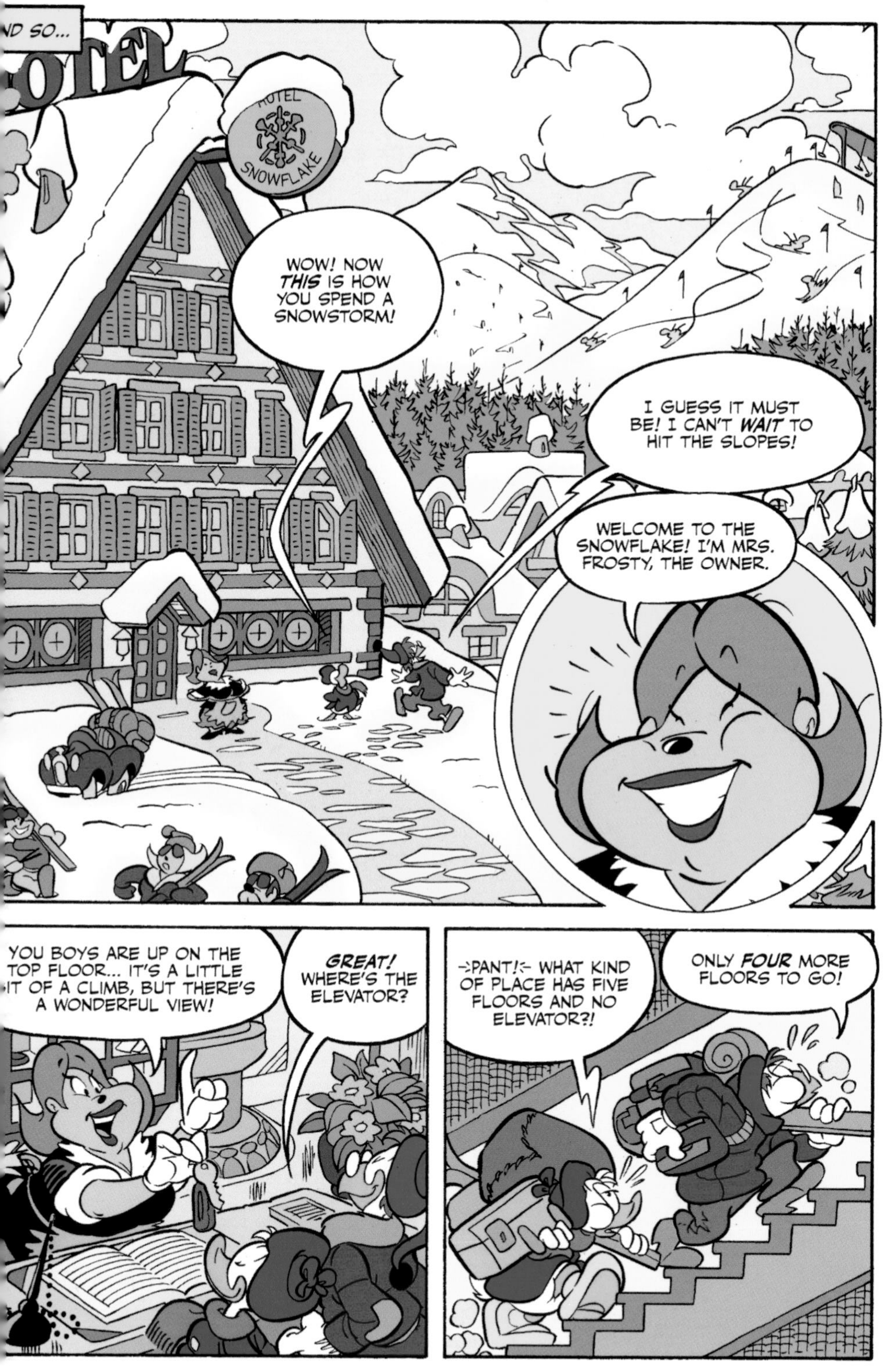
ND SO...
HOTEL
HOTEL SNOWFLAKE
WOW! NOW THIS IS HOW YOU SPEND A SNOWSTORM!
I GUESS IT MUST BE! I CAN'T WAIT TO HIT THE SLOPES!
WELCOME TO THE SNOWFLAKE! I'M MRS. FROSTY, THE OWNER.
YOU BOYS ARE UP ON THE TOP FLOOR... IT'S A LITTLE IT OF A CLIMB, BUT THERE'S A WONDERFUL VIEW!
GREAT! WHERE'S THE ELEVATOR?
PANT! WHAT KIND OF PLACE HAS FIVE FLOORS AND NO ELEVATOR?!
ONLY FOUR MORE FLOORS TO GO!

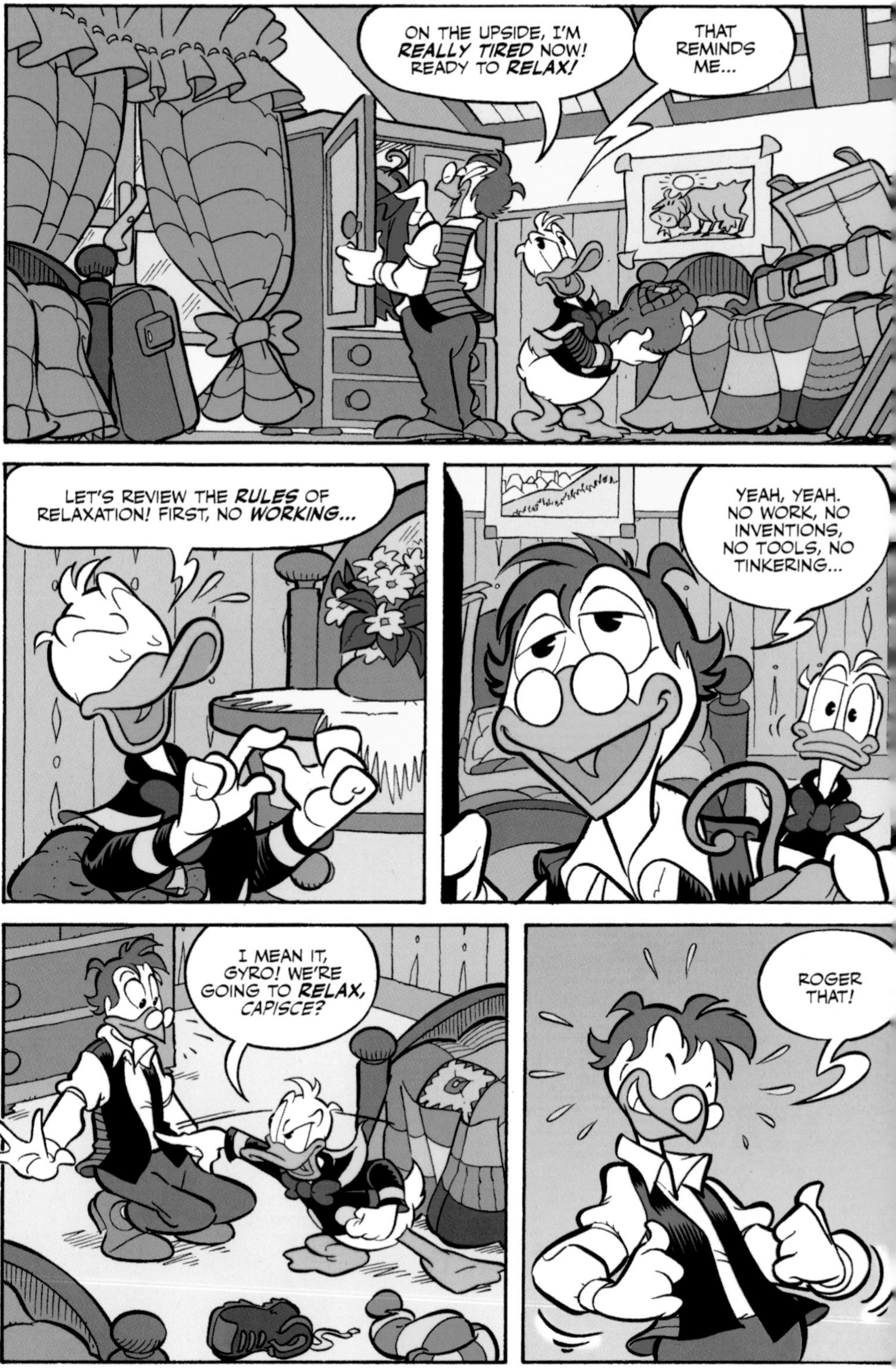

ON THE UPSIDE, I'M REALLY TIRED NOW! READY TO RELAX!
THAT REMINDS ME...
LET'S REVIEW THE RULES OF RELAXATION! FIRST, NO WORKING...
YEAH, YEAH. NO WORK, NO INVENTIONS, NO TOOLS, NO TINKERING...
I MEAN IT, GYRO! WE'RE GOING TO RELAX, CAPISCE?
ROGER THAT!

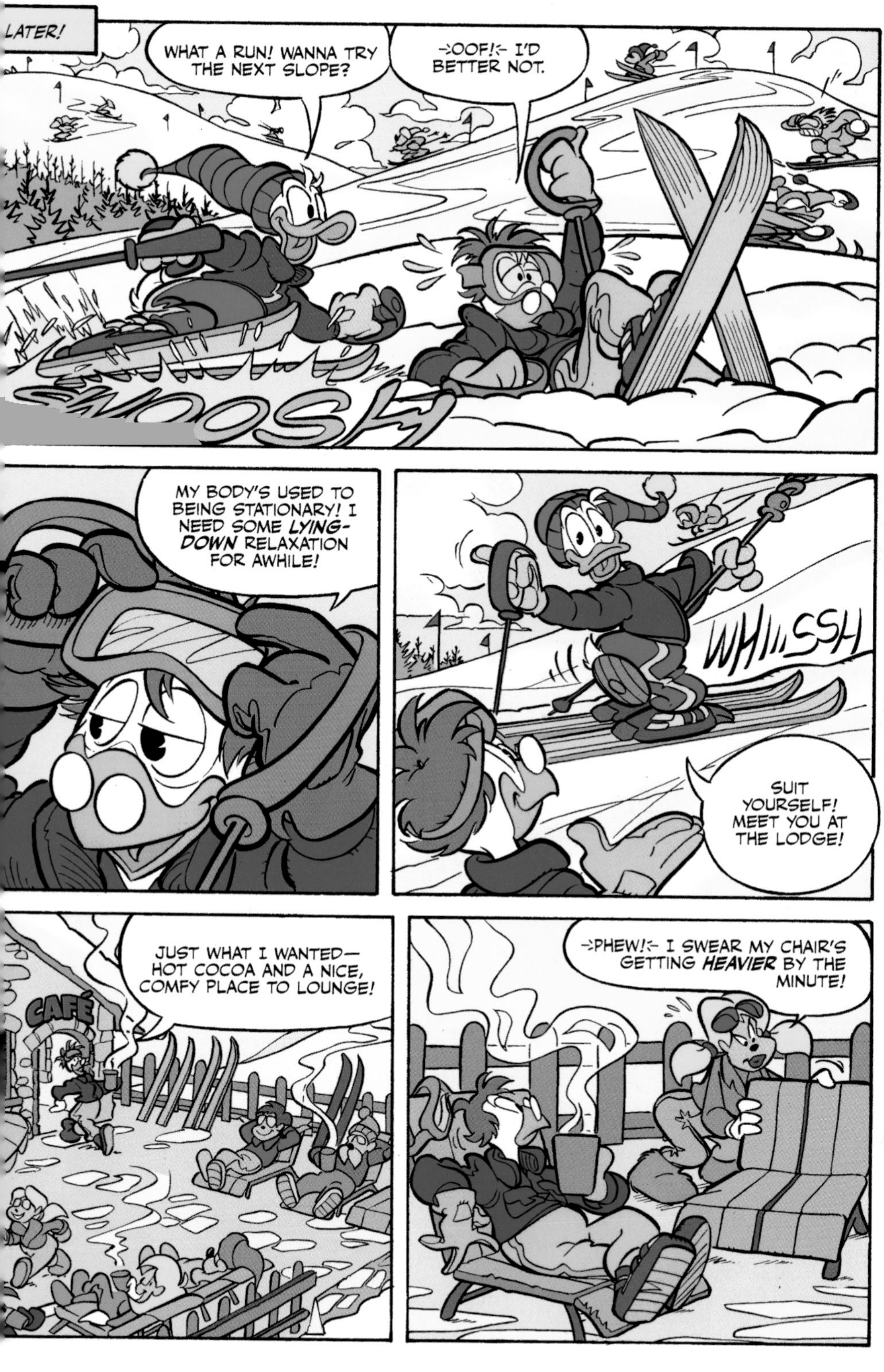
LATER!
WHAT A RUN! WANNA TRY THE NEXT SLOPE?
-›OOF!‹- I'D BETTER NOT.
SWOOSH
MY BODY'S USED TO BEING STATIONARY! I NEED SOME LYING-DOWN RELAXATION FOR AWHILE!
WHIIISSH
SUIT YOURSELF! MEET YOU AT THE LODGE!
JUST WHAT I WANTED— HOT COCOA AND A NICE, COMFY PLACE TO LOUNGE!
CAFÉ
-›PHEW!‹- I SWEAR MY CHAIR'S GETTING HEAVIER BY THE MINUTE!

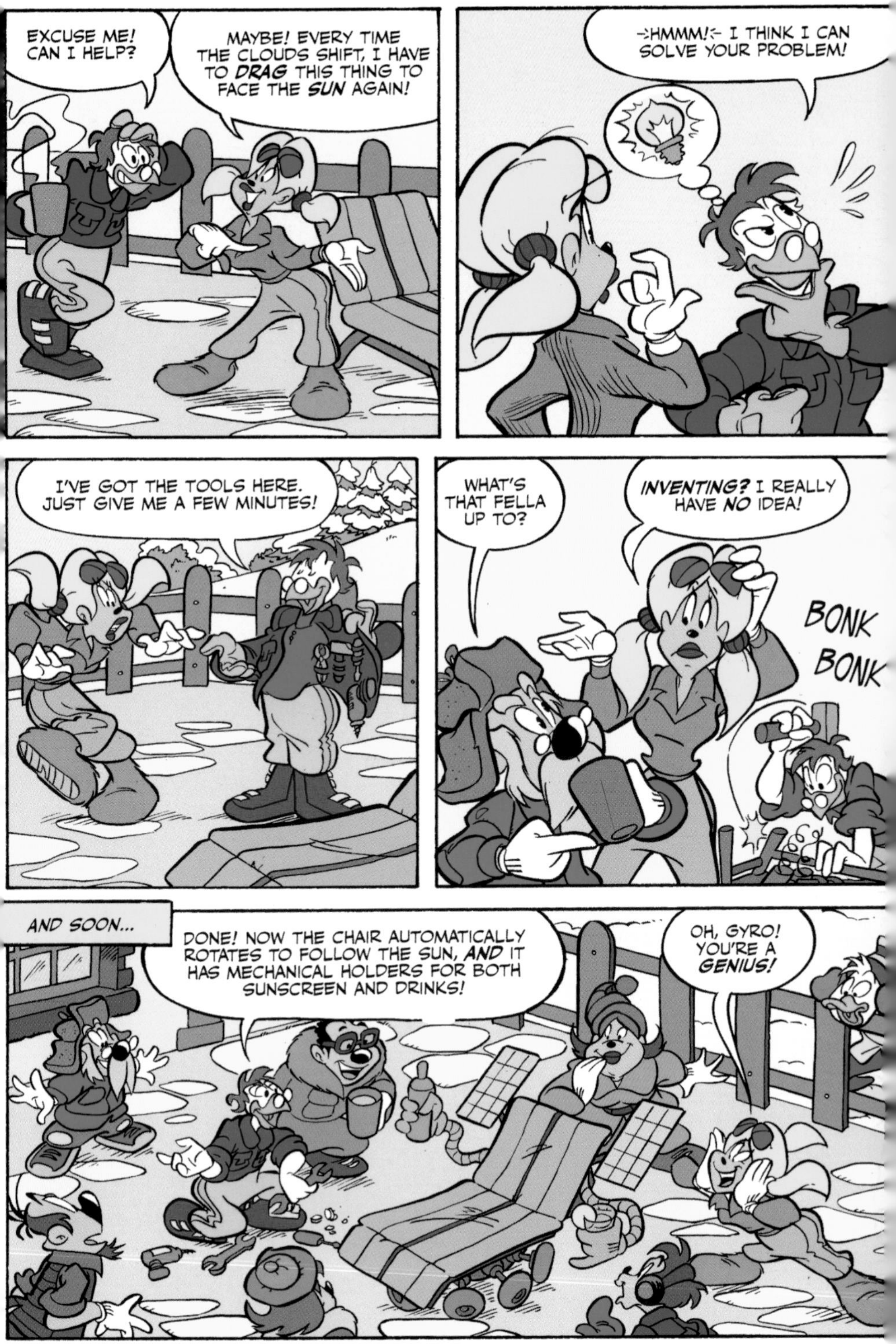

EXCUSE ME! CAN I HELP?
MAYBE! EVERY TIME THE CLOUDS SHIFT, I HAVE TO DRAG THIS THING TO FACE THE SUN AGAIN!
HMMM! I THINK I CAN SOLVE YOUR PROBLEM!
I'VE GOT THE TOOLS HERE. JUST GIVE ME A FEW MINUTES!
WHAT'S THAT FELLA UP TO?
INVENTING? I REALLY HAVE NO IDEA!
BONK
BONK
AND SOON...
DONE! NOW THE CHAIR AUTOMATICALLY ROTATES TO FOLLOW THE SUN, AND IT HAS MECHANICAL HOLDERS FOR BOTH SUNSCREEN AND DRINKS!
OH, GYRO! YOU'RE A GENIUS!

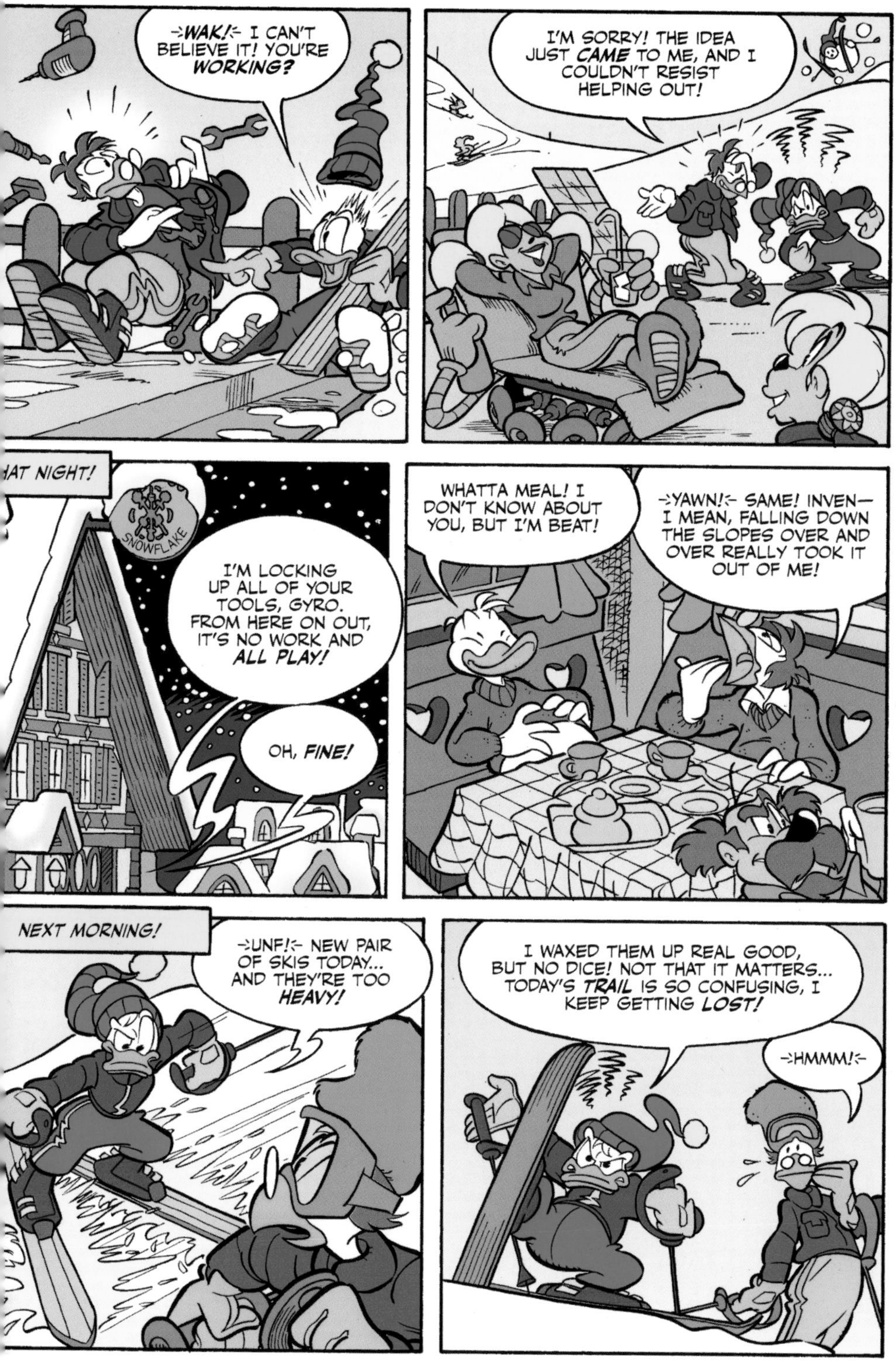
-WAK!- I CAN'T BELIEVE IT! YOU'RE WORKING?
I'M SORRY! THE IDEA JUST CAME TO ME, AND I COULDN'T RESIST HELPING OUT!
HAT NIGHT!
SNOWFLAKE
I'M LOCKING UP ALL OF YOUR TOOLS, GYRO. FROM HERE ON OUT, IT'S NO WORK AND ALL PLAY!
OH, FINE!
WHATTA MEAL! I DON'T KNOW ABOUT YOU, BUT I'M BEAT!
-YAWN!- SAME! INVEN— I MEAN, FALLING DOWN THE SLOPES OVER AND OVER REALLY TOOK IT OUT OF ME!
NEXT MORNING!
-UNF!- NEW PAIR OF SKIS TODAY... AND THEY'RE TOO HEAVY!
I WAXED THEM UP REAL GOOD, BUT NO DICE! NOT THAT IT MATTERS... TODAY'S TRAIL IS SO CONFUSING, I KEEP GETTING LOST!
-HMMM!-

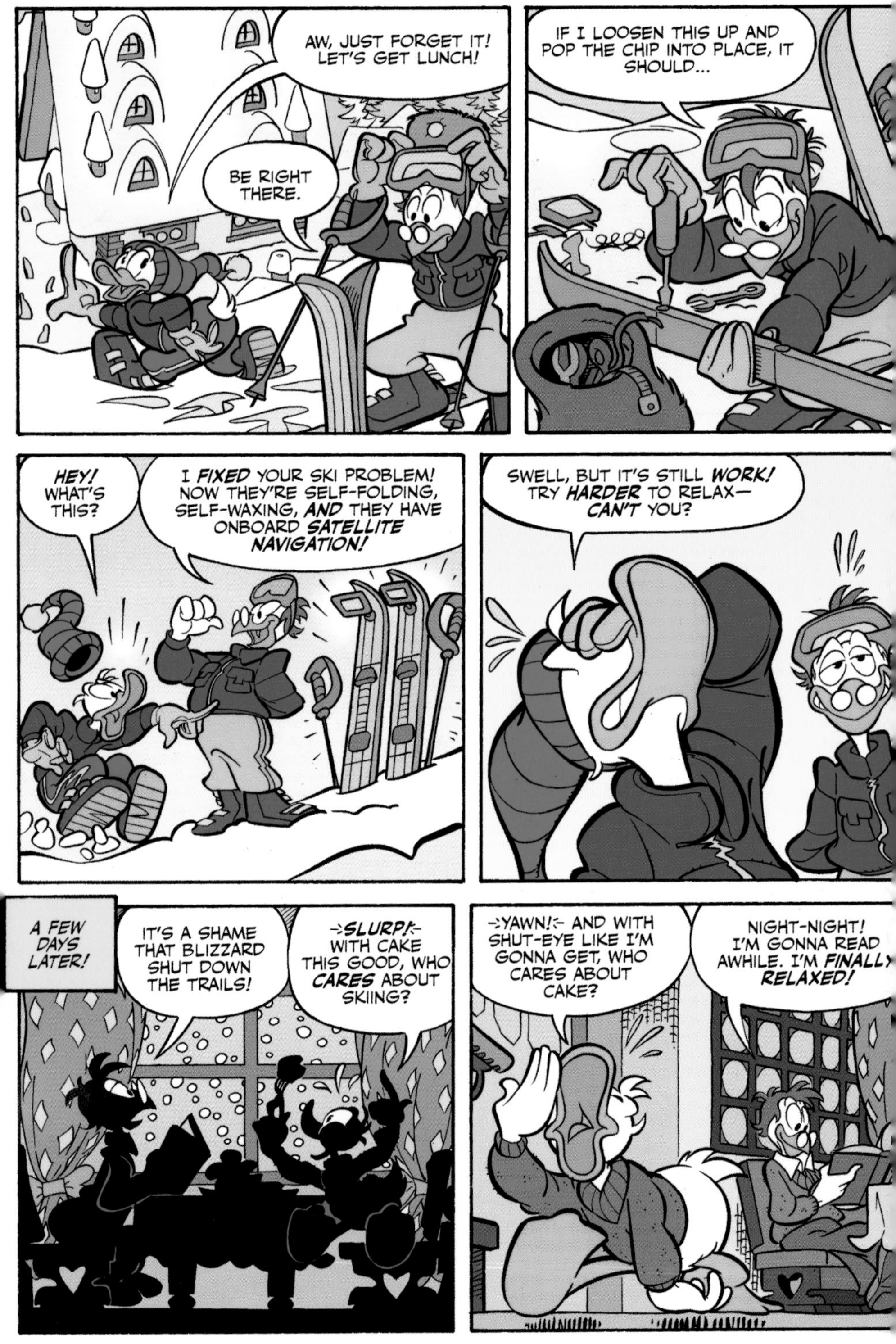
AW, JUST FORGET IT! LET'S GET LUNCH!
BE RIGHT THERE.
IF I LOOSEN THIS UP AND POP THE CHIP INTO PLACE, IT SHOULD...
HEY! WHAT'S THIS?
I FIXED YOUR SKI PROBLEM! NOW THEY'RE SELF-FOLDING, SELF-WAXING, AND THEY HAVE ONBOARD SATELLITE NAVIGATION!
SWELL, BUT IT'S STILL WORK! TRY HARDER TO RELAX— CAN'T YOU?
A FEW DAYS LATER!
IT'S A SHAME THAT BLIZZARD SHUT DOWN THE TRAILS!
-SLURP!- WITH CAKE THIS GOOD, WHO CARES ABOUT SKIING?
-YAWN!- AND WITH SHUT-EYE LIKE I'M GONNA GET, WHO CARES ABOUT CAKE?
NIGHT-NIGHT! I'M GONNA READ AWHILE. I'M FINALLY RELAXED!

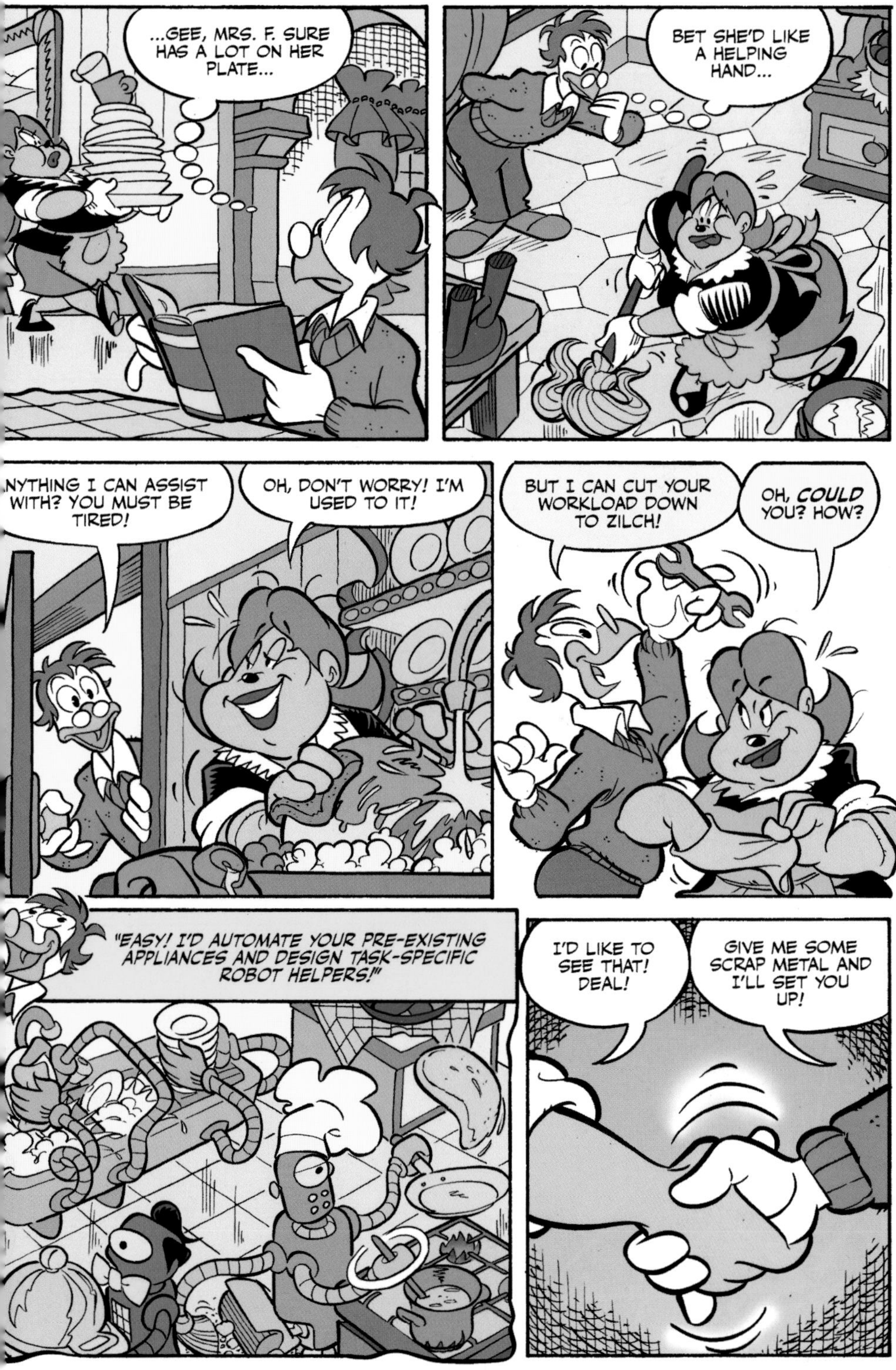
...GEE, MRS. F. SURE HAS A LOT ON HER PLATE...
BET SHE'D LIKE A HELPING HAND...
NYTHING I CAN ASSIST WITH? YOU MUST BE TIRED!
OH, DON'T WORRY! I'M USED TO IT!
BUT I CAN CUT YOUR WORKLOAD DOWN TO ZILCH!
OH, *COULD* YOU? HOW?
"EASY! I'D AUTOMATE YOUR PRE-EXISTING APPLIANCES AND DESIGN TASK-SPECIFIC ROBOT HELPERS!"
I'D LIKE TO SEE THAT! DEAL!
GIVE ME SOME SCRAP METAL AND I'LL SET YOU UP!

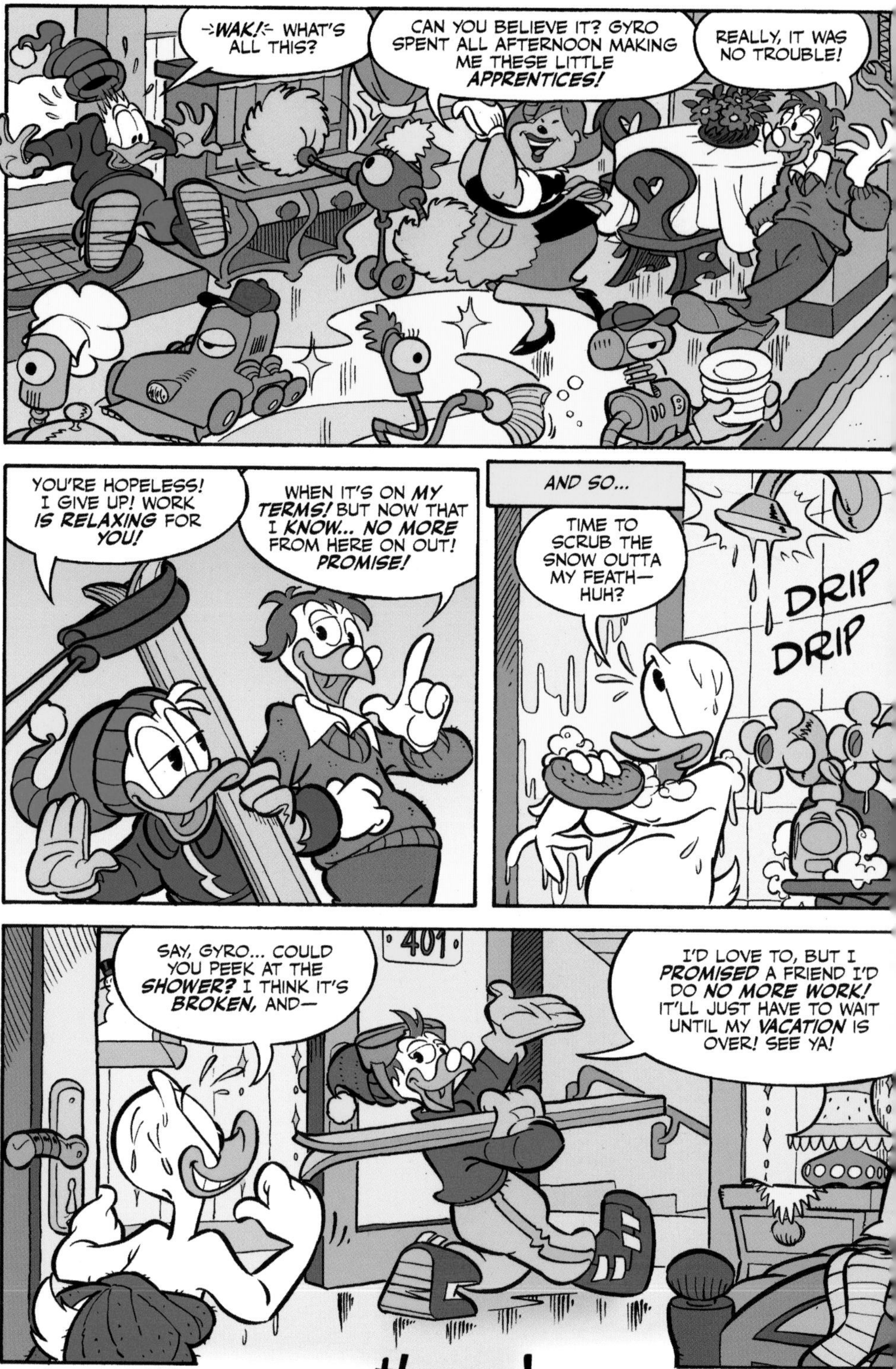

-WAK!- WHAT'S ALL THIS?
CAN YOU BELIEVE IT? GYRO SPENT ALL AFTERNOON MAKING ME THESE LITTLE APPRENTICES!
REALLY, IT WAS NO TROUBLE!
YOU'RE HOPELESS! I GIVE UP! WORK IS RELAXING FOR YOU!
WHEN IT'S ON MY TERMS! BUT NOW THAT I KNOW... NO MORE FROM HERE ON OUT! PROMISE!
AND SO...
TIME TO SCRUB THE SNOW OUTTA MY FEATH— HUH?
DRIP
DRIP
401
SAY, GYRO... COULD YOU PEEK AT THE SHOWER? I THINK IT'S BROKEN, AND—
I'D LOVE TO, BUT I PROMISED A FRIEND I'D DO NO MORE WORK! IT'LL JUST HAVE TO WAIT UNTIL MY VACATION IS OVER! SEE YA!

the end

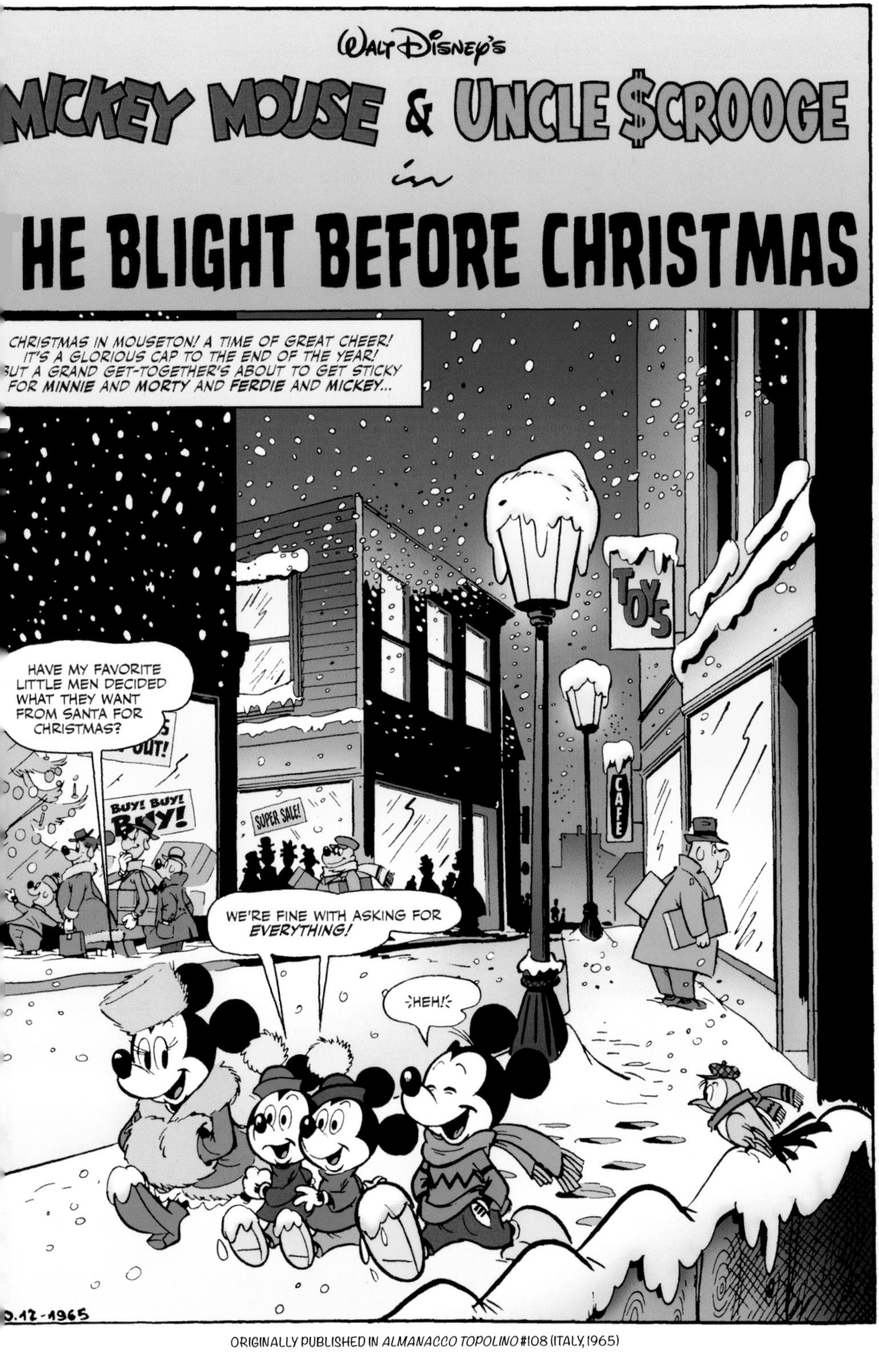

WALT DISNEY'S
MICKEY MOUSE & UNCLE $CROOGE
in
HE BLIGHT BEFORE CHRISTMAS
CHRISTMAS IN MOUSETON! A TIME OF GREAT CHEER! IT'S A GLORIOUS CAP TO THE END OF THE YEAR! BUT A GRAND GET-TOGETHER'S ABOUT TO GET STICKY FOR MINNIE AND MORTY AND FERDIE AND MICKEY...
TOYS
CAFE
HAVE MY FAVORITE LITTLE MEN DECIDED WHAT THEY WANT FROM SANTA FOR CHRISTMAS?
OUT!
BUY! BUY! BUY!
SUPER SALE!
WE'RE FINE WITH ASKING FOR EVERYTHING!
HEH!
D.12-1965

ORIGINALLY PUBLISHED IN *ALMANACCO TOPOLINO* #108 (ITALY, 1965)

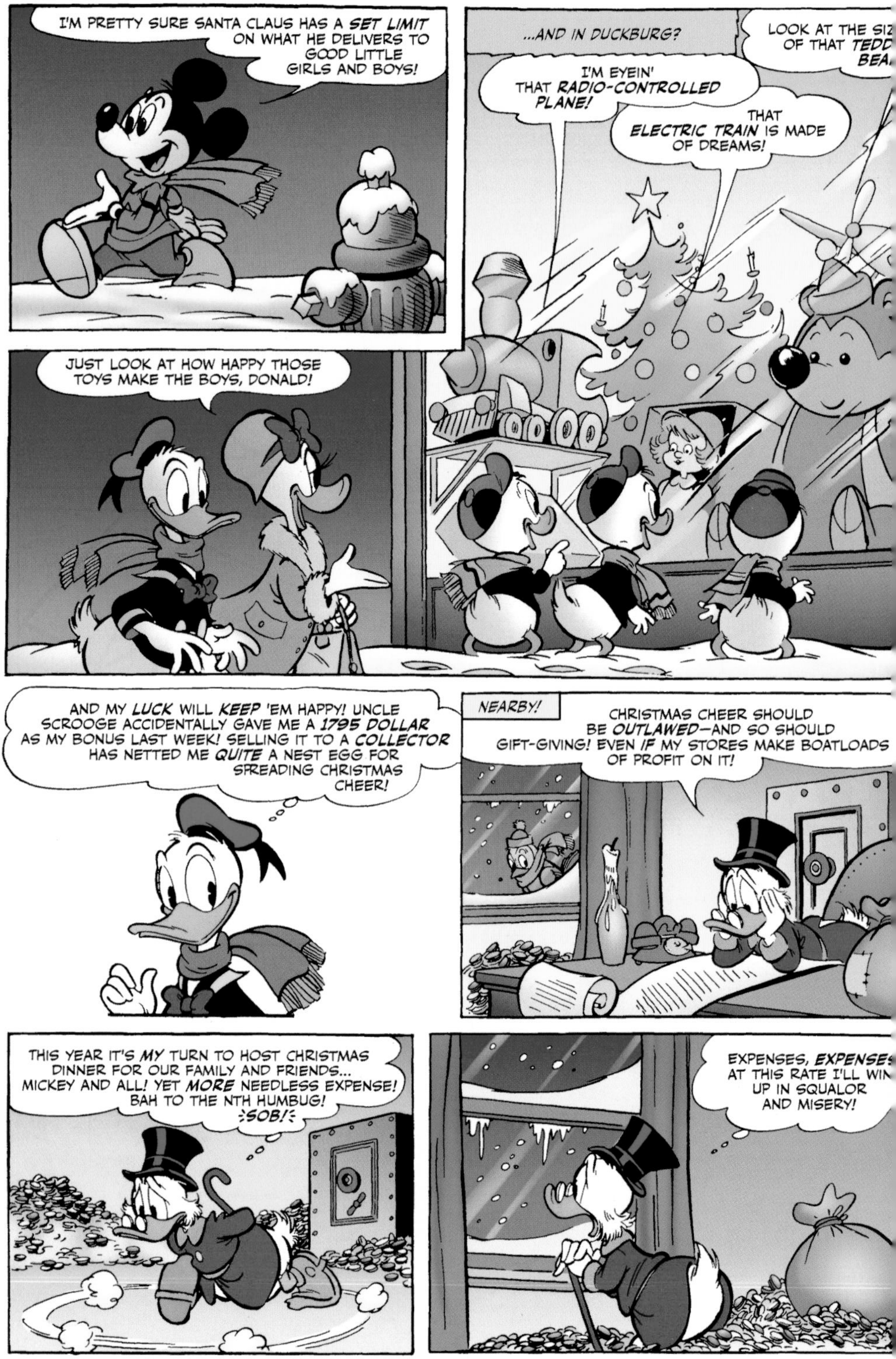
I'M PRETTY SURE SANTA CLAUS HAS A SET LIMIT ON WHAT HE DELIVERS TO GOOD LITTLE GIRLS AND BOYS!
...AND IN DUCKBURG?
I'M EYEIN' THAT RADIO-CONTROLLED PLANE!
THAT ELECTRIC TRAIN IS MADE OF DREAMS!
LOOK AT THE SIZ OF THAT TEDD BEA
JUST LOOK AT HOW HAPPY THOSE TOYS MAKE THE BOYS, DONALD!
AND MY LUCK WILL KEEP 'EM HAPPY! UNCLE SCROOGE ACCIDENTALLY GAVE ME A 1795 DOLLAR AS MY BONUS LAST WEEK! SELLING IT TO A COLLECTOR HAS NETTED ME QUITE A NEST EGG FOR SPREADING CHRISTMAS CHEER!
NEARBY!
CHRISTMAS CHEER SHOULD BE OUTLAWED—AND SO SHOULD GIFT-GIVING! EVEN IF MY STORES MAKE BOATLOADS OF PROFIT ON IT!
THIS YEAR IT'S MY TURN TO HOST CHRISTMAS DINNER FOR OUR FAMILY AND FRIENDS... MICKEY AND ALL! YET MORE NEEDLESS EXPENSE! BAH TO THE NTH HUMBUG! :SOB!:
EXPENSES, EXPENSE AT THIS RATE I'LL WIN UP IN SQUALOR AND MISERY!

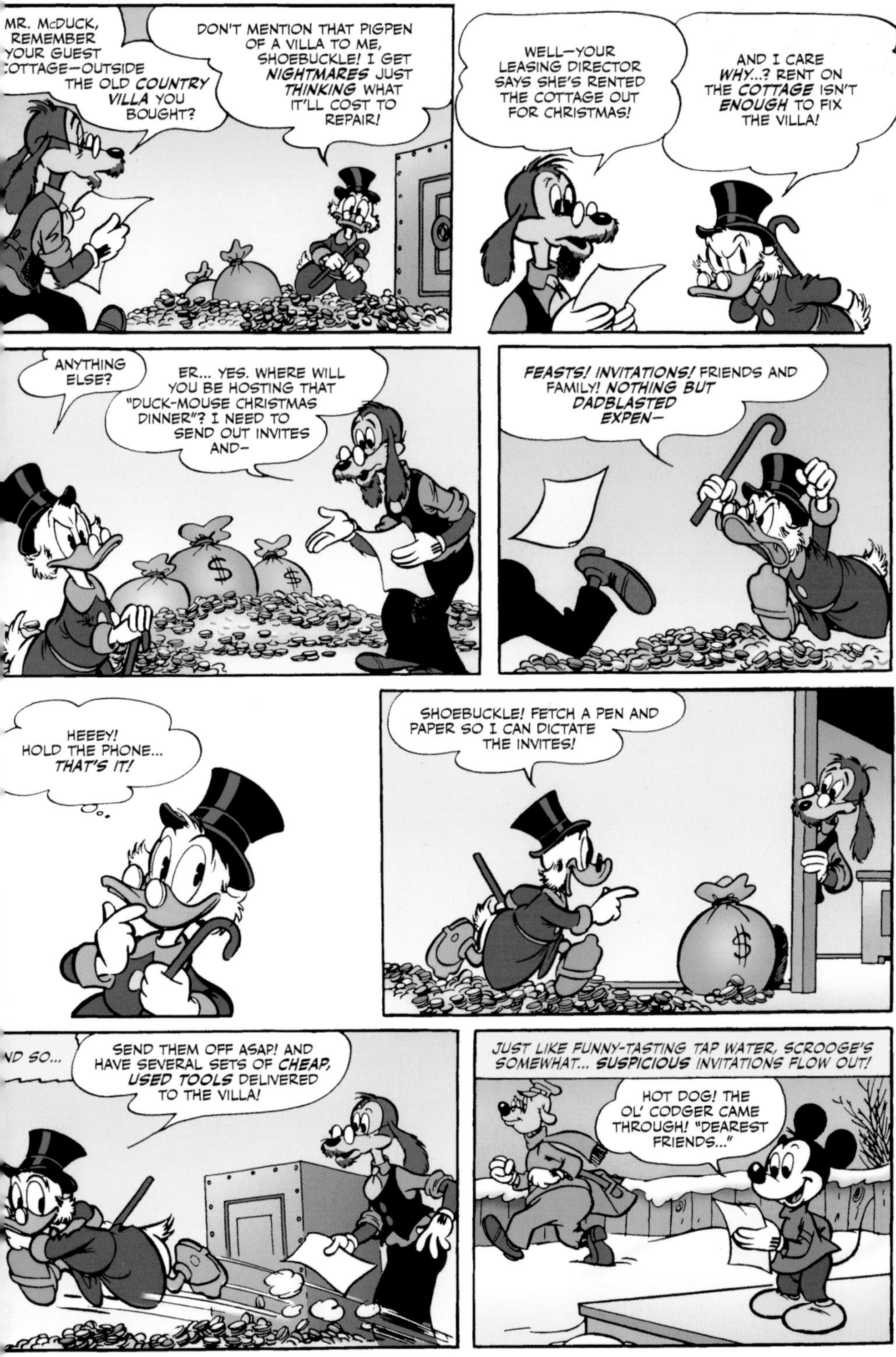
MR. McDUCK, REMEMBER YOUR GUEST COTTAGE—OUTSIDE THE OLD COUNTRY VILLA YOU BOUGHT?
DON'T MENTION THAT PIGPEN OF A VILLA TO ME, SHOEBUCKLE! I GET NIGHTMARES JUST THINKING WHAT IT'LL COST TO REPAIR!
WELL—YOUR LEASING DIRECTOR SAYS SHE'S RENTED THE COTTAGE OUT FOR CHRISTMAS!
AND I CARE WHY...? RENT ON THE COTTAGE ISN'T ENOUGH TO FIX THE VILLA!
ANYTHING ELSE?
ER... YES. WHERE WILL YOU BE HOSTING THAT "DUCK-MOUSE CHRISTMAS DINNER"? I NEED TO SEND OUT INVITES AND—
FEASTS! INVITATIONS! FRIENDS AND FAMILY! NOTHING BUT DADBLASTED EXPEN—
HEEEY! HOLD THE PHONE... THAT'S IT!
SHOEBUCKLE! FETCH A PEN AND PAPER SO I CAN DICTATE THE INVITES!
AND SO...
SEND THEM OFF ASAP! AND HAVE SEVERAL SETS OF CHEAP, USED TOOLS DELIVERED TO THE VILLA!
JUST LIKE FUNNY-TASTING TAP WATER, SCROOGE'S SOMEWHAT... SUSPICIOUS INVITATIONS FLOW OUT!
HOT DOG! THE OL' CODGER CAME THROUGH! "DEAREST FRIENDS..."

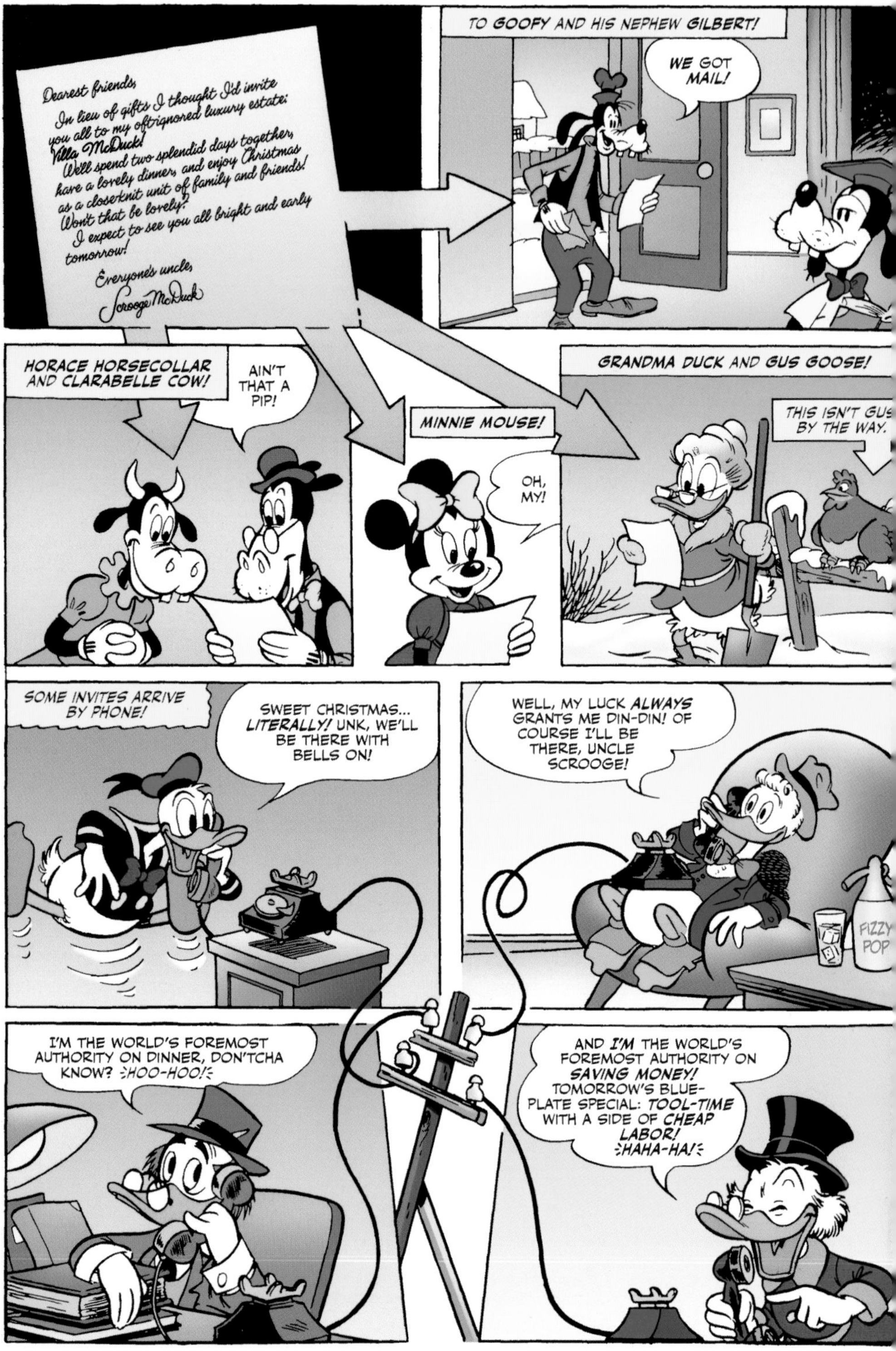

Dearest friends,
In lieu of gifts I thought I'd invite you all to my oft-ignored luxury estate: Villa McDuck!
We'll spend two splendid days together, have a lovely dinner, and enjoy Christmas as a closeknit unit of family and friends!
Won't that be lovely?
I expect to see you all bright and early tomorrow!
Everyone's uncle,
Scrooge McDuck
TO GOOFY AND HIS NEPHEW GILBERT!
WE GOT MAIL!
HORACE HORSECOLLAR AND CLARABELLE COW!
AIN'T THAT A PIP!
MINNIE MOUSE!
OH, MY!
GRANDMA DUCK AND GUS GOOSE!
THIS ISN'T GUS BY THE WAY.
SOME INVITES ARRIVE BY PHONE!
SWEET CHRISTMAS... LITERALLY! UNK, WE'LL BE THERE WITH BELLS ON!
WELL, MY LUCK ALWAYS GRANTS ME DIN-DIN! OF COURSE I'LL BE THERE, UNCLE SCROOGE!
FIZZY POP
I'M THE WORLD'S FOREMOST AUTHORITY ON DINNER, DON'TCHA KNOW? HOO-HOO!
AND I'M THE WORLD'S FOREMOST AUTHORITY ON SAVING MONEY! TOMORROW'S BLUE-PLATE SPECIAL: TOOL-TIME WITH A SIDE OF CHEAP LABOR! HAHA-HA!

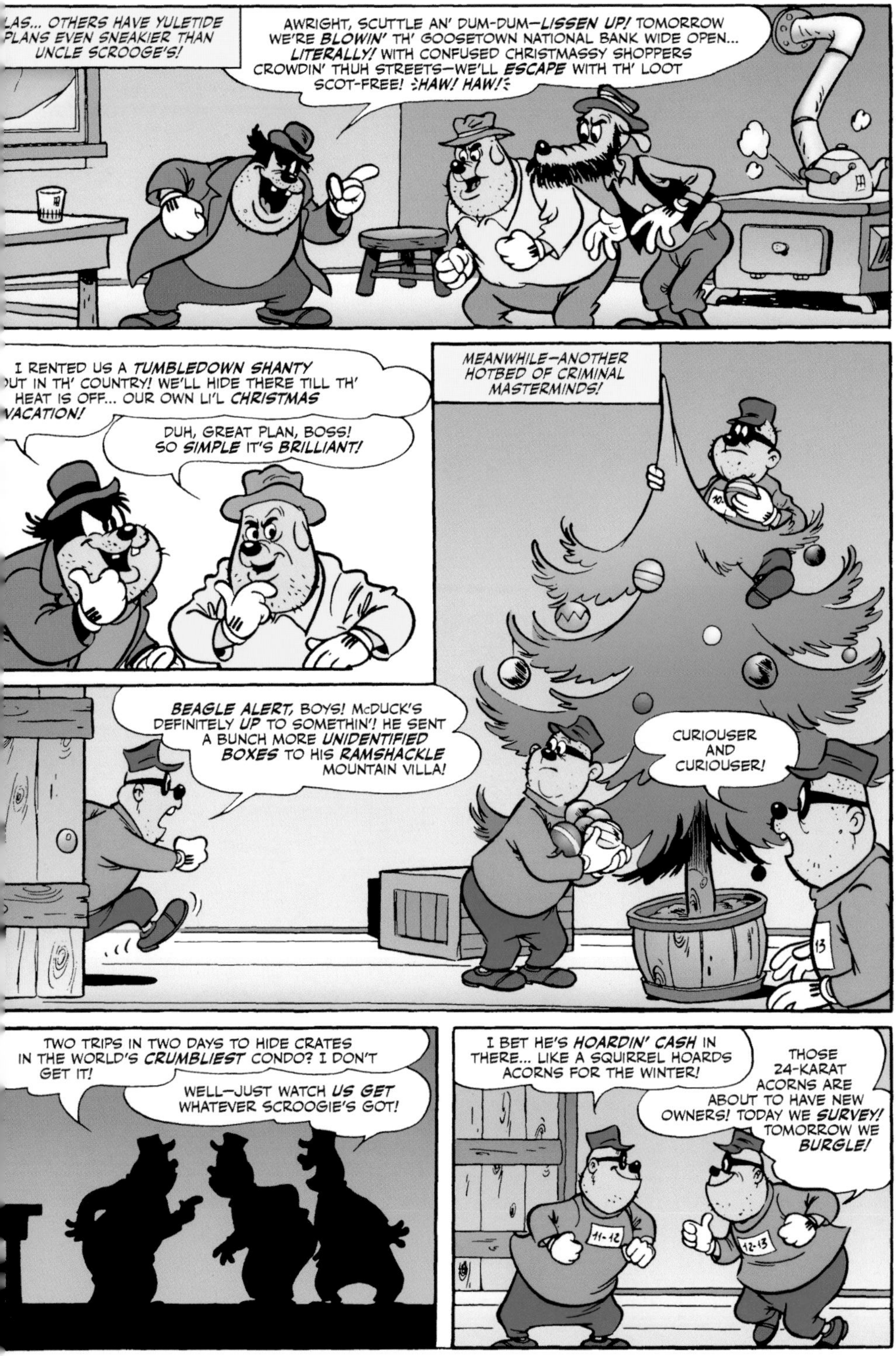

LAS... OTHERS HAVE YULETIDE PLANS EVEN SNEAKIER THAN UNCLE SCROOGE'S!
AWRIGHT, SCUTTLE AN' DUM-DUM—*LISSEN UP!* TOMORROW WE'RE *BLOWIN'* TH' GOOSETOWN NATIONAL BANK WIDE OPEN... *LITERALLY!* WITH CONFUSED CHRISTMASSY SHOPPERS CROWDIN' THUH STREETS—WE'LL *ESCAPE* WITH TH' LOOT SCOT-FREE! *HAW! HAW!*
I RENTED US A *TUMBLEDOWN SHANTY* OUT IN TH' COUNTRY! WE'LL HIDE THERE TILL TH' HEAT IS OFF... OUR OWN LI'L *CHRISTMAS VACATION!*
DUH, GREAT PLAN, BOSS! SO *SIMPLE* IT'S *BRILLIANT!*
MEANWHILE—ANOTHER HOTBED OF CRIMINAL MASTERMINDS!
BEAGLE ALERT, BOYS! McDUCK'S DEFINITELY *UP* TO SOMETHIN'! HE SENT A BUNCH MORE *UNIDENTIFIED BOXES* TO HIS *RAMSHACKLE* MOUNTAIN VILLA!
CURIOUSER AND CURIOUSER!
TWO TRIPS IN TWO DAYS TO HIDE CRATES IN THE WORLD'S *CRUMBLIEST* CONDO? I DON'T GET IT!
WELL—JUST WATCH *US GET* WHATEVER SCROOGIE'S GOT!
I BET HE'S *HOARDIN' CASH* IN THERE... LIKE A SQUIRREL HOARDS ACORNS FOR THE WINTER!
THOSE 24-KARAT ACORNS ARE ABOUT TO HAVE NEW OWNERS! TODAY WE *SURVEY!* TOMORROW WE *BURGLE!*

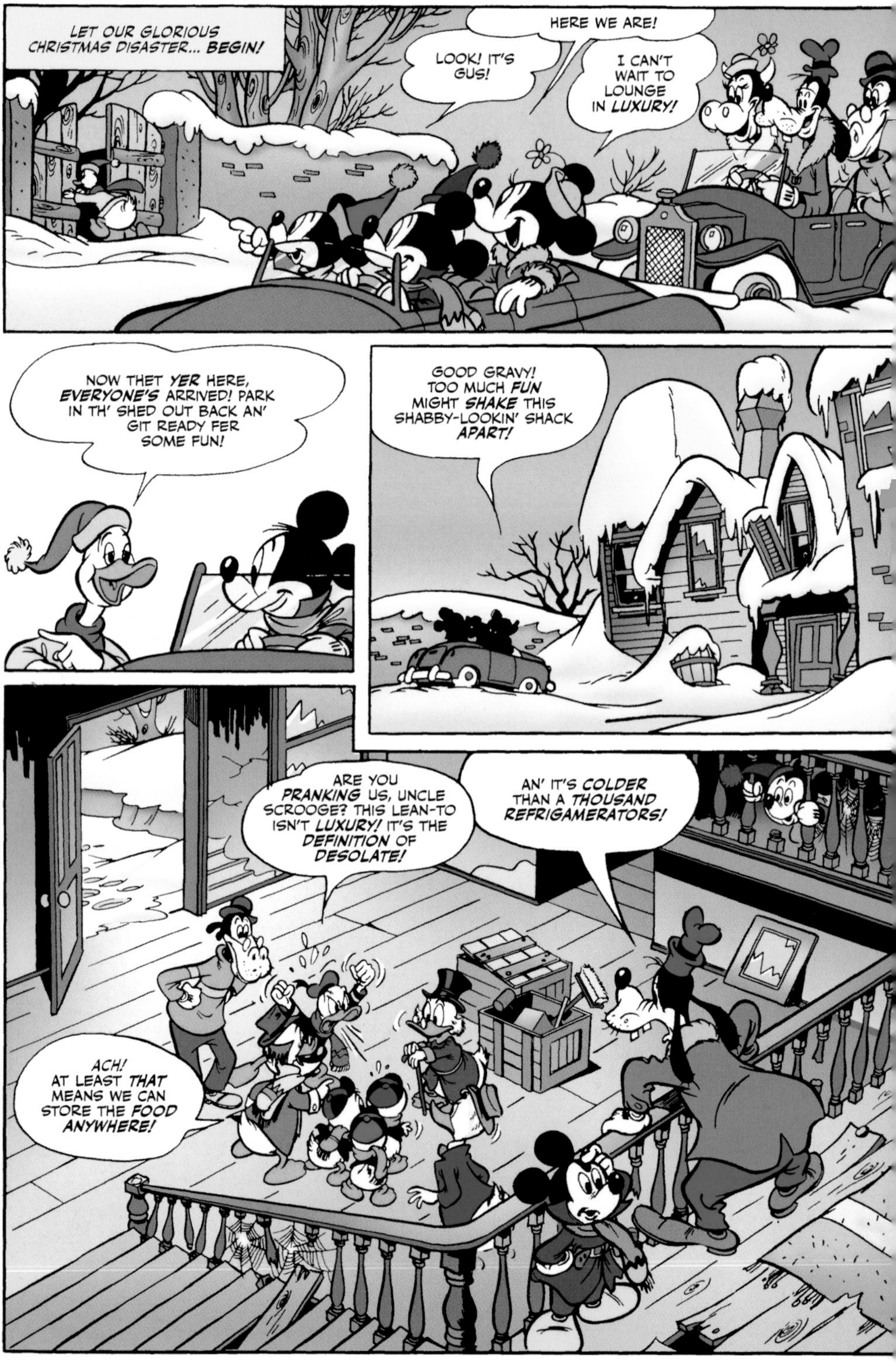
LET OUR GLORIOUS CHRISTMAS DISASTER... BEGIN!
LOOK! IT'S GUS!
HERE WE ARE!
I CAN'T WAIT TO LOUNGE IN LUXURY!
NOW THET YER HERE, EVERYONE'S ARRIVED! PARK IN TH' SHED OUT BACK AN' GIT READY FER SOME FUN!
GOOD GRAVY! TOO MUCH FUN MIGHT SHAKE THIS SHABBY-LOOKIN' SHACK APART!
ARE YOU PRANKING US, UNCLE SCROOGE? THIS LEAN-TO ISN'T LUXURY! IT'S THE DEFINITION OF DESOLATE!
AN' IT'S COLDER THAN A THOUSAND REFRIGAMERATORS!
ACH! AT LEAST THAT MEANS WE CAN STORE THE FOOD ANYWHERE!

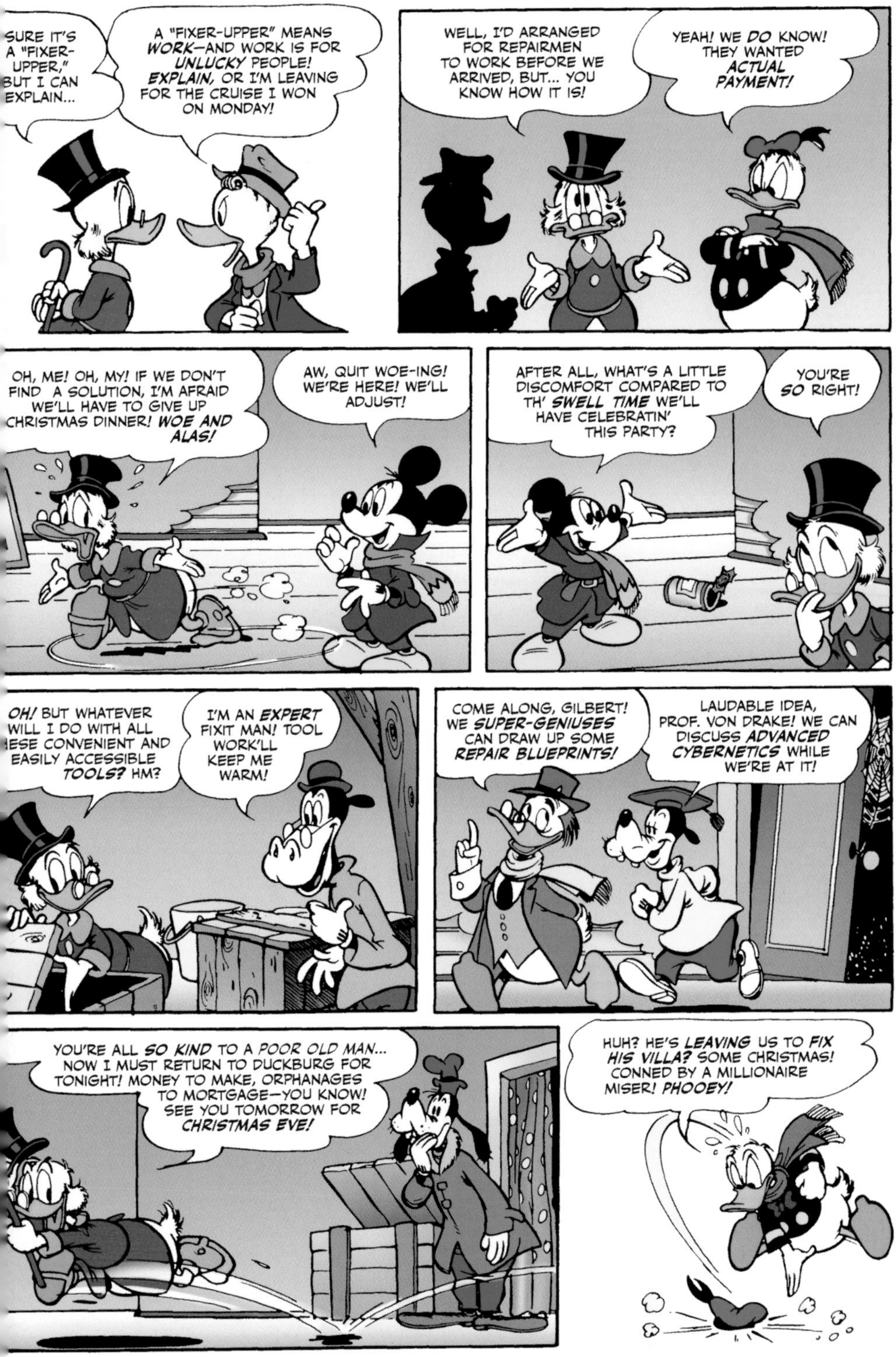

SURE IT'S A "FIXER-UPPER," BUT I CAN EXPLAIN...
A "FIXER-UPPER" MEANS WORK—AND WORK IS FOR UNLUCKY PEOPLE! EXPLAIN, OR I'M LEAVING FOR THE CRUISE I WON ON MONDAY!
WELL, I'D ARRANGED FOR REPAIRMEN TO WORK BEFORE WE ARRIVED, BUT... YOU KNOW HOW IT IS!
YEAH! WE DO KNOW! THEY WANTED ACTUAL PAYMENT!
OH, ME! OH, MY! IF WE DON'T FIND A SOLUTION, I'M AFRAID WE'LL HAVE TO GIVE UP CHRISTMAS DINNER! WOE AND ALAS!
AW, QUIT WOE-ING! WE'RE HERE! WE'LL ADJUST!
AFTER ALL, WHAT'S A LITTLE DISCOMFORT COMPARED TO TH' SWELL TIME WE'LL HAVE CELEBRATIN' THIS PARTY?
YOU'RE SO RIGHT!
OH! BUT WHATEVER WILL I DO WITH ALL ESE CONVENIENT AND EASILY ACCESSIBLE TOOLS? HM?
I'M AN EXPERT FIXIT MAN! TOOL WORK'LL KEEP ME WARM!
COME ALONG, GILBERT! WE SUPER-GENIUSES CAN DRAW UP SOME REPAIR BLUEPRINTS!
LAUDABLE IDEA, PROF. VON DRAKE! WE CAN DISCUSS ADVANCED CYBERNETICS WHILE WE'RE AT IT!
YOU'RE ALL SO KIND TO A POOR OLD MAN... NOW I MUST RETURN TO DUCKBURG FOR TONIGHT! MONEY TO MAKE, ORPHANAGES TO MORTGAGE—YOU KNOW! SEE YOU TOMORROW FOR CHRISTMAS EVE!
HUH? HE'S LEAVING US TO FIX HIS VILLA? SOME CHRISTMAS! CONNED BY A MILLIONAIRE MISER! PHOOEY!

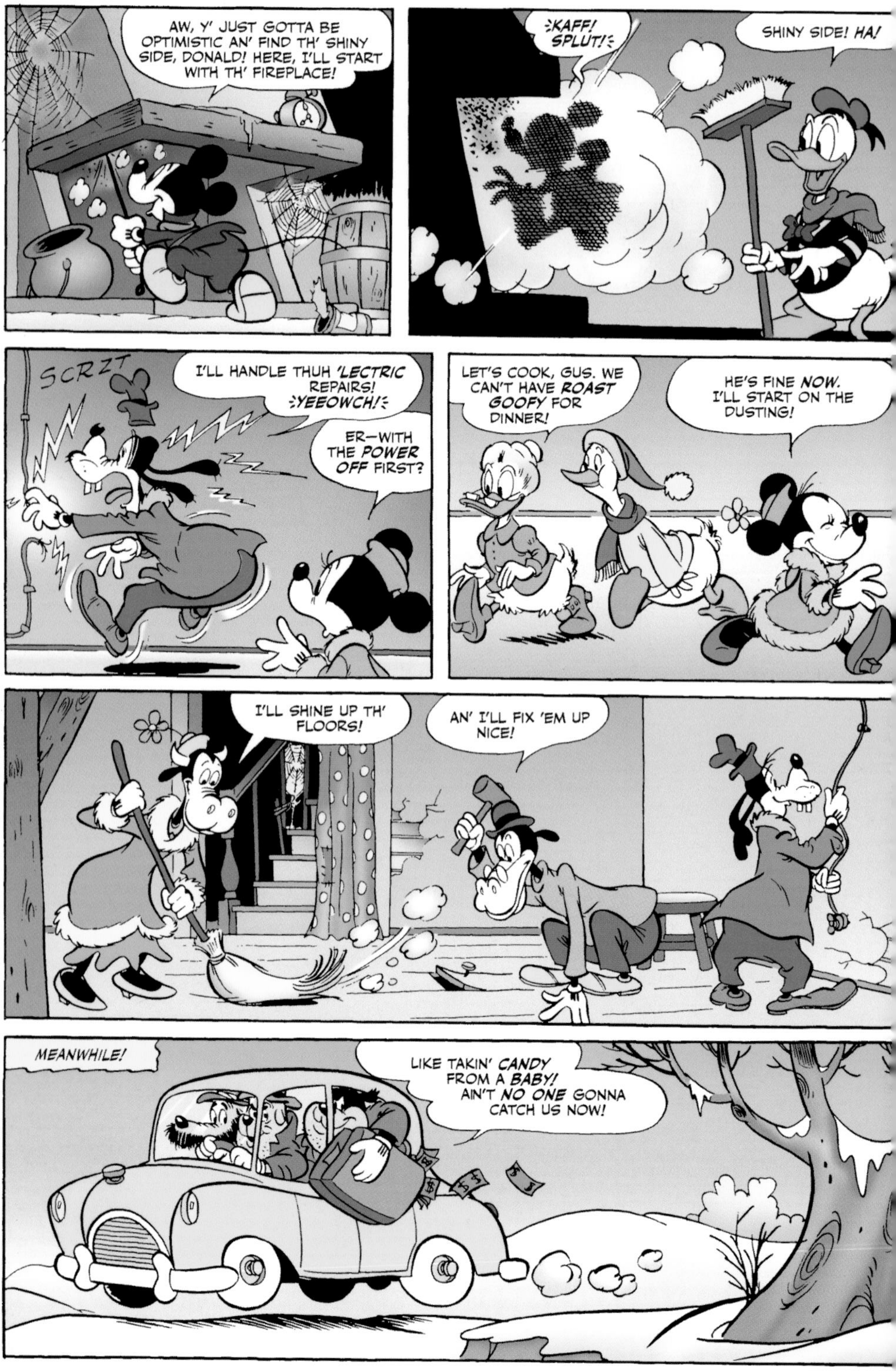
AW, Y' JUST GOTTA BE OPTIMISTIC AN' FIND TH' SHINY SIDE, DONALD! HERE, I'LL START WITH TH' FIREPLACE!
KAFF! SPLUT!
SHINY SIDE! HA!
SCRZT
I'LL HANDLE THUH 'LECTRIC REPAIRS! YEEOWCH!
ER—WITH THE POWER OFF FIRST?
LET'S COOK, GUS. WE CAN'T HAVE ROAST GOOFY FOR DINNER!
HE'S FINE NOW. I'LL START ON THE DUSTING!
I'LL SHINE UP TH' FLOORS!
AN' I'LL FIX 'EM UP NICE!
MEANWHILE!
LIKE TAKIN' CANDY FROM A BABY! AIN'T NO ONE GONNA CATCH US NOW!

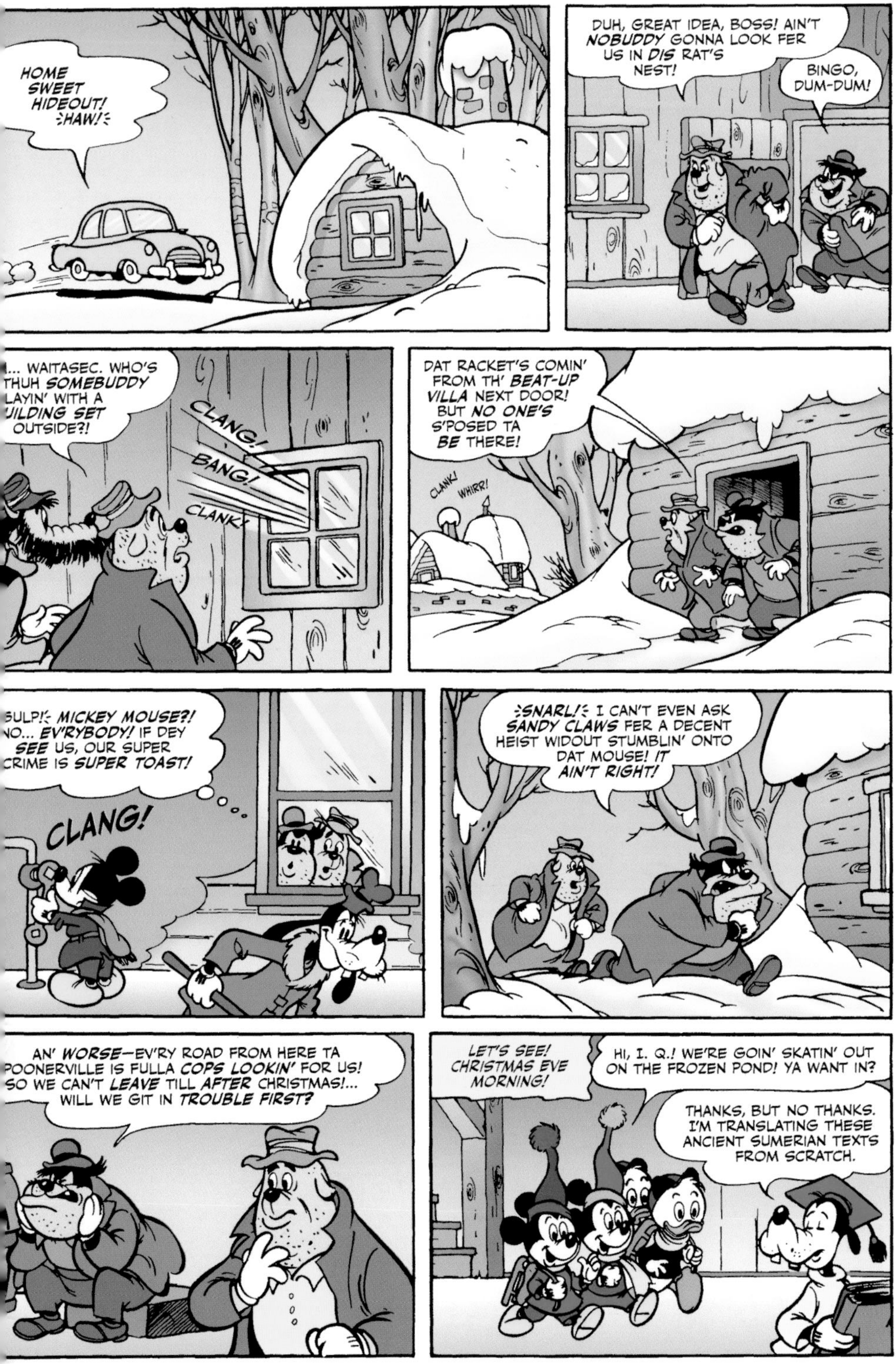
HOME SWEET HIDEOUT! HAW!
DUH, GREAT IDEA, BOSS! AIN'T NOBUDDY GONNA LOOK FER US IN DIS RAT'S NEST!
BINGO, DUM-DUM!
... WAITASEC. WHO'S THUH SOMEBUDDY LAYIN' WITH A UILDING SET OUTSIDE?!
CLANG!
BANG!
CLANK!
DAT RACKET'S COMIN' FROM TH' BEAT-UP VILLA NEXT DOOR! BUT NO ONE'S S'POSED TA BE THERE!
CLANK!
WHIRR!
ULP! MICKEY MOUSE?! O... EV'RYBODY! IF DEY SEE US, OUR SUPER CRIME IS SUPER TOAST!
CLANG!
SNARL! I CAN'T EVEN ASK SANDY CLAWS FER A DECENT HEIST WIDOUT STUMBLIN' ONTO DAT MOUSE! IT AIN'T RIGHT!
AN' WORSE—EV'RY ROAD FROM HERE TA POONERVILLE IS FULLA COPS LOOKIN' FOR US! SO WE CAN'T LEAVE TILL AFTER CHRISTMAS!... WILL WE GIT IN TROUBLE FIRST?
LET'S SEE! CHRISTMAS EVE MORNING!
HI, I. Q.! WE'RE GOIN' SKATIN' OUT ON THE FROZEN POND! YA WANT IN?
THANKS, BUT NO THANKS. I'M TRANSLATING THESE ANCIENT SUMERIAN TEXTS FROM SCRATCH.

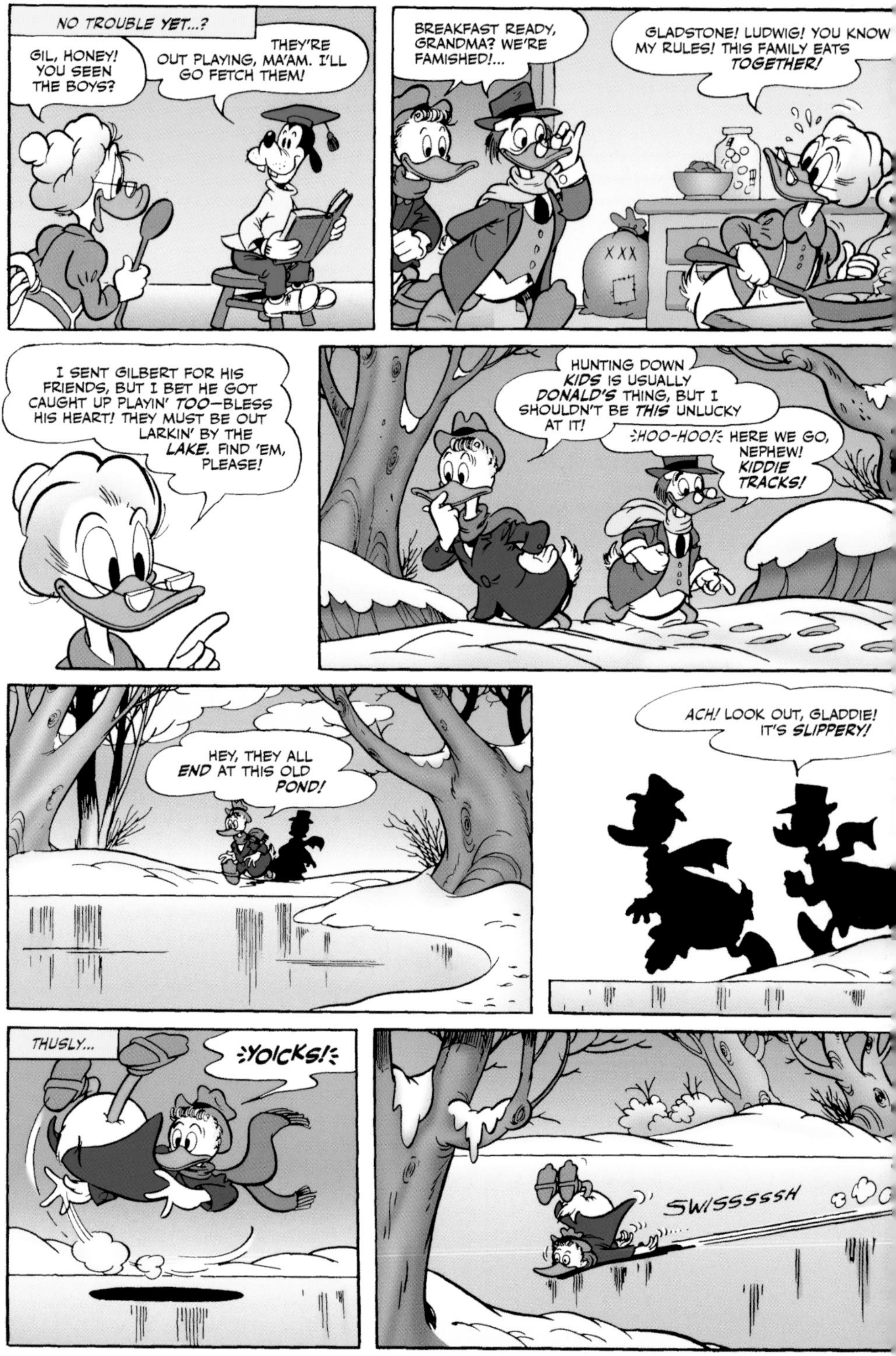
NO TROUBLE YET...?
GIL, HONEY! YOU SEEN THE BOYS?
THEY'RE OUT PLAYING, MA'AM. I'LL GO FETCH THEM!
BREAKFAST READY, GRANDMA? WE'RE FAMISHED!...
GLADSTONE! LUDWIG! YOU KNOW MY RULES! THIS FAMILY EATS TOGETHER!
XXX
I SENT GILBERT FOR HIS FRIENDS, BUT I BET HE GOT CAUGHT UP PLAYIN' TOO—BLESS HIS HEART! THEY MUST BE OUT LARKIN' BY THE LAKE. FIND 'EM, PLEASE!
HUNTING DOWN KIDS IS USUALLY DONALD'S THING, BUT I SHOULDN'T BE THIS UNLUCKY AT IT!
HOO-HOO! HERE WE GO, NEPHEW! KIDDIE TRACKS!
HEY, THEY ALL END AT THIS OLD POND!
ACH! LOOK OUT, GLADDIE! IT'S SLIPPERY!
THUSLY...
YOICKS!
SWISSSSSH

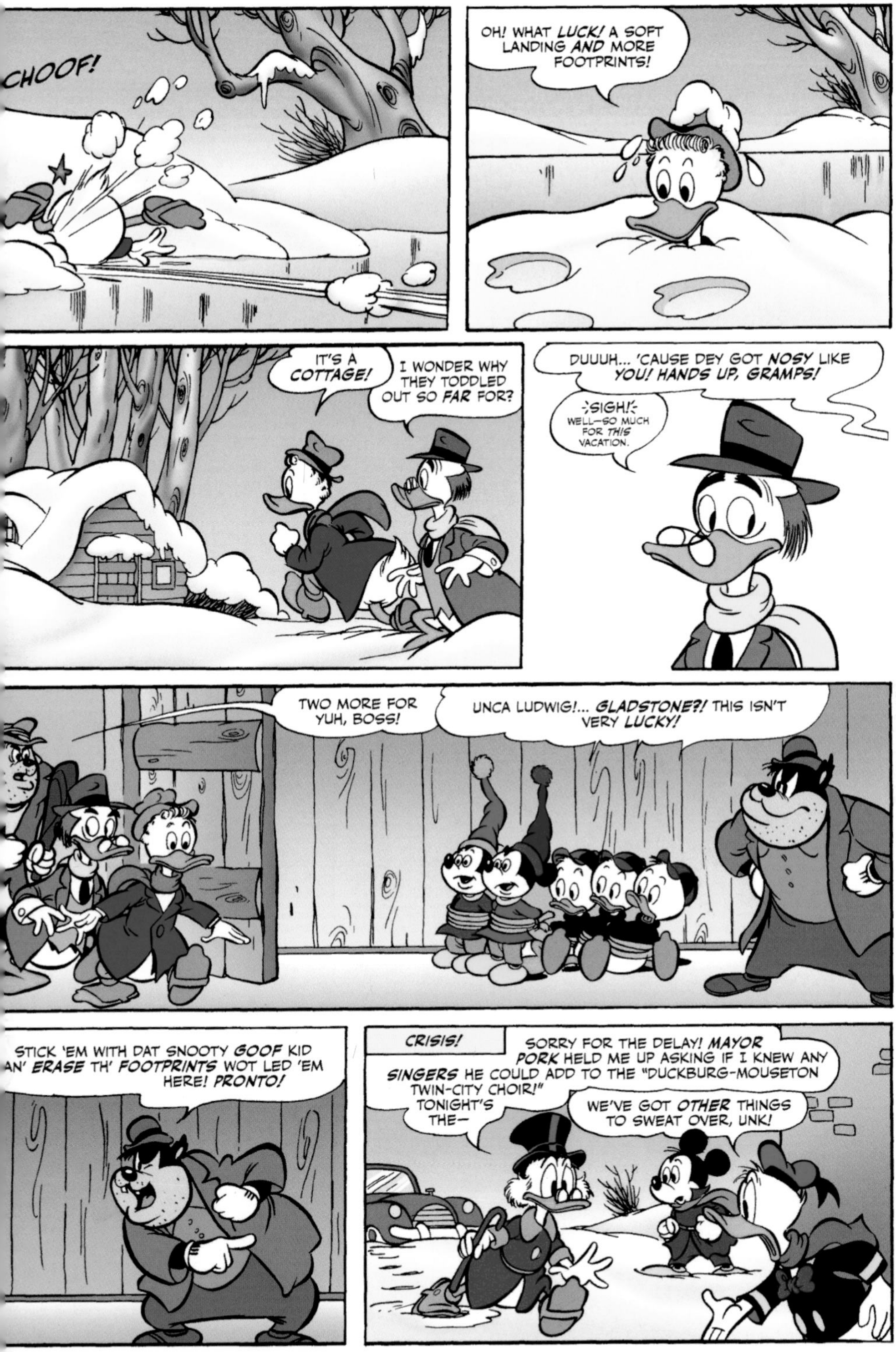
CHOOF!
OH! WHAT LUCK! A SOFT LANDING AND MORE FOOTPRINTS!
IT'S A COTTAGE!
I WONDER WHY THEY TODDLED OUT SO FAR FOR?
DUUUH... 'CAUSE DEY GOT NOSY LIKE YOU! HANDS UP, GRAMPS!
SIGH! WELL—SO MUCH FOR THIS VACATION.
TWO MORE FOR YUH, BOSS!
UNCA LUDWIG!... GLADSTONE?! THIS ISN'T VERY LUCKY!
STICK 'EM WITH DAT SNOOTY GOOF KID AN' ERASE TH' FOOTPRINTS WOT LED 'EM HERE! PRONTO!
CRISIS!
SORRY FOR THE DELAY! MAYOR PORK HELD ME UP ASKING IF I KNEW ANY SINGERS HE COULD ADD TO THE "DUCKBURG-MOUSETON TWIN-CITY CHOIR!" TONIGHT'S THE—
WE'VE GOT OTHER THINGS TO SWEAT OVER, UNK!

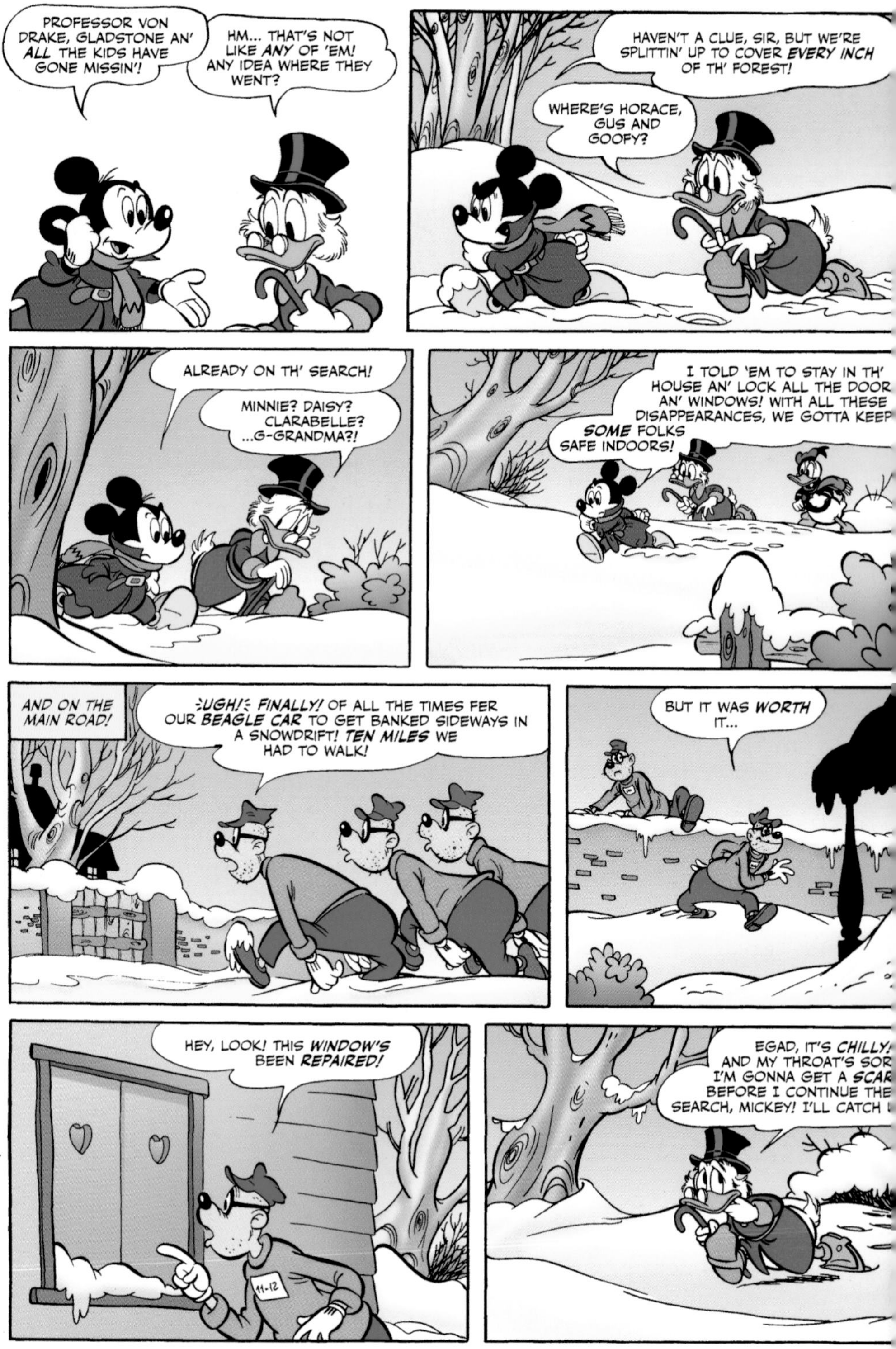
PROFESSOR VON DRAKE, GLADSTONE AN' ALL THE KIDS HAVE GONE MISSIN'!
HM... THAT'S NOT LIKE ANY OF 'EM! ANY IDEA WHERE THEY WENT?
HAVEN'T A CLUE, SIR, BUT WE'RE SPLITTIN' UP TO COVER EVERY INCH OF TH' FOREST!
WHERE'S HORACE, GUS AND GOOFY?
ALREADY ON TH' SEARCH!
MINNIE? DAISY? CLARABELLE? ...G-GRANDMA?!
I TOLD 'EM TO STAY IN TH' HOUSE AN' LOCK ALL THE DOOR AN' WINDOWS! WITH ALL THESE DISAPPEARANCES, WE GOTTA KEEP SOME FOLKS SAFE INDOORS!
AND ON THE MAIN ROAD!
UGH! FINALLY! OF ALL THE TIMES FER OUR BEAGLE CAR TO GET BANKED SIDEWAYS IN A SNOWDRIFT! TEN MILES WE HAD TO WALK!
BUT IT WAS WORTH IT...
HEY, LOOK! THIS WINDOW'S BEEN REPAIRED!
11-12
EGAD, IT'S CHILLY AND MY THROAT'S SOR I'M GONNA GET A SCAR BEFORE I CONTINUE THE SEARCH, MICKEY! I'LL CATCH

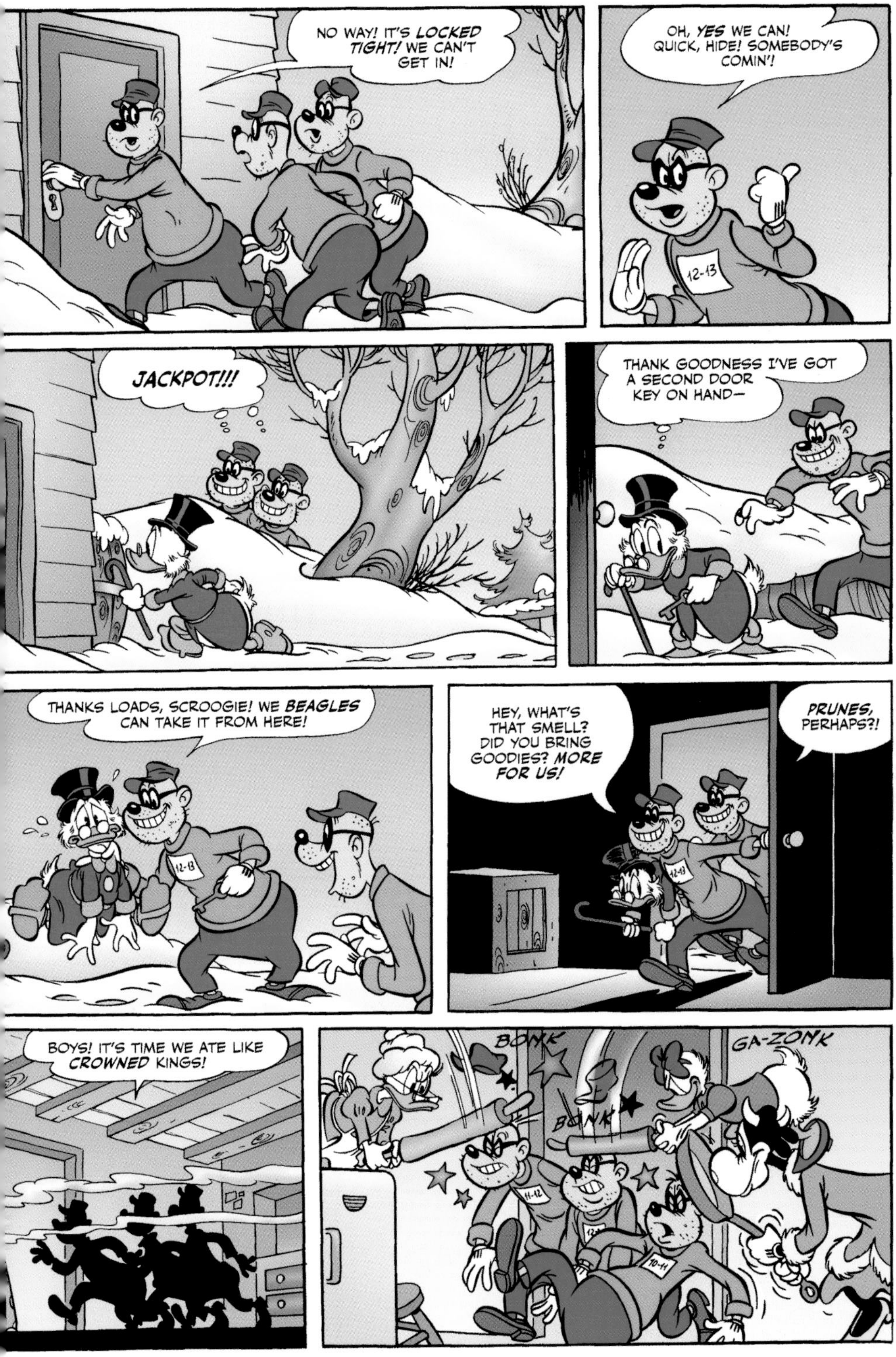
NO WAY! IT'S LOCKED TIGHT! WE CAN'T GET IN!
OH, YES WE CAN! QUICK, HIDE! SOMEBODY'S COMIN'!
12-13
JACKPOT!!!
THANK GOODNESS I'VE GOT A SECOND DOOR KEY ON HAND—
THANKS LOADS, SCROOGIE! WE BEAGLES CAN TAKE IT FROM HERE!
12-13
HEY, WHAT'S THAT SMELL? DID YOU BRING GOODIES? MORE FOR US!
PRUNES, PERHAPS?!
12-13
BOYS! IT'S TIME WE ATE LIKE CROWNED KINGS!
BONK
GA-ZONK
BONK
11-42
10-11

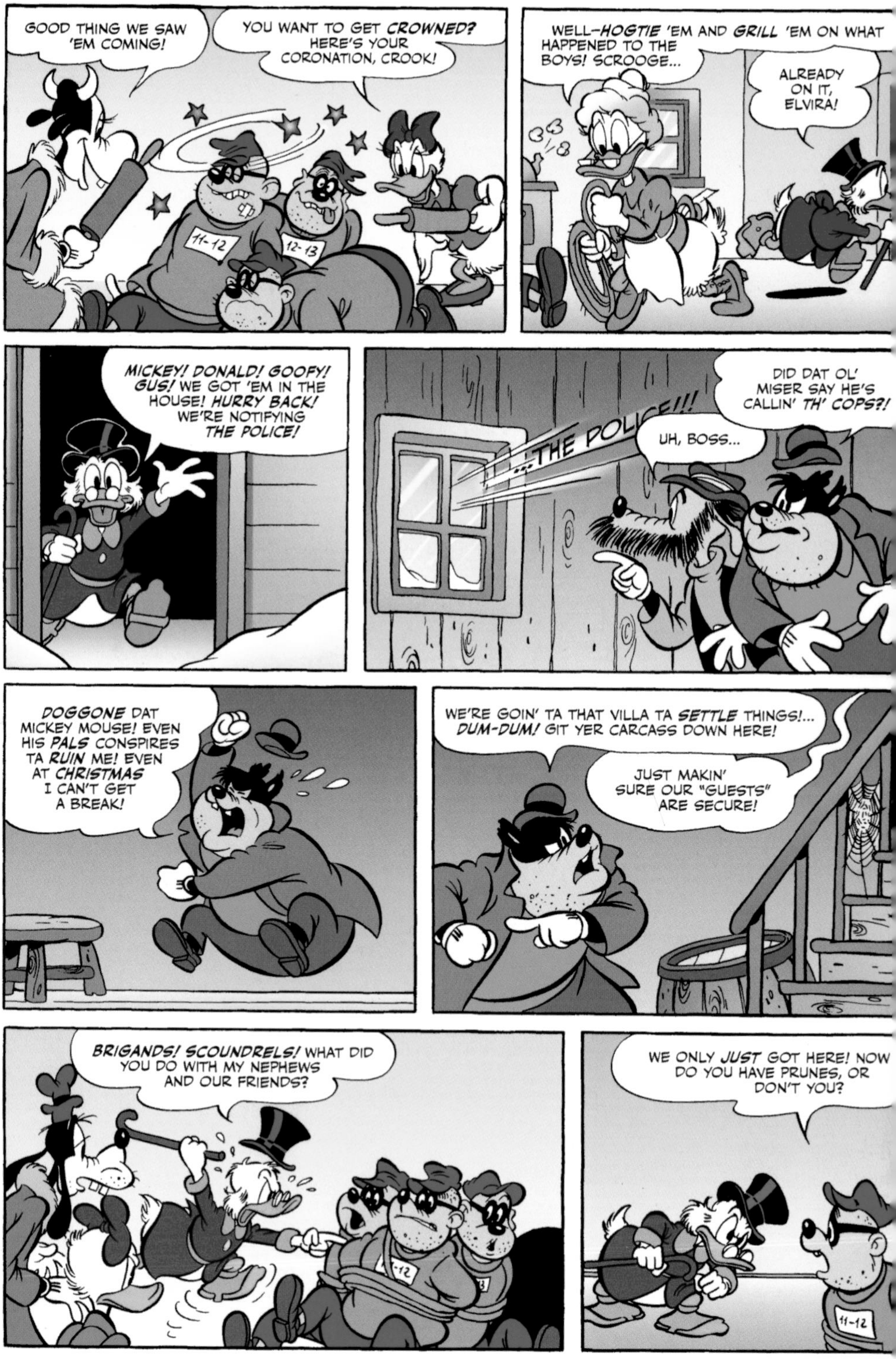
GOOD THING WE SAW 'EM COMING!
YOU WANT TO GET CROWNED? HERE'S YOUR CORONATION, CROOK!
WELL—HOGTIE 'EM AND GRILL 'EM ON WHAT HAPPENED TO THE BOYS! SCROOGE...
ALREADY ON IT, ELVIRA!
11-12
12-13
MICKEY! DONALD! GOOFY! GUS! WE GOT 'EM IN THE HOUSE! HURRY BACK! WE'RE NOTIFYING THE POLICE!
...THE POLICE!!!
DID DAT OL' MISER SAY HE'S CALLIN' TH' COPS?!
UH, BOSS...
DOGGONE DAT MICKEY MOUSE! EVEN HIS PALS CONSPIRES TA RUIN ME! EVEN AT CHRISTMAS I CAN'T GET A BREAK!
WE'RE GOIN' TA THAT VILLA TA SETTLE THINGS!... DUM-DUM! GIT YER CARCASS DOWN HERE!
JUST MAKIN' SURE OUR "GUESTS" ARE SECURE!
BRIGANDS! SCOUNDRELS! WHAT DID YOU DO WITH MY NEPHEWS AND OUR FRIENDS?
WE ONLY JUST GOT HERE! NOW DO YOU HAVE PRUNES, OR DON'T YOU?
11-12

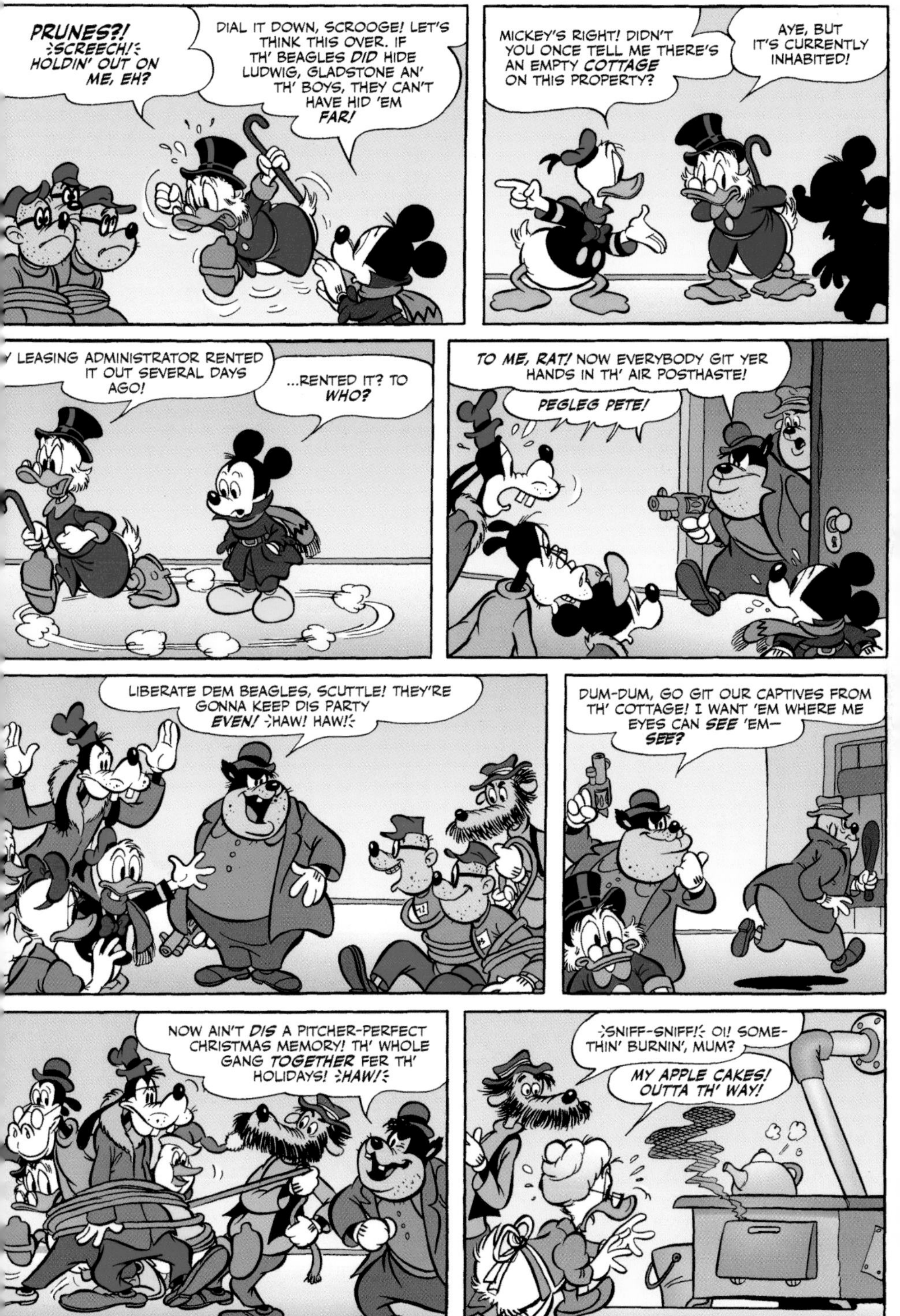
PRUNES?! ⁂SCREECH!⁂ HOLDIN' OUT ON ME, EH?
DIAL IT DOWN, SCROOGE! LET'S THINK THIS OVER. IF TH' BEAGLES DID HIDE LUDWIG, GLADSTONE AN' TH' BOYS, THEY CAN'T HAVE HID 'EM FAR!
MICKEY'S RIGHT! DIDN'T YOU ONCE TELL ME THERE'S AN EMPTY COTTAGE ON THIS PROPERTY?
AYE, BUT IT'S CURRENTLY INHABITED!
Y LEASING ADMINISTRATOR RENTED IT OUT SEVERAL DAYS AGO!
...RENTED IT? TO WHO?
TO ME, RAT! NOW EVERYBODY GIT YER HANDS IN TH' AIR POSTHASTE!
PEGLEG PETE!
LIBERATE DEM BEAGLES, SCUTTLE! THEY'RE GONNA KEEP DIS PARTY EVEN! ⁂HAW! HAW!⁂
DUM-DUM, GO GIT OUR CAPTIVES FROM TH' COTTAGE! I WANT 'EM WHERE ME EYES CAN SEE 'EM— SEE?
NOW AIN'T DIS A PITCHER-PERFECT CHRISTMAS MEMORY! TH' WHOLE GANG TOGETHER FER TH' HOLIDAYS! ⁂HAW!⁂
⁂SNIFF-SNIFF!⁂ OI! SOME-THIN' BURNIN', MUM?
MY APPLE CAKES! OUTTA TH' WAY!

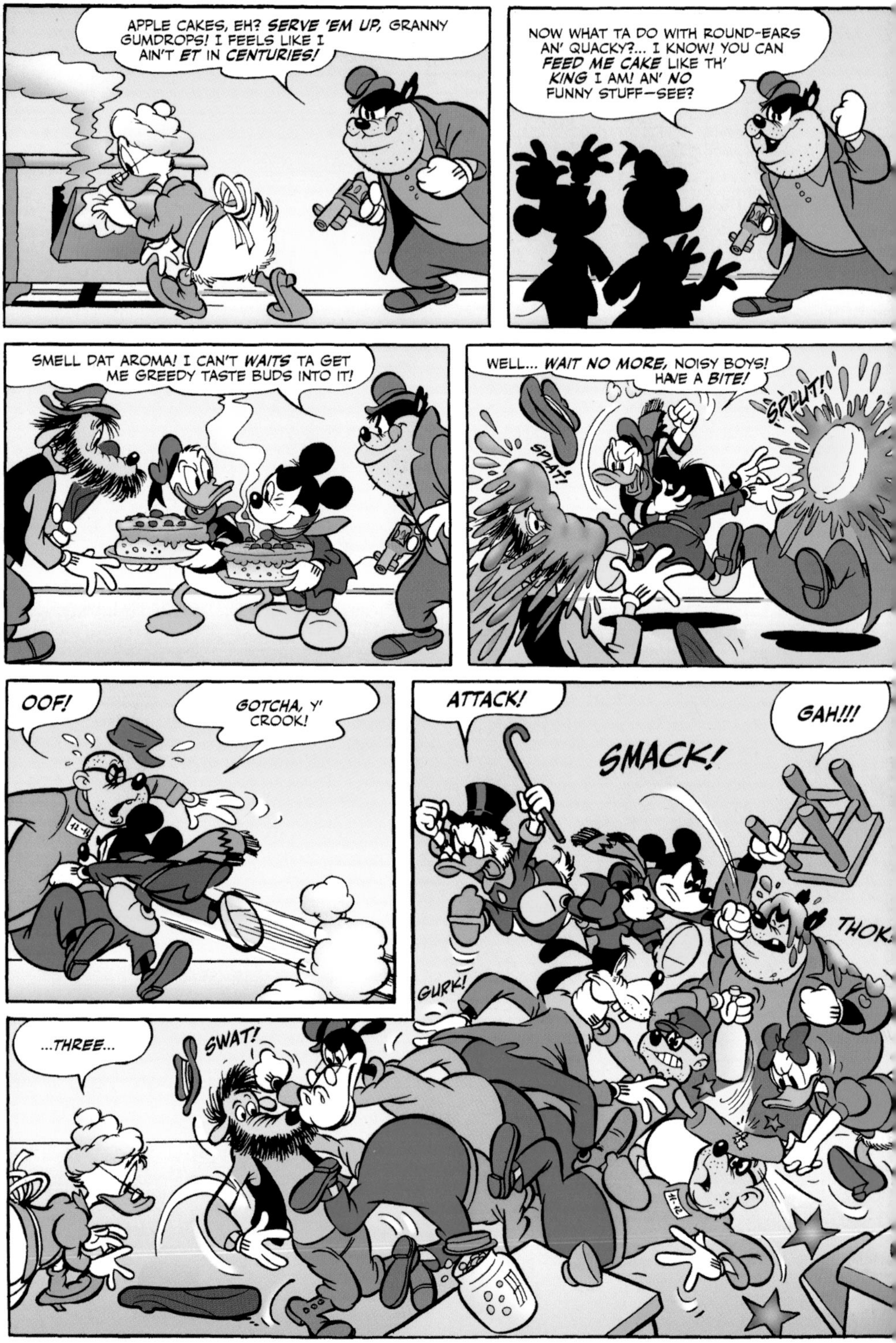
APPLE CAKES, EH? SERVE 'EM UP, GRANNY GUMDROPS! I FEELS LIKE I AIN'T ET IN CENTURIES!
NOW WHAT TA DO WITH ROUND-EARS AN' QUACKY?... I KNOW! YOU CAN FEED ME CAKE LIKE TH' KING I AM! AN' NO FUNNY STUFF—SEE?
SMELL DAT AROMA! I CAN'T WAITS TA GET ME GREEDY TASTE BUDS INTO IT!
WELL... WAIT NO MORE, NOISY BOYS! HAVE A BITE!
SPLUT!
SPLAT!
OOF!
GOTCHA, Y' CROOK!
ATTACK!
GAH!!!
SMACK!
THOK
GURK!
...THREE...
SWAT!

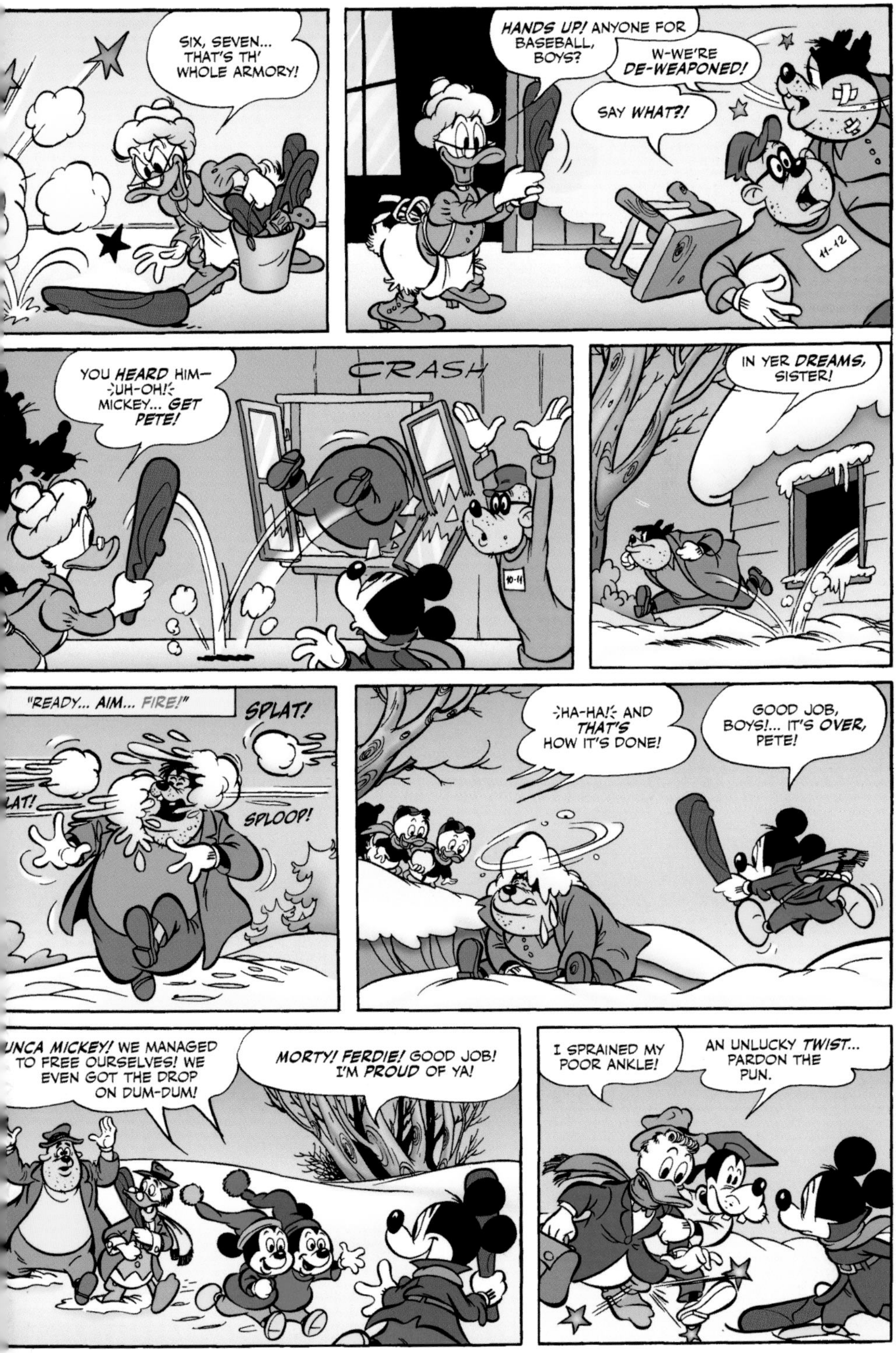
SIX, SEVEN... THAT'S TH' WHOLE ARMORY!
HANDS UP! ANYONE FOR BASEBALL, BOYS?
W-WE'RE DE-WEAPONED!
SAY WHAT?!
11-12
YOU HEARD HIM— -UH-OH!- MICKEY... GET PETE!
CRASH
10-11
IN YER DREAMS, SISTER!
"READY... AIM... FIRE!"
SPLAT!
LAT!
SPLOOP!
-HA-HA!- AND THAT'S HOW IT'S DONE!
GOOD JOB, BOYS!... IT'S OVER, PETE!
UNCA MICKEY! WE MANAGED TO FREE OURSELVES! WE EVEN GOT THE DROP ON DUM-DUM!
MORTY! FERDIE! GOOD JOB! I'M PROUD OF YA!
I SPRAINED MY POOR ANKLE!
AN UNLUCKY TWIST... PARDON THE PUN.

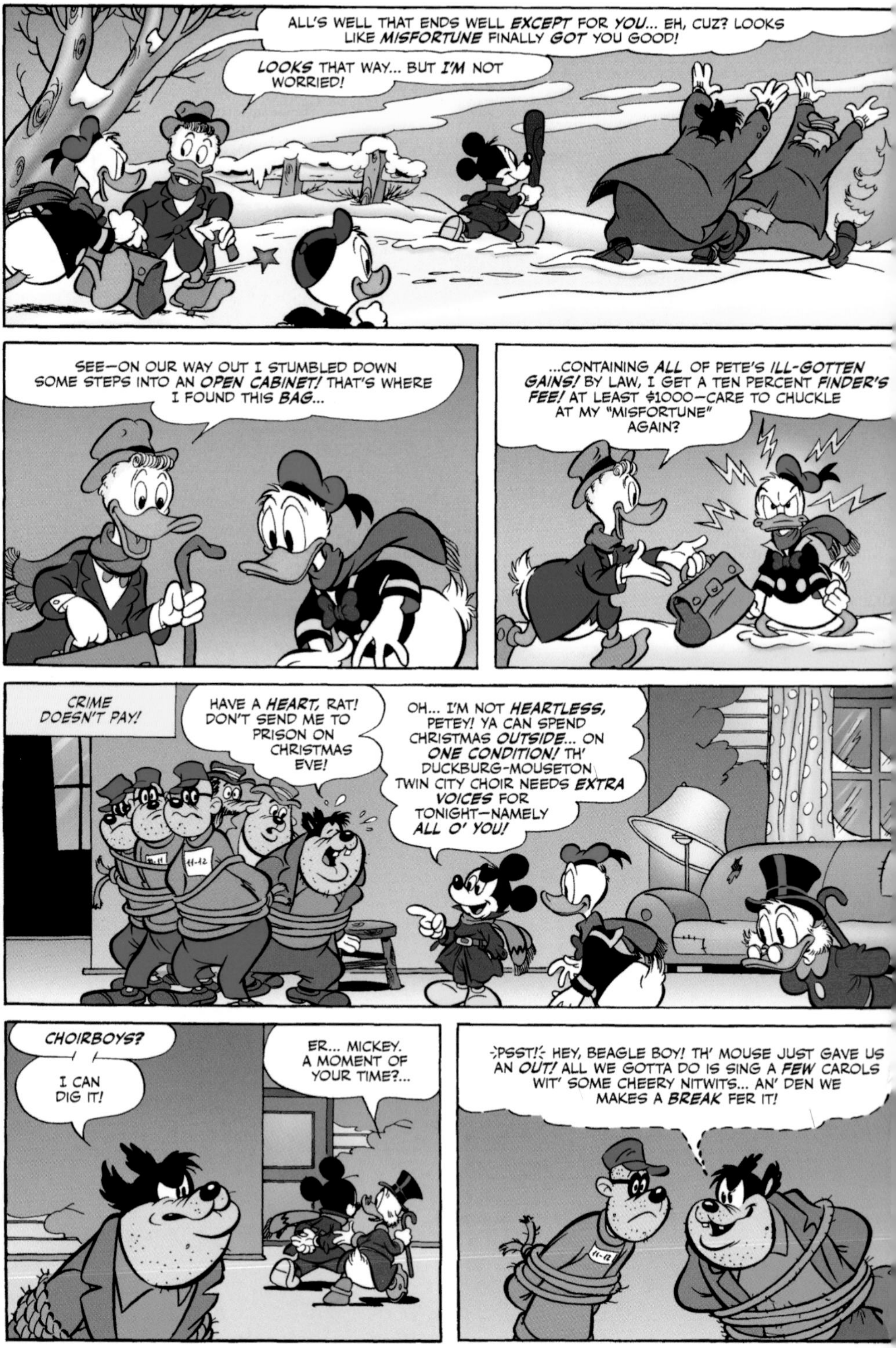
ALL'S WELL THAT ENDS WELL EXCEPT FOR YOU... EH, CUZ? LOOKS LIKE MISFORTUNE FINALLY GOT YOU GOOD!
LOOKS THAT WAY... BUT I'M NOT WORRIED!
SEE—ON OUR WAY OUT I STUMBLED DOWN SOME STEPS INTO AN OPEN CABINET! THAT'S WHERE I FOUND THIS BAG...
...CONTAINING ALL OF PETE'S ILL-GOTTEN GAINS! BY LAW, I GET A TEN PERCENT FINDER'S FEE! AT LEAST $1000—CARE TO CHUCKLE AT MY "MISFORTUNE" AGAIN?
CRIME DOESN'T PAY!
HAVE A HEART, RAT! DON'T SEND ME TO PRISON ON CHRISTMAS EVE!
OH... I'M NOT HEARTLESS, PETEY! YA CAN SPEND CHRISTMAS OUTSIDE... ON ONE CONDITION! TH' DUCKBURG-MOUSETON TWIN CITY CHOIR NEEDS EXTRA VOICES FOR TONIGHT—NAMELY ALL O' YOU!
CHOIRBOYS?
I CAN DIG IT!
ER... MICKEY. A MOMENT OF YOUR TIME?...
PSST! HEY, BEAGLE BOY! TH' MOUSE JUST GAVE US AN OUT! ALL WE GOTTA DO IS SING A FEW CAROLS WIT' SOME CHEERY NITWITS... AN' DEN WE MAKES A BREAK FER IT!

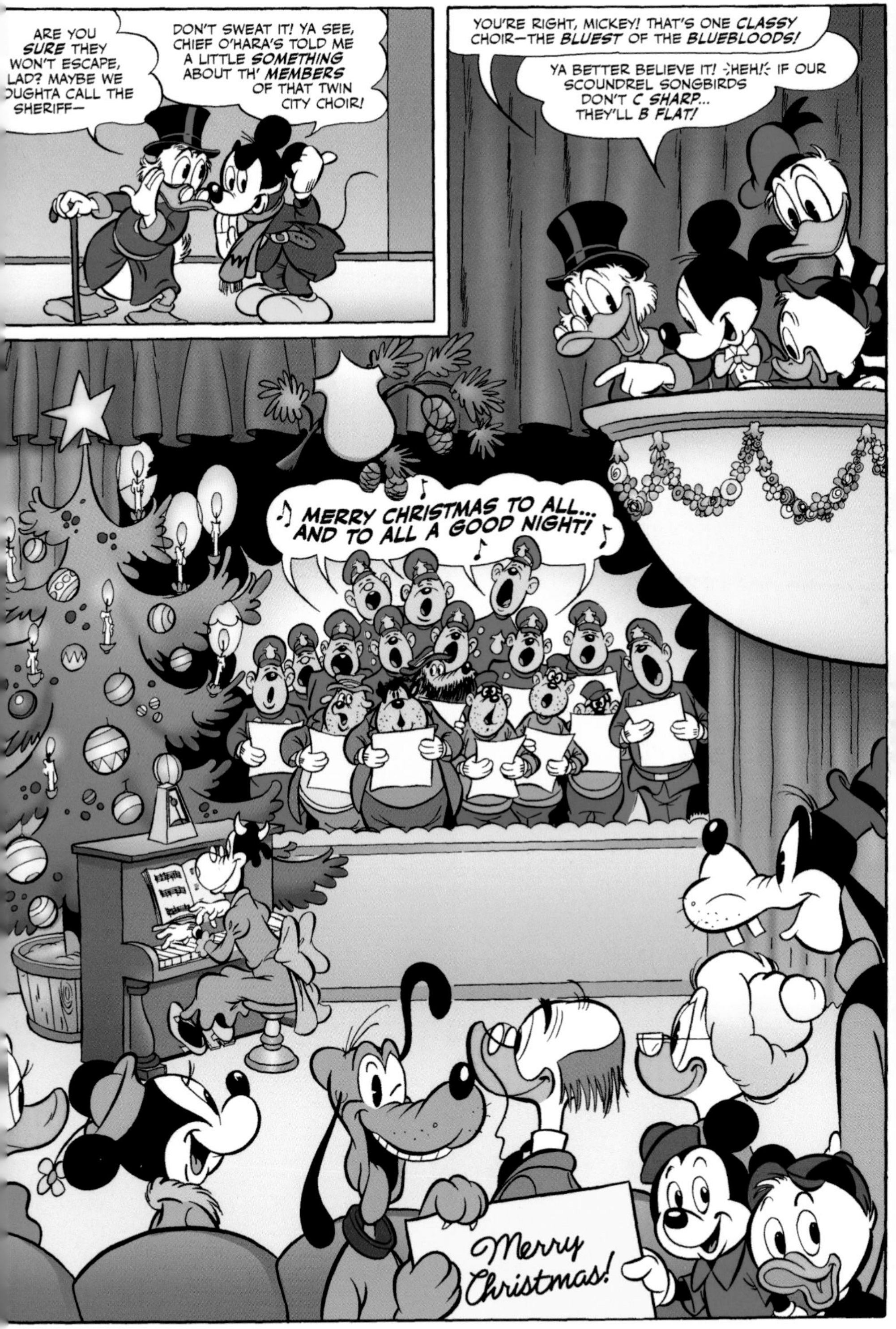

ARE YOU SURE THEY WON'T ESCAPE, LAD? MAYBE WE OUGHTA CALL THE SHERIFF—
DON'T SWEAT IT! YA SEE, CHIEF O'HARA'S TOLD ME A LITTLE SOMETHING ABOUT TH' MEMBERS OF THAT TWIN CITY CHOIR!
YOU'RE RIGHT, MICKEY! THAT'S ONE CLASSY CHOIR—THE BLUEST OF THE BLUEBLOODS!
YA BETTER BELIEVE IT! HEH! IF OUR SCOUNDREL SONGBIRDS DON'T C SHARP... THEY'LL B FLAT!
MERRY CHRISTMAS TO ALL... AND TO ALL A GOOD NIGHT!
Merry Christmas!

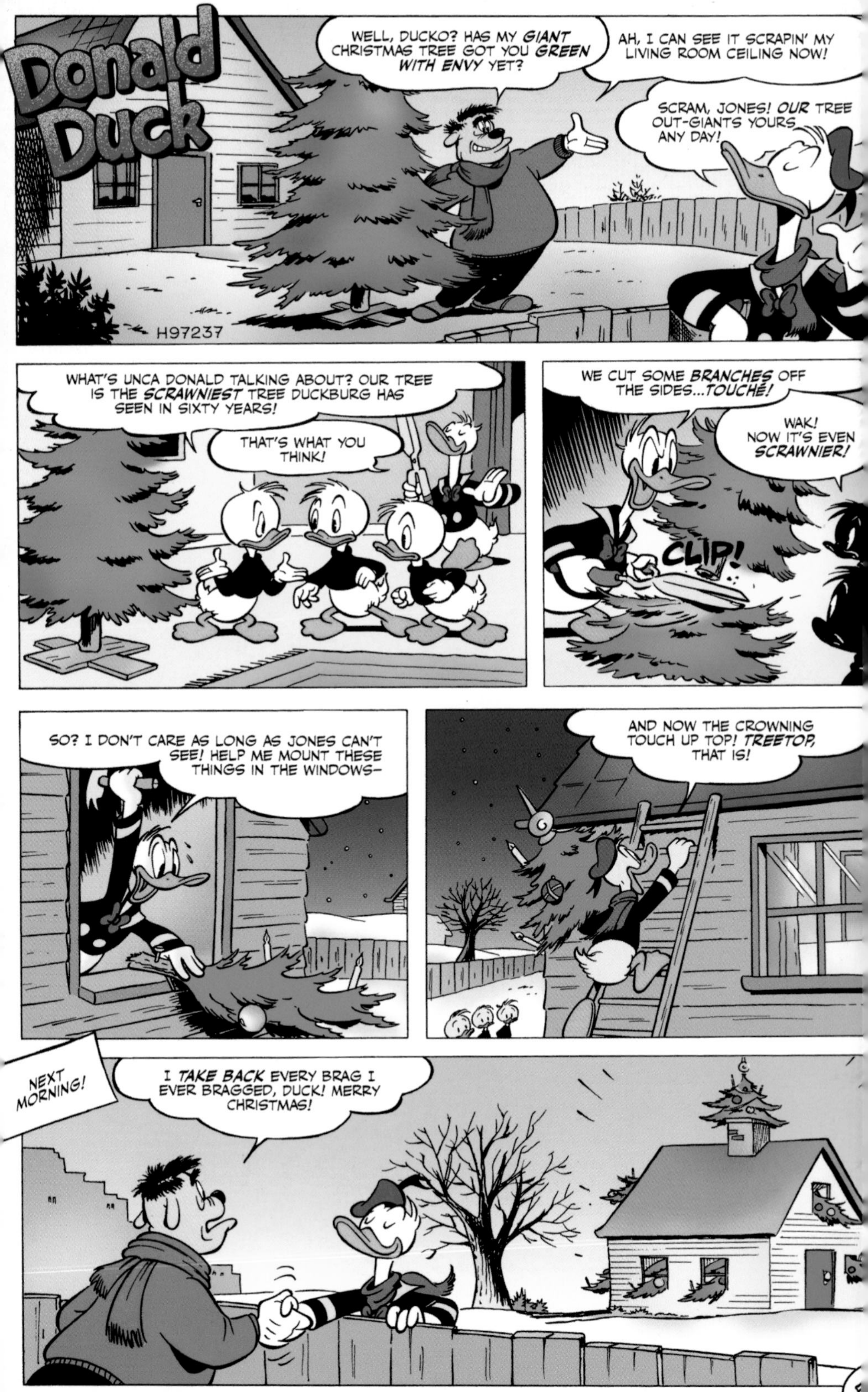
Donald Duck
H97237
WELL, DUCKO? HAS MY GIANT CHRISTMAS TREE GOT YOU GREEN WITH ENVY YET?
AH, I CAN SEE IT SCRAPIN' MY LIVING ROOM CEILING NOW!
SCRAM, JONES! OUR TREE OUT-GIANTS YOURS ANY DAY!
WHAT'S UNCA DONALD TALKING ABOUT? OUR TREE IS THE SCRAWNIEST TREE DUCKBURG HAS SEEN IN SIXTY YEARS!
THAT'S WHAT YOU THINK!
WE CUT SOME BRANCHES OFF THE SIDES...TOUCHÉ!
WAK! NOW IT'S EVEN SCRAWNIER!
CLIP!
SO? I DON'T CARE AS LONG AS JONES CAN'T SEE! HELP ME MOUNT THESE THINGS IN THE WINDOWS—
AND NOW THE CROWNING TOUCH UP TOP! TREETOP, THAT IS!
NEXT MORNING!
I TAKE BACK EVERY BRAG I EVER BRAGGED, DUCK! MERRY CHRISTMAS!

ORIGINALLY PUBLISHED IN *DONALD DUCK* #51/1997 (NETHERLANDS, 1997)

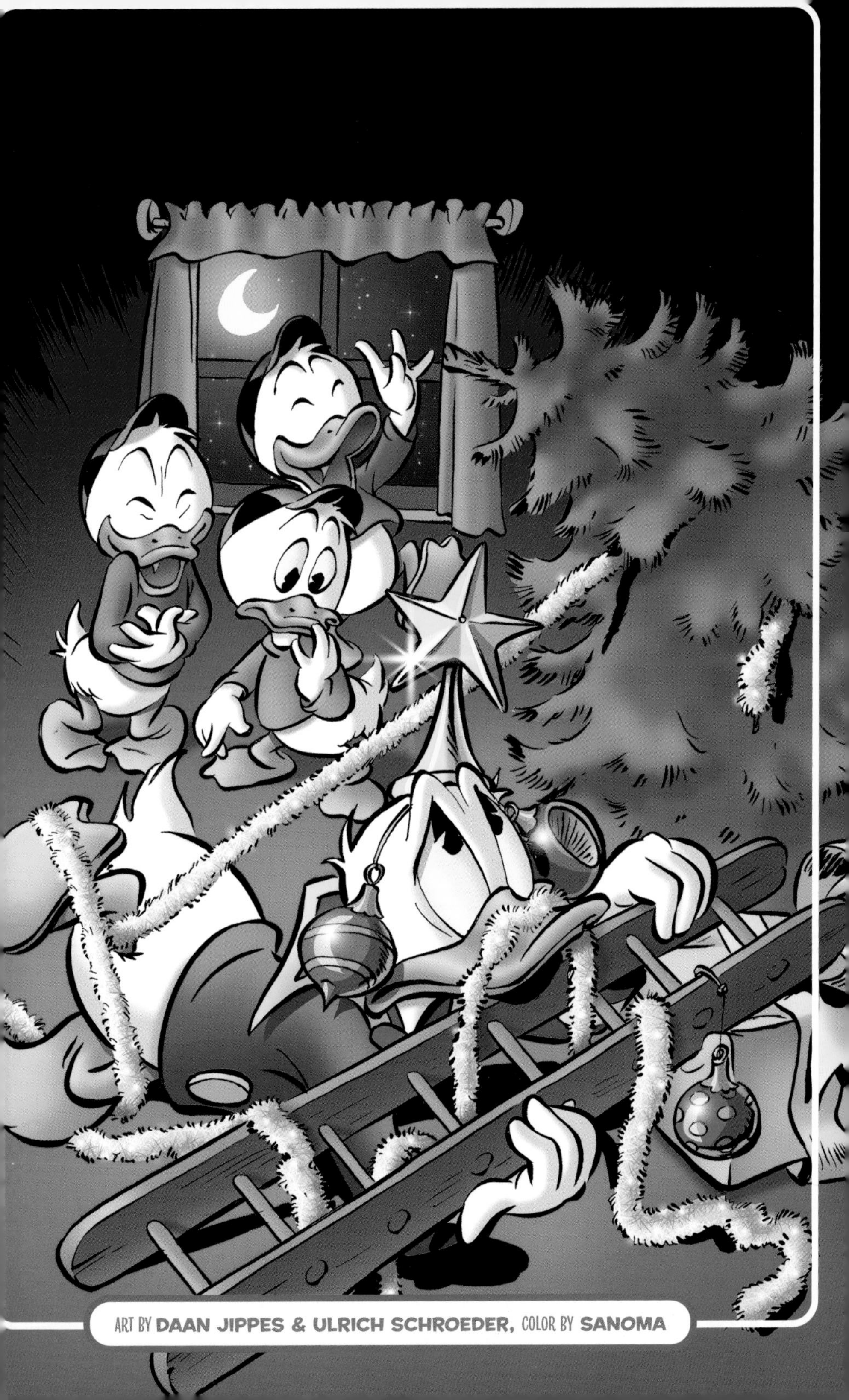

ART BY **DAAN JIPPES & ULRICH SCHROEDER,** COLOR BY **SANOMA**

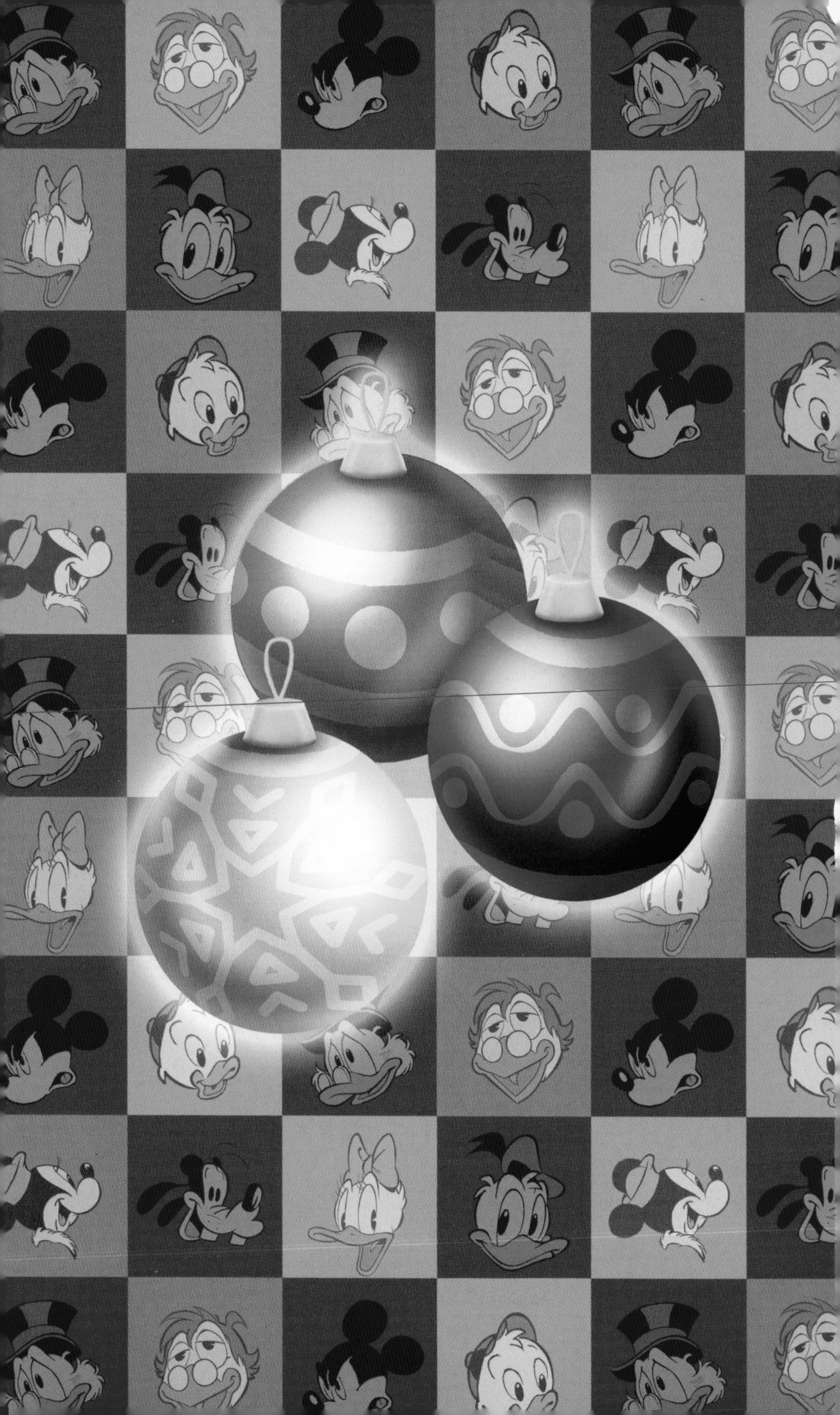